What readers say abo

James A. Cox, Edito

A deftly crafted and impressively reader involving narrative storytelling style made an inherently fascinating novel that vividly tells the complex and roller-coaster of a ride story of how those 'brave men and women in blue' ultimately solved the problem of departmental leaks that wreaked havoc on their station and their lives. "Betrayal In Blue" is the stuff from which block-buster movies are made, and unreservedly recommended for community library Police Procedural Mystery/Suspense collections.

Jeanne C. Stein, New York Times Best-selling Author

Fans of Sue Grafton will enjoy C. R. Downing's *Betrayal in Blue*. This police/PI procedural takes place when detectives had to rely on their wits and instincts more than gadgets. It's a roller coaster ride that will keep you guessing to the end.

K. Newman, Former Homicide Detective

Betrayal in Blue grabs the reader's attention from the opening pages and never lets go. Downing spins a web of relationships and develops characters and events that leave one wondering what is behind the next door. If you love a great mystery, *Betrayal in Blue* will not disappoint!

P. Tschida – Retired Sheriff

Betrayal in Blue is definitely a book I would buy and read and recommend to someone else to read. It held my interest throughout. It flows in a very natural sense. Sometimes when a person authors a book similar to this one, the author goes all wild and crazy with scenarios that just really in real life and aren't going to happen. That's not the case here. I started my career in law enforcement in1975 when the drug problem was as bad or worse than it is now. The scenarios in the book are realistic—unfortunately. Despite his best efforts, Mamba did not catch the big guy. Or maybe that's the message that we rarely do catch the big guy, and that is another very true statement.

C. Gaughan: Master's Degree in Forensic Science
Betrayal in Blue is absorbing and suspenseful with a well thought out story and complex characters revolving around the treacherous drug trade, law enforcement efforts to fight the drug war and the dangers they face not only from the outside, but from within. As a fan of thriller/mystery books and having an advanced degree in Forensic Science, I appreciate the care taken to portray accurate and realistic police procedures and situations in this exciting thriller. An excellent addition to my library!

Renee Bautista, Avid Reader
A well detailed crime mystery with characters you'll want to root for, and a few you'll love to hate. Phil Mamba is an ex-cop turned private investigator with friends on the force and on the streets. Set in the 1980's the references to times and places made the settings easy to picture in the mind's eye. I enjoyed how the personalities played off each other, a good mix of humor with the darker aspects of crime.

K9Mom
I tend to judge a book, not by its cover, but by how quickly it pulls me into the story and whether it keeps me there. From the very first chapter, the reader is privy to the complexity of the web of deceit and treachery, a fly on the wall, if you will. The writing makes you feel like you're an accomplice, knowing who the bad guys are, and cheering on the detectives as they work their way to the truth. The characters are rich and relatable, and their lives intertwined so beautifully. I found myself disappointed if I didn't have time to read before bed each night and haven't been so eager to get back to a story as I have with *Betrayal in Blue.*

J.L. Rizzo, Avid Reader
Typically, I would not be interested in a crime novel with the backdrop of the drug trade. Oftentimes, there is graphic or gratuitous violence and a sensationalistic "seedy" undercurrent that are not inviting to me. This novel is different. There are a number of characters introduced that become the focus of the storyline and together they reveal the complex dynamic and effects of human emotions and choices [betrayal, suspicion, greed, integrity, justice, truth-seeking]. This novel does leave you with unanswered questions and a desire to know "what happens next" with key characters.

Joe Balleweg, Public School Educator – Director of Curriculum, Instruction, and Assessment

Amidst a backdrop of drug trafficking deceit and deeply rooted corruption, C.R. Downing introduces private investigator Philip Mamba, and shows us that betrayal is no match for the powerful bonds that are forged through integrity, friendship, & love.

The twists and turns of the narrative pulled me through the story wondering which of the contrasting powers, corruption & betrayal or integrity & love, would win the day. But in the end, it was the character of Philip Mamba that kept me coming back for more. The private investigator from another time, embroiled in a life and death struggle, perhaps highlights what matters most in an all too brutal and fast moving world. He loves his wife; he values his friends; he honors his commitments; and he protects the weak. And for all of these things he made me feel as though everything is going to be just fine.

Miss H. Downing, Teacher and Book Aficionado

Betrayal in Blue is a fascinating fictional story inspired by an actual police task force situation. I enjoyed the mystery, the pace, and the unforgettable characters. The clues dropped throughout the story and the interesting web of intrigue kept me guessing and enthralled until the end. I was drawn into a world of private detectives, underground cartels, innocent victims, and internal moles.

Cody Jelsovsky, Passionate Reader

The men and women in blue… to protect and serve… but what happens when they don't adhere to the motto? What happens when they do, but not for the public good? What happens when they protect the criminals? When they serve their own interests? *Betrayal in Blue*! The book is more than imagination, more than elaboration, it's a story taken from real events involving real people. It's a story of people who forget their oath and the officers who won't give up until they have stopped those people. The story takes the reader into the world of backstreet characters and underworld deals. A great crime story that kept me on edge, hoping for redemption and finding the honor we expect from those who wear the uniform.

Debbie Ray, English Teacher
Betrayal in Blue details accounts of police intervention in the stopping of violent crimes. The reader feels like a ride-along in the backseats of the vehicles of both a PI and Manzanita Police Department officers. The fast paced action gives the reader the adrenaline rush of a wide-eyed observer. At the same time, C.R. Downing tugs on the reader's heart strings as he weaves the lives of men and women together dedicated to the safety and well-being of others as well as a family of law enforcers. The heart of the story revolves around the destruction of betrayal and the commitment to exposing the truth.

Bayda Julihn, Avid Reader
This book had me hooked from the first page. The characters are skillfully interwoven with each other in a storyline full of surprises. The suspenseful plot kept me engaged and wanting to find out how the story was going to end.

Cindy Anderson: Avid Reader
Betrayal in Blue is an action-packed novel about law enforcement and the dangerous drug cartel. You'll be introduced to characters you'll think about long after you've finished reading. The twists and turns will keep you on the edge of your seat all the way to the end!

D. Jones
What I love about reading is finding great characters that I can follow as they develop over a book or a series of books. Of course a good mystery doesn't hurt either. *Betrayal In Blue* has both of those qualities. I was also excited to see that the next book is coming soon. I love finding great characters I can follow as they develop. A good mystery doesn't hurt either. *Betrayal In Blue* has both.

Kim Kahler
Interesting and enjoyable read. Encourages you to read on to find out what happens next. References to other books in the series compels you to read them also.

Marnie Rogers, High School Teacher
Phil Mamba and his wife are truly the heart of this story. They have a relationship that feels like a real marriage and is believable. They both have characteristics that make me wish I was friends with them while, at the same time, not wanting to be mixed up in the craziness they live through. The story flows well, with a great cast of characters of all types. I found myself cheering on Mamba as he figures out what is going on and searches for the source of the problem. His sense of integrity and desire to find the actual truth make him a great hero for this story.

Jordan Eagles, Editor-Author
Betrayal in Blue deals with drug trafficking while the police force and private detectives try to locate the drugs and the people associated with them. This gives the story many themes that I enjoy including trust, good versus evil, and a bit of a mystery. Although a longer book, the pace and writing style made it seem like a quick read. One of my favorite aspects of *Betrayal in Blue* was the characters. I fell in love with them. I thoroughly enjoyed reading Downing's *Betrayal in Blue* and encourage other readers to pick the book up.

Dr. Cynthia Purviance, Murder Mystery Aficionado
This story takes off right from the beginning and pulls the reader in immediately. The characters are fully developed and you feel as if you really get to know them. There are delicate layers of stories upon stories woven into this book that keep you going deeper throughout the entire book. You cannot miss a minute – cannot put the book down once you start. Highly entertaining and enjoyable read.

Nicole Schultz, Writer
Based on a true story, *Betrayal in Blue* gives an inside look on the world of private investigating. Phil Mamba is a gritty, intelligent character who faces a challenging case.

f

Betrayal in Blue

Mamba Mysteries

By

C. R. Downing

ISBN 9781686141041

Betrayal in Blue is a work of fiction. All characters and locations, certain procedures, and the ultimate ending of this story are fictional. With the exception of verified historical events and persons, all incidents, descriptions, dialog, and opinions expressed are the products of the author's imagination and are not to be construed as real.

Any resemblance to actual events, police officers, criminals, or other characters on either side of the legal system is entirely coincidental.

In the late 1970s, a police officer in a city in the western United States was part of a task force against a violent criminal gang. The summary report from that task force to the police department was five pages long. The first four pages were a narrative of the task force's actions and results. It was released to the media for their use.

The fifth page was a list of task force members with annotations of their specific contributions. It remained in-house, at least it was supposed to remain in-house.

Somehow, a copy of the fifth page found its way out of police headquarters. Several task force members and their families were targets of anonymous threats, vandalism, and drive-by shootings. One member of the task force was directed to leave the city and his career in law enforcement after his family home and personal vehicles were riddled with bullets. The police department could not guarantee his family's safety.

That incident is the inspiration for this story.

Dedication

To Leanne

Chapter 1

"Hand me the bomb." Sid Brewster's voice was calm. He extended his hands without turning his head. The stocky sat cross-legged in the street beside the left front wheel of a Matador Red 1968 Camaro RS. His skill ensured detonation after the driver was inside before the Camaro pulled away from the curb.

"Don't make me look at you."

His helper flinched at each word before handing over the bomb. "You want the duct tape now?"

"I don't need tape."

"How you gonna keep the bomb where you want it?"

In answer, the bomber grunted, stood, and brushed off the seat of his pants before pointing into the wheel well.

"I don't see it."

"You're not supposed to. These tires are big and wide. The bomb is on top of this tire."

"What if it falls off?" The skinny man jumped back in anticipation of an explosion.

"It won't fall off, at least, not until someone's inside. Then, it's supposed to fall off. That's when it blows."

* * *

The two men waited in the lengthening late afternoon shadows in an alley across the street from the Camaro. With the bomb in place, their job was to confirm the hit. The target was a male cocky enough to deal his drugs personally on their boss's turf.

"Look." Brewster pointed across the street.

"That the guy?"

The bomber nodded.

The skinny man squinted to get a clear view of the target. What he saw was a lone figure weaving his way through the shadows over the uneven sidewalk in a rundown neighborhood of what was once the city center of Manzanita, California.

No one watching the mysterious man would connect him to the Camaro. The already classic vehicle had over 100,000 thousand miles on it, but the exterior was pristine. The condition of the owner reflected the wear and tear of a drug-filled life.

Thanks to Brewster, this rogue dealer was on his boss's radar. The amateur supplied pills to students at the three junior high schools, two high schools, and one community college in Manzanita. Sales were down. They dropped on Ash Wednesday and stayed down through Lent.

It was April 16, 1984, the Monday after Easter. Brewster's sales should be up because students back from vacation had cash and a need for speed. However, speed was something the rogue dealer offered at the lowest prices on the streets. Brewster's highest boss ordered the irritating amateur eliminated, which is why the two men waited to close the book on the renegade.

The free-lancing dealer's product was cheaper because it was less potent than what his competition offered. Lower doses meant buyers consumed more pills to get the desired effects, which led to more sales. Inferior product notwithstanding, he cleared more than enough money to feed his own heroin addiction. His current mental and physical conditions were the result of a recent heroin hit.

The line between daylight and darkness edged into gray and made it difficult to see. The two observers stepped out of the alley to improve their view.

When the supplier reached the Camaro, he stopped, swaying from side to side.

"This is taking forever."

"Patience," the bomber advised. "The guy's a junkie. He'll be lucky to find the pocket with his car keys in it."

"When will the bomb explode?"

"Might blow when he slams the car door. Might blow when he starts the car. For sure it will blow when the tires roll. Whatever makes it fall to the ground, the car and the driver are toast."

"Explain—"

"Shh. Looks like show time. Get your skinny butt to that payphone." He pointed to a booth a block away. "Now!"

It took six attempts at getting the door key into the lock before the supplier unlocked the door, opened it part way, and yanked the key out of the lock. After a pause, he pulled the door completely open.

Nothing.

He slid onto the driver's side bucket seat and slammed the door.

Nothing.

Sid Brewster raised his hand and gave the signal to make the call.

Brewster's assistant nodded and swiped at his comb over.

The supplier turned the key in the ignition.

Nothing.

The supplier pushed in the clutch and turned the key.

Nothing.

He stepped on the accelerator. His foot slid off the clutch pedal. The car lurched forward.

The bomb on the driver's side front wheel dropped to the ground.

A glass tube filled with Mercury broke on impact.

Mercury spread between two electrodes, one linked to a detonator, the other to the explosives.

Less than two seconds after the car lurched forward, the bomb exploded. Windows in the empty building behind the bomber crashed inward. The folding door on the phone booth rattled and shook.

Parts of the Camaro and pieces of human body rocketed away from the detonation. A tire bounced off the wall of the building sheltering Brewster. White smoke erupted from the vehicle. It reminded Brewster of photographs taken from airplanes flying over Alaska's Mt Augustine when she blew her top. He swelled with pride.

On the sidewalk side of the car, shrapnel forced its way into the diamond-shaped openings in a chain-link fence. Slabs of sidewalk lifted, shifted, and returned to earth as a pile of rubble.

"9-1-1. What is your emergency?"

"I don't know how to—" the man in the phone booth paused for dramatic effect.

A second explosion announced the obliteration of the Camaro's gas tank. Enormous tongues of blue flame lit the sky. Orange and green flames came and went as sodium and copper ignited and burned away. Brewster found the sight compelling.

Glass rained down on the sidewalk where the bomber stood. He backed into a doorway, mesmerized by the havoc he created.

The door to the phone booth slammed open trapping the skinny man's size 14 shoe behind it. He yelped and yanked his foot from its impromptu trap. The heel of his left foot crashed into his right ankle. He winced in pain.

"Sir, are you still there? Are you hurt?"

"I think I just saw a man die!" the assistant choked out.

"Why do you think someone's dead?"

"He was . . . The car he was in exploded. There's fire everywhere!"

"Where are you calling from?"

"I don't know," he lied.

"Sir?"

"I'm not from around here. I turned onto this street from a street called Los Ojos." The man mispronounced the Spanish words intentionally.

"Is that Los Ojos, sir?"

"I guess so. We don't have words like that in Des Moines. I was going West and passed Legion Road. Then I turned left. I was trying to find Hillside Drive."

The operator paused. Static crackled in the man's ear.

"I've got two squad cars on the way. Please wait."

The call ended with a resounding click as a gloved hand slammed the handset into the holder.

"You got all your gettin' from me, sister." He stepped out of the booth, winced, and gave a cursory wave toward his partner.

His partner waved back.

The skinny man limped away from Brewster, cursing every time his right foot hit the sidewalk and jolted his bruised ankle.

The bomber watched only long enough to ensure his partner was following the plan then turned and took several steps in the opposite direction. He stopped involuntarily when the charred metal frame of the Camaro was across from him. He felt goose bumps form under his jacket sleeves and hyperventilated with excitement at the view.

"I gotta go," Brewster said to the Camaro after inhaling and exhaling a calming breath. "Don't worry. I won't forget you."

He began a brisk walk toward the corner of his street and Los Ojos Road. He turned left on Los Ojos. He'd stop at the first pay phone he came to before he got to Hillside Drive.

He dialed a collect call to Chicago.

"Collect call from Manzanita, California. Will you accept the charge?" The nasal tones of the long-distance operator recited Ma Bell's required verbiage.

"I accept."

"Go ahead, sir."

"This is Sid, um, Sidney Brewster. I guarantee the target is dead, sir. I watched him blow up."

Sid listened.

"Thank you, Mr. Garmel. Goodbye, sir."

As Sid Brewster hung up the payphone, he visualized a successful future in Garmel's operation in his mind's eye.

Chapter 2

"How much longer?" Anthony Garmel asked the stewardess in a tone of voice that reflected only a small part of his negative feelings for his mode of transport.

"Not long, sir. We should begin our descent momentarily."

Garmel knew not long could be another half an hour. He sighed and focused on the shapely female as she returned to the galley.

A jab in his rib by the seat partner to his right brought his attention back from the swiveling hips of the stewardess.

"How's the view?" the female voice of that passenger inquired.

"Not as good as this one." He patted the leg of Jana, his traveling secretary, and sometime paramour. "And those aren't just empty words."

She smiled and turned to look out the window.

He looked at the Estate Rolex Daytona Cosmograph that adorned his left wrist. With three dials and two push buttons, the bulky timepiece was more show than go for the drug lord. He hadn't pushed either button since the day he picked up the watch at the high-end jewelry store in downtown Chicago. As he rotated his wrist and admired the reflected light coming off the synthetic sapphire crystal, he knew those around him were covetous of his $25,000 adornment.

Most of the time, Garmel's life as a drug lord was a life he loved. He lived in a penthouse in a high-rise along Lake Shore Drive in Chicago. His view of Lake Michigan was spectacular. His standing in an expanding illegal narcotics syndicate assured his lifestyle would get better, if it changed at all.

He tried to focus on the reasons for this trip to St. Louis. What he accomplished there should help him monopolize the fast-growing California market. He tried to remember the name of the man he was meeting and failed.

Garmel sighed again. The passenger in 2A gave him a raised-eyebrow look. He shrugged in response. Resigned to his situation, he reclined his seat and closed his eyes.

Once on the ground, Garmel gave a cursory wave to the man he knew was his driver. He stood in a common area between gates in the terminal and, much to Garmel's satisfaction, blended into the crowd. He didn't know the man's name, and didn't care.

"Jana, you grab a cab and check into the hotel. I've got to check where we'll be working. I'll join you for dinner."

Jana shrugged. She was used to being dismissed. She walked out of the gate area without looking left or right, a porter trailing behind her. She waited while a cabbie opened her door and the porter loaded her suitcases into the trunk. She tipped the porter and gave the name of a new jewelry store getting rave reviews to the cabbie.

The cabbie nodded and started the meter running.

Garmel joined his driver. The two men walked to the livery section of the terminal's passenger pickup area. When they arrived at the correct Lincoln limousine, the driver opened the back door. Garmel climbed in and slid across the back seat. Without thinking, he reached for a bottle of wine and a glass.

"I have the address of one of our properties in the industrial district as your drop point, Mr. Garmel. Is that correct?" the driver asked.

"Sounds like what I remember. Just get there, quickly."

"Of course, Mr. Garmel."

The ride was smooth, quiet, and swift. Although the neighborhood was less than desirable, the self-appointed executive was glad he'd be out and about soon.

Despite his bubble of euphoria, Garmel merely nodded to his driver as he stepped out the back door of his limo into the already warm St. Louis morning. The sun played hide and seek behind the cumulus clouds. They were all that remained of the fast-moving, low-pressure system that was on its way out of town, leaving behind a hangover of humidity that brought beads of sweat to his upper lip.

He walked up the sidewalk towards the door to the remodeled industrial suite that the St. Louis branch of his drug syndicate called home. Garmel was glad he had the foresight to bring a second shirt with him. He could already feel the trailblazing drops of sweat traveling down the sides of his trim body.

He reached the suite. Before he could knock, the door swung open. A man stepped aside, allowing his boss full access to the doorway.

"Gene, right?" Garmel asked as he passed.

"Yes, sir, Mr. Garmel. Gene Marcotti."

Now that he saw the man, Garmel remembered Gene from previous visits. He was what the locals called a lieutenant. The man could be brutal. Garmel witnessed what he'd done to a customer with an overdue payment. He knew the man was a dedicated employee who would take a bullet for him, if necessary.

Copper! The metallic smell of dried blood assaulted his nose. He scanned the room and saw the cause of the odor. Ten pairs of handcuffs were secured to rods in one wall. Each hung with one cuff open.

"What do you call this place?"

"The Confessional, Mr. Garmel."

"What happens if someone's reluctant to confess?"

"We've anticipated that. Let's just say that only happens once to a customer." Gene gestured to a drain in the concrete floor.

Garmel reflexively made the sign of the cross at those words. Although he held control over all branches of the drug trafficking syndicate from Chicago to New Orleans, he was devoted to the outward evidence of his religious affiliation.

"May God have mercy," he mumbled when he concluded his demonstration of piety.

"I didn't catch that, sir."

"It was nothing. I was just talking to myself."

"That could be dangerous, sir. Think what might happen if you were to talk in your sleep."

"You ready to see the copies?" Garmel asked, ignoring his lieutenant's cautionary statement and carefully sliding a stack of papers out of the envelope he carried. He placed the stack on the glass-covered top of one of the few flat surfaces in the room.

"I am."

The syndicate boss motioned to Gene and stepped back from the table.

"Mind if I glove up?" the man asked as he pulled two latex gloves from his jacket pocket. "I thought I might be asked to check the forgeries, so I came prepared."

"Good idea."

After a bit of a challenge in pulling the reluctant gloves over sweaty fingers, the lieutenant lifted the papers and began his inspection.

Garmel watched the man he inherited as part of his takeover of the St. Louis branch. While he didn't particularly care for his tendency to speak his mind, Gene was an asset. Although the way he carried himself made him an imposing figure, the close look revealed something; the man was average height. He wondered what Marcotti wanted out of life.

"Take more than a look. I tell you, these are good, real good."

"I suspected as much, sir. The price we paid for them was steep."

"What stands out to you?" Garmel asked after the man stopped surveying and began scrutinizing the pages.

"Same paper. Same typewriter element style. Even the edges of the pages are beat up a little so they look like they've aged as the rest of a file has. These should fool anyone who's not looking for forgeries."

"I am certain that they'll fool any jerkwater cop in California who checks them out." Garmel knew that someone in the Manzanita Police Department would read the entire file, not just the pages he had before him. They were copies reproduced as originals—with modifications. He took the papers back and, as he turned to put them down on the large oak desk behind him, added, "I'll stake my life on that."

"You know, we may be doing just that," Gene muttered.

"What did you say?"

"It wasn't important. But, I was wondering about the delivery guy. These perfect forgeries of yours are of no value unless the courier's in our pocket."

"There's no problem there," the boss assured him. "His son has leukemia. He needs money for medical bills."

"A sick kid?" The man's face morphed into a sadistic smile at the thought of the deliveryman's misfortune. It wasn't much, but the grin was enough for Garmel to realize that the man before him was most likely in charge of all confessions held in the room.

"Sick kids are great for insurance."

Garmel's eyes narrowed as he glared at Marcotti.

He wasn't sympathetic to the plight of others, especially others that could be used by him. Gloating only perpetuated the traditional myth of the brainless, classless Mafia-type Garmel despised. Anthony Garmel considered himself anything but stereotypical. He considered himself as a Renaissance man among savages.

The clandestine drug lord always dressed impeccably. Clean shaven and smelling like expensive men's cologne, he was not to be mistaken for one who wrestled in the trenches.

Casual linen slacks and expensive silk shirts were his preferences. Overall, Anthony, never Tony, Garmel, formerly Garmelli, looked like a model for an exclusive men's shop. He didn't dwell on the unsavory parts of the family business; the necessary evils were collateral damage.

He wasn't sorry for the things he did, but he disliked it when others spoke of him as a criminal. He preferred the title businessman. To Anthony Garmel, distributing drugs was no more than a profitable business. He provided a good living for his employees in exchange for unwavering loyalty.

"We have to swap out the forgeries before the package arrives." Garmel paused and checked the address on the envelope. "Arrives in Manzanita, California, wherever that is."

"Why do we need leverage on a cop that far out west?"

"We might not. Brewster seems to have things under control. But this file's for a cop that is leaving St. Louis. These pages go in his St. Louis file."

"Seems like you've got all bases covered, sir."

"I'm confident we do, for all I've gone over so far. But, we also have an exact replica of the envelope that the originals are in." Anthony hefted a large, padded manila envelope. "And I have every brand of tape, glue, staple, or fastener produced in America. Once we open the original envelope and insert our pages of enhanced information, we'll seal this envelope exactly like the one picked up at the 9th Precinct."

"When's the exchange going down?"

"Tomorrow morning. The delivery truck picks up the envelope from Precinct Headquarters on," Garmel pulled a folded paper from his shirt pocket, unfolded it, and read what was written on it. "The pickup's on Juniper Avenue at eleven o'clock. We intercept the truck six blocks later at the light on 48th Street. We bring the envelope here and switch out the papers. We send our envelope to an unscheduled pickup point where it's returned to the delivery truck. Next stop is the airport where the delivery man drops it off."

"How can you be sure that the plane won't leave without our package?"

"I have it on good authority that the gyroscope on that plane needs repairs, and they will not be completed until this is on board." He displayed the padded manila envelope.

"I'm not an expert on gyroscopes, but I know that all this work is of no value to Mr. Brewster and the others out on the coast if something happens and that envelope isn't delivered."

"Don't worry," Garmel patted his colleague on his broad shoulders. Fire with fire was Gene's go to strategy. It made him an invaluable asset that needed boundaries.

He slid the papers back into the envelope. "Nothing's going to go wrong."

* * *

Weyland Krebs pulled his Security Express van to the curb outside the brick façade of the St. Louis Police Department's 9th Precinct Headquarters building. The place was alive with activity. He was glad that most of his downtown stops had designated parking spaces right in front for deliveries. Businesses that lacked those spaces destroyed his company-imposed timeline and extended his workday without paying him overtime.

He sat in the driver's seat staring at the door to the building he was about to enter. He liked his job, but he hated what he was doing today. His head throbbed. He'd gone through four extra-strength headache pills in three hours, but his head still felt like he'd squeezed it in a vise. He dumped another tablet into his hand, tossed it into his mouth, and swallowed it with the last swig from a cup of cold coffee.

He inhaled deeply, and his resolve solidified. He opened the door of the van and slid out.

He smiled and nodded at each police officer he passed. The last thing he needed was some cop remembering him because he looked preoccupied or uptight.

As the glass door swung shut, Krebs shot a quick look at his watch. He could spare only five minutes or the whole plan was in jeopardy. He offered silent thanks for the designated parking space.

"Anything for me today, Charlie?" the driver asked the Desk Sergeant.

"Hey, Weyland. How goes it?"

"Pretty good."

"You sure? You don't look so hot."

"Headache. Probably sinuses acting up." He rubbed his right temple with two fingers in a circular motion.

"You're not contagious, are you?"

"Naw, nothing like that. So, you got something for me or not?"

"Well, there's this." The Sergeant handed a padded manila envelope down from his raised desk.

Krebs took the package and feigned an entry in his log. The envelope was what he was getting paid under the table by Anthony Garmel to deliver.

"You sure that's all?"

"Yep. Nothing but one lonely envelope," the Sergeant answered. He wiped his brow with a large handkerchief. "Not that I'd mind going where it's headed."

"Where's that?" Krebs asked as his heart rate slowed with the news of only a single item to account for in his log. The question indicated good manners on his part; however, the tone of the delivery of that question suggested a lack of interest in the Sergeant's answer.

This was not the first time Anthony Garmel swooped in from out of town and told him what to do to earn the money he needed to pay for his leukemic son's treatments. But, it would be only two more months until he would be eligible for Security Express's medical coverage. Then he would stop taking the money from Garmel—forever.

A sharp pain shot through the deliveryman's head. A burst of light flashed like fireworks inside his brain. He prayed it wasn't the start of a migraine.

"I figured you guys always checked out where the stuff you picked up was going."

"Sometimes," Krebs admitted with a weak smile, which was the best he could muster through his headache. "Today my route's so tight that I've got to keep moving."

"Too bad," the Sergeant commiserated. "That baby's going to Manzanita, California."

"Sounds like a pretty nice place to visit."

"Anyplace without humidity sounds like a pretty nice place to me, and I've heard California is one of those places."

"Yeah. No humidity does sound inviting," Krebs said with a hint of envy in his voice.

"Inviting is just the word." The Sergeant closed his eyes as he visualized palm trees and cactus, swimming pools, and short-shorts.

"Hey, Sarge, wake up," Krebs called over his shoulder as he left.

* * *

At the stoplight on the corner of Juniper Avenue and 48th Street, a white pickup truck with Hal's Handyman Service printed on the doors pulled up behind the stalled Security Express van in the right-hand lane.

"Need a hand, buddy?" the driver of the pickup called as he walked up to the driver's window.

"Looks like it," Weyland Krebs admitted. "You know trucks?"

"Enough to keep mine in top shape."

"I've got some tools in the back," Krebs offered. The pickup driver's answer to the question about knowing trucks was the correct one. He was thankful for that small favor. He rummaged around in the back of his van until he found the tool pouch provided by the company.

He took a deep breath, reached up to a shelf for the padded manila envelope, and stuffed it inside the tool pouch.

"Hope you don't mind," the pickup driver said. "I got my toolbox out of my truck."

"No problem." Krebs' sat his tool pouch beside the stranger's toolbox.

"Hand me a flat blade screwdriver, will ya?" the pickup driver called from under the short hood of the van. "The yellow-handled one."

Krebs complied and then rubbed both temples simultaneously.

"This one's too long," the handyman/mechanic complained. "Could you get the one with the yellow and black handle?"

"Sure thing." Krebs' hands were sweating as he reached not into the toolbox but into his pouch and removed the padded manila envelope. He slid it into the toolbox of the pickup driver. When his hand emerged, the envelope was gone and he held a screwdriver in its place.

"Here you go."

The handyman took the offered tool and disappeared under the hood again. "Give it a try now," he called less than a minute later.

With his head pounding harder than ever, Krebs climbed into the van and turned the engine over. The motor roared to life.

"Thanks," he called.

"No problem," the handyman called back as he slammed the hood of the van. "Here you go," he picked up both sets of tools and handed the tool pouch through the window to Krebs.

"Thanks again," Krebs said to the back of the man as he headed toward his pickup. The good Samaritan dismissed him with a perfunctory hand gesture.

Krebs took a deep breath and exhaled slowly as he pulled into traffic. That was one more obligation he could cross off the list.

* * *

It was early afternoon and Anthony Garmel was back at The Confessional. Final delivery of the packet to the suite was by a man in a white sports car. That man picked it up from a young lady in a cab who plucked it from a trash bin where the handyman in the white pickup deposited it.

Garmel focused on the task at hand. He didn't notice the metallic smell that hung in the air, a fragrant reminder of the room's primary purpose.

His latex-gloved hands removed layers of tape from the back flap of the manila envelope. The tip of his tongue protruded from between his teeth in intense concentration.

He finished peeling back the fourth and last strip of tape. He spoke to Jana who wrote down his words verbatim as she had for each preceding step in the process.

"The fourth layer overlaps the flap edge by…" he used a ruler to measure the amount of overlap and reported, "Half an inch. Metal brad is folded under the flap not poking through the hole in the flap. The flap is glued only at the center."

With the envelope open, Garmel's gloved hands removed the contents. After substituting his forged pages for their originals in the same locations in the files, he listened while Jana read aloud in reverse, the descriptions she had noted concerning the seal on the envelope. He duplicated the layers of tape exactly on his replacement envelope.

A forger brought in by the St. Louis branch reproduced the address from the first envelope before he arrived. Garmel held the package aloft. After careful scrutiny, he came to a conclusion.

"Only the police officer in the 9th Precinct who stuffed the original envelope might be able to detect the switch."

Gene, always ready to help the big boss, leaned over and stared hard at the envelope.

"It's very good. Even a policeman with forensics training might miss this one. You think they have forensics cops in California?"

"Who's the first courier?" Garmel asked Jana, ignoring the frivolous question.

Jana pointed in the direction of a fidgeting young man in jeans and t-shirt who'd raised a hand in answer to the boss's question about the courier.

"Put your hand down," Garmel snapped. "You know where the drop is?"

"Yes, sir."

"Get going," Garmel directed as he handed over the envelope. "And, remember, this package is worth a whole lot more than you are."

The young man shivered, nodded, and fled.

The forgery changed hands three more times on its route back to the Security Express van. A tan, long-legged blonde in tight, white short-shorts, who knew only that she was doing her roommate's boyfriend a favor, delivered the duplicate envelope to Krebs. The driver logged in the parcel at 3:35 p.m. the next open time slot in his log.

Not coincidentally, the mechanic installing a new gyroscope in the Security Express jet scheduled for the Los Angeles run finished his repair seconds after all California-bound parcels from Kreb's van were hustled into the hanger.

Chapter 3

A bright orange Security Express Delivery van dropped Garmel's package within the guaranteed timeframe at Manzanita Police Department's central offices. Before the morning break mandated by the Police Officers of Manzanita contract, the sergeant in charge of the records division opened the package, scrutinized the contents, and determined the final resting place for the file.

She made a mental note about the origin of the file. The Manzanita Police Department didn't get many newbies from east of Colorado. This made two from the same city in the Midwest in around five years.

After paper-clipping a note to the envelope directing the document room clerk to file it in the appropriate location, she dropped it in the tray for interoffice delivery. She reached for the next item in her In box when she realized she'd skipped one step.

Grabbing a packet of Post-it notes and a Sharpie, she printed in bold letters, "Copy only when requested in writing!" on the sticky square and slapped it on the envelope just below her previous message.

Satisfied, she returned the envelope in the Out tray.

* * *

The first time Becca heard about a speedy party was in the hallway at school. She opened her locker door on clean out day. A half-page flyer floated off the shelf and onto the corridor floor.

She read it aloud.

"This summer you'll feel the need for speed! Good friends. Good time. Good stuff. Drop in for some fast-paced action. We're partying at 1542 Coulter Street. The last Wednesday of June, the last Wednesday of July, and the last Wednesday of August. The speedy party starts when you get there and ends when you leave!"

Embarrassed by the content of the flyer, she looked left and right. After a sigh of relief when she saw no one close to her, she decided to toss the flyer into the trashcan at the end of the bank of lockers on her way to the Council Area, the official name of the school's open quad.

Manzanita High School's nickname was "The Judges." Someone named common areas of the school for places in a courtroom. Their mascot was a giant gavel.

"Eloise, like wait up!" she called to a friend as she turned the last corner waving the flyer like a semaphore.

Seconds later the flyer was still in her hand but the party forgotten as the conversation turned to what Gerald, who sat two seats in front of Eloise in U.S. History, might be doing over summer vacation.

* * *

"I need to leave my undercover assignment."

"I'll need more than that. You've gotten more leads than any five previous undercover officers together at the high school."

That was a backhanded compliment from Sergeant Stallings. Although she was thirty-one years old, the female officer passed her undercover-self off as a seventeen-year-old Junior at Manzanita High.

"Thanks. I think."

"I still haven't heard a reason to end your assignment."

"Some kids, but more teachers are noticing things."

"Things?"

"I'm not up on the latest slang."

"So? That's fixable."

"I use out of date references too often. My U.S. History teacher suspects something. I'm sure of it. And he teaches Civics, too. I'll probably have him next year."

"I'll contact the Principal and have her talk with the history teacher. What's your alias, again?"

"Eloise. Eloise Cooper. I'm sure I saw something suspicious today."

"That's better."

"There is one girl, Becca, that's bonded with me. She's shy, kind of a loner." The undercover cop pursed her lips and wrinkled her brow as she formed her next sentence. She wanted to say the relationship had potential, but wasn't sure girl had the same outlook.

"I saw a flyer for a series of parties today." She held out her hand in a stop gesture to keep the sergeant for interrupting her. "They're called 'speedy parties.' I didn't get a good look at the flyer, and there wasn't time to ask for a look with locker clean out and all."

"Good." Stallings ignored the locker comment. "I'll put you on a cushy parking enforcement assignment over the summer. That will protect your cover. Keep in touch with that girl. You've got a phone number for her, right?"

This morning, Petula awoke to an empty bed. It was far from the first time, and, as much as she hated this feeling, she hoped it would not be the last. Some times together were better than no times together, even though fraternization within the Manzanita Police Department hierarchy—particularly the kind between two people, in secret, in the dark—was a dismissible offense.

She didn't know that she loved Rogers. She looked forward to their trysts. But, deep down, she didn't think she could live with his aura of pompous arrogance day after day, and, he had a wife in St. Louis.

She stretched, threw the covers back, and headed toward the master bath. When she flipped on the light, she found a note taped to her mirror. "Call Andy from my private line. Message: Pressure's on my hire. It's time for you to make your move."

Petula sighed. In spite of the Police Chief's interest in her physically, mornings after his visits were far from amorous. It took almost an hour for her to remove or disguise evidence of the man's presence in her apartment.

She'd grown to hate the one-sidedness of the affair and the morning after a night with Dwight routine. After throwing a dirty pair of argyle socks into her clothes hamper, she slammed the top closed.

Satisfied with her clean-up, she climbed into her sports car and made the short commute to Manzanita's Central Police Complex. She parked her car in her labeled space and closed the convertible top. After a brief primping glance in the rear-view mirror, she slid out of the driver's seat. She closed and locked the car door before smoothing her uniform skirt. She made sure the tight skirt hugged her hips provocatively even though it was a uniform.

She vowed to take control of her relationship with the Chief. With that thought in mind, she paraded across the parking lot. Once inside the building, she made her way to Rogers' office suite, exuding confidence with every step.

The suite was a two-room design with a comfortable waiting area and reception desk in the first room. This was Petula's domain. Among the accouterments was a hotel room refrigerator—with Perrier and sodas—and a coffee maker. On days when appointment volume was high, she ordered pastries from the local bakery as a courtesy to the Chief's visitors.

The inner sanctum, as everyone called the Chief's private office, was impressive. The desk, credenza, bookcase, and conference table were polished cherry wood. Two secure filing cabinets with five-digit combinations and a paper shredder built into the back of the credenza completed the furnishings.

Once inside her office, she made coffee and checked her message machine. After annotating each message, she listed them by time and topic on a cover sheet. She placed the list of messages in the tray mounted to the wall outside his door. No one entered the Chief's office when he was not inside. Not even the cleaning crew had a key.

On her way back to her desk, Petula locked the hallway door. What she was about to do was for her eyes and ears only.

She pulled the note from Rogers from her purse and read the message twice. Satisfied that she had all the information correctly added to her memory, she shredded the note. Then she made the call.

"Mr. Anderson, please."

"I'm sorry, he's on a long-distance call. Would you like to leave a message?"

"I have instructions only to leave messages on Mr. Anderson's private machine."

"Not a problem. I'll connect you."

There was a click, a brief period of silence, another click, and then the greeting began.

"This is William Anderson. I do regret missing your call. Please leave a detailed message. If you have a specific time you'd like me to return this call, include it in your message. I will do my best to accommodate your wishes. Thank you for calling Anderson Pharmaceuticals."

Well versed on the protocol involved in these calls, Petula repeated her boss's message verbatim and hung up. Her surreptitious task completed, she yanked the pages from the previous two weeks from her desk calendar.

Her tasks completed, she unlocked the office door and returned to her desk. Once again, she smoothed her uniform skirt before and sat down. She was ready to face the day.

Chapter 4

Hope Mamba was not a fan of public transportation. She understood the need to conserve fuel, but she remembered the 70s, sitting with her parents in their Ford Galaxy waiting for their turn to buy gas on an "even" day. She was sure today's circumstances were the cause of that memory.

She sighed and looked down at the mystery novel that lay open on her lap. *A is for Alibi* by Sue Grafton adorned the cover. She checked it out from the "Female Detectives" section at the library. Kinsey Millhone was a tough, smart private investigator. Since Millhone's fictional hometown of Santa Teresa was in Southern California, it was fun to imagine what she might have accomplished had she become a female version of Phil Mamba, her private eye husband.

Today, the ride to the office of Mamba Investigations was taking far too long. The office housed her husband's business. It was her place of employment as well.

She wished she had her car. However, her car was in the shop because she ignored a warning light on the dashboard. She had no idea when the light began glowing amber. That frustrated Phil.

All had been fine until he took her car to the grocery to get some Pedialyte for their son, Jimmy. He'd been running from both ends all day and needed hydration. Since it was a Saturday, Phil agreed to stay with Jimmy the entire afternoon while she went to the mall with two girlfriends.

She'd pulled into their driveway after shopping. Phil greeted her at the door.

"Hi, sweetie," he said and gave her a kiss. "Jimmy's sleeping. I'm taking your car, because it's blocking the garage door, and running down to Thrifty Drugs. I think he can keep fluid down now, and we're out of that Pedi-something his doctor recommends."

"Pedialyte," Hope finished the name of the liquid. "Get a half-gallon of chocolate malted crunch ice cream, too."

"I knew I married you for more than your spectacularly good looks," Phil grinned and patted her bottom as he passed by.

Chocolate malted crunch was her husband's favorite ice cream, bar none. She liked it mostly because it was chocolate ice cream. The malt balls infusing the confection were okay. But the chocolate malt was to die for. Besides, she'd heard that chocolate was an aphrodisiac, and she was ready, willing, and able to have another child.

Phil returned from his shopping trip. She heard the front door and turned from watching *Facts of Life*.

"How long's the warning light been on?"

"Ummm," was the best she could do.

He lectured her on the reason cars have warning lights. It was something about people never understanding the gauges in older cars.

Phil dropped her car off early Monday morning and rode the dealer's shuttle home. He transferred from the shuttle to his car and drove to work. She'd been riding the bus since then.

Hope exited the bus two blocks from Mamba Investigations. She strolled along the sidewalk, giving cursory glances to various window displays before arriving at the office.

She was proud of her husband, his work, and his office. She smiled a devilish smile as she finished her list of prideful things with, a long look at the logo adorning the front window.

She had to admit that the idea for the logo on the window was Phil's. But, the logo itself was all hers.

She met Phil while he was still a detective with the Manzanita Police. He'd been investigating the death of her first husband. She remembered his awkward attempts at neutral conversation. She knew her feelings and suspected his. She moved to her left until she could see herself in the office window.

As satisfied as she could be with her appearance, she unlocked the front door, stepped inside, and flipped on the lights. Her desk was the focal point of the reception area. She'd decided on that design element when she began working for him. Working for him was her idea.

At first it had been good mental therapy. She enjoyed the work of coordinating the loose ends for a private detective—and there were plenty of loose ends to coordinate. But, in retrospect, she realized that there was more to her offer than the work.

She was certain that Phil liked her. Not in the romantic way she hoped for, perhaps, but they developed into a good team. Their relationship continued to develop, until the bomb went off. Glass shards flew everywhere including her leg. She shuddered at the horrific memory.

After the explosion, she awakened in a panic unable to form coherent words. Finally, she'd managed to ask if her baby was all right.

Just after they handed her a baby boy, Phil arrived, and the horrific memory evaporated.

A smile replaced the shudder as she poured herself a cup of the coffee, added sugar and cream, and went back to her desk. It was time to get her official workday going.

Chapter 5

Guillermo Arcenas was born in the state of Chihuahua, Mexico and raised in the home of Martín Arcenas, the head of one of the largest drug cartels in that area. A precocious child, he was conversationally bi-lingual in English and Spanish by age three.

By the age of seven, he was bilingually fluent in speaking, reading, and writing. Capable of speaking either Spanish or English as a native gave his father an opportunity to expand his drug empire North of the Mexican border. Sent to America before his eighth birthday, Arcenas' surrogate parents groomed him for the position he now held.

Guillermo was as blond as any Scandinavian. No one in California knew Arcenas was born in Mexico. No one in California knew how he entered the United States illegally, crossing the U.S./Mexico border stuffed behind the back seat of a dilapidated sedan. Also unknown was that he legally assumed his mother's maiden name, Anderson, and used the Anglicized William as his given name. His application for a U.S. passport was granted without question. William Anderson became the legal American name of Guillermo Arcenas.

Although a bonafide citizen of the United States, William Anderson was also a citizen of Mexico as Guillermo Acenas. Now in his mid-thirties, William Anderson was a reputable prescription drug manufacturer. His business model was solid, expanding only to production of additional drug lines after the market proved them viable. William wore a suit and tie everywhere as was proper for one of Manzanita's major employers.

When Anderson chose to be the thirty-something Guillermo Arcenas, his title was not CEO. Arcenas was a drug dealer. His plans included running the drug trade in all Southern California—Mexico to the Grape Vine and the Pacific to Arizona. His wardrobe featured short-sleeve dress shirts, always worn with at least two buttons open, and linen trousers. Guillermo didn't own a tie. Neither did he have an office in Manzanita.

As Arcenas, the man spent blocks of time on both sides of the border studying Mexican drug cartels and possible pipelines for importing illegal drugs. Arcenas, the drug dealer, used intimidation to get what he wanted.

However, he was not opposed to using selected strategies of persuasion when intimidation proved inadequate.

Anderson and Arcenas were light and dark reflections of the same image—two men with a single body. The glow of legitimacy from Anderson's persona as the respectable drug manufacturer masked the shadowy actions of his alter ego, Arcenas.

When William Anderson sat at his massive desk, a colossal credenza filled the space between his chair and the back office wall. Enormous bookcases dwarfed the commissioned oil painting hiding the door of a wall safe. A bank of file cabinets mirrored the bookcases on the opposite wall. An oversize conference table and six king-sized, leather-covered chairs completed the imposing décor.

The room was always under-lighted. Those admitted to his office were never allowed an adequately illuminated look at any part. He followed the same precaution with his personal information. He granted acquaintances and friends minimal access to details of his life.

Those invited to his office lost any sense of superiority when they sat on chairs designed to keep the feet of all but the longest-legged visitor dangling at least half an inch off the floor. The massive pieces of the office suite furniture and the inadequate illumination combined to generate a sense of insecurity.

Only those who gained Anderson's trust ever met with him outside this office.

Today was a day when Guillermo Arcenas, not William Anderson, sat in the big chair behind Anderson's desk. He snatched the phone from its base, selected the phone line dedicated to him, and punched in a number, and waited impatiently for his party to answer.

"I need a disposable asset."

"Most of the junkies in this area have hitched their wagons to Garmel's syndicate," reported the feminine voice.

"I don't want excuses. When this is finished, Garmel, if he's still a player, will try to find new users but fail. We'll have them all in our house."

"Okay. When and where shall I have someone make contact?"

"Tomorrow night. At the factory office. Call me with information on your selection. I need to customize the place for his arrival."

"It might take a couple hours. The beat cops are all at a training session on how to deal with the homeless."

If quiet has emotions, this silence was most unhappy at that news.

"As soon as I have a name, I will call," Petula Jacobs promised. "Do you want Rogers to know?"

The click of the handset contacting the cradle concluded the conversation.

"I'll take that as a . . ." Petula informed the dial tone.

* * *

Hours later, Arcenas was still in his office. He'd told Anderson's wife he had to take an important call there. She'd been pouty, but he'd make up for his perceived gaff by bringing home a bauble for her. The phone rang. Arcenas answered.

"Speak."

"The guy's named Reed," Petula said.

"First name or last?"

"Far as I can tell, that's it. Just Reed."

"Presumptuous of him," was the facetious comment from a man with an inflated ego.

"If you say so. The guy's a musician. Pretty good from what I've heard. But, that's only when he's not high, which isn't all that often."

"Sounds perfect. What time will he meet me?"

"You want him delivered."

"Is that a question?"

"No. You want him delivered to the factory office. I'd say that's the only way you have a chance of getting him there on time."

"Do it."

"Yes, sir. Is there anything else?"

"I have some materials to stash in Mr. Reed's residence. Call in a month."

As was his preference, it was Arcenas' handset that hit its cradle first.

* * *

William Anderson stared out the one-way window that flanked the private door to his office. Few people knew that the window existed. Anderson liked it that way. It allowed him to do what he was doing at that moment—observe without fear of discovery.

A limo pulled into the Vice-President's space next to Anderson's car. The back door opened and a scraggly looking man climbed out before the driver could perform the expected door opening service.

Seconds later, Reed and the driver stood in the breezeway outside the office door. Anderson recognized the driver. The man acted as the courier between Petula and his alter ego, Guillermo Arcenas. Anderson didn't know the driver's name. He didn't want to. His associates assured him of the driver's loyalty by assuring the driver catastrophic injuries to his wife and children if he ever went to the police about his work.

The driver pushed the speak button on the intercom hidden in the molding surrounding the door and window.

"I appreciate promptness."

"Thank you, señor Arcenas." The response was impressive since it followed a startle reaction to the sound of the ethereal voice.

"Do not use that name again."

Blood drained from the driver's face. He staggered back to keep his balance.

"Which of you is Mr. Reed?" Anderson ignored the driver's physical distress and asked only to find out if Reed was strung out.

Jerky movements of the disposable asset showed he needed a hit. A half wave of his right arm implied his mental facilities were at accessible.

For the next ten minutes, Anderson tried to explain his expectations to Reed. It proved more difficult than Anderson planned. Reed was transfixed by talking to an unseen voice through the intercom. Anderson decided it was time to end the conversation.

"Can you tell me what I want you to do?"

"If I'm hearin' right, you want me to, uh, to break in and steal some drugs from your factory. That right?"

"In a crude way, yes. But, you won't really be breaking in. We'll make it look like a break-in for insurance purposes. That will happen after you are long gone. And you're not really stealing. I'm giving you whatever drugs you want. After you've got the drugs, leave through the same door you came in. Your driver will take you home."

"Righteous!"

Anderson sighed and continued, "Listen carefully. This last part is critical."

Reed scrunched his face into what he considered a look of concentration.

Anderson shook his head. Until now, he'd never seen the ultimate end of addiction to his drugs up close. It was disgusting.

"I will report the robbery to the police."

"What? I ain't goin' to jail for not stealin' somethin'. No way! I'm out!"

"Your only way out, Mr. Reed, is to die." Anderson's tone was granitic. He needed Reed to follow his instructions to the letter. "You will do exactly as I say, or the police will find out who stole my merchandise. And, you will go to jail for a long, long time. Is that clear?"

"I hear ya. But I thought you said you was givin' me…" Reed's voice trailed away. Figuring he heard the man wrong, he said, "Tell me what I'm doin' again. Okay?"

Anderson complied. After a final review, he directed the driver to take Reed to the factory employee entrance.

"There's a latex glove dispenser outside the door. Make sure Reed is wearing them from before he opens the door until he closes it on his way out. I want the police to spend time and effort on this investigation."

Reed looked confused.

"Mr. Reed. Follow your driver. Put gloves on when you get to the door. Go inside. Get your drugs. Come outside. Close the door. Get in the limo. The driver will take you home."

"Do I get to keep the gloves?"

Anderson sighed.

"No. Leave them in the limo when you get out. Any questions, driver?"

"About the timeline—"

"Give him fifteen minutes, then call for him to come out. Do not—I repeat, do not go in after him. If he's still there in twenty minutes, leave. He's on his own."

"Yes, sir. Thank you, sir."

"Questions, Mr. Reed?"

Reed shook his head. He followed the driver to the factory entrance and put on his gloves. The driver watched while his passenger took a first hesitant step, then shuffled across the threshold and over to a stack of containers filled with bottles of pills.

Anderson watched through the window until the pair turned the corner at the end of the office complex. Thirty minutes later, he heard the limo pull away. He smiled a knowing smile, walked to the factory door, locked it, got in his car, and drove home.

It was not quite midnight.

* * *

At 2:30 a.m., two figures in clean suits stood outside the factory door. One of them raised the sledgehammer he carried and took several swings at the door before it finally popped open. The pair entered the building. Their instructions were to make the storage area look like one or two people searched for something specific. They could open boxes, remove pill bottles and drop them, or pull boxes off pallets to the floor. The task was to create disorder not chaos.

They took fifty-seven minutes to complete the assignment.

* * *

William Anderson lay on his back on his side of the California King-size bed in the Spanish style bedroom in his villa in Las Piñas Estates. Las Piñas was a desirable and expensive community in Manzanita. Up and coming movers and shaker living there lobbied for and received, a distinct zip code. Senders now addressed mail to Las Piñas Estates, CA.

He looked at his wife. Nearly ten years his junior, she had been a bombshell when they married. Time and malaise had taken its toll. He frowned and pulled the sheet up over the dimpling in her bottom.

He looked at the clock on his nightstand. The number 5:57 changed to 5:58 as a tile flipped down to reveal the numeral beneath it. He returned his gaze to the ceiling.

The phone rang.

"I've got it, sweetie," he whispered to his wife as he picked up the phone and climbed out of bed.

"Yes?" Anderson said doing his best imitation of a man just awakened from his slumber.

"This is Jameson, down at the factory. I'm sorry to call so early, sir, but there's been a break-in."

Anderson swore.

"Something wrong, Bill?"

"It's the factory," he replied covering the phone's mouthpiece with his hand. "I'll take it downstairs. Just hang up when you hear me tell you to."

He handed the phone to her and hurried downstairs to the den.

"Okay, Sweetie. I've got it."

"Oh, good. I'm not ready to get up yet." The distinctive click of the phone handset being placed on the base unit was clear. Anderson resumed his conversation with his factory foreman.

"Touch nothing. And, whatever you do, don't let anyone in the building. We want the police to have the most evidence they can find."

"Um, sir."

"What is it?"

"Two of us have already been in the building."

"I see. Well, don't go in again. And keep everyone else out! I'll head down there now."

"Do you want me to call the police, sir?"

"No!" Anderson realized he over-emphasized that directive. "I mean, don't bother. I'll call the police after I've seen the damage."

"Yes, sir."

The pharmaceutical mogul left a note for his wife, hopped in his Mercedes, and drove to his factory. He conducted a cursory inspection as soon as he arrived. That satisfied his foreman and verified what he already knew.

"I'll take it from here," he said. He entered his office and phoned the police.

* * *

Two weeks passed without an arrest in the Anderson Pharmaceuticals break-in. Anderson was pleased. An arrest was something he helped delay. He decided enough time had passed to warrant the hiring of a private investigator. When looking for someone to do a job for him, he always began with the M's in the phonebook. It was a nod to his biological father's given name.

Mamba Investigations was the top name on the list.

Chapter 6

He was trying hard not to be, but private investigator, Philip "Dancer" Mamba, was bored. It wasn't any one thing that pushed him off the precipice of interest into the marsh of tedium in which he now found himself. It was the combination of many small aspects of his current, and only, case that was conspiring against him. He was on the phone with that client.

Times like these when he was stuck on the phone with a client who enjoyed listening to his own voice, that he almost regret becoming a private investigator. He knew that wasn't true. The ultimate reason for his career choice was based on a case involving Hope Tanner. She was now his receptionist, and his wife.

He refused to believe that Hope's first husband's death was an accidental electrocution. When his Captain demanded he close the case listing that as the cause of death, he opted to close all his police cases. He quit the force and went to work on his own for Hope. The end result was a conviction of murder in the first degree, and he hadn't looked back.

A vision materialized in his mind's eye. The vision was familiar.

At the end of his first case as a private investigator, as he walked down the hallway away from her appointment, he admitted Hope Tanner was a very pretty woman and decided he should give her a call someday to be sure she was doing all right.

Instead, she called him wanting to be his secretary, since the combined stress of being widowed and pregnant was driving her stir crazy. He hired her. Things went well for a while and would have gone better if it hadn't been for the bomb that detonated in his office while she was there.

Doctors took her baby via Cesarean section and she had extensive surgery on one leg. Long story short, they married as soon as she could walk, although she used him as a crutch during the ceremony. The baby was now his adopted son. Hope was still his secretary. She limped when it was cold and damp because of her leg injury from the bomb blast.

His life was good.

Something his client said cut his contemplation short. The vocal inflection sounded like it might have been a question. Even though he hadn't heard the words, he was sure he could give an appropriate answer. William Anderson was nothing if not consistent. He picked up where he left off in the conversation certain Anderson wouldn't realize he hadn't been paying attention.

"Mr. Anderson, my next move is to follow up on the chemical analysis of the material scraped from the front threshold of your factory's office. Without a thorough examination by an analytical chemist, I won't know whether it warrants further investigation."

Anderson did not respond.

As the silence inexplicably continued, Mamba's mind wandered. That wasn't uncommon. He did much of his best detective work while lost in thought.

William Anderson was notorious for his lack of patience, and the PI's investigation of a burglary at his pharmaceutical factory was in its second week. The explanation he just gave his client for the lack of progress on the case was an example of why Dancer was Mamba's nickname. He was renowned for his verbal choreography while circumventing the delivery of unpopular news to a client, or a suspect.

More words from his client invaded his consciousness and refocused his attention.

"I want an arrest," Anderson said without inflection. Finding the burglar was of paramount importance to the man. That was understandable, but something bothered Mamba about Anderson's fixation with that idea. There was concern for justice, and then there was neurosis. Mamba was still on the fence about his client's location on that continuum.

"I don't see how I can go to the police without the chemical analysis. That's the only hard evidence I might have against my suspect. And even if the police arrest someone, that doesn't guarantee a conviction. And definitely not without solid evidence."

"I'll agree to the analysis only on the condition it provides some of your hard evidence. No evidence and I pay only half the cost of the report."

"That's not an acceptable position," Mamba explained, simulating patience he did not possess. "I could have had the analysis done myself two days ago, but that testing costs money. As a man who deals with chemicals and their development and testing, you know that." He played his trump card with a touch of annoyance for effect.

"I don't see how you can avoid additional break-ins without that lab report."

The sound of silence filled the phone line. Mamba hoped that he hadn't beat the horse too hard.

Anderson could not deny the truth about the cost of anything dealing with chemicals, knowing that would raise a giant red flag. And, the detective had a point about the possibility of future break-ins. He berated himself for forgetting that detail. But, he hated the thought of giving in to anyone. Giving in was against William Anderson's principles.

After a rambling mental monolog, and although the results of this lab test could also undermine the plan he set in motion, Anderson decided to go along with the PI.

"I'll pay for only seventy-five percent of the cost of the analysis if it provides no evidence," Anderson conceded.

"Fine. But, if we get the results I'm expecting, you'll pay the rest, or I release only seventy-five percent of the results to you."

"I refuse to be—"

"That's the way it's going to be, if you want me to continue working for you. There are other detective agencies in town. I'll be glad to have my secretary provide a list of alternatives."

The brief sound of angry breathing ended with Anderson clearing his throat.

"My secretary will send you a form detailing that provision in the expense voucher," the man growled. Mamba erroneously visualized Anderson's teeth grinding as he forced those words out.

After ending the call, Mamba's client muttered into the handset, "You are lucky, señor Mamba, that you are dealing with William Anderson and not Guillermo Arcenas. Señor Arcenas is much less accommodating of such presumptuous behavior as yours."

* * *

The pharmaceutical factory owner was aggravating, but not impossible to deal with. Mamba found guilt to be most effective in working with Anderson types. And, seventy-five percent of the cost of the analysis was a cheap way to buy time if nothing came from the results. If the analysis paid off, it was cheaper still, since Anderson picked up the whole tab.

Mamba hung up the phone and buzzed his secretary.

"Yes, Phil?"

"Call the lab and tell them to go ahead with the analysis, and then come in for a minute, will you? I need you to take a memo to Mr. Anderson."

"Is this your idea or his?" Hope asked as she entered the office a few minutes later. She smiled as she leaned over the desk, kissed her husband on the cheek, and added, "I'm running out of room in his file folder."

"Believe it or not, this memo was my idea," Mamba grinned. "We can start volume two of 'The Anderson Files,' if you want to."

The PI's eyes followed his wife as she pulled up a chair opposite him and opened her steno pad. She was not skinny. Neither was she fat. She called herself petite, which he thought meant something completely different from whatever her definition was.

He told her she should quit working for him after their wedding. He considered that expedient considering the bomb blast destroyed their old office. She was adamant. Little Jimmy was at Grandma's house fifteen-twenty hours a week, much to grandma's satisfaction, while Hope supervised the office, and him.

"I'm all set." Hope broke into his thoughts.

He dictated the necessary memo for William Anderson. When he finished, he leaned back in his chair.

"What's the matter, Phil?" Hope asked.

"Oh, nothing." He startled her when he leaned forward in his chair and ordered, "Get Reed on the phone. We have a number on file for him, right?"

"Not Mr. Reed." Hope grimaced. Requests like this one were not why she stayed on as her husband's secretary. Most of Phil's clients were regular people in need of help. A subdivision of his associates was not.

"He's such a . . ." she paused while searching for the correct word in her mind.

"Slimeball?"

"Well, yes." It was against her nature to belittle anyone. Mom, Dad, and a succession of Sunday School teachers had seen to that.

"I know you don't approve of him, but he provides a service from time to time. I'm going to twist him a little."

The confused look on Hope's face reminded Mamba that not everyone spoke police jargon, which he still did at times. It was difficult to break certain habits, even after over two years off the force.

"I think he's responsible for the Anderson Pharmaceutical burglaries," he explained. "But I won't have any hard evidence until that chemical analysis comes back, and maybe not then. By twisting the truth a little, I hope I can wring some information from him free of charge."

"Oh. So, you pretty much get to be yourself," Hope responded as she rose to leave. She understood the nature of her husband's business forced certain compromises between fact and fiction from time to time. She also knew that Phil would never lie if he was the only beneficiary from the falsehood. Even so, some of the details to which she'd been privy bothered her.

"I'll see if I can reach him."

"Thanks. If he's not at his place, try Tug's Pub down on 22nd Street."

"Will do," she said with a careless salute. She turned a sloppy about-face and sauntered back to her desk.

Chapter 7

Manzanita Chief of Police Dwight Rogers entered the conference room reserved for him each Tuesday morning and removed copies of the meeting's agenda from a manila folder. He walked around the conference table placing one agenda on the table before each chair.

The highest-ranking officers from each key cadre in the Manzanita Police Department and Deputy Chief Nolan Chalmers comprised the Rogers' Leadership Team. Captains from Northeast, Central, Western, and the Internal Affairs Divisions, and the Lieutenant of the department-wide Records Division had been hand-picked or intentionally promoted to their current positions by Rogers. Chalmers was not his selection; he worked his way up the ladder and was a favorite among the rank and file. They were a loyal, hardworking team.

"Morning, Chief," the Captain of Northeast Division, the perennial first to arrive, called his greeting as he entered the conference room, coffee mug and yellow legal pad in hand.

The Chief turned to greet the first of his six confederates.

"Good morning back at you, Captain."

As the others arrived, Rogers' demeanor turned serious. RossAnn Gilroy, a local pillar of the community was the newly appointed leader of Manzanita Unified School District's fledgling "Just Say No" anti-drug campaign. Their Superintendent requested police support at the kick-off rallies during in the school year. She was the final agenda item for the day. He knew he had to come across as a champion of the anti-drug movement. That was not going to sit well with his strongest, if anonymous, supporters.

* * *

"I don't know if you should wait up, Liz," Sergeant Franklin Stallings said as he unlocked the door of his g-ride, the nickname for every Crown Victoria assigned to an officer in any division of the Manzanita Police Department. Within limits, they allowed him to use the car as he saw fit.

"You know I will, no matter what you suggest." Lizbeth sighed as her husband opened the driver's door.

Franklin looked as his wife. She was tall. He was medium. He was athletic, playing soccer as a kid because of the Nigerian refugee contingent in his neighborhood. She was an athlete. She'd played college basketball at Kent State until suffering a career-ending knee injury.

Today, she wore an Afro wig. She was in chemotherapy for ovarian cancer, and the process had taken its toll on her. Her hair, normally shoulder length and moderately kinky fell out early in the treatment series. She'd shaved her head and "gone 'fro," as she called it, with the wig. Contrary to her opinion, he thought her flawless ebony skin made everything she wore look spectacular.

"That's why I love you." He heard the sigh, and he'd been married long enough to know he did or said something untoward in her opinion.

"If that's your only reason." She left the threat hang.

"It's not," he assured her. "Given enough time, I'm certain I could come up with one or two more."

"Not funny," she called as he slammed the car door. She reached down, grabbed the newspaper off the porch, and launched it towards the now moving car.

"Airball. Ouch!" he chided as the paper fell short of the mark. Then, he grinned, waved, and blew her a kiss.

She grimaced, returned the kiss, sighed again, and trudged after the paper certain that five months ago that paper would've smacked the car's windshield, she thought and shook her head. By the time she returned to the porch, she was breathing heavily. She hated cancer.

* * *

As is typical in every central to southern California city, rain transformed a normal commute into a giant bumper car ride. Stallings made scores of unscheduled stops, starts, and turns on his trip to the division office. All the while, his thoughts drifted back over the past year.

The house they lived in now was significantly smaller than their home in St. Louis. His commute to work was longer because of traffic, not distance, but, the weather was glorious compared to the Midwest, except for today.

He was glad he accepted MPD's offer. He knew they based the offer, at least to some degree, on Manzanita's need to move toward compliance with Federal Affirmative Action mandates. But, since he'd been on duty, he'd experienced little internal prejudice, neither overt nor covert, because he was an African American.

He asked himself why he was angry so often. As was his habit, he formulated his answer as a list.

His wife had cancer.

He was exhausted.

His caseload was huge compared to his previous positions.

He did not know who was real and who was playing him.

He was being pressured by someone sending him untraceable, threatening memos.

He jammed the brake pedal of his sedan down to the floorboard. Tires squealed. Bumpers came to rest mere inches apart. Imprecations flew. Gestures were exchanged.

Stallings drove the rest of the way to work thinking about nothing but his driving. By the time he passed the Desk Sergeant, his mood was bad, and headed to worse.

* * *

After letting the phone at Reed's only known phone number ring over a dozen times, Hope Mamba moved to Plan B. She sighed and dialed the number for the hangout suggested by her husband for the stealthy Mr. Reed.

"Tug's Pub. The tug's in port. This is the Cap'n."

"Is Mr. Reed there, please," Hope asked with as much professional demeanor she could manage after the bartender's standard telephone greeting. Making phone calls to places like this was an uncomfortable, but necessary part of her job.

"Mr. Reed?"

"Yes. My, uh, husband, Phil Mamba, asked me to call."

"Dancer?"

"Yes, I guess. I know some people call him that."

"You say you're his wife?"

"Yes, but—"

"Blow me down!" the Cap'n shouted into the phone. Hope then heard him bellowing in the background. "Ahoy, Mates! Dancer Mamba's got himself a female first mate."

She tried to figure out what she could say to reclaim the bartender's attention. She failed in her deliberations and just held the phone away from her ear until the noise in the bar subsided and the Cap'n returned to his end of the connection.

"Little lady, if you've managed to hook the Dancer, I'll try to find a Mr. Reed or Miss America or anyone else you and he wants." The Cap'n's voice reverberated in the phone's receiver.

"This man has worked for him before."

"You mean Reed?"

"Yes, Mr. Reed."

"Well, he's never been no mister, and he's not here—" he paused. "Blow me down! He's comin' aboard now."

"Hold on a moment, please, Mr. Mamba wants to talk to him." She didn't care if anyone heard her or not. She buzzed her husband as she spoke.

"I think Mr. Reed's on the phone now."

"Thanks, Hope." The private detective punched the outside line button on his phone.

"Reed?" he asked. There was no immediate answer. The detective could hear the Cap'n instructing someone to, "Take the phone if you know what's good for you."

Mamba smiled with understanding at Hope's previous remark. He asked again, "Reed?"

"Yeah," was the slurred reply. "Who wants to know?"

"This is Dancer. I want you. Five o'clock this afternoon. Write down this address."

"I ain't got no paper or pen."

"Put the Cap'n back on."

No response.

"Reed!"

"Sure. Sure. Put the Cap'n back on."

"This you, Dancer?"

"Ahoy, Cap'n," Mamba greeted the bartender. He rushed to continue before the man could ask questions. "I want you to write down this address and give it to Reed."

"Anything you want," the bartender promised, dropping the sea-going jargon he used to promote the name of his bar. He recognized the tone of Mamba's voice. He'd heard it before and knew the detective wanted no questions about his orders. "Go ahead."

After Mamba gave his office address to the bartender, he asked, "Is Reed flying?"

"Not on my booze. He just got here."

"Will twenty dollars keep him that way until five o'clock?"

"Twenty-five would guarantee it."

"You're a pirate, you know."

"That's a mite strong, Mate," the Cap'n pouted, grateful that Dancer had opened the door back to his nautical slang. "Not a full-fledged pirate, but, maybe a cabin boy on a pirate ship."

"Close enough," Mamba laughed. "Put him in a cab at four thirty for the extra Lincoln."

"Drop anchor on that, mate," the Cap'n agreed. "Say who's this Mrs. Mamba?"

"Later. Just get Reed in that cab."

"Like a steamer into port, Mate."

"Goodbye, Cap'n."

Mamba sat lost in thought after he hung up the phone. If he met Reed tonight, the possibility of a quick solution to the Anderson case might increase by a significant percentage.

"Honey," Hope stage-whispered from the office doorway.

"Huh?" Mamba shook his head as he recovered from the brief start his secretary caused him.

"I'm going to pick up Jimmy and go on home," she continued. "When can I expect you?"

"Reed's coming at five," he mused aloud. "It shouldn't take long. I should be home by six or six thirty."

"Why didn't the bartender know whom I wanted when I asked for Mr. Reed?"

"You asked for Mister Reed?"

"Of course."

"That's the problem," Phil smiled as he went to his wife and hugged her. "I don't know what Reed's name would be if anyone called him Mister. We call him Reed because he plays a mean tenor sax when he's sober."

"I'll never keep up with all the nicknames your acquaintances use," Hope complained good-naturedly. The term acquaintances was a deliberate choice over a less polite, but equally accurate term she considered. She brushed her husband's cheek with a kiss as she departed. "Call me, if you'll be late. I might wait up, if I'm in the mood."

She left Phil alone in his office with his thoughts about the kind of mood he hoped Hope would be in when he got home.

* * *

Reed sat in the back seat of a cab. At least that's what it looked like to him. Of course, this far into a bottle of cheap whiskey, he might not have left Tug's yet.

He belched. The cabbie shook his head in disgust and prepared to demand a sizeable tip for this fare.

Reed told no one his given name. Most assumed the brain cells that had stored that information had drowned in a sea of alcohol or burned away by drugs years before. As a young man, the jazz community in and around Mobile, Alabama considered him a rising star. His future looked as bright as it could for any black man in Alabama in the late 1950s.

With success came more gigs. With more gigs came more jazz joints. With more jazz joints came more women—and more booze, and drugs. He did fine with the extra gigs until the combination of more women and a lot more booze and drugs turned him into an unreliable sot who used to be someone who could light up a saxophone.

In recent years, he remained sober only long enough to play a couple of sets two nights a week in low-end bars along the Central California coast. Somehow, he managed to hold a ratty apartment in Manzanita through it all.

Reed knew for certain that he would go to Dancer Mamba's office as directed. As a Manzanita police officer, Mamba threatened to run Reed in for miscellaneous misdemeanors, mostly drunk and disorderly or creating a public nuisance. Only on rare occasions did Reed get involved in physical altercations. No matter how drunk or high he was, he retained an understanding of the importance of intact fingers in his line of work.

Because he never booked Reed while he was a police officer, Mamba squeezed him as a confidential informant, a CI. In exchange for reliable information from Reed, he let the man skate on his offenses since they harmed no one but Reed himself.

Deep in Reed's nearly pickled brain he knew that's where he was headed this evening. Dancer Mamba would squeeze him for information.

At 5:02, Mamba paid Reed's cab fare, including a sizeable tip, and led him into his office.

"I've got enough from the Anderson job for the narcs to nail you," he lied as he waded right in with a frontal assault on the informant. "Either you give me names of the friends you're working for or you are going to fall. Hard."

"You got nuthin'!"

"I scraped the office threshold, Reed. It's at the lab now. When they confirm what I suspect, that'll do it."

The sweat trickled down Reed's face. The color in his gaunt features faded from dark to milk chocolate as the implications of Mamba's words soaked in. He mustered his final defense.

"That resin could've come from anywhere. Not just the floor of The Jazz Machine has sawdust on it. Besides, I just got back in town from up in Oregon."

"I've got witnesses that place you at The Jazz Machine last week," Mamba lied again. He had only a rumor about Reed's presence in town, but he needed information quickly. Leaning back in his chair, he studied the shaky figure before him while he contemplated the mention of resin in Reed's statement. He suspected fresh asphalt sealer for the sample from Anderson's lab, but resin was a possibility. He pressed harder.

"Face it, Reed, you're taking the fall if I want you to."

Reed's body slumped forward at Mamba's pronouncement. He thought that only the manager knew of his visits to The Jazz Machine during off-hours. Now it was clear somebody else saw him going in or coming out. Dancer still didn't miss a thing. He had to tell him what he wanted to know, because he knew he'd never survive prison.

"What do you want to know?" the informant asked in a hoarse whisper.

"You know what: names, dates, places, where the stuff's going and who's taking it."

An hour later, Reed was gone. Mamba sat in shocked silence. Lying on the desk before him were four pages of detailed information on drug dealers and deals in Manzanita and two neighboring cities. Twisting Reed hadn't produced a trickle of information. What he'd wrung out of the man was a flood.

Even if only a few names Reed had provided were trafficking narcotics, the police could cripple local drug dealers for quite a while with a systematic series of raids. Mamba wondered what was waiting for Reed in prison.

He decided to wait until morning to go to the police. His former partner, Pat Kerrigan, would be on duty then. Mamba wanted to run the information past his old friend before anyone else learned of the bonanza. Kerrigan deserved that.

After slipping the unfolded sheets of notebook paper into a large envelope, Mamba placed them in his briefcase. Hefting the briefcase, he locked up the office, glad that he would be home for dinner with his family, but wishing it was tomorrow already so he could unload what he got from Reed.

As he drove home, he knew he would not sleep that night.

Chapter 8

Pat Kerrigan, Lieutenant of Homicide Detectives, looked up from his desk as the door to his office opened. The lines of worry that creased his brow even at this early hour smoothed out when he recognized his friend and former partner, Phil Mamba. He stood and extended his hand.

Not long ago, this room was Lieutenant Mamba's office. He was a rising star in the Manzanita Police Department. His conviction rate was the envy of all and discussed with an almost mythical reverence in the locker room.

Kerrigan knew Mamba as a classmate at the regional police academy, where they met. The attraction was not mutual at the start. Phil Mamba took some time to grow on you.

Mamba's impressive conviction rate was not achieved by luck. The man was relentless.

"It's good to see you, Phil!"

"Good to see you, too, Pat." Mamba glanced around the small cubicle he once occupied. Stacks of paper created disorderly piles in every available open space. Kerrigan was not on top of the paperwork required of a police lieutenant. To Mamba, it appeared his friend had barely started his climb toward the top of that part of his job. "How's it going?"

"I think you know." Kerrigan grimaced as he watched Mamba visually scrutinizing the office disarray. "How'd you get the paperwork under control?"

"I found prayer a big help." Mamba grinned. Then he added, "The truth is that it just takes experience. And long hours. Of course, it doesn't hurt to have a second in command that's a dynamite typist."

"I figured you had some kind of secret," Kerrigan accused. "Who did your typing?"

"Officer Phillips, before she resigned to have her baby," Mamba confessed. "After she left, MPD switched to civilian secretaries." He held up his hands, "From then on, these babies did all the key pounding, since civilians have restricted access to classified documents and reports."

Kerrigan's face fell.

Mamba allowed his friend to suffer for several seconds. Captain Martin would have called the revelation about doing his own typing a "character builder." Since he'd never liked Martin, Mamba added the rest of the truth for his friend. "And, I took a night class in typing at the Adult School when Phillips told me she was leaving in five months."

Pat perked up at that information.

"Think they still offer that class?"

"The Adult School usually has one going. Can you spare the time?"

"To save time in the long run and to help get this mess cleaned up a little, believe me, I'll make the time!"

"I'll shut the door if you don't mind." Mamba pulled the handle on the wood rimmed glass partition.

"Must be serious business." Kerrigan frowned as he returned to his chair. "What've ya got?"

"It needs a little checking, but I think I've got a laundry list of information on the drug traffickers in the area." Mamba snapped open his briefcase and removed the envelope with the pages of names and locations Reed supplied.

Kerrigan took the papers and made a cursory inspection of each. When he finished page four, he leaned back in his chair with a soft whistle.

"If even half this list is legit, it's worth more than a stack of gold bullion. Mind if I have copies of these made?"

"I figured you would."

Kerrigan pushed the intercom button on his desk phone.

"Can you come in here, please, Peggy."

By the time Peggy Wallace, the civilian department secretary appeared at the door, Kerrigan was waiting for her, lists in hand.

"Get Sergeant Edwards to copy each of these. Tell him it's Code 3."

She nodded and made an immediate exit. Although Code 3 was the code for use of lights and sirens by police vehicles when responding to a call, in the Manzanita Police Department it had come to mean the same as ASAP in other organizations.

* * *

"Hey, Eddie," Peggy called to Sergeant "Eddie" Edwards, the officer of rank in the Records and Copies section.

"Hi, Peggy. What brings you down here?"

"I need copies," she deadpanned.

"Then you've come to the right place," Edwards answered with a huge smile. He walked from the copy machine he was using to the counter that marked the limit of public access to the copy room.

"One copy of each," she said and handed over Mamba's lists.

"You want fries with that?" Edwards didn't follow-up his most common quip when he finished his quick visual scan of the first page. He almost always checked out what he was copying. What started as casual routine became an essential adjustment to Edwards' activity. He was looking at a hornet's nest of names of people he knew about, and names that certain people didn't want others to know about.

"You okay, Eddie?"

"Huh? Oh, yeah." He cleared his throat. "Must have got something down the wrong pipe."

He went back to the large copier he was using when Peggy arrived. He repeated four sequences of lifting the copier lid, placing a page on the glass, closing the lid, pushing a button, and then removing the page. Those actions produced a copy of each page of the list. He knocked the four sheets together on the top of the copier to align them in the stack. Without preamble, he swore loudly.

"Hang the maintenance sign on this one," he growled to his assistant as he crumpled the four copies he'd just made. "We got to get a service guy down here immediately." Turning to Peggy he held up all four of her lists and said, "I'll take these to the smaller machine. Just be a minute."

"No problem."

Edwards disappeared through the door to the back half of the copy room. He pulled the door closed behind him and went to the metal desk on the back wall of the room. He lifted the phone and removed a page of numbers and notations from beneath it. He dialed the number at the top of the page.

"Manzanita Copy and Fax."

"This is Edwards over in Northeast. I need an emergency service call."

"What's the problem?"

Edwards ran his finger down a column on the page titled, PROBLEM.

"Far as I can tell, we need a new toner cartridge."

"I see. What model number was that machine? I want to be certain our technician brings the correct cartridge."

As he ran his finger down the page a second time, but this time in the column titled DESIGNATION, he answered.

"It's the five thousand."

"Glad I asked. That model take's a special cartridge."

"How long will the machine be down?"

"I've got a service van in the area. Maybe ten minutes from the time the technician arrives."

"Have him ask for me, Sergeant Edwards." As promised, he made the requested copies on the machine by the desk and delivered the copies and the originals to Peggy.

"Thanks, Eddie. I don't know how we survived without copy machines."

"I try not to think about that," he answered with a wave, but he. He called to her when she reached the door to the copy. "Oh, Peggy, tell the Lieutenant he owes me a cup o' Joe, from a diner, for the expedited service."

"Sure thing, Eddie."

* * *

Kerrigan closed his door and returned to his seat before he began asking his questions about the lists of names.

"Where'd you get those?"

"I heard it from a reliable source," was the conveniently elusive answer.

"You don't have to dance for me, Phil."

"Ingrained habit."

Kerrigan grimaced. "Anyone I know?"

"You might. He's been around."

"Do you use him often?"

"When it's appropriate."

"You're not going to tell me who it is, are you?"

"No." Mamba grinned.

"Okay." Pat smiled, too. "I had to try."

"I know."

A knock on the door ended the litany of questions.

"Come in," Kerrigan called.

Peggy did just that. She handed the now eight-page stack to the Lieutenant.

"Sgt. Edwards says you owe him a cup of real coffee for the fast turnaround," she said, paraphrasing the man's words.

"Thanks, Peggy. I'll keep that in mind."

After the secretary was gone, Mamba remarked, "I'm impressed."

"By what?"

"That was seriously fast turnaround time on those."

"Edwards is a good man. Now, about this list," Kerrigan held up the pages as he turned the conversation back to the original track. "Have you checked out any names?"

"I haven't had time. Just got them last night about 6:00."

"You know I can't go to Narcotics without verification."

"I'll check it out, if you want," Mamba offered. "I just wanted to be sure you were interested."

"More than interested. How about by Tuesday? I'm already scheduled on Wednesday into a task force meeting that includes the Narcs."

"Um," Mamba hesitated as he played out the time in his mind. Next Tuesday gave him four full days plus the rest of today. That would provide enough time since he wanted to report back to William Anderson by then anyway. "Sure. Tuesday's fine."

"You're not being altruistic about this are you?" Kerrigan stated as much as asked.

"What?"

"How much will this help you on whatever case you're on?"

"Pat, I'm hurt!"

"Come off it." Kerrigan refused to be conned. "This reeks of something you're working on for a client."

The PI shrugged and remained silent. It was best to let his friend's fertile imagination run rampant. Revealing Anderson as his client would do no good and could possibly harm his investigation. He gave Kerrigan what he uncovered. That was enough.

"Okay, you're in—for the time being."

"Then, I'd better get started," Mamba announced as he selected two of the pages of names Reed supplied him and shoved them into his briefcase. He slid the remaining six pages into the manila envelope he brought with him and dropped it on Kerrigan's desk. He turned to leave.

"Tuesday," Kerrigan reminded. Then he pointed to the envelope. "Thanks."

"Tuesday," Mamba confirmed. "And, you're welcome." After a beat, he added. "Try not to lose the envelope in this black hole of yours."

He pulled the door shut as he left. As he walked away from Kerrigan's office, he wondered how long would it take for Pat to contact the FBI's current database. He remembered it used to be known as INVSTAT. He also remembered that it wasn't always helpful.

After grimacing at Mamba's office clutter innuendo, Kerrigan roused the department secretary on his intercom a second time.

"Peggy, get me INVSTAT on the phone, please."

"Yes, sir, Lieutenant."

Once again, Kerrigan leaned back in his chair and shut his eyes. He knew why Mamba left two of the original lists of names. He and Mamba would not duplicate searches. He expected his friend to do some checking on his own. Mamba would expect them back on Tuesday.

INVSTAT, the Federal Bureau's acronym for their Status of Investigations system, kept track of all the local investigations of which they were aware. The FBI was capable of running any of the names on the list and would provide Kerrigan with information concerning any past or pending investigations involving that person. It was a handy, reliable, and quick way to verify certain pieces of information.

Of course, the downside was the Feds then knew of your interest in every case with potential of becoming their case. The bottom line: INVSTAT was more often a hindrance than it was a help to local law enforcement agencies.

"For the greater good," Kerrigan mumbled as the phone buzzed.

"Lieutenant Kerrigan," he stated slowly and distinctly.

"Code, please," a mechanical voice intoned.

"Rosencrantz," Kerrigan responded with the week's code of access to the INVSTAT files.

"Counter code," was the next emotionless request.

"Zero-Seven-Two-Seven-Zero-Five," completed the necessary access information. Each local police agency had its unique access number. Both the code and counter code number had to be correct, or the computer would hold the line open until a trace was made on the initiating phone's location.

There was a significant time delay while the confirmation was granted. Pat knew enough about computers to know that it did not take that much time to process his information. He was convinced that INVSTAT traced all calls it received. He couldn't blame the Feds, especially with terrorist types around.

"What can we do for you, Lieutenant?" were the first human words Kerrigan heard from the INVSTAT.

"Can you run a couple of drug suspects for me?"

"That's what we're here for," was the too perky reply. "Spell the names slowly, please."

Kerrigan complied. He picked one name from each page and meticulously spelled each name using the standard alphabet codes.

"That all?"

"That'll be enough, if it pans out."

"I hear you. We'll TELEX the report by fourteen thirty hours California time tomorrow."

Customers on any TELEX exchange could deliver messages to any TELEX machine around the world. To lower line usage, TELEX messages were first encoded onto paper tape and then fed into the line as quickly as possible. The system normally delivered information at sixty-six words per minute. The messages were encoded using the International Telegraph Alphabet No. 2, adding a minimal level of security to each message.

"That long?" Kerrigan asked facetiously as he flinched a bit at the reference to his time zone knowing they traced the call.

"The machine's been sick."

"Until tomorrow then."

The click of the receiver in Kerrigan's ear confirmed that the conversation was over.

"Peggy," Pat buzzed the secretary a third time.

"Yes, Lieutenant."

"I need a Teletype hook-up." Kerrigan preferred the older version of the machine's name. Anything with an EX at the end sounded suspicious to him.

Peggy did a quick calculation of the amount of time she would need to set up a viable link with the temperamental TELEX system.

"Give me fifteen minutes to clear a line."

"That's fine." Kerrigan did some time calculating of his own. Fifteen minutes would be just long enough to get a fresh cup of coffee, hit the men's room, and check on the progress of the primary homicide investigation he was involved with.

Seventeen minutes later, taking extreme care not to make any typographical errors, he punched at the keys of the TELEX machine. The terminal was tied into the central computer of the Criminal Identification and Information, CII, division of the State Government's Justice Department. The information available from this source differed from that of INVSTAT by providing only prior criminal records with no consideration of their current status with the law.

Kerrigan entered the same names that he gave the INVSTAT investigator into the CII terminal. He paused then added two additional names from Mamba's CI's list, hoping to increase his chance of obtaining concrete background information on someone listed on the handwritten pages on his desk.

The TELEX response from CII was usually instantaneous. After Kerrigan stared at the silent printer for five minutes, he decided that the system must be "down" on the other end. With an evil glare, he pushed his chair back from the terminal.

He stalked away from the recalcitrant device and stopped at Peggy's desk.

"Keep an eye on that printer."

"Yes, sir!" She replied. "Do you want to know when it comes in or do you just want me to collect it for you?"

"I'll pick it up later," he decided. "It's not life and death."

"Very good, Lieutenant. I'll keep it here for you."

"Thanks, Peg." Kerrigan checked his watch. "I've got to get to that meeting with the Captain. It may be tomorrow before I pick up that printout."

"No problem. I expect to be here."

"Sure. That's okay," the Lieutenant remarked absently. He turned his thoughts toward the agenda of his next meeting.

Chapter 9

Phil and Hope Mamba lived in a split-level house in the middle-class neighborhood of Manzanita Heights. The house was a short commute up Hillside Drive to Las Piñas Road. There was nothing special about the place. That was thanks to the Manzanita Heights Home Owners Association. It looked like any other of its cookie-cutter clones in their neighborhood. The only distinctive feature was the front door wreath, which Hope changed on the first day of each month.

It was Monday night. Monday nights for Phil Mamba meant Monday Night Football. Contrary to her husband, Hope Mamba was not a fan. It invaded a night in Phil's crowded schedule. Tonight, she would have traded her husband's preoccupation with some unknown situation for his usual interest in whoever those two or three men were that announced the play-by-play. Their insight, wit, and colorful descriptions were wasted on the entire Mamba household this Monday.

"Anything you want to share?" she asked as she looked over at the tense form pretending to relax in the recliner.

"Huh? What?"

"I was wondering if you wanted to share whatever it is you're concerned about with me." She invited her husband over to her side with a pat of her hand on the cushion of the couch.

"I wish I could," Phil confessed as he brought the recliner to the upright position. He usually bounced ideas off Hope's brain. It was wired differently than his in many places. Often, input as a result of those different pathways provided the perspective he needed to determine the importance of a piece of evidence. Their dialogs helped him visualize while building his case.

It was too early to speculate on the significance of what he gave Kerrigan. Until he had verification of Reed's list from law enforcement sources, it was best if he was the only Mamba worried about the case. He qualified his refusal to accept Hope's help.

"But, I've got to keep a tight lid on this until the police investigation ends." He concluded as he plopped down on the sofa beside her. She snuggled close. His voice trailed away as Hope's softness conformed to his contour.

* * *

It was a refreshing and relaxing commute. Having taken only surface streets because of the continuing threat of rain, Mamba arrived at the Northeast Division's station early for his meeting with Kerrigan.

He parked in the visitor's lot and walked across the street to the small coffee shop there. "Open 24 Hrs" flashed on and off on a sign in the window. Mamba thought that the sign was the highlight of the establishment's décor.

This morning, it was coffee he was after. He ordered a "coffee with extra cream to go." With Styrofoam cup in hand, he strolled down to Las Piñas and back.

He checked the time on his watch, tossed his cup in the receptacle outside the front door to the station, and walked directly to Kerrigan's office.

"You got your four days. What'd you find out?" The door clicked shut behind him.

"Me?" Kerrigan's feigned innocence was no more convincing than Mamba's had been in their previous meeting.

"Which alphabet gave you the most? Feds or State?"

"California came through. It was CII. In spades! I almost called you."

"Almost, is right. I bet you wanted to be sure that I earned my client's money."

"Just looking after your interests. How'd you do?"

"Same-o, same-o. A hit every time I checked."

"I'm surprised by the quality of your information." Kerrigan put both elbows on his desk and leaned forward. "You still going to sit on the Confidential Informant's name?"

"You know I can't give you the name. It means we need each other now." Although Mamba smiled as he spoke, his tone was all business.

Kerrigan nodded. He understood the fragile relationship between a cop and his informants. They were called "confidential informants" for a reason. He cleared his throat and asked, "Can you still find interrogation room 4 without help?"

"Unless you moved it. Why?"

"Remember that I told you I have that meeting with the Narcotics boys Wednesday?"

Mamba nodded.

"Well, it got bumped up. They'll be there in half an hour…" Kerrigan let the sentence hang.

"And if I just happen to show up, you won't send me away," Mamba finished. "See you in thirty."

Chapter 10

Mamba figured a five-year-old designed the Northeast Division station. There were no frills. Straight hallways connected with other straight hallways. Doors alternated on the left and right sides of those hallways.

Traversing the halls gave Mamba the sensation of a condemned ancient Greek citizen approaching the River Styx. The dearth of architectural features was oppressive, a clear contrast to the open space outside the station.

While walking from the men's room to the site of his meeting, an involuntary shiver stopped him in his tracks. He looked left, right, ahead and behind him in quick succession and wondered how long his confidence would last if he was the one escorted through those hallways in handcuffs.

Kerrigan was waiting outside the door of Interrogation Room 4 when Mamba arrived. He opened the door and held it open.

Mamba gave a head nod in return, his trip through the hallways still the focus of his thoughts.

"Geez, Phil. It's just a meeting with Narcotics. They're not charging you with anything." Kerrigan shook his head before following his taciturn friend into the room.

As Mamba cleared the doorway into his destination, he gave the space a quick visual scan, something he did subconsciously to every room he entered. Nothing changed in the two years since he severed ties with the Manzanita Police Department.

Interrogation room 4 was small with a table and four chairs. A two-way mirror dominated the wall that faced the doorway. A curtain covered the mirror now, and the electronic listening devices had been de-activated on Kerrigan's order. Mamba was only vaguely conscious of the details as waited for the other principals in the drama about to unfold.

For a moment he couldn't decide whether the room smelled stale, musty, or, then it hit him. Urine! This place smelled like the men's restroom. He felt his nose wrinkle at the thought.

The sound of the door opening roused Mamba from his introspection. An African American in a neatly pressed sergeant's uniform entered. His dark skin and hair were stark contrasts to Kerrigan's red-blonde hair and Irish complexion.

The newcomer's eyebrows rose as he spotted Mamba, but he settled himself into a chair across from the private detective without comment. Kerrigan spoke from where he sat next to his friend.

"Sergeant Stallings?"

"I'm Stallings." The man had a résumé that included stints in three Midwestern cities. Hired out of the St. Louis PD, he distinguished himself in leadership roles. Kerrigan knew of the man, but no matter whom he talked to, no one seemed to know the man himself.

"Kerrigan. Homicide." The Lieutenant introduced himself. "I've seen you around."

"Yeah, me, too," Stallings replied. He pointed to the ebony skin on the back of his hand and added, "I'm kind of hard to miss in this place."

Mamba perked up at the gesture and the accompanying comment.

"I know the feeling," Kerrigan said. He stood to his full six and one-half feet and pointed to his reddish hair. "I'm kind of hard to miss, myself."

The hint of a smile flickered on Stallings' lips, but he said nothing. He appreciated the lieutenant's effort.

"That's Phil Mamba," Kerrigan continued while he pointed to the PI. As he sat down, he explained, "He's the source of the information."

"I see," was Stallings' non-committal reply. He wondered how a civilian that looked like a cop got invited to this meeting and hoped the guy wasn't a private eye.

"Where's your man?" Kerrigan asked as he sat down in the chair next to Mamba.

"He'll be along. He was on the street most of the night."

"Do I know him?"

"You might. He transferred from here to Southern a couple years ago. Took the sergeant's exam once. I borrowed him about six months ago when Chief Rogers began his big anti-drug campaign."

"Borrowed?" Mamba asked.

"That's the way I put it. When I looked at my narcotics people, there wasn't anyone who looked like he might have any connection with a Mexican cartel. Made undercover work almost impossible."

"You profiled your own people," Kerrigan said. "That's gutsy."

"It's a fine line between gutsy and—"

There was a commotion in the corridor. Kerrigan started to stand, but Stallings waved him back down.

"That sounds like my guy."

The door burst open and the tail end of an off-color joke delivered in a thick Spanish accent reverberated down the hallway. A giant filled the doorway. Detective Enciso Martinez had arrived.

"Buenos dias, amigos," the giant bellowed a greeting in his native tongue. A completely shaved head wrapped in a blue and yellow bandana topped the man's six-foot-four inch, two-hundred-fifty-pound frame.

A large gold hoop dangled from one ear and a diamond stud pierced his right nostril above a black brush of a mustache. Each arm sported a dazzling tattoo. Faded, skin-tight blue jeans, a sleeveless yellow muscle shirt, and heavy leather boots were his uniform. Three gold chains surrounded his size twenty-one neck.

Mamba straightened up in his seat at the sight of the near caricature of an undercover officer.

As the door closed behind him, Martinez spoke.

"Sorry, I'm late, Sarge. I know I should be more time conscious." The change in the man's demeanor was more than dramatic. Gone was the bravado. There was no trace of an accent. He wedged himself between the arms of the last remaining chair.

"Gentlemen, this is Detective Enciso Martinez. Let's get started," Stallings began without acknowledging Martinez's apology. He respected the detective's work. He admired his skill and his ability to drop into and out of character in an instant without missing a beat. But, his professed need to be more time conscious was a stretch. The detective had yet to show any evidence of time consciousness.

Mamba shifted his weight. He was uncomfortable with Stallings' attitude. On the one hand, he had appreciated the dry humor when he announced the arrival of Martinez. On the other hand, the Sergeant appeared to be an overbearing bore with his almost insolent attitude toward the Hispanic American.

He knew Martinez more by reputation than in person. The detective deserved more courtesy than Stallings had just shown. He wondered if that was Stallings' attitude toward everyone.

"Mr. Mamba came as a friend last week," Kerrigan began with an introductory nod toward the private detective. He, too, was ill at ease at the combination of Stallings' manner and Martinez's physical presence. He was eager to get the attention focused on the matter at hand. "He provided me with a list of names."

Kerrigan produced the manila envelope and dug out the two pages of notes he kept. Mamba snapped open his briefcase and produced his two pages. They tossed the pages onto the table.

"We ran selected names of these lists through INVSTAT, the CII, and local sources," Kerrigan continued as Stallings and Martinez read through the names. "Every name we checked is known to deal pot, cocaine, heroin, assorted varieties of pills, or worse. That's where you come in, Sergeant Stallings."

"Yeah," Stallings agreed. He tapped the paper in front of him. "I know at least three of the guys on this page by rap sheets."

"And I've had contact with three times that many," Martinez added a deliberate underestimation. "They're all dirtballs."

"Then we can count on your help in running this thing to the end?"

"I don't see why not. What do you think, Martinez?"

"I'm in." The big man shrugged. "We might as well get 'em now if we can."

"You're hired," Kerrigan said as he glanced at Mamba.

"I might know more of those scumbags, but I'm not too up on the spelling of your gringo names," Martinez spoke as he shifted his bulk in his chair. "You know that they all look the same to me."

"You got a point, Martinez?"

Mamba shook his head. Stallings either missed or ignored the sarcastic nuance in his agent's comment.

"One contact is in a gang I'm working on right now. He has dealings with a middle management dealer named Weston. That's the third name on this page." He tapped a beefy finger on the list and winked at Mamba as Stallings' gaze shifted toward the table.

"You don't say." Stallings leaned forward and picked up the page. "I guess we'll be checking this out pronto."

"Sí. Pronto." Martinez's teeth flashed a dazzling white against the olive complexion of his mustachioed face.

Kerrigan and Mamba exchanged meaningful glances. Stallings appeared unaware of Martinez's humorous intonation as he repeated the sergeant's Spanish term. Mamba shrugged. Kerrigan flashed a warning gesture.

"I think you need to keep these original lists safe," Stallings decided. "I'll get copies made. Officer Martinez, I believe you've got other places to be."

"Yes, sir," the mammoth Hispanic replied. He shook hands with Kerrigan. As he turned to Mamba, he said, "You're outside your normal space, Lieutenant."

"I'm surprised you remember me. But, I consider myself back in familiar territory," Mamba answered and offered his hand.

"Sounds like me. Let's exchange stories about our returns to Northeast," Martinez said as he shook hands and moved toward the door.

"Gentlemen, it's been a pleasure." Stallings opened the portal and exited to the copy room to get Mamba's lists copied. Martinez took a deep breath, turned, and threw a wink at the two remaining men.

"An' the oo-ther man says, 'You chood've seen her seester!'" he bellowed and laughed uproariously. Another wink preceded his final, "¡Adios!"

Kerrigan shook his head. Mamba looked at him and laughed. It would be difficult to convince a sane group of unbiased observers that what had just transpired in Interrogation Room 4 was official police business. They killed time with a discussion of the Dodgers' Mexican phenomenon, Fernando Valezuela, while they waited for Stallings' return.

Ten minutes later, a female officer looked into the interrogation room.

"Lieutenant Kerrigan."

"Yes."

"Sergeant Stallings sent these down to you," she explained as she handed Kerrigan Mamba's four original lists.

"Thank you."

"Strange bird, that Stallings," Mamba said as he prepared to leave.

"Strange is not the word," Kerrigan corrected.

"Hey, we should have had Stallings make me copies." Mamba snapped his fingers as he realized that the two of them had only the original list and a single copy between them.

"No problem," Pat told him. "The copy room is on the way out for you. I'll go along and we'll get you copies. I'll keep the originals in a secure location."

Sergeant Edwards recorded Kerrigan's badge number. He pulled the copy counter key for the Homicide Department and ran the copies.

Kerrigan took the originals and handed the set of copies to Mamba. The two men continued along the corridor to the stairs that led down to the street.

"It looks like we're underway."

"Sure does."

"Kind of like old times."

"They were good old times," Mamba amended with a firm shake of Kerrigan's hand. "Thanks, Pat."

"What are friends for?" Kerrigan asked. "And, this one helps everybody. See you soon." He turned and headed back inside the police station.

* * *

After a long month listening to complaints about the stupidity of Manzanita's parking metering, Eloise Cooper called her high school friend. The conversation was short. There would be a total of four girls from their lunch clique at the speedy party the last Wednesday in August.

She called Stallings.

"That's right, Sergeant. I'll be arriving last. I'll call in as soon as I confirm the drugs. The three other girls are totally going to the party next Wednesday."

"Totally what?"

"I'm sorry, sir. Looks like I use more school slang than I thought. It just slipped out. It won't happen again."

* * *

Becca knocked on the door of 1542 Coulter Street. It was mid-afternoon on August 29.

No answer.

"Tap. Tap. Tap, tap, tap. Tap!"

"Yeah?" The word rasped through the spyhole in the door.

"I hear this is like the place to find L. A. Ice."

"Who says that?"

She repeated the name of the kid just off her high school campus. She'd seen the flyers in the boy's hand and asked what she should buy at the party.

The door opened.

"Let's see how well-funded you are."

A hand reached out, palm open and up.

She couldn't see the voice's face. While that bothered her, she complied. Unzipping her fanny pack, she pulled out a small roll of bills and held them in up to the spy hole.

"What's the holdup?"

"I'm holding my money. Move so you can see it."

"Funny. Hand it over!" The bodiless hand bounced up and down in a show of frustration.

"Eat my shorts."

"What?"

"You heard me. I'm not giving any money to you. This money is for L. A. Ice."

"Listen—"

"Either let me in dude, or I'm going straight to the police."

The door swung all the way open.

"Chill, girl."

"Hank?"

"Shh!" Hank stepped onto the porch and pulled the door closed behind him.

"No names! Didn't your source tell you anything about what's totally cool here?"

"Sorry. But, I'm not the one talking all funny trying to disguise his voice, dude. You knew who I was from when you talked through the spyhole." The girl clipped each word into an individual insult to the boy.

"Okay. Okay. Show me your money, and I'll let you in."

"I changed my mind."

"What? Why?"

"If you're part of this party, I know inside this house is no place I want to be."

She shoved the money back in her fanny pack and stomped off the porch.

"Have a cow, why don't ya," Hank said beneath his breath and rejoined the group inside.

The party deteriorated into a scene from a low-budget horror film. Bodies littered the furniture and carpet. Most were unconscious. Some were barely breathing. It was hard to tell how many vomited and now lay in their own vomit and how many fell into the vomit of others.

Hank looked around and realized he was one of only two partygoers still able to walk, and he was losing that ability quickly. He staggered across the room, grabbed a pill from an end table, and swallowed it dry. Three minutes later he passed out.

* * *

"I think our friends are in trouble."

Eloise recognized the voice on the other end of the phone. It was Becca.

"Where and why do you think that?" Eloise demanded. The girl's words triggered her police instincts. This was no time to pretend to be someone she wasn't.

"At the party. The other two girls are there. They went early and promised they would be home by now. They're not home. I went back and knocked on the door to the party house. No one answered."

"Where are you?"

"In my house."

"Stay there. Stay there until I call you or a police officer calls you or comes to your house!"

Silence.

"Do you understand?"

Becca's answer was a click and a dial tone. She felt belittled by Eloise and relieved someone else was taking over her other friends' plight. She didn't know which was least appropriate.

* * *

"Call in for a bus. Code 3! No, make that as many as they can send. It looks like there's maybe twenty kids here. Most are unconscious," the undercover detective yelled to the first officer that joined her in the party house. She called the cavalry when she learned some girls didn't make it home.

The newcomer put out an all points call for emergency medical help, then ran into the house.

"What happened here?" the newcomer asked after a quick look around. "These kids are in bad shape!"

"This kid's beyond bad. I can't get a pulse." She pulled the dying boy off the sofa onto the floor. Kneeling, she began the CPR sequence.

"I'll check the others!"

The undercover officer didn't stop her CPR.

The first paramedic truck skidded to a halt in the driveway. Two paramedics grabbed emergency equipment and entered the house.

"Here!" The single word echoed through the front room.

"Whatta we got?" One paramedic asked as he opened the defibrillator and flipped the ON switch.

"No pulse or breathing for seven minutes."

"Any break in your CPR?"

"Negative."

The paramedic nodded. A single beep announced the defibrillator was fully charged. After lubricating the paddles, he signaled his readiness.

"Clear!"

The undercover officer stopped her compressions and leaned back while the defibrillator delivered its charge.

"Again!" the second paramedic barked.

"Clear!" Another electric shock jolted the teenager's body.

"We've got sinus rhythm," the second paramedic announced.

"Roger," his partner responded and secured an oxygen mask on the boy.

Over the next several minutes, three additional paramedic trucks and a dozen ambulances arrived at the house with lights flashing and sirens blaring. They transported fifteen high school students to Manzanita's two Emergency rooms. Police cited six partygoers for possession of a controlled substance, treated, and released them into parental custody.

One of the fourteen through eighteen-year-olds died. Another was in a coma for over a month. Six suffered permanent mental impairment. Every partygoer had some abnormal reaction to the drug they ingested.

Laboratory analysis confirmed the contamination of all pills seized in the bust. There were traces of five potentially lethal contaminants in the samples. Mercury and talc were the primary impurities.

* * *

The Manzanita Daily News ran five days of guest editorials condemning drug traffickers and drug use. Local television coverage focused on those in rehab after the overdoses and contaminated drugs. RossAnn Gilroy was vocal in her role as anti-drug champion as often as she could.

Manzanita was a city in conflict. Mourning, outrage, fear, and blame fought for prominence. Tension throughout the city was palpable.

Chapter 11

During the week after Stallings got copies of his list, Mamba worked the Anderson Pharmaceuticals burglary. As Reed had unintentionally tipped him, chemical analysis of the scrapings from the office door's threshold verified the presence of resin. While resin was not a conclusive link between Reed and the burglaries, it provided a circumstantial link between the list of names and a specific crime.

Reed's acknowledgment of recent time spent at The Jazz Machine strengthened that link. The permanently temporary stage of the club/bar was constructed from planks of rough-cut pine. Once the lab confirmed the substance recovered at Anderson's factory as resin, placing Reed at the crime scene was simple. A test of resin from The Jazz Machine's stage matched the crime scene sample. Time spent working the street confirmed the connection.

Mamba's gut told him to play his hand close to the vest with his client. He held a strong belief that results of his work belonged to him, even if those results were achieved while someone else was paying for his time. He withheld nothing essential to resolving a matter he investigated from his clients. Non-essential discoveries were those he held close to his vest.

Mamba classified some of the lab results as non-essential, although he couldn't explain why. It wasn't long after that decision that Hope buzzed his line.

"William Anderson, right on schedule, and holding."

"Put him through." Anderson's weekly Monday morning update on the progress on the break-in at his factory was underway.

Preliminary back-and-forth conversation between client and private investigator proceeded as usual. Anderson signaled he was ready to move on to current events when he asked, "Don't the police have a list of suspects in this case?"

"The police do have a list of suspects they're following up." As Mamba spoke, a tiny alarm went off in his head. Why was he confirming a list of suspects to his client? He mentally filed the query and said, "I'm confident that there will be at least one arrest before long."

"And what of the chemical analysis I am paying for?"

"It confirmed my suspicions. The results of the analysis led to the observation of a particular suspect." Mamba said, blending truth with strategic falsehoods and insinuation in another evasive maneuver.

"So, you finally have a solid suspect. I was beginning to question my choice of investigators. I'll have a check cut for the balance of the cost of the testing."

"Thanks." Mamba made a mental note to tell Hope to look for the check before offering an update on the investigation. "I'm looking at a candidate for primary suspect. But it appears as though there is an unusual amount of interplay between several known drug traffickers going on. I'm not willing to put all my eggs in one basket yet."

"I see." Anderson didn't agree with the decision and couldn't help wondering if the PI knew about Guillermo Arcenas' involvement. "When do you estimate resolution of this matter by the police?"

"Well," Mamba hedged. "If you pushed me for an estimate, I would guess by the end of the month at the earliest."

"I will expect to hear from you then, if not before." Anderson accepted the time estimate and hung up.

Mamba replaced his phone and shook his head. He would never understand a man like Anderson. On the one hand, how could any reasonable person expect someone to predict when a case would wrap up? On the other hand, Anderson decided that the chemical analysis was worth paying full price.

The PI shrugged. He had enough other concerns, not the least of which was the silence from the Narcotics Unit about the list.

He was waiting for word on their plans for a raid. Stallings and Martinez seemed eager to get started. But now it looked like they were stonewalling.

Because of the delay by Manzanita Police Department, Mamba set up an appointment with another snitch. Flatly Broke was the man's nickname. All who knew the man understood the appropriateness of the moniker. The PI had no clue of the man's given name.

Flatly was a former boxer with a weakness for ladies of the evening. The weakness was one Mamba would exploit. The rumor that Sherleen Hobbs, a hooker, was seeing the doctors at the downtown clinic would guarantee Flatly's attention.

"Phil, there's a, um, gentleman here," Hope told him after he flipped on his office intercom unit. "He says he has an appointment, but your calendar doesn't show one."

"I set this one up," Mamba confessed. "If he's about five-nine with chocolate brown skin and a pushed in nose, send him in."

"He's on his way," Hope announced. "But I don't think he appreciated the crack about his nose."

"He'll get over it."

The door to the office opened and Flatly Broke walked in. The black man was stylishly appareled, but the appearance of style was an illusion. It took only a not-so-close inspection to reveal threadbare spots in the shirt and pants and serious sweat stains on the fashionable hatband. Flatly Broke was usually just that.

"What you want, Dancer?"

"Let's start with a little conversation. Pull up a chair."

"How come you wanna talk to me?" The man sat down without enthusiasm.

"Later, Flatly, later," Mamba promised. "Would you like some coffee or maybe a soda?"

"Well, I would like a beer."

"No beer here at the office. Your choices are soda, coffee, or tea."

"Got any ginger ale?"

The detective nodded.

"With lots of ice?"

Another nod.

"Okay, that's what I'll have." The former fighter's smug look showed his pleasure with the result of his negotiating.

Mamba called out the order to Hope along with an iced tea for himself. The two men talked about experiences from the time when the private detective had been a police lieutenant. The most memorable of those experiences was nowhere near what Mamba had in store for the man now.

Hope interrupted their reminiscing with the cold drinks.

The interlude of congeniality lasted a few minutes more. Then Mamba provided the boxer with the purpose of the meeting with a series of jabs to the heart.

"I've got a tip for you, Flatly."

"That's a switch," the man chuckled. "Usually I got sumpin' you want."

"That's still the way it is."

"But you said—"

"I'm offering a trade. Something you need for something I want."

"What you got I want?"

"I have important information you need," Mamba corrected. "It's about one of your female friends."

"Ain't none of my lady friends been pinched in months." Flatly sipped his ginger ale through a smug expression. "You can't tie me to no vice at all."

"Not vice," Mamba agreed. He leaned forward in a practiced maneuver and stared hard at the man before casually asking, "How about AIDS?"

"AIDS!" Ginger ale sloshed onto the carpet as the snitch reacted with a start. "I got nothin' t'do with them diseased hookers, man. And I don't do no fags, either. I tell you, I'm clean!"

"Maybe you used to be," was the ominous response. "But I know one of your contacts was exposed to AIDS." Mamba presented the innuendo as fact. Flatly's reaction had been all that he hoped for. He added some fictional background as an embellishment to the scenario, ending with, "And she was exposed before your last experience with her. I'd get to a doctor if I were you."

"I will. I will!" The man promised as he made a move to stand. "I'll go to the clinic right now."

"Not quite yet." He motioned the man back into his chair. "You still need the rest of my information." He paused. "And, I want you."

"What's the rest of your info'mation?"

"Who it is." Mamba watched the small man's eyes. They widened second-by-second as the words registered in Flatly's brain. "That's right. If you don't know who exposed you, you're still in jeopardy. Unless you become a priest or find all new lady friends."

"You right. As usual." Flatly's shoulders slumped, his head dropped forward, and his eyes stared vacantly at the carpet. He'd taken enough punches in the ring to know when he was beaten. "What I gotta do to find out who she is?"

"Make a buy for me."

"You crazy, Dancer? I don't do no drugs!"

"I want you to make a buy while you're wearing a police wire," Mamba ignored the protestations. "It'll only be coke, so the dealer won't suspect anything."

"I tol' you, man, I don't do no drugs!"

"And I don't breathe air."

"Okay, man. I snort some coke. But only at parties. I ain't no addict. No way I could afford no habit."

"That's why people steal things," Mamba reminded the boxer. "I'm going to the station this afternoon to set up the time and place for your buy."

"Please, man," Flatly whined. "They'll kill me, if they ever find out I'm workin' for the cops."

"There's no bargaining. You want the name, you wear the wire."

"But they'll kill me."

"They might kill you. AIDS will kill you. Take your pick."

"Ooohhh, man." Groans escaped from between the gnarled fingers of the hands that covered Flatly's frightened face. "I wish I was already dead."

"I'll contact you through the Cap'n down at Tug's," Mamba continued, ignoring the theatrics of his newly recruited associate. "You be there tomorrow for lunch. There'll be food and a new set of clothes."

"New threads?" Flatly's head jerked upright. Clothes were important to the man. New clothes were the stuff of dreams. His eyes narrowed. "You serious, man? You start talkin' new clothes, and you best be serious."

"Dead serious."

"Can I pick 'em?" Flatly asked after missing Mamba's sarcasm.

"Leave a list of the clothes you want and your sizes with my secretary on your way out. I'll spring for up to one-hundred and fifty."

"Dollars?"

Mamba nodded.

"I get a hundred fifty U. S. dollars' worth of new threads? You really serious about this, ain't you?"

"I want this to work and you not to get hurt."

"Thanks, man," the fighter gushed. The promise of brand-new clothes pushed the threat of disease, and everything else into the deep recesses of his addled brain.

Mamba brought him back to reality with a single comment.

"You'll get the woman's name after the buy."

"You being straight with me, Dancer?"

"Haven't I always been straight?" Mamba asked as he showed Flatly to the door. "You be at Tug's tomorrow at noon, understand?"

"I do, man," Flatly's reality was short-lived. Mamba's offer of clothing resurfaced in his thinking, once again masking the threat of disease. "You ain't never lied to me. My new threads'll be at Tug's, right?"

"With the tags still on, Flatly." He patted his new informant on the shoulder and watched as the excited man inundated Hope with the information needed to purchase the promised wardrobe.

Mamba could have gotten Flatly's cooperation without stretching the truth. He shook his head.

You never knew.

* * *

After the boxer left, Mamba took Hope out for tacos at one of the new food trucks that parked off the street in the Peacock Valley Park lot. The hot sauce was just that, and they ended up stopping for an ice cream cone to cool the fire in Hope's mouth. He left for the Northeast Division station after dropping her back at their office.

The station was less crowded than it often was. Mamba remembered that usually meant one of two extremes was about to occur: a leisurely afternoon and an on-time trip home, or an afternoon that lasted long into the night.

"Are they stonewalling us?" the PI asked Kerrigan. "Shouldn't we have heard something by now?"

"I would think so. But Narcotics has to work at its own pace. You remember."

"Yeah, yeah. But maybe we could encourage them to speed it up a little. I have a plan."

"And, I'm not surprised. What do you have in mind?"

"Trust me."

Kerrigan grimaced. "Way too often."

"That's cold." When Kerrigan ignored his quip, he continued, "Can we meet with Stallings right now?"

"I'll check," Kerrigan picked up the phone and dialed the extension number of the Narcotics Sergeant.

Fifteen minutes later, Mamba and Kerrigan sat in Stallings' office. The Sergeant looked haggard. His uniform's pristine appearance was a memory. It was clear it had been a long week for the man since their last meeting.

Stallings hated this part of his job. He enjoyed the thrill of the hunt. He also enjoyed luring foe and friend alike into a false underestimation of his ability by his staged appearance of disorganization. But, sitting and waiting while information was verified drained him. He knew that some of this delay was his own making. He hated the reason for that most of all.

"Lieutenant, I am not dragging my feet on the investigation." Stallings sighed as he responded to Kerrigan's opening question. "We've been working full time on a marijuana smuggling ring. It broke last night." He sighed again, "I'm just beginning the paperwork."

"We're not accusing you of anything, Sergeant. In fact, we might be able to help you out on the investigation of that list of names."

"What's on your mind?"

"Mr. Mamba has an idea," Kerrigan answered with a motion toward the PI.

Stallings hoped the suggestion by a civilian was the low point of the meeting. Despite his negativity, he kept a poker face as Mamba began.

"I have a snitch who is willing to wear a wire. Can you set up a coke buy?"

Stallings straightened up in his chair. His expression made it clear that he wanted more information before he agreed to anything. In case Mamba missed the visual clue, he asked, "How do you know we can trust the guy?"

"He's worked for me and never gone off the reservation. Besides, I've got a hook in him pretty deep. He's scared enough to do whatever I ask."

"Fear's a strong motive," Stallings agreed. "But, I'm not so sure."

"If we set this up properly, we won't have to worry about Mamba's man doing anything to mess it up," Kerrigan chipped in. "For instance, it'll have to be the right time and place."

"No, actually, I was thinking more of the right dealer," Mamba corrected. He made eye contact with Stallings and continued, "Wasn't there a name on my list you knew was tied to some current dealings?"

"Um," Stallings rubbed the stubble on his chin as he tried to remember the names on the list. "Martinez is working in a gang associated with a Martin, no, Milton Brown."

Mamba rummaged through his briefcase and produced his copies of the original lists. He scanned them in his search for the name of Milton Brown. That name was not on any of the four pages.

"No go. No Brown's on the list."

Stallings muttered a profanity. "That's right. Brown is Martinez's contact. He's got to be a bottom feeder. What was his supplier's name?" He closed his eyes and massaged his forehead as he mumbled, "Farrel—no! Weisman. Uh, Westlake. Weston."

"It's here! Weston's our man. How long before you can set up a meeting for a new buyer?"

"You better give me a day," Stallings decided after several seconds of silent thought. "Martinez is here sometime each afternoon. If all goes well, we should be on for tomorrow night."

"I'll plan on having my man here at least four hours before the buy," Mamba said. "That way we'll have plenty of time to check and double check the equipment before we leave. I want him to feel secure before the buy goes down."

"Good enough. I'll see you tomorrow." Stallings pointed to his office door with his thumb, swung his desk chair around, and began typing information on the page in his typewriter.

It was obvious the meeting was over.

"Thank you, Sergeant," Kerrigan said as he rose and started to leave. "Come on, Phil. It's in good hands now."

"I think we've just been thrown out of the game," Mamba mumbled as he followed Kerrigan out of the room.

"I feel better about Stallings now after that little outburst, profanity and all," Kerrigan said as the two men walked down one of the arrow-straight hallways.

"Tossing us out of his office with an umpire's out signal was unexpected, but I kind of liked it. And, it was good to see that he actually works."

"Even all night sometimes like the rest of us."

"Uh, huh. My first impression was desk jockey all the way."

"I checked around. Stallings is a solid cop. He's just still a little new to the department."

"Oh?"

"Yeah. He hired in from somewhere in the Midwest."

"That explains why I don't know him. How about Martinez? I don't remember much about him."

"You wouldn't. He came over from the Sheriff's Department about the time you left the force. Transferred to Southern. You heard why he's back. Word around the department is he's one of the best."

"I knew he wasn't a new cop. I have a vague memory of crossing paths with him on some case. Thanks, Pat, for sticking by me."

The pair walked in silence to the station's main door, each man content to mull his own thoughts. Kerrigan broke the silence.

"You know, if I thought you were wrong, I'd be turning you down."

"I know."

"This will help the whole city if it works. I should thank you."

"You got that right," Mamba agreed with a mischievous smile. He dodged a punch, moved down the stairs, and headed for his car. As he reached the sedan, he turned. Kerrigan was nowhere to be seen. He climbed in, closed the car door, and breathed a prayer of thanks for friends.

That night, Chief Rogers televised a statement about the tragic death of a Manzanita High School student. The victim died after ingesting contaminated drugs at a party attended by Manzanita High School students. Nearly all party-goers showed signs of physical or mental injuries. Several of the students would never be the same again.

A tired and frazzled-looking Franklin Stallings stood respectfully to the left and slightly behind the chief. Rogers reiterated his pro-anti-drug position ending with, "Sergeant Franklin Stallings and his narcotics team are committed to severing the arteries that supply illegal drugs to our neighborhoods."

Citizens took the chief at his word. The city needed to believe in someone, or something.

* * *

"Did you see Chief Rogers' statement, Mr. Brewster?"

"I did."

"And?"

"I have no problem with the police helping us by clearing out our competition. Anyone sloppy enough to make and sell bad product deserves whatever comes their way."

"Can I get you anything, sir?"

"Coca Cola in a bottle. Those cans leave an aftertaste in my mouth."

Chapter 12

Tug's Pub was a throwback to watering holes of the past. It avoided becoming a coffeehouse in the 1950s and 60s. More important to the owner, Cap'n Tug, was the avoidance of even a hint of disco influence in the 1970s. Today, it was a hangout for a slice of the local population often overlooked. Shady and scary were adjectives genteel folks used to describe "those people."

The reality of Tug's was neither complex nor scary. Cap'n Tug ran a tight ship, literally. If a customer needed to be cut off, he or she was. If they protested but left after arguing, there was no problem. However, fighting and lewd or crude behavior resulted in a lifetime ban of those involved. The only way back in after the lifetime ban was verified proof of completion of a behavior remediation program. While there were shady types in attendance every night, Tug's Pub was the place to enjoy passible food and drinks in a genuinely friendly environment.

The décor was nautical to the extreme. And, even in this day of emerging women's rights, the bar was decidedly male.

Dancer, as they knew Phil Mamba in this part of town, entered the dark interior of Tug's Pub at 11:30 a.m. He stood for a moment while his eyes adjusted to the darkness and he gave the bar and tables that crowded the interior of the pub the once over. The scan was a ritual he learned as a police officer. It was ingrained in his nature and carried over into his current profession, which wasn't a bad thing. It was early enough that only one table and three stools at the bar were occupied.

"Ahoy, Dancer!" The Cap'n bellowed his greeting to the PI.

"Permission to come aboard," Mamba called.

"Permission granted! Welcome aboard!"

"Glad to be here, Cap'n."

"Your boy's not in port yet. Navigate over here. Whatever you want is on the house."

"Sparkling water with a twist of lime." He piled a plainly wrapped package and two boxes on the bar to his right. "I want to be on my toes."

"Can't say I blame you. You always wanted that, and, you never can tell what's going on in Flatly's beat up noggin." The Cap'n plopped a glass down on the bar.

Mamba realized the Cap'n had taken his usual tack of accepting all interactions at face value until the situation required other interpretation. He responded by slapping five, five-dollar bills beside the glass. He took a sip of his drink to cover his smile.

"What's this?" the Cap'n asked. Then he broke out in a gap-toothed grin. "Now I remember. This is my Reed money."

"I want people to know I keep my word."

"No worries there, Dancer," the Cap'n assured him. "Everybody knows you're good for whatever you say."

"I plan on keeping it that way."

"Hey, Cap'n!" A cry from the doorway broke into the conversation.

"Who wants boarding privileges?" the bartender demanded.

"It's me, man." A body emerged from the light beyond the doorway and gave substance to the voice. "You gotta know me, man."

"Right on time, Flatly," Mamba answered for the bartender. "Come on in, I've got your clothes."

"All right!" The ex-fighter jogged to where Mamba stood, grabbed the packages off the bar in a remarkably agile move. "Let's have me a look."

"Not here." Mamba slid off his stool and put one hand on Flatly's shoulder.

"But you said—"

"I've got us a booth. It's more private than here."

"Ohh. I get it. I'm goin' to need to look like no one who's ever seen me before. Right?"

Mamba laughed and led the way to a booth in the back corner. Flatly placed the objects in his hands on the table. His movements were gentle. This was a special occasion.

Mamba slid into the booth and watched while the man ran his gnarled hands over the material of the shirt and slacks. Flatly's mouth dropped open when he lifted the lid of the shoebox and inhaled the scent of new leather. But, his biggest reaction was for the hat. A large purple feather decorated the flashy felt fedora he placed on his balding head with reverence.

"Thank you, man," he breathed.

"You'll earn it." Mamba's simple phrase brought reality back into the scene. Flatly deflated.

The PI realized he needed to re-inflate the man or the whole plan could fail.

"Go ahead. Put the new threads on. Then we'll have some lunch and head on down to the station."

"So soon?" the informant moaned. "It's still early."

"We'll go over the plan a couple of times with everybody at the station so there won't be any mistakes."

Flatly's brow furrowed while he processed the words as fast as his battered brain cells allowed. Seconds later, he nodded to himself.

"Hey, Dancer, that's a real good idea. I don't want no foul-ups."

Mamba watched the ex-boxer enter the dingy men's room to change into his new clothes all the while thinking he felt the same way.

After lunch, they left Tug's through the back door into an alley and climbed into Mamba's car. Prying eyes reporting Flatly's new wardrobe qualified as a foul-up that they successfully avoided.

* * *

The ride in Mamba's sedan from Tug's to the division station was a quiet one. Neither man knew what might be an appropriate topic for conversation between them outside the business at hand. But, after Mamba parked the car, as the two men were walking towards the station's front door, the trip became a study of Flatly Broke's persona.

Mamba knew the man well enough to predict his silence during the ride. He expected nothing different until they were working on the plan for the sting. The first ten yards of their walk across the parking lot did not alter his thinking.

However, the closer he got to the station, the more swagger Flatly added to his steps. Mamba smiled as the swagger evolved into a strut.

By the time the men crossed the last of the open asphalt before the station's entry, the boxer was nodding and pointing at or waving to everyone who looked his way, playing to the crowd like a celebrity.

It was all Mamba could do to maintain the state of mind he knew the rest of the day required. He dropped back and allowed the full wattage of Flatly's imaginary spotlight to envelop the man.

Once they entered the reception space, Mamba moved beside his charge.

"You wait here. I'll find out where they're waiting for us."

"It's all smooth," Flatly replied with a gesture mimicking rubbing his hand across a tabletop. He looked around. Once sure of an audience, he gave his feather a manly swipe.

Mamba shook his head and went to the front desk leaving the man to preen in peace. After a brief conversation with the Desk Sergeant, the PI led the boxer down a hallway.

"Whoa, Dancer? What we doin' here?"

Mamba placed his hand on the interrogation door handle.

"This room is for criminals! I ain't no criminal!"

"When the police don't have any criminals, they use these rooms for meetings. This is where our meeting is." He held the door open.

Flatly tip-toed through the portal.

Kerrigan, Stallings, and an officer unknown to Mamba were already in the room.

"Mr. Mamba, how long are you planning on supervising us on this operation?" Stallings asked.

Mamba felt the hair on his neck bristle. He hadn't wanted to start the meeting with attitude showing on either side.

"I have no desire to do anything more than make sure my CI understands what's going on before he's thrown into the breach."

"I see. What's going down later, it wouldn't have anything to do with one of your cases, would it?"

Mamba's mind clouded with emotions from revenge to persecution when Stallings played the PI card. It was obvious that some prejudices extended across the country. He decided it was best for all concerned for him to take a neutral position.

"I'm not going to lie. I asked another CI for information. He gave up the lists you got to start this party. It was part of an investigation I'm conducting for a client. Turning the lists over to Manzanita Police Department wasn't motivated by untainted altruism. Although, scum like the names on those lists need to be scraped off the pond and disposed."

Stallings stared at the PI for several seconds. He felt himself react to the term altruism. He hoped Mamba missed it, although he doubted that.

Kerrigan felt his shoulder muscles tense as the stare-down continued.

Flatly was looking back and forth between Mamba and Stallings, much like a spectator at a ping pong match. Finally, the Sergeant gave a quick nod. Kerrigan thought he heard the breaking tension drop to the floor.

"Now, to more directly answer your question," Mamba began.

Stallings raised his hand in the universal STOP gesture. As soon as it was clear that Mamba understood the action, Stallings switched gears.

"I did some investigating into your background, Mr. Mamba. I uncovered several interesting tidbits."

Mamba set his jaw. He ran scenarios and responses through his mind.

"First," Stallings continued as though he hadn't noticed Mamba's change in body language. "You were a seriously good cop."

The PI's eyebrows shot up.

Stallings facial contortions were evidence of his fight to keep from smiling at the reaction to his first revelation. He cleared his throat and reset his jaw before continuing.

"Second, you're pretty much relentless for following what you think is a good lead on a case. In fact, if the scuttlebutt around here is true, your Captain's opposition to just such a decision on your part is why you are no longer employed by the City of Manzanita."

"That's a reasonable description of the breakup," Mamba offered.

Kerrigan relaxed. The monochromatic Stallings was showing his true colors.

Flatly Broke stopped listening at Stallings' use of the term tidbits. He yawned—it was many an athlete's answer to stress.

"Anything else?" Mamba asked, although he figured there was.

"Quite a bit. But only one for public consumption."

There was a dramatic pause.

"About your nickname, is 'dancer' your second job?"

This time, it was Mamba who choked back a laugh. Kerrigan grinned. The unknown cop looked lost.

"Oh, no!" Flatly answered Stallings' question. "I've never seen a white cop what could dance a lick. He's Dancer because he—"

"I think the Sergeant knows more than he's letting on." Mamba cut off the boxer. "Am I right?"

Stallings shrugged. But he smiled, too. Mamba took that as an invitation to get back to the meeting's agenda.

"I don't think I know you," Mamba said to the unfamiliar cop.

“He’s from Information and Surveillance,” Stallings answered for the man.

“New unit?” Mamba asked.

“Yeah. It’s partly my idea. There’s so much change in the equipment used for both information-gathering and surveillance that the street cop can’t keep up with the advances. The I and S unit spends the time to learn the latest about the greatest. Then they teach and monitor the use of new equipment until officers are comfortable using them.”

Mamba introduced Flatly all around.

Only then did the I and S officer begin the meeting.

“This device is an SK-90,” he said as he held up a small electronic transmitter. “It is the most sophisticated piece of equipment of its type we have.”

“It’s a Fargo, Flatly,” Mamba interpreted. He’d watched his CI’s eyes widen during the description of the transmitter so he translated for the technician.

“Hey, man, so that’s what one of them looks like.” The boxer reached for the device. A nod from Stallings gave permission. The technician handed it to the boxer who held it between his thumb and index finger. “Sure causes bunches of trouble out on the street.”

The technician took the device back from the informant. “You’ll be wearing this when you get to the meeting.”

“I know. I know,” was the half-hearted reply.

“Do you want me to continue?” the technician asked.

“No. It’s okay. I’ve used this before,” Stallings answered. The I and S officer gave head nods all around and left.

“Take off your shirt,” Stallings ordered Flatly without preamble. He reached toward the ex-boxer.

“You be careful, man.” Flatly’s left hand shot out and caught Stallings right hand as it approached. It was a reflex. He’d deflected scores of punches similarly in the ring.

Stallings stiffened. The boxer pushed Stallings’ hand away from his chest and unbuttoned buttons. “These are new threads.”

Stallings rolled his eyes and leaned back against the table behind him. Flatly removed his shirt and hung it with care over the back of a chair.

Stallings never worked narcotics as a street officer. His duty stations included several areas of Crimes Against Persons—robbery, assault, even a stint in homicide. Dealing with street people was not his forte. There were too many uncontrollable variables when working with civilians. He preferred to implement, not micromanage events, as he called situations like today's.

Mamba stole a look at Kerrigan, and they both smiled at Stallings interaction with Flatly. He wondered how the man landed in narcotics. Several of his mannerisms didn't fit someone in that assignment. After a moment of contemplation, he shrugged off the thought.

After minimal discussion, they attached the transmitter to Flatly's chest just below his pectoral muscle. Stallings used a long strip of adhesive tape to hold the device in position.

"Now drop your pants."

"Hey, man, watcha goin' to be doin' with my pants down?"

"See the wire that's hooked onto the Fargo?" Mamba asked. Flatly looked down at his chest and nodded.

"That goes to a power supply, like a battery. The Fargo's no good without a power source. Can we show him the battery pack?" Then he turned to Stallings. "Another tidbit I'm certain you uncovered is that I like to be involved with my cases."

"Just color inside the lines, Mr. Mamba," Stallings said before he reached behind him and picked up another tiny piece of equipment from the table. He handed it to the detective.

"Understood, Sergeant," Mamba said before addressing Flatly, "We have to tape this power source to you, too. Without the battery, the transmitter doesn't send us anything."

"You guys use them special alk'line batteries?" Flatly asked. "I want to be sure there's extra power in this sender. I want it to keep goin' and goin', you know. Like that bunny rabbit on TV."

There was laughter all around.

"These are better than alkaline batteries," Stallings assured the informant. "You won't have to worry about losing power during the deal."

"How come I got my pants down?" Flatly returned to his earlier question.

"We don't know if you'll be searched tonight or not," Stallings continued the explanation. "If someone searches you, we don't want them to find our transmitter."

"You don't! Hey, man, I don't want that at all!"

"When I said we, I meant all of us here." Stallings defined his position as best he could with a wave of his hand around the room. He turned to Kerrigan for help.

"I can't think of anyone who would be more concerned than he would," Kerrigan deadpanned. "What do you think, Phil?"

"I'm sure Flatly is the most concerned of the group," Mamba corroborated Kerrigan's position as he fought, with only partial success, to suppress a smile.

"Thanks," was Stallings' sarcastic expression of feigned gratitude. He turned back to the informant. "Nothing will go wrong if we get this placed properly. Your pants, please."

"Well, I don't know," Flatly hesitated. He appreciated Stallings as a target. Usually he was the one squirming at the expense of other people. He was enjoying watching someone else on the hot seat. He stalled a little longer.

"You better show me how this is gonna look on me," he announced. "Why don't you take your pants off?"

The laconic Stallings chuckled at that. He turned to Mamba and Kerrigan as the friends roared.

Flatly was grinning, but he was standing in only his boxer shorts with his hands on his hips and his pants puddled atop his shoes when Stallings looked back at him.

With exaggerated care, the Sergeant taped the battery pack high in Flatly's groin area. Unless the person searching Flatly was an adventurous female, or a far too friendly male, there was no way the power pack for the device would be discovered.

They taped the thin wire from the pack in place beside the navel on the former boxer's still reasonably flat stomach. With the transmitter taped discreetly off center on the man's chest, there was the least chance for someone to detect the Fargo.

With the wire in position, Flatly put his clothes back on while discussion of the procedure for the buy began.

"While you're wired, you only answer questions," Stallings told Flatly. "Let my man do most of the talking."

"I understand." The informant nodded. "Last thing I want is a problem with these dudes. Hey, man, I don't do drugs. Those users are strange people."

"Hola, amigos," boomed from the doorway as Martinez arrived at the debriefing. Flatly gave a start at the boisterous entrance. Mamba signaled thumbs up to his CI and hoped he was up on the meanings of current gestures. When he flashed his raised thumb in response, Mamba relaxed.

Meanwhile, Martinez closed the door behind him. "Is the wire set?" he asked in his most professional voice.

"He's ready," Stallings answered.

"Yeah, I'm ready," Flatly answered for himself. "You another cop?"

"Detective Enciso Martinez, Narcotics." He extended an enormous paw to the diminutive fighter. "Are you my new partner, amigo?"

"Sí," Flatly answered

"¡Muy bien!" Martinez bellowed. "You call me Cue Ball whenever we're together. Got it?"

Flatly's confusion was evident.

"I met Weston in a poolroom. I shoot a mean game of rotation." Dazzling white teeth exploded into a gigantic smile as he added, "My head helps solidify the name, too." He pulled off the brightly colored bandana and rubbed his shaved skull with some relish.

"Sure, Man. That'll be easy cuz that bald head of yours surely looks just like," the CI paused. His brow wrinkled in concentration before announcing his conclusion. "You know, cuz you're a Mexican and all, you look more like a seven ball than a cue ball, right?"

Martinez burst into laughter. Stallings, Mamba, and Kerrigan smiled.

"We're going to do just fine tonight, amigo!" Martinez decided.

"You know, Cue Ball, Flatly's not the only one to notice the resemblance," Mamba said. He was glad to see the positive attraction and relaxed interaction between his CI and Martinez. It boded well for the success of the sting.

"We need to get on with the business at hand." Stallings stopped the conversation cold. "We've only got three hours before the buy."

"Plenty of time."

"Never the less, I want this to go down smooth. Real smooth."

"Yes, sir," the undercover officer responded.

"Give me a hand, will ya?" Kerrigan asked Mamba as he grabbed one end of a table pushed against a wall.

With only a nod in answer, Mamba walked to the other end of the table. Together the two friends muscled the large piece of furniture into the middle of the room.

"Bet you coulda done that by you'sef, right?" Flatly asked Martinez.

"With one hand and holding a burrito in the other," he answered with a grin and a flex of both biceps.

Stallings chose the head of the table. He opened a manila folder and spread several papers in front of him. Then he motioned for the others to find a seat. Chairs scraped across the tiled floor as each man grabbed a chair and sat.

"What's those papers for?" Flatly asked as he took his seat.

"Just some names and a general outline of the procedure we'll use during the buy."

"Do I got to know all the stuff you got written down?"

"No. Your part is to say two or three things to make them think you're for real," Mamba answered as he placed his hand on the fighter's shoulder. "You know, like a real drug buyer."

"You sure?"

"Mr. Mamba is correct," Stallings acknowledged but shot Mamba a look and picked up where he left off.

"We'll go over the whole procedure, so you'll know what's going on. Then we will practice what we want you to do. Got it?"

"OK, man," Flatly decided after additional brow furrowing. "But, don't forget the practice."

"Just think of this as going a couple of rounds with a sparring partner," Mamba grinned, interjecting his comment was another reminder that the whole scenario resulted from his work. "Tonight's the main event."

"Right," Flatly grinned back. "I got that action, Jackson."

Ignoring Mamba's interjection and Flatly's response, Stallings began at the top of one of his pages of notes.

"We send Martinez and your man into the apartment complex at about eight o'clock. We'll use two cars, one with you two in it." He motioned at Mamba and Kerrigan. "I'll be in the other car with a uniform."

"How close will we be?" Kerrigan asked.

"In the street beside the main entrance to the complex."

Flatly jerked his head toward Kerrigan. The whites of the boxer's eyes seemed to occupy his entire forehead.

"We'll be close enough to get to you in plenty of time—if anything goes wrong. Right, Stallings?"

"No problem. We'll be at the apartment door before the buy's completed."

"Remember, I'll be there, too," Mamba said. He shot Stallings a look. The Sergeant nodded his approval.

"Besides, amigo," Martinez placed a meaty hand on Flatly's shoulder. "Cue Ball will be in the room with you. Ain't no way they'll get us both before our helpers arrive." He winked at Flatly.

"Thanks, man." Flatly relaxed at the words from the mammoth undercover agent and the weight of his hand on his shoulder.

"Two squad cars and another undercover vehicle will act as backup." Stallings continued his narration as though there had been no interruption. "Once the buy is set, we move into position and bag Weston."

"You figure he'll talk?"

"I think we can wring enough from him to establish grounds for a warrant or two, Lieutenant," Stallings answered. "Then this takes off like a pyramid scam."

"Remember the guy we're dealing with tonight knows me as Cue Ball," Martinez picked up the story.

"Did you have a point you were trying to make, Officer?" Stallings soured the air with his tone. "Or were you just practicing your story-telling?"

"No, sir. I wanted our CI to know enough to make him comfortable with anything I say."

"Hey, man, you got me all comfortabled up. We're partners!"

"Continue," was Stallings succinct directive.

"They think I'm a renegade biker. I'll arrive on my Harley."

"How will I get there?" Flatly asked. "I don't ride no Harley, Cue Ball."

"If you were just buying for yourself, what would you do?"

"Take a cab, Man," was Flatly's immediate response. His eyebrows shot up as he realized that the answer sounded too spontaneous, so he added, "Not that I'd be doin' any of this without it bein' the Dancer's, uh, idea and all."

Four men exchanged skeptical looks while they fought to suppress smiles at that comment.

"All you have to do is follow my lead," Martinez explained. "I'll give the dealer some background on you. Then he'll ask some questions you have to answer to his satisfaction."

"That's all there is to it," Mamba confirmed. "Just remember who you're supposed to be and answer any questions like you would if you really were that person."

Flatly's brow furrowed again. The conversation was moving faster than he was used to listening, and the vocabulary in use far exceeded his. After several moments, he pursed his lips and nodded.

"Sounds easy enough. Just who am I goin' to be?"

Mamba relaxed.

"A friend of Martinez."

"That's Cue Ball," Flatly corrected.

"Right," Stallings said consulting his notes again. "You have a place that Cue Ball uses to crash from time to time."

"Like an apartment?"

"Probably a house."

"Oooeeee," Flatly whistled. "I been workin' for the police for only a few hours and I already owns me a house."

"But not too nice of one." Martinez punched him gently in the arm. "Otherwise, you wouldn't be seen with someone like me."

The boxer sat up straight in his chair. With the gravest of expressions on his face, he turned and scrutinized the undercover officer. His brow wrinkled with the intensity of his concentration. After a beat, he leaned back in his chair before he spoke.

"I'm just sayin', Cue Ball, you look so bad I'm not sure if it's cool to be seen wit you, anyway."

It took all Mamba's self-control to stifle his laughter at the candid comment.

"I am offended." Martinez crossed his arms and stared hard at the CI.

"I'm only kiddin'," Flatly said with a smile. He reached over and punched his newfound compadre.

Mamba and Kerrigan leaned back in their chairs. This was going well. Stallings flashed another brief grin at the realization that the boxer played Martinez.

"Gentlemen. Since we have only two hours until we have to be at the apartment, it might be appropriate if we did some rehearsing." Stallings frowned his emotionless statement. Mamba wondered if the man used sternness as a tool to control the direction of conversations.

"Yes, sir," was the response. But this time it was a choral response from Martinez and his new partner.

Stallings shook his head—his frown frozen in place. He was tempted to say something about the importance of the following of procedure, but he figured it would only confuse the punch-drunk man with a foolish grin on his face who sat beside his undercover officer. Besides, he'd been pleasantly surprised at the CI's mostly appropriate spontaneity.

He relaxed his frown to a neutral expression.

Chapter 13

Kerrigan sat at his desk staring at the phone in front of him and wondered if being single—as so many police officers were by choice or divorce—was the route he should have taken. He loved his wife, and he was looking forward to having kids. In fact, Kate was going off her pills after her prescription ran out.

Because he liked to think he had a life, he hated stake-outs and covert action assignments. With a sigh of resignation, he picked up the handset and punched in a number.

"Looks like a long one tonight, honey."

"You told me that this morning." She sensed the disappointment in his voice. That emotion always showed through, no matter how hard he tried to mask it.

"I know, but, well, I hoped I might not be involved in this operation."

"That's not true. You wouldn't miss this chance to work with Phil Mamba again for the world."

"You're right. As usual. I'm glad you're around to keep me honest with myself."

"Hey, Pat!" Mamba's voice echoed through the small office. "I'm starving. Let's get moving. Everybody else has already gone off to eat."

"Be right there," he called to his friend. Then he returned his focus to his wife. "I've got to go. See you later, sweetie." He hung up the receiver.

"You'd better," she breathed her almost inaudible response as she eased the handset into its plastic cradle.

* * *

Flatly arrived at the designated address in a cab driven by a police officer wearing street clothes. He clambered out of the taxi about a block away from the correct address. As directed, he walked toward the site of the buy.

The sound of a motorcycle brought the boxer to a stop. He turned in time to see Martinez round the corner behind him. In seconds, the undercover man parked his ride and stood beside his new partner.

"I don't know about the hat."

"What you mean? This is a stylin' hat," Flatly responded indignantly.

"I know it is. But, how will you keep it on when you're riding with me on my bike?"

"I been thinkin' 'bout that." Flatly moved behind the behemoth. Once in position, he saluted from the top of his head into the back of Martinez. Flatly's hand struck the Latino midway between his shoulder blades.

"Man, I could ride behind you a long way and never even feel the wind. Ain't no way my hat gets blow'd off. You as big as one of them cruiser-weight fighters. How'd you get so big?"

"Clean living and Mexican food," Martinez answered as they crossed the small lobby, climbed a flight of stairs, and approached the door to the buy site.

The door was unremarkable. The surface was flat, but there was a knocker. Martinez saw a viewing hole just below the knocker. That was common throughout the building.

"You ready?"

"I can go a full ten if I need to."

"Who am I?"

"Wha— Oh, you're Cue Ball."

Martinez nodded and hoped Flatly was as cool as he sounded.

"All right then, it's show time!" Martinez rapped the doorknocker in a specific sequence.

The interior cover of the viewing hole opened.

"Good to see you again, Cue Ball," a voice from inside said. Then, in a worried tone, "You got someone with you?"

"This is my number one house man." Martinez introduced Flatly Broke. He slid the boxer in front of him and maneuvered him to the most visible place for the viewing hole. "He's always got room for a man to sleep it off."

"Does your house man have a name?" the drug dealer asked.

Mamba twisted knobs on the top of the tape recorder that was recording the transaction. Martinez came through loud and clear on the headset. That was a good sign. The seller's words were garbled, and the voice spoke only short questions or phrases.

"Golly, Ned! Keep him talking." Mamba muttered beneath his breath.

Kerrigan turned toward his friend. Phil Mamba did not use profanities or vulgar language. That phrase and "Geeze, Louise" were as close as he ever got. He wondered what was wrong. He considered tapping Mamba on the shoulder and asking him but decided against it as the conversation continued in his earphones.

"Come on, man," Martinez answered. "Sometimes it's better to have no name, isn't it?"

"Sometimes," the dealer admitted. "Why'd you bring him here? I thought we agreed that only clear people would come to my place."

"My amigo is, what you call it? Clear," Martinez assured. "I have said he is okay."

"Well, I'm not so sure."

"Hey," Flatly interrupted. "It's cool, Cue Ball. If the dude doesn't want me here, I'll just go and buy someplace else. Let's beat feet."

"Good job," Kerrigan whispered to Mamba, who smiled and nodded. Flatly's first words were delivered perfectly. They also recorded nicely.

"Buy?"

"I tol' him you had primo coke," Cue Ball said in a stage whisper.

"How much do you want?" The change in attitude was dramatic.

"Quarter K," Flatly repeated the rehearsed amount. The only sounds caught on tape were a sharp inhalation of breath from the dealer and the creaking of the front door hinges.

The door swung open. A disheveled man of indiscriminate age stood in the doorway. Martinez confirmed his identity as the Weston whose name was on Mamba's list. Weston shot a furtive glance from Martinez to Flatly and back. He looked worried.

"Hey, Man, if that's too heavy for you . . ." Flatly let the sentence hang. He watched the man sweat. He figured that the dealer must have looked about the same as he had back at the station when first heard the amount of coke he was to buy. Half a pound of the white powder was more than he'd seen in his whole life added together.

"You sure you want a full quarter kilo?"

"Does your friend have a hearin' problem?" Flatly asked.

"No, man." Martinez fought back a snicker. "He's just bein' certain. ¿Sí?"

"Yeah. Yeah. I'm just making certain. That amount is no problem." The dealer assured his new customer, before qualifying his interest with, "If you've got the bread."

"Right here," Flatly said. Mamba heard movement as their informant displayed the wad of marked cash the Department supplied. "But, it ain't stayin' long. You understand?"

Enciso Martinez relaxed as the small, wiry man standing beside him threatened to take his money and walk out. Flatly Broke was doing the job. He wondered what Mamba had on the man to get him to compromise himself like this. He decided that whatever it was, it must be serious.

The script they practiced for the buy was going as planned. It was as though everybody, even the supplier, rehearsed their parts.

Then it started to unravel.

"Let's go," the dealer announced.

"Go?" Martinez's mind began to race. If they left the house, the odds of the deal ending in trouble were high.

"Yeah. I'll take you to the stuff. I don't have that much around here."

"But—" Flatly glanced at Cue Ball in his panic. The undercover agent gave the informant a meaningful look and a sharp jab to his arm. The boxer choked off the rest of his protest.

Mamba hoped his informant stopped at a sign from the undercover cop and not from a move by the supplier.

"Tell me where we're goin'. I'll follow you on my bike, man. I can't leave it here."

"No way you're taking your bike, Cue Ball. It's too noisy. That makes it too obvious," was the blunt rejoinder. "We'll go in my car. It's downstairs in the garage."

It was Kerrigan's turn to swear. The garage was the underground parking structure upon which the apartment complex was built. The major issue was that the garage had three exits. He pulled off his headset in frustration.

"We can't lose them," Kerrigan spoke the needless words. He snapped the radio microphone from its holder on the dashboard. His mind raced as it organized details.

"I know. I know," Mamba responded, but the Lieutenant wasn't listening; he was barking into the radio's microphone.

Mamba paused the tape recorder, waited for his friend to sign off, and asked, "Got a car at each exit?"

"They're on their way," Kerrigan muttered. "You and I have the south one!"

"Let's go."

Martinez grabbed Flatly by the arm and guided him as they trailed their host towards the elevator.

"Don't worry," he whispered in the boxer's ear. "They'll be right behind us all the way." He hoped he sounded convincing, because he wasn't completely convinced. He didn't mind surprises. But, right now, he had a civilian to worry about.

"Whatever you say, Cue Ball," Flatly answered in a hoarse whisper, his unlimited confidence in the giant Latino showing through. "I'm with you."

"Good man," Martinez murmured. Then he called to Weston, "Wait up! You tryin' to leave us here?" He had to stall until all exits from the parking structure were covered by the time they arrived at whatever transport vehicle Weston had in mind.

The drug dealer slowed his pace.

"Sorry. I've never dealt a quarter-K before. I guess I'm a little nervous."

"Well, you just de-nervous yourself," Flatly said. "I don't want no nervous Nellie driving me in a car."

Martinez relaxed a bit. The boxer was more than holding his own in this fight. He'd already landed a body blow that knocked the confidence out of Weston. Now he was frustrating the drug dealer with an occasional verbal jab.

"I'll be all right," Weston assured his buyers. "We're in luck. The elevator's here already." He reached out and held the door as the trio entered.

Weston directed the men to a sorry-looking green Bonneville coupe. He pulled the hinged back of the driver's side bench seat up to the steering wheel and directed Martinez and Flatly to climb into the back seat.

"Sorry about all the crap back there, Cue Ball," Weston called over his shoulder. "I wasn't expecting any passengers."

"No problem," Martinez lied as he shoved at least a week's worth of fast food lunch remains off the seat cushion and onto the back-seat floor. "We've got lots of room."

Despite the aged appearance of the Bonneville, it roared to life with the first turn of the key. Weston slammed the car into reverse and accelerated backward out of the parking space. After screeching to a stop, he jammed the transmission into drive and left black skid marks for fifteen feet as he sped out of the underground parking area.

Kerrigan pulled his car out of its parking space and crept along the curb. He eased the car's front fender into their assigned driveway.

"Pat!" Mamba's shout startled Kerrigan into a reflex jerk of his leg. This led to an abrupt stop that sent the PI's head snapping forward.

A battered, once two-tone green coupe roared toward the unmarked police car. It missed the front of their car by no more than a few inches.

Martinez ~~saw~~ Flatly blanch as the already dented right front fender of the Bonneville narrowly missed the front bumper of a car entering the driveway as they roared out of the garage. But a sideways glance by the undercover man two seconds later saw no lingering evidence of the scare.

Weston flipped off the other driver and added a nasty laugh. The Latino's eyes sparked to life as he recognized the occupants of the offending car. He flashed a grimace to Kerrigan and collapsed back in the seat hoping they realized the expression indicated he recognized them.

"Dancer," he whispered to his back-seat companion.

Flatly started to look over his shoulder. Martinez shook his head no. The boxer nodded and leaned against the back cushion.

"You bet that guy's a bastard," Weston called over his shoulder after misunderstanding Cue Ball's comment to Flatly.

"There's too many drivers should be shot these days," Martinez offered.

"You got that right," the dealer agreed. He made a hard right turn onto 22nd Street.

"Phil, that's Martinez in the back seat," Kerrigan shouted.

"I know. Did you see the grin on his face as they passed us?"

"It wasn't the happiest look I've ever seen. I'm not so sure he was glad to see us."

"He couldn't afford to let on that he recognized us. All he needs right now is suspicion from the supplier."

"I hope your man doesn't let on that he noticed anything," Kerrigan said after missing Mamba's rationalization.

"Flatly's not a pro, but he's not dumb, either," Mamba assured his friend. "He wants to get out of this in one piece. Believe me."

"Suspect vehicle coupe. Bonneville, late sixties, green on green. Significant damage to both front fenders. License number," Kerrigan barked into his microphone. He turned to Mamba.

"George Queen Sam Niner Zero Zero," Mamba told Kerrigan, then stopped talking as his friend repeated the plate number.

"Suspect headed west on 22nd Street. Report immediately when you make it."

"This is one-Adam-seven. We've got him!" The voice of a patrolman in one of the black and whites crackled in the radio speaker. "Still west on 22nd, Lieutenant. We're turning on his tail."

"Roger," Kerrigan acknowledged. He learned that the passage of time in situations like this vacillated between speeding so fast he couldn't keep up with the action to slowing until time stood still. The switch from one speed to another was frequent and random.

"Stallings!" Kerrigan snapped during one of the millisecond lulls. He'd decided to run rotation for the street surveillance of the green coupe. His brain raced as he visualized which patrol car would alternate with the unmarked cars available to him. Stallings response broke his concentration.

"Here!"

"Run parallel on 21st for two blocks, then move in behind Adam-Seven." Kerrigan placed Stallings' g-ride second in the rotation.

"Roger that. Who picks us up?"

"Then we go in rotation by car number." That was the easiest method of deployment of the cars in the sequence of the tail.

"We'll follow car—" He paused and looked over at Mamba who scanned the roster of cars assigned to the detail.

"Fifty-seven," Mamba said.

"We'll follow car five-seven. So, they're picking up from you," Kerrigan reported. "That should give the dealer time to forget he almost rammed us in the parking garage."

"What about the black and whites?" the Sergeant asked. "You sure you want to include them in the tail?"

"We'll work them in periodically." Kerrigan's mind continued to race as he considered the question. "Adam-Seven's already on the suspect and car fifty-seven is in the queue. Everybody's been followed by a cop at some time or another. Especially at night."

"Good," Stallings said. As the ranking narcotics agent, Stallings was technically in command of the operation. But, Kerrigan was a Lieutenant and had a vested interest in the situation. Besides, the plan for the tail was a good one.

As Kerrigan pulled away from the curb, Mamba clicked the tape recorder back on.

"Hey, man," Martinez called. "You know where you're goin'? We've been on Sixteenth Street already."

"I know where I'm going," Weston retorted. "Just sit back and relax."

Cue Ball sighed. He wasn't going to be much help to the tail. Weston was in no mood for conversation. He tried four more times in the next forty minutes to get some clue of their destination from Weston. He was no more successful on those than he'd been on the first. He risked only two other attempts after being directed to, "Shut up!" a second time.

The PI breathed easier with each of those reports. However, a sharp, "Shut up!" from the driver reduced the trickle of information to one drop at a time.

For over an hour, five police vehicles changed positions irregularly behind the dilapidated green Bonneville. The supplier followed a circuitous route that passed through a lower-middle-class neighborhood. At the moment, Weston's car was less than two miles as the crow flies from the apartment where the buy didn't take place.

"This guy's paranoid," Kerrigan said as a tail car reported the coupe slowing after turning down a side street.

Mamba nodded his response. There had been little conversation in the Bonneville as it maneuvered through traffic.

Flatly seemed to be holding up well in spite of the drastic change in the planned procedure of the buy. The tone of his occasional comments revealed neither overt fear nor panic. Mamba hoped that the man's composure continued to hold when the men arrived at the new buy site.

The green Bonneville finally slowed as it turned down a cul-de-sac. The tailing car, with Stallings and a uniformed officer inside, continued past the intersection after reporting the anticipated stop to Kerrigan.

The boxer completed the relaxation technique he began during the rehearsal and dozed off long before the green Bonneville turned onto the cul-de-sac. As they slowed, he stirred a little. When the car finally stopped, he jerked awake.

"Where we at?" he asked Martinez.

"Give me a second," Mamba said. "I want to change this tape out. I hope this is where we pick up where we left off back at Weston's."

"Yeah. Good." Kerrigan had no idea what he just agreed to, or that he agreed to anything for that matter.

Chapter 14

The dilapidated Bonneville pulled into the driveway of a house. After a visual sweep of the area, Martinez was certain that the house was outside Weston's neighborhood. The style of homes on the street reeked of suburbia. The yards were far too wide and the houses too far apart to be anywhere but the suburbs. He settled on one of Manzanita's older neighborhoods.

"We're here," Weston announced. He cut the ignition and climbed out.

"'Bout time. I thought we were gon' to drive all night long." Martinez grunted as he extricated himself from the doorless back seat and stretched his arms and legs.

"Can't be too careful," the supplier called over his shoulder. "Come inside."

"Wait up!" the undercover man stalled. "My backside's asleep, and your buyer's still climbing out of this heap."

"This better go down pretty fast," Flatly called as he climbed out of the car. "I been tryin' to buy for a long time. My time's valuable, ya know."

"Things will go fast enough once we're inside," Weston promised. "Hurry up!"

"We're coming! Don' blow a gasket," Martinez called as he winked at Flatly.

The unlikely pair walked along the slightly sloped driveway. Martinez noted the house number enshrined in a lighted metallic box attached to the stucco exterior close to the garage door.

"Five nine five seven. I like those numeros. I think I'll play them in the lotto next week."

"Thanks, Detective," Mamba whispered as that information came through his headset. The batteries in at least one transmitter still had charge. He called out the address to Kerrigan who broadcast it to the team.

* * *

Weston waited until the two men reached him, and the trio arrived together at the front door of an unpretentious stucco dwelling. There was little to distinguish it from fifty others in the same tract.

The house was good cover for the drug dealer. Martinez wondered how many neighbors were on the payroll to keep the place anonymous.

Once on the porch, Weston rapped out a coded knock on the door. He paused then added a single knock to end the series. One ring of the doorbell and a repeat of the knocking pattern finished the ritual.

Martinez felt sweat run down his sides as though attempting an escape from his muscle shirt. Flatly shivered involuntarily as they waited for the door to open. Instead of creaking hinges, a female voice called through a small wrought iron grate in the door at Weston's eye level. The grate nestled behind four spindles of darkly stained wood, homage to an architectural style popular in the 1960s throughout Southern California. Yet, there was something not kosher about the spindles and the viewing grate. That bothered Martinez.

"I never open the door after dark." Although she delivered the words with perfect inflection, the adrenaline in the speaker's veins had her heart racing. She reacted this way whenever a new player entered her house. She wondered if the racing heart and shallow breathing were normal. She had no experience with which to compare. She couldn't remember a time she considered herself normal.

"Smart move," Weston said. "You never know who might be knocking. Is the party over?"

"Not yet. Can I take a message to someone inside?"

"I brought a friend."

"Do I know him?"

"No, but you'll like him. You both like to spend your money on the same things."

Martinez avoided standing on porches when undercover. It exposed him to all who walked or drove by.

"I got to use the baño."

"Shut up, Cue Ball!"

The woman in the house laughed.

"That'll be all right. Come on in."

After the clicking sounds of locks disengaging, the door opened.

* * *

Kerrigan's patience was nearly exhausted. The time spent in tailing the Bonneville had taken its toll. For the last twenty minutes, he methodically pounded the steering wheel with his fist. Mamba was sure he didn't know he was performing the act.

"Pat, I think—"

"Suspect vehicle stopped." The static-riddled crackling of Stallings' voice cut Mamba off.

Kerrigan wrenched his microphone from its holder with a spastic movement of his right arm.

"Where?"

"Third house on the right down Henry Court off Livingstone."

Mamba flipped to the index of the loose-leafed map book he used to trace the route of the beat-up coupe. He found the page listed in the index and tried to locate Henry Court.

"I can't find it, Pat."

"Repeat that name, will you?" Kerrigan barked.

"The sign says Henry Court." Stallings' voice had an edge of its own.

"I've got it!" Mamba cried. His finger punched at the open map page with angry irritation. "It's a dead-end street."

Martinez's voice crackled through his headset.

"Five nine five seven. I like those numeros. I think I'll play them in the lotto next week."

Mamba repeated the numbers loud enough for Kerrigan to hear.

"Martinez says the house number is five nine five seven."

"Roger!" Stallings reported. The other cars involved responded in kind.

"We've got Henry Court as a dead-end, Stallings. Can you confirm that without blowing the tail?"

"Yeah, the street ends in a big circle maybe a hundred-and-fifty yards from the corner."

Mamba shook his head as he spoke. "These guys are so sure of themselves that they deal from a dead-end street."

"Only one exit isn't the traditional set-up," Kerrigan agreed. He asked into the microphone, "What's the back look like?"

"Hold on a minute." One of the patrol cars involved in the tailing rotation pulled forward and turned left down the next street. Kerrigan resumed his attack on his car's steering wheel while he waited.

"Looks like it opens into the back of two yards on the next cul-de-sac."

"Thanks. Stallings, you sit tight. I'm calling in more back up. We'll be there in two minutes."

Kerrigan switched to an open channel and requested cars and officers for the houses on either side of the suspect's home. A moment later he added units for the two houses that bordered the property in the rear. He pulled his car up to the corner of Henry Court and Livingstone Drive. Stallings walked across Livingstone and leaned into the driver's window.

"It's all yours now," Kerrigan told Stallings.

"We're on top of it. You want to be a part of the bust?"

"I didn't sit on my butt for two-and-a-half hours not to!" Kerrigan growled as he clambered out.

"Pat?" Mamba called from the passenger side of the car where he stood, looking across the roof.

Kerrigan looked at Stallings. Stallings nodded.

"Come on, since you're already here," Pat said. "You don't enter until we've cleared the building."

"Wouldn't have it any other way."

Kerrigan turned to Stallings. "Take us in, Sergeant!"

* * *

Mary Carstairs was a native Californian, born in the Northern Cal quasi-coastal town of Ukiah. Her father was a logger, her mother an elementary school teacher. Precocious and smart, the brunette was a neighborhood favorite. It wasn't uncommon for Mary to be the focus of attention of groups of varying ages as she sang, danced, or told a story to entertain.

Growing up as an only child, Mary had lots of time on her hands, time that required decisions on how to fill it. In elementary grades, after-school programs were the easy choice. She was an honor student. Expectations of teacher and family were high. Unfortunately, those expectations were dashed in a single afternoon.

Mary's father died in a logging accident.

The lumber company's insurance settlement was enough to pay off the Carstairs' home but left little money for day-to-day living. Mary's mom taught in a private school. The pay was low. To make ends meet, she took a second job, leaving Mary alone nearly every day.

Left to decide how to spend her free time, by eighth-grade, Mary's choices degraded from innocence to unsavory. The most common choices were smoking and beer drinking. Borderline passing grades replaced her once stellar academic performance.

In high school, Mary cleaned up her act enough to become a solid performer on the Ukiah High School Wildcats' volleyball team. To stay eligible for athletics, she made sure her grades were above C level. She played the system with just enough B-grades to balance the D-grades.

School days were full of positive activity. Besides playing volleyball, she was part of the school's drama program. Mary was good enough on stage that the drama teacher allowed her to act more often than to work as crew.

Unfortunately, weekends and off-season days, and nights, saw Mary revisiting her past discretions. By spring of 1978, her senior year, she thought she'd perfected living a double life. It took only one event to prove how wrong that assumption was.

Her last drama production ended in disaster. It was the final performance of the run, the only performance on a Saturday. Mary showed up late for her call time with a buzz on, a combination of weed and beer. She missed cues and blew lines.

Embarrassed and ashamed, in the days that followed she began skipping school. Her grade in drama class plummeted. She barely passed the course that was once her only A grade.

After barely graduating from high school, Mary dabbled in higher education at Mendocino Community College. She dropped completely out of school after three semesters, accumulating a GPA of 1.9 with only 12 credits on her transcript.

She left Ukiah with a boyfriend in 1980. The pair traveled up and down Highway 101 working odd jobs and camping for the better part of a year. After leaving her boyfriend, Mary fell in with a group of punks. They became her pipeline for marijuana, but she was never arrested for possession or distributing *Cannabis.* During those years, she and the group with whom she ran were on the verge of extended periods of incarceration most of the time.

At twenty-two, she moved to Manzanita, California because she liked the sound of the name. Over the next two years, she ensconced herself in Sid Brewster's local drug trafficking organization. She was bright with savvy business skills. Pretty enough to be desirable to her supervisors, and to her buyers, she did what she needed to when she needed to do it. Insightful, with an outward aura of calm, she rocketed up the organizational ladder.

Now, her flirtatious personality and skewed, but strict, morality made Mary a desirable tease and an unrivaled drug seller. She never had a serious relationship with anyone in the organization, although several males dreamed of how things might end up. Those men misjudged Mary Carstairs.

Every man who dated Mary knew she was not available for anything more than food, maybe a joint or two, and some fully clothed cuddling. The only exceptions to that trifecta came if she invited further advances.

Men who tried unsolicited advances left her home in pain. Mary saw to that by punctuating her displeasure with her kneecaps, elbows, or fingernails. Always bruised, and sometimes bleeding, none of those men spent time alone again with her.

By the time Flatly and Martinez landed on her front porch, she'd built a reputation as levelheaded and motivated. She was an audacious flirt. Those within the organization agreed that if she had a weakness, it was her special attraction for muscular men of color.

* * *

As soon as Weston, Martinez, and Flatly were inside, Mary Carstairs slammed the door behind them. Martinez noted two deadbolts on what appeared to be a steel door in the brighter light of the entryway. That explained why the spindles looked out of place. The owner added them to the door to help disguise its metallic construction.

The steel door worried him. Large metallic objects wreaked havoc with the signals from the department's wires. His head swiveled from side to side, looking for sanctuary.

Before he had a chance for more casual observations or to finalize his plan, the woman snapped at Weston.

"What're you doing bringing strangers here?" Her voice hardened, and her congeniality disappeared as she slammed deadbolts into place.

"Don't worry, Mary. This is gonna be worth your while." Weston turned to Flatly and asked, "Right?"

"I hope so, man. So far, all I got from you is th' run-around. I ain't seen no crack yet."

"You brought them here for crack? And you gave them my name? Weston, I should wring your neck!"

"Hey, just hold on." Weston held up his hand and shifted his weight nervously from one foot to another at Mary's reaction.

Martinez made a mental note that Mary was the alpha dog in the pack.

"They want more than I had at my place. More than I've ever had at my place," Weston whined in explanation. "Tell her, Cue Ball."

"Sí, señorita," was Martinez's startled rejoinder. He composed himself and added, "My frien' wants a quarter K."

Mary's composed demeanor evaporated, but only for an instant. Her resolute glare re-materialized quicker than it dissipated. The amount requested was a major buy, even by her standards. She visualized a career move as the possibility of a new drug source registered in her mind.

"Maybe I was hasty. I'll get our supply. You can check the quality." Mary was back in full emotional control. She mentally berated herself for not checking the details before harassing Weston and for losing her cool. She needed to get to where Brewster could hear this through the bug her boss had planted in the house.

"Perdóname." He interrupted her as she turned away from the men. Things were moving too fast. "My amigo and I still have to use your baño. I already tol' señor Weston that." Stallings and the team needed time to deploy. He had to get away from the steel door to update his status.

"What?"

"They asked, Mary. I forgot," Weston admitted with more feet shifting.

"Get a grip, Weston. Big man, I heard you through the security hatch," Mary said. "I was in no hurry, though. Truth be told, I'm kind of hoping for a show of your dance moves."

Martinez shrugged, forced his knees together, and rocked back and forth, all with a grimace on his face.

"That'll do," she snorted through a laugh. "It's the second door down the hall."

"¡Gracias!" The relief in Cue Ball's voice was genuine even though it was not for the reason the drug dealers thought. "Come on, amigo. We'll feel more like dealing in a few minutes."

He grabbed Flatly by the arm and directed him toward the hallway.

"Hold on!" Mary called before they'd gone three steps.

Martinez neck hairs stiffened. He felt his muscles tighten.

"You got a name, big man? You already know I'm Mary. Mary Carstairs. But no parent ever named a kid Cue Ball."

"Everybody's got a name," Martinez replied without turning around. It took all his self-control to keep his relief out of his voice. He knew he'd never be able to mask his facial expression.

"Everbody calls him Cue Ball," Flatly said as he ran his hand over his partner's skull. He looked up at Martinez and shook his head before he turned toward Mary. "But who he's gonna be is Wet Pants if we keep standin' here."

Mary snorted a second laugh and gave Flatly the go-ahead gesture.

* * *

The transmission from Flatly's wire was less than stellar. Kerrigan shed his headphones and joined the ranks of the first-in officers. Stallings directed Mamba, the only remaining monitor of the transmissions from Martinez and his CI, to apply all the tricks he knew to the surveillance equipment.

"We need more recon from the inside."

Mamba nodded.

"Once we're a 'go,' you're backup for the bathroom boys. And I mean far back."

"Rear echelon all the way," Mamba promised.

Stallings grunted an unintelligible response. Then he used hand signals to position his men around the house. Normal night noises predominated. Whispers of essential communication escaped the lips of the assembled ~~men~~ only on the rare occasions when there was no signal for what had to be done.

Kerrigan followed Stallings' gestures as best he could. He hadn't been on a silent protocol assignment in a long time, and it showed. He bore down even more as his ulcer flared.

Between adjustments to the radio and his headset, Mamba strained to see what was happening outside the house. The crackle in the earphones returned his complete attention to the men inside.

Over the last several minutes, the only conversation he overheard, and only parts of that, was the antagonistic interplay between Weston and a woman named Mary. Comments by the two undercover men were infrequent and hard to hear. At first, Mary was unhappy with Weston for bringing Martinez and Flatly to the house. She'd mellowed when she learned the amount of product they wanted to buy.

Martinez's voice was the clearer of the two undercover men, but sounds of running water muffled it now. Mamba strained to catch each individual syllable.

"We're going in for the buy," Martinez said into Flatly's Fargo. "You guys be ready because I'm not gonna let this go too far."

"Hey, man, you better be more than ready," Flatly added. "I think you pushin' how much I owe you, Dancer."

The sound of running water ended. As he exited the car, Mamba smiled a grim smile at his CI's candor. He left the door open to avoid any unnecessary sound when it closed and hurried to the first officer he saw. He touched the man on the shoulder and whispered, "I've got information for Stallings or Kerrigan."

The response was a gesture to his left. The officer's attention was riveted on the bathroom window. Mamba glanced up as he left. The light went out. Mamba hurried to his friend's side.

"Pat!"

"What is it?" Kerrigan snapped as part of his startle reflex. "You scared about three years of life out of me! This better be important, really important!"

"Martinez and Flatly are about to make the buy." Mamba ignored Kerrigan's tone. He'd been in this situation and knew nerve endings were exposed and raw. Focus was your closest friend and best chance for success. "You better take this." He handed Kerrigan the headset.

Kerrigan mumbled something as he accepted the apparatus.

Mamba knew better than to ask him to repeat the comment. Instead he asked, "You know where Stallings is? I need to let him know what I heard."

"No. I haven't looked for him since he stationed me here." Kerrigan slipped the headset on without taking his eyes off the house. "I'll look for him now."

"I'm going to the side yard," Mamba whispered. "Stallings told me to run back-up on bathroom duty."

"Make sure they're close enough to move in as soon as we're inside." He turned and looked at Mamba for the first time. "And you stay backed up! Understood?"

"The officer in charge is all over it." Mamba hustled away.

* * *

Martinez left the bathroom with Flatly following close behind. He stopped when his saw an empty entryway.

"Hey, amigos!" He shouted. "Where'd you go?"

"We're in the living room." Mary stuck her head through the suspected opening. "What're you drinking?"

"Tequila." Martinez smiled.

"No tequila, I'm afraid." Mary smiled back inexplicably drawn to the man. She tore her gaze away, looked at Flatly, and asked, "How about you?"

"I could use a beer," Flatly replied. "Draft beer," he added after considering what his undercover persona would drink.

"We've only got draft in a bottle."

"Well," Flatly pondered. "I guess that'll haf t' do."

"Make it two drafts then," Martinez decided his partner had been a terrific counterpuncher in the ring. His calm decision-making was impressive.

Mary stepped back into the living room.

Martinez and Flatly followed their hostess through the opening and found themselves in a snug, formal living room. Mary directed them to a pair of matched overstuffed chairs. She continued over to the wet bar to get the beers.

Martinez surveyed the room. Mary, in tight jeans and a loose blouse, crouched down as she rummaged around in a small refrigerator at the end of the bar, hoping the Latino was watching.

Weston was at a bookcase fingering a book. An unknown third person sat on a barstool. From the back, it was difficult for Martinez to determine the sex of the person. The haircut was one of those unisex jobs that expensive salons specialized in. Jeans and an untucked T-shirt disguised the shape of the body perched on the stool.

Martinez leaned back and decided that whether it was a wimpy guy or an underdeveloped female was unimportant. Who it was, was the critical issue.

"When do I get to check my stuff," Flatly asked with a slight waver in his voice.

Martinez sensed the boxer's confidence was waning and prayed that the beer didn't push him too far the other direction. Overconfidence was a cardinal sin in undercover work.

"Right away," Mary said as she handed Flatly a long-necked brown bottle. She sauntered over to the Latino, smiled invitingly, and offered him one of the two beer bottles she gripped by their long necks with one hand.

She found herself more than a little excited by the size, demeanor, and clothing of the man she now looked in the eye. She wanted more of this interesting man's attention.

"Gracias, señorita," Martinez murmured. Mary was one hundred percent eye candy, and she knew it. It was all he could do to extract one bottle from between her fingers with calm precision.

Martinez felt Mary's eyes roam over his body. She pursed her lips. A wink completed the come-on.

He stared at the woman. Designer jeans with a contoured design over-stitched in white thread squeezed her legs. She ran her index finger down the entire length of the beer bottle.

He licked his lips.

"Good brewski," Flatly stifled a burp as he wiped his lips with the back of his hand, destroying the moment. He set the bottle on the table between the two chairs.

"I'm glad, amigo," Martinez roused himself in response to the informant's comment and reminded himself he wasn't Cue Ball.

At the sound of the bottle touching the wooden top of the table, the mystery figure at the bar turned and fixed Flatly with a dour glare.

"Mary, get that bottle, will you?" It was more a demand than a request.

As Mary prepared to bus the bottle, she berated herself for letting the Latino distract her. Her live-in drug dealing partner's bat-like ears never missed the sound of a bottle hitting the end table without a coaster.

"Right away, Billy." Mary broke off her unfinished visual invitation to the undercover cop. She picked up the empty bottle and flaunted her tight jeans as she sauntered out of the living room heading for the bathroom.

"How much coke do you want?" Billy inquired. Martinez gaze locked onto the man, but his head never moved. His mind raced as he mentally scrolled through Mamba's list of names. He hadn't found a Billy before Flatly answered.

"A whole quarter K." The CI enjoyed the feeling of power advertising for such a large quantity of cocaine gave him.

"That won't be a problem," Billy responded. "But, I need to see some sincerity on your part."

"Huh?"

"He has the dinero with him, señor," Martinez interjected the desired response. "Let him see your money, amigo."

The former boxer obliged and produced his roll of bills.

Billy slid off the barstool and walked to where Flatly sat, removed the bills from the boxer's hand, and rifled through the stack of currency.

"This all you got?"

"It's more than I need," Flatly snapped as he grabbed the money back from Billy.

Martinez shook his head. His partner continued to amaze him. A minute ago, he appeared lost. Now he reacted perfectly when the pressure came down on him.

Billy backed off half a step but never changed expression. He called to Weston.

"Bring it over here."

Weston pushed the EJECT button on the VCR on the shelf where he stood. A videocassette emerged from the bowels of the recorder. Martinez nodded in appreciation. Using a dummy videocassette to hide drugs was slick.

The undercover agent stood. He intercepted Weston.

"Let me take a look, amigo." Martinez waved his beer bottle towards Flatly in an invitation to join him in the middle of the room. The sound transmission of this part of the conversation would be perfect. He also wanted the officers involved in the bust to see everyone in the room with one glance as they entered the house.

Billy shot a look at Martinez as he took the cassette from Weston. He wasn't comfortable around the giant Mexican, but money was money. As Martinez and Flatly watched, Billy worked the end of the black plastic case loose with his penknife. He used the same knife to slit open the sandwich bag that lined the inside of the fake videotape. Completing a trifecta of uses, he stuck the knife into the white powder and offered it to Flatly.

The boxer's hand trembled only slightly as he licked his right index finger and dabbed it in into the powder. He stared at the drug-coated digit before he put a tiny taste into his mouth. He ran his tongue over his lips before he spoke.

"Good stuff."

"Can I test it? Por favor, don't think I don't trust you, señor Billy. The palate of mi amigo is not as sophisticated as mine." Martinez bragged. He would give the prearranged signal only after he was sure of the drug's quality.

With a shrug, Billy offered the other side of the tiny blade to the agent. The stuff was most likely high-mid-grade quality, but still better than the flashily dressed boxer ever used.

Martinez sniffed the powder. He was not about to lick his finger and try a taste. If it wasn't cocaine, it could be anything. If it was cocaine, there was no way to know the purity or strength. He squeezed a pinch between the tip of his thumb and his middle finger. He held his index finger just above the powder, blocking Billy's vision of his sleight of hand. He rubbed the side of his thumb and index finger together and studied the supposed result with a critical eye.

"The color is good," was his determination. Only then did he lick his index finger, harmlessly mimicking Flatly's taste test before nodding at his partner.

Flatly dutifully handed the role of cash to Billy completing Billy's sale of illegal drugs.

Chapter 15

Seconds that seemed like hours ticked by for those waiting for the confirmation phrase that would send the collection of police officers into Mary Carstairs' house. Some men fidgeted; others shrugged their shoulders repeatedly. Still others intentionally controlled the in/out of their breathing. Whatever the method, the objective was the same for all: relax enough to have a next level adrenaline rush when the bust began.

The sour feeling in Kerrigan's stomach intensified with each passing minute. He stifled a belch and fumbled through his jacket pockets for a package of chewable antacid tablets.

Flatly exclaimed, "Good stuff."

"Stallings," he hissed.

Stallings turned halfway around. The Lieutenant held up his hand in a gesture that stifled any response. Kerrigan's eyes were unfocused as he concentrated on the conversation in his headset.

Stallings felt his anger spike and Kerrigan's dismissal. He inhaled a deep breath and exhaled.

"Can I test it?" Martinez asked. The next words Kerrigan heard could open the floodgates of activity.

Silence answered Martinez's question. The knot in Kerrigan's stomach tightened.

Kerrigan called Stallings' name. The Sergeant's face mirrored the questions he had in his mind. Something was happening inside the house, but all the communication he received from the Lieutenant was an open palm, a furrowed brow, and rivulets of sweat.

After what seemed half of eternity, Kerrigan heard Martinez's signal, "The color is good."

"It's a go!"

Stallings spun away from Kerrigan. He raised the two-way radio and barked, "We're going in!"

The collective tension of a dozen men spiked. Weapons were triple and quadruple checked. Breathing, previously halted by unconscious nervous action, resumed with muted whoosh sounds.

"Now!"

A grim smile turned the corners of a burly patrolman's mouth. After a quick change of his grip on the handle, he hefted an eight-pound sledgehammer. He moved with surprising speed from his position behind a shrub to the left of the porch and climbed the two steps up in stealthy silence. After taking careful aim, oversized arms swung the hammer in a mighty arc toward the doorknob.

With a metallic *smack,* the hammer made contact. The doorknob shot through the entryway and ricocheted off the half wall inside the house. A second swing between the deadbolts splintered the doorjamb. It was a mistake on the dealers' part to replace only the door with steel.

Stallings, Kerrigan, and two uniformed officers exploded through the shattered doorway. Shouts of identification by the entering policemen and curses by the home's occupants filled the rooms of the small house.

Mamba broke the bathroom window with a nightstick, cleared the glass shards from the edges of the frame, and stepped aside. A uniformed officer removed the bowling ball from the bag he carried. Leaning through the window, he dropped the ball into the porcelain bowl of the toilet. No drugs would be flushed away from searching officers tonight.

At the sound of the sledgehammer crashing into the door, Martinez grabbed his partner and threw him to the ground. Without explanation, as the second sledgehammer strike echoed, he pulled Flatly's shirt from inside the waistband. In a deft maneuver, he jerked the microphone from the boxer's body and stuffed it under a sofa pillow. The duo was still on the floor when the police entered the living room.

Mamba was last to enter the house. Even without Kerrigan's directive, he would have allowed the guys who got paid for this kind of risk-taking to lead the assault. By the time he walked into the living room, it was over. Four men offered little resistance when confronted with drawn service weapons.

After frisking, Martinez and Flatly were handcuffed and rousted until they were facing the wall to the left of the door. They confiscated Martinez's gun and folding knife. They did not find the power supply for Flatly's wire. Officers searched and cuffed Weston and the man called Billy and hustled them out for Mirandizing and transport.

A uniformed officer dragged a snarling Mary into the room. In dramatic contrast to her male associates, she was a study in non-compliance.

"She was trying to flush this," the officer held up a plastic bag filled with smaller bags of white powder. "She's had her rights."

Mary assumed the role of crazed drug chick. She'd decided to play as many roles as she needed as damage control by taking her cues from the officers.

"What's a matter?" Stallings asked her. "Plumbing problems?"

"Shut up, pig!" Mary spat her answer at the Sergeant. She knew this would not end well for any of those in the house. She thought her best bet was the role of the frightened victim. She decided, when she saw the bowling ball in her toilet, to assume the role of a Sybil-like character instead. So, she'd shown the police her first persona as she made her grand entrance.

"Cuff her and get her out of here," Stallings ordered. "Get the two scumbags by the door out of my sight, too!"

Mary's demeanor transformed as the handcuffs closed around her wrists. Tears welled up in her eyes and rolled down her cheeks. Her shoulders shook with soundless sobs as she was turned and escorted toward the door.

Mary's legs collapsed, and she sank to the floor drawing their focus to her.

The phone rang.

Mamba was closest to the phone. He looked at Kerrigan. The phone rang a second time. Kerrigan looked at Stallings. The third ring brought a nod from the Sergeant. Mamba picked up the receiver.

"Yeah."

"I need Mary," the emotionless masculine voice stated.

"Hold on," Mamba stalled while he formulated an excuse. "Billy says she's out shopping for more beer."

"What's Billy doing there?"

"Right now, he's waiting for a beer."

The voice laughed. Mamba relaxed. He'd played the sarcasm card out of habit.

"Could you send over two bricks of Acapulco Gold?"

"You gotta work through Mary."

"I'll do that," Mamba promised. "You want to leave a message?"

"Tell Mary to call Sid as soon as she gets home. She's got the number."

"Tell Mary to call Sid," Mamba reiterated. "Sure thing."

Mary feigned an attempt to speak.

Kerrigan watched from the kneeling position he took beside Mary after her collapse. He remained beside her as Mamba worked the phone routine. The name Sid sparked his prisoner's interest. She started to call out, but Kerrigan's hand slapped across her mouth.

Mamba hung up.

"Quiet!" Kerrigan barked before asking, "What'd you get?"

"My guess is her supplier."

Kerrigan felt Mary's shoulder stiffen beneath his hand. Mamba was right on track. With a barely perceptible movement of his head, Pat nodded confirmation to the private investigator. He knew that there were few better than Dancer Mamba at pulling information from a suspect, so he let his friend continue.

Mary's mind raced as she tried to determine the pecking order of the cops still around her.

"Too bad we don't have more information on this Sid," the cop/civilian began. "Leashing the top dog in this kennel, well, that'd get attention all the way to the chief."

"Yeah," Kerrigan picked up the cue after the briefest pause. "We could sure use the help of an informant to nail this guy." He stood and helped Mary to her feet. "Come on, uh, Mary, isn't it?"

She nodded.

"I don't like taking a woman downtown," Kerrigan mused.

"Hey, you've got to bust the ones you catch, Lieutenant," Stallings forced his way into the conversation. He'd followed the repartee. It was clear that Mamba and Kerrigan worked together before. He'd been content, until now, to let them do their thing. Now, he needed them both to remember who was top dog in the police kennel on this bust.

"I know, Sergeant," Kerrigan conceded with feigned reluctance. "But, it still bothers me."

"Wait a minute," Mamba snapped his fingers. *Please!* His eyes called to Stallings in a quick glance.

Stallings returned the smallest of nods.

"Do you know how to contact this Sid?"

Kerrigan felt Mary stiffen again. He wondered if sobs had been an act. But there was no time to worry about that. What might come if she agreed to help them was the prize.

"What are you doing?" Kerrigan asked Mamba with what he hoped was just the right edge to his voice to keep the play going.

"Sorry, Lieutenant. I just thought if she knows something and will talk—"

"You've got no right offering a deal."

"I said I was sorry," Mamba spat back.

"How much is Sid worth to you?"

Heads turned in Mary's direction.

"Depends what information we get." Stallings commandeered the conversation. It was time for Narcotics Division to do what it did.

"If the Sergeant here says it's okay, the right information might help reduce charges for the source of that information," Kerrigan conceded.

"What's with this? You just said no deal to me," Mamba complained.

"I said you couldn't offer a deal," Kerrigan corrected.

"And you can?" Mary asked her cop-confessor.

Kerrigan gestured to Stallings.

"Like I said, if we get the right information."

"What type of information?"

"What Sid deals and where he's at!" Stallings snapped.

Mary's brow furrowed in concentration.

"Two small pieces of information that could be the difference between a long stay or a very short stay in jail," Stallings prodded.

"I'm scared," Mary whispered.

"No doubt," Kerrigan said. "I, uh, we can promise you protection, if we nail Sid."

Mary hesitated then responded.

"Sid deals in anything I want. But, I only know a phone number. I don't know where he is." The words spilled out in a torrent of syllables. Mary's breathing was rapid and shallow as she finished.

"No games," Stallings warned.

"No games. I'm too scared to lie," she lied.

"Shut up, chica," Cue Ball hissed from the wall. "They will kill you for sure now."

"Jenkins! Mamba!" Stallings pointed to Martinez and Flatly. "I thought I told you to get those two out of here!"

"Yes, sir," Officer Jenkins replied. He grabbed Cue Ball by the arm.

Mamba did the same to Flatly and stifled a laugh. It was obvious the uniform hustling Martinez to the car did not know he was manhandling an undercover officer.

Mamba slowed his steps. The zealous Jenkins kept hustling his charge toward the patrol car as quickly as he could push the belligerent, oversized Mexican.

In conspiratorial tones, Mamba asked the boxer, "Are you okay?"

"I'm fine, man," was the reply. Mamba had to signal him to lower his volume. "But what you doin' hustlin' me off to the slammer, Dancer? I'm one of the good guys, man!"

"You've got to stay under cover until we get you to the jail. You don't want certain people to know your part in this. Do you?"

"I dig, man. I dig!"

"You did great." After a closer look at his CI, he asked, "What happened to your clothes?"

"Cue Ball pulled the Fargo," was Flatly's emotionless response. But, he added with a catch in his voice, "I think he ripped a button off."

"I'll have my wife fix that," Mamba promised. Despite all that had gone down, the boxer's main concern was that Martinez damaged his new shirt.

"Maybe we're even now?" Flatly's question brought Mamba back to the moment.

"More than even."

"Who's the lady?"

"What?"

"The lady with AIDS, man."

"First thing in the morning," Mamba promised as he put that conversation on hold when he realized he'd forgotten how he hooked him into wearing the wire.

"I'll load this one first," Mamba said as he walked to the passenger's side of the black and white.

"Okay."

Mamba opened the back door, placed his hand on Flatly's head and eased the ex-boxer into the back seat. Finished, he winked at his charge.

As he walked back around the police car, he snuck a wink at Martinez as well. While Flatly smiled in return, Martinez sign of recognition was much less courteous.

Mamba smiled a knowing smile and returned to the house. When he arrived at the living room, he found Mary on the phone. Kerrigan sat beside her, his head as close to the telephone receiver as Mary's. Stallings was nowhere to be seen.

"Two bricks of Acapulco Gold. Can I pick them up tonight?"

"Why? I always come through."

"I know. But my buyer's got an extra bill for both of us, if I deliver tonight."

"I have a two hundred dollar minimum on rush orders," Sid fabricated the amount. He'd learned he could milk extra cash from anyone in a real hurry.

"Hold on. I'll check with my buyer." She put her hand over the mouthpiece.

"He wants two hundred dollars for himself," she told them.

"I heard. Agree to whatever you have to. We want that address."

She nodded. "He says one C-Note and a single Grant is his limit," she told her supplier.

Kerrigan grimaced.

"Okay," Sid agreed. "But tell him the next time it's two hundred flat, on top of the price of the product."

"Where can I get the merchandise?"

"10123 Lexington. Just north of Main."

"I'll be there in . . ." Mary looked at Kerrigan. He held up ten fingers and flashed them three times. "It'll take me thirty minutes."

"Don't be late." Sid hung up.

Mary stood holding the phone.

"I got it all on the bedroom extension," the Sergeant announced as he reentered the living room. "You call it in from here. I'll pick up the warrant and meet you there. And, thanks for the half hour."

"Don't mention it. We'll be right behind you." Kerrigan knew it would do no good to arrive before the warrant. He hoped thirty minutes was enough time for Stallings to find a sympathetic judge.

"I can't believe I crossed him," Mary mumbled in feigned disbelief. "Why did I do it?"

"Maybe you're a better person than you think," Kerrigan offered.

"What about my deal?" She asked her question with just a hint of an edge to her voice.

"Tomorrow. After we've booked you and we know what we got from your cooperation."

Mary's eyes narrowed and daggers shot towards Kerrigan as another officer hustled her away. She'd expected some dodge by the police; she'd been through this before in another city. She hoped her expression was suitably menacing.

Mamba punched in a number on the phone. As soon as he heard it ringing, he tapped Kerrigan on the shoulder and handed him the receiver as he turned.

"Division Office. Edwards."

"Eddie?" Kerrigan asked. "What're you doing at the front desk?"

"Copier's down and Smitty's gone home sick. Something wrong?"

"No, I just didn't expect you. We're setting up a bust for 10123 Lexington. Just north of Main," Kerrigan told the Sergeant. "Send three cars. But tell 'em to sit tight. Stallings is on his way with a warrant. I'll be there, too. Shouldn't take us more than half an hour to get set."

"10123 Lexington. Just north of Main. Thirty minutes. Check!" Edwards repeated. "Good luck!"

"Thanks." Kerrigan placed the receiver back into its cradle. He turned to Mamba, "You still with me?"

"All the way, partner. All the way!"

* * *

Sidney "Sid" Brewster's house was alive with activity. A shipment of marijuana arrived earlier in the day. A select group of his employees was weighing and packaging the product. Brewster was finishing his personalized packaging of Mary's Acapulco Gold.

Back in Manzanita Police Department's Northeast Division's station, Eddie Edwards dialed a familiar number.

The telephone rang. This annoyed Brewster. But, then, almost everything annoyed Sid Brewster. However, it was unusual for the telephone to be an annoyance. He did nearly all his business over the phone lines.

By the sixth ring, Brewster knew that whoever it was wasn't hanging up until he answered. He put down the handful of high-grade marijuana he was stuffing into a plastic bag, and reached for the receiver.

"10123 Lexington," was all Edwards said.

"Where'd you get that address?" Brewster demanded. He recognized Edwards' voice and knew that information was far above his paygrade.

"I didn't get it. But, you're lucky I'm here tonight. A lieutenant just called in a request for backup at that address. Since he used the term bust in his demand, and I know he's at a buy-bust, I assumed it had to do with merchandise you specialize in. So, I called. Without me, you'd be a sitting duck," Edwards finished in a condescending tone.

Brewster seethed. Nobody talked to him like that.

"Make it quick," he snapped. "I'm busy!"

"You'll have lots of time if you don't clear out," Edwards advised. "Narcs are on the way. And they're pulling a warrant."

"How long before they get to that address?" Brewster's mind raced. He began a mental list of what to take and what would have to be left behind and cursed into the phone.

"They didn't have the warrant in hand when the Lieutenant called me. Thirty minutes minimum. They've got to find a judge."

"Spare me the explanation. I'll get to work clearing this place. You, I expect you to do everything in your power to slow that search warrant."

"I'm not a miracle worker."

"That's not what you imply more often than not. Just do what you're getting paid to do."

There was a click. The line went dead. Brewster held the phone in his hand, mesmerized by the information he received. Another click followed by a high-pitched whine from the receiver in his hand yanked him back to the reality of his present situation.

He slammed the receiver down with a violent explosion of profanity. He figured he'd have to lie low for the next several days. He turned away from the phone and shouted instructions to his crew. They began to stack and then to load merchandise into boxes and bags.

Brewster collected money and small packets of drugs he could quickly and easily convert to cash. He glanced at his watch and stopped collecting and packing.

"Get everything in boxes out of here! Take bags, too, but boxes have priority. Use whatever transportation you can find. We'll meet in the parking lot of the Roadhouse, the one south of town on 101. If you're driving, talk to the other drivers. I want time and space between cars as they leave this street. And, don't all of you exit onto King Road. I want at least half of you to use Los Ojos. Understood?"

Everyone within earshot acknowledged the directive and lifted, pushed, or pulled boxes and bags out of the house. Once outside, they stuffed the containers into trunks and back seats of sedans and coupes parked along the lengthy driveway.

When the bustle slowed, Brewster surveyed the room a final time and cursed. What happened was unacceptable in his mind. He was paying too much for information to get notified of a raid on such short notice.

He turned on his heel and headed towards the front of the house. He pulled up short at the door. More profanity did nothing to change the facts, although it placated him somewhat. In his haste, he'd forgotten that Mary was on her way over. With a shrug, he continued through the portal.

As he closed the door, he stopped short a third time. He'd forgotten about the shipment coming in later that night. He hurried back inside the house.

He stopped in the common bathroom and snapped on the light over the sink. That was the sign to his supplier that something was amiss and to abort the delivery.

After he pulled the front door closed for the second time, he patted his jacket pocket. At least he'd put only sixty percent down on the current shipment. Even if the delivery boys got busted, he wouldn't suffer a total loss.

Back at the station, Edwards sat for several seconds after ending the call contemplating his choices in response to Brewster's bravado. He concluded it would be easy to flip on the man when needed.

He picked up the phone from the base unit. He wasn't thinking about revenge. He was thinking about what he could do to slow down Stallings procurement of the search warrant.

He made a call to a fellow Manzanita Police Department employee.

Chapter 16

The officer who unceremoniously escorted him from Mary's house made certain the tattooed, bandana-capped Latino knew who was leading whom. By the time the pair reached the driveway, Martinez was close to the limit of his patience.

Martinez's handler followed the same physical actions that Mamba had with his prisoner. However, the term eased did not apply to a single aspect of the loading of prisoner number two into the patrol car.

After a delay while the officer called in, he climbed into the driver's seat and started the vehicle. As they pulled away from the curb, Martinez called out.

"Pull over after the first cross street."

"Shut up!"

"I want you to pull over after the next cross street so we can get these cuffs off."

"I told you to shut your mouth!"

"If you want to keep this cushy patrol car assignment, you will pull over and uncuff us both."

"Just who do you think you are?"

"Undercover Narcotics Detective Enciso Martinez, Officer," was the stone-cold reply. He paused a beat to let the driver process what he just heard. "Check it out with Stallings."

"You're a detective." Sarcasm oozed from each syllable of the officer's statement. He wasn't about to call in about some addict's claim.

"Do it!"

"Just shut up, Punk!"

"Call Dispatch then. Ask Nina about Detective Martinez. I'll give you my badge number if Nina wants it."

The patrol car slowed. The driver reconsidered. Nina was the name of the dispatcher on night duty. It was possible that someone not on the force might have seen Nina's name on a duty roster. The giant in the back seat pronounced the name, "Nine-uh," the dispatcher's preference.

The car pulled to curb. The officer made the call.

Less than two minutes later, Martinez and Flatly were rubbing their wrists with unshackled hands while they listened to apologies from their driver.

"No worries, amigo. You did what you should have until we checked out."

The officer offered a weak smile of thanks. "Let me buy you coffee?"

"Another time." A beefy hand reached past the steering wheel and grabbed the patrol car's radio. "This is Martinez. Patch me through to Stallings."

"Sorry," the female voice was apologetic. "He's after a warrant. I assume my glowing praise of your expertise a moment ago was sufficient."

"What?"

"I said, I suppose—"

"Not that. What did you say about Sergeant Stallings?"

"He's got another bust set up. He's getting the warrant for a search."

"Where's the bust?"

"I just sent two squads over to Lexington as back-up."

"Who asked for it?"

"I guess Lieutenant Kerrigan did," Nina offered as her best explanation. "The Desk Sergeant called it over to me. The Lieutenant must have phoned in the request. He's with the Sergeant tonight. Right?"

"Yeah." Martinez imagination was running full speed. He ran through a dozen scenarios in seconds. The last one struck a chord. "They must have scored off that phone call Mary got."

"Repeat that, will you Detective?"

"It's not important. Get me Kerrigan, por favor."

"Sure thing."

"And thanks for getting me out of the bracelets."

"Anytime. The Lieutenant's on the line."

After a brief exchange between Martinez and Kerrigan, Martinez directed the patrol car to the street outside Weston's apartment. Martinez told the transporting officer to return to Mary's place, remove and catalog the power supply for Flatley's wire. Call a cab for the boxer to take the CI home. Give the receipt to me."

"On it."

"Oh, and I pulled the transmitter off my partner before they stormed the palace," Martinez added as an afterthought. "It's under one of the sofa cushions. Take it back, too. There's no way I'm having the cost of that deducted from my next paycheck."

The officer, now willing to do just about anything to gain Martinez's good graces, nodded and headed back to Mary's house.

With all known loose ends tied off, Martinez climbed aboard his motorcycle and roared toward Lexington. The house number wasn't important. Lexington was less than five blocks long. It's primary purpose was to connect King Road and Los Ojos Road. It also provided access and egress to the three cul-de-sacs attached to it. There was only one cross street.

* * *

Nights on Lexington Street reminded passers-by of film noir. Homeowners in the upscale community preferred stars to streetlights when they looked out their oversized picture windows.

Twenty-eight minutes from the time they left Mary's house, Kerrigan and Mamba arrived at the Lexington address. Mamba gave a low whistle. Whoever Sid was, he lived in style. This was one of the most prestigious houses in an emerging neighborhood.

Twin brick columns flanked the entrance to the long driveway. An ornate light fixture topped each. The numbers "1-0-1-2-3" were back-lighted in recessed cases on both columns. The driveway ended in a large circle around a massive fountain.

Two police cars maneuvered until they sat as sentinels, one close to each column. They were far enough back that there was no chance of being seen from the house. Each faced the other with a clear view of the driveway's entrance. No car coming down the driveway could exit without being intercepted.

"I don't see Stallings."

"He had to get the warrant, Pat."

"I know. But that should have been a piece of cake. The judge already knew about the wire and buy-bust." Kerrigan rubbed his stomach in an unconscious attempt to quell his acid reflux.

Mamba looked at his watch. "It's just now been thirty minutes."

"From when we left," was Kerrigan's impatient rejoinder. "Stallings must have been almost five minutes ahead of us."

"Take it easy. I can name three things that could cause a delay on a warrant." The Lieutenant's face was a pasty hue that could have been the poor street lighting.

"I know," the sullen Kerrigan admitted. "I guess I'm just tired."

"And anxious."

"Yeah," the Lieutenant snorted a small laugh. "And anxious." He winced and reached for his roll of antacid tablets.

Martinez approached Kerrigan and Mamba after parking his motorcycle at the Los Ojos Road corner. A uniform stopped him, confirmed his identity, and escorted him to Kerrigan's car. The detective climbed into the back seat. No one said a word.

Tension wrapped itself around each man and sucked out even the memory of calm confidence. Mamba's leg began to twitch. Martinez cracked each of his knuckles in turn. Kerrigan groaned periodically and pushed in on his ulcer.

Finally, forty-five minutes after leaving Mary's house, Stallings arrived. A second car followed the black-and-white that delivered him. Nine officers and Mamba assembled just off the driveway.

Stallings exited his car, displayed the warrant he obtained, and waved them all to follow. The group started up the driveway in a ragged V formation.

"What kept you?" Kerrigan demanded when he caught up to the Sergeant.

"Later. After we're through here."

Mamba, although having no intention of becoming part of the operation once it moved inside the house, tagged close behind Kerrigan. As he walked, he made a mental note of the brief conversation between Stallings and his former partner.

Kerrigan, although surprised and irritated by Stallings' tone of voice, couldn't argue with his decision to delay his explanation. There was plenty to do.

While it had taken longer than it might have for Stallings to arrive, once on the scene, he deployed men quickly and efficiently. A scowl and muttered profanity hinted at the irritation he felt at the small number of officers assigned to him.

No one answered the front door in response to Stallings' announcement of the presence of the police. Nerves wound tighter.

Mamba would reprise his role at Mary's if needed. He tagged behind a small cadre of officers headed to the backyard. The cadre leader motioned for his followers to spread out and do a thorough visual reconnaissance.

"This door's open," Mamba called softly when he arrived at the sliding back door. Two officers materialized at his side. One officer verified Mamba's report. The other stage-whispered the news into his radio. Tension ratcheted up a notch.

Based on what Mamba heard of the conversation between the officers at his location and either Kerrigan or Stallings—he couldn't hear that voice—initial ingress to the house would be through the sliding glass door by the swimming pool, his location. Mamba smiled as he imagined the displeasure of the officer responsible for using the sledgehammer.

"I'm going in," Martinez whispered and tapped Mamba on the shoulder. "Can I use your weapon, amigo? I don't have mine right now."

"Sure." Mamba handed his Colt .38 Special to the detective. The more he worked with Martinez, the more he admired him. The big man was a professional. He was also one heck of an undercover operative.

"Gracias," was the distracted response as he accepted the gun without taking his eyes off the patio door. He snuck a glance at the snubbed barrel of the weapon in his hand and gave a quick head shake at the size of the gun. He pointed as he said, "One of you to the right., the other go straight in and wait on the right side of the door until 'm in position. I'm going three steps left, and then I'm on the floor. I'll cover the hallway."

Grunts from the two officers confirmed their roles. Martinez took a deep breath, slid the glass door aside, and stepped through.

One officer followed on his heels and stopped as directed. The last man slipped inside and spun to his right. At Martinez's signal, the two officers cleared the kitchen and dining room while the detective provided cover against approach from the bedroom area from his prone position.

"Clear the living room and let the Sergeant in," Martinez directed, nodding toward the front door as he stood.

The front door opened. Stallings entered with his phalanx of officers.

"We need to clear the bedrooms," the officer who opened the door reported.

With a gesture, Stallings dispatched three from his group down the hallway.

Moments later, “Clear!” echoed through the hallway.

“This guy, uh,” Martinez began when he and Stallings entered the kitchen.

“Sid,” Stallings filled in the name.

“Thanks. Anyway, Sid was into leftovers or something illegal.”

“How so?” Stallings moved closer.

“Sink’s full of these.” Martinez used a table fork to hold aloft a small plastic bag with a pressure-sealing top. He dropped the bag back in the sink and waved his hand toward an open base cabinet door. A uniformed officer pointed inside as he kneeled there. Several boxes of the storage bags were in plain sight.

Stallings squatted down and surveyed the interior of the cabinet.

Mamba waited by the patio door. He gloved up and examined the door’s hardware. He was working the latch when a hand on his shoulder startled him.

“Sorry,” Kerrigan apologized. “I left two uniforms to hold the fort in front. I didn’t mean to surprise you. Watta ya got?”

“Look at this.”

“Hmm,” was the extent of Kerrigan’s response as he studied the hardware.

“This latch is impossible to lock.” Mamba pointed to an empty slot in the mechanism. “There’s no hook to catch on the door frame.”

“Odd.”

“I don’t think the latch is broken. I’d say they disassembled it. This doorway has a lot of heavy traffic.” Mamba motioned to the floor. “Look at the wear pattern.”

Kerrigan studied the high-end vinyl flooring. The worn surface of the vinyl marked a path from the doorway through the open end of the kitchen to the hallway that led to the bedrooms.

“My guess is this is the delivery door for drugs,” Stallings offered as he arrived at the doorway.

“That’s a distinct possibility.” Kerrigan unbent his lanky frame and turned to survey the moonlit yard. “I wonder where that pathway leads beyond the pool?”

"I'll bet it goes right down the slope to whatever street is parallel to Lexington. They can unload there and haul the product up here without suspicion," Mamba offered.

"The living area is clear," an officer reported. "In fact, it's squeaky clean, even the garage."

"And there's nobody in the bedroom area," another uniformed officer, reported. "But there is about fifty pounds of this." He held up a brick-shaped wad of dried plant material.

Martinez took the brick and sniffed. "Good quality."

Stallings' face contorted in a fierce frown. He brought his fist down with a resounding smash on the kitchen counter.

"We had this Sid guy dead to rights!"

Silence.

With an obvious effort, Stallings composed himself before he asked, "Did you find anything else?"

"A couple nickel bags."

"Sergeant!" An officer outside in back interrupted with a stage whisper.

"What?"

"Looks like someone's coming up the slope behind the pool." All eyes turned to the backyard. Flashlight beams were visible as they swung back and forth, then up and down.

"Kill the lights!" Stallings snarled.

Mamba ducked below the kitchen counter.

"The bathroom light was on when we arrived," an officer reported.

"That's usually the signal to kill a deal," Martinez muttered as he slid the back door shut.

"We'd better leave some light on."

"How about a bedroom light, Sergeant?"

"No!" Stallings' mind raced. "Living room light only. Kerrigan, you take two uniforms. Wait on the far side of the swimming pool in case whoever's approaching bolts. Martinez, grab another uniform and stay in here with me. Everybody find a place and hide!"

"I gave my weapon to Martinez," Mamba said.

"Then get your butt out the front!"

Seconds later, quiet reigned. No one climbing the back slope could know what awaited them.

Three figures appeared between the oleander bushes beyond the pool. Each carried an armload of something. Panting breath patterns implied that the loads were heavy or the slope steeper than it looked.

"Where's Brewster?" One figure grunted.

"He never meets us outside," answered a second figure.

"He never meets us outside when we have anything that weighs anything," corrected the third.

"Humph."

"Let me up front," demanded the second figure. "I can get the door open."

"Be our guest." Two figures stepped to one side so the second could pass.

Figure number two used one index finger to slide the door open. He entered the house. Numbers one and three followed him. Kerrigan and Martinez filled the doorway as soon as the third deliveryman cleared it, weapons in hand.

"Welcome, gentlemen," Stallings greeted the trio as he switched on the kitchen light. Three surprised heads swung back and forth from one police officer to another. "I think you're surrounded."

"Set the packages on the table, kneel, and place both hands on your heads," Kerrigan instructed from the doorway. To Stallings he added, "We'll cover these guys. You search and cuff 'em."

They handcuffed the deliverymen in less than a minute.

"They must have a truck down the slope," Mamba offered as he reentered the kitchen.

"I'll bet someone's in that truck waiting for these three." Martinez rubbed his chin as he spoke. "It'd sure be nice to wrap this thing up in a neat package."

"What're you driving at, Martinez?"

"If we could get three of us back down the slope in place of these flunkies, Sergeant, we might pick us up another partner."

"It's plenty dark enough," an officer added. "If we wear the jackets these guys are wearing when we go down, there's a good chance of making it to their vehicle before the driver realizes we're not who he's expecting."

"Not so fast. The driver could be armed. Besides, Martinez is bigger than two of these dirtbags together. He'll never squeeze into one of those jackets."

"I've got my vest on," the uniform said.

"So do I," a second uniform chimed in. "And Richter outside has hers, too."

"OK," Stallings agreed. "Kerrigan and Martinez get a car down there as cover. Block the truck's exit if possible, but only if you can do that without being seen."

"No problem," Kerrigan said. "You and Mamba get to babysit, Sergeant?"

"Yeah, I guess that's what it is," Stallings admitted. Turning to the three uniformed officers now donning the deliverymen's jackets, he said, "If it looks like it's falling apart, you bail!"

"Right away, Sergeant," one uniform conceded. "I've got no desire to die tonight."

"Not even funny. Kerrigan, you go first. I want that car in position to stop any vehicle from leaving this scene."

"On our way," Martinez called as the two men headed to the front of the house where Kerrigan parked his car.

* * *

Martinez and Kerrigan peered through the darkness at the base of the slope below the swimming pool of the Lexington house. They found a spot from which they could see the suspected delivery truck. They were out of sight of the truck driver unless it moved. It was too dark to for a positive ID of three figures struggling down the slope.

A silence that grabbed you from behind and squeezed your chest until you felt you were suffocating imposed itself on the scene. Martinez rolled his massive shoulders to shake the sensation. Kerrigan rubbed the back of his neck with his left hand while he jabbed his ulcer with his right.

A high-pitched snarl that ended in a yowl and a yelp announced the end of an encounter between two members of the local feline population. Both men jumped at the unexpected racket. The tension broke when each caught the quick glance of the other trying to see if his partner had noticed his reaction. They exchanged sheepish grins before Martinez leaned forward and pointed beyond the windshield.

Three minimally disguised police officers trudged down the narrow path that cut a steep diagonal down the hillside. Despite an excessive amount of slipping and sliding, all three arrived at the end of the path without falling.

The sound of a truck engine roaring to life and the light from two headlights brought Martinez and Kerrigan full alert. The Lieutenant reached for his car's radio microphone.

"Stallings!"

"You got something?"

"Looks that way. Keep this channel open."

"10-4."

The jacket-wearing police officers arrived at the headlights. The sound of the engine ended. The interior light of the truck cab went on as the driver's side door opened. Kerrigan saw a figure climb out of the truck with its hands in the air.

"Looks contained from this end," Kerrigan reported. "The driver's out of the truck and in custody."

"Good!" Stallings sounded pleased. "Check the truck."

"Already on it."

Fifteen minutes later, four suspects were on their way downtown. They refused to answer questions about their presence or activity. The delivery truck was under police guard until they could tow it to the station as evidence.

While the arrest of the delivery truck driver was in progress, the search continued inside Brewster's house. Two additional bags of marijuana were found inside pillows on one bed. No other drug related discoveries were made.

"Detective, you need to see this."

"See what?"

"There's broken glass on the carpet." The uniformed officer knelt and pulled the shag fibers apart.

The detective removed a pen from his pocket and used it to sweep a larger piece of glass from beneath a nightstand.

"Do you think that's part of this?"

"It was." The detective stood. "Bag and tag this." He dropped a glass cylinder into the gloved hand of the officer.

"Yes, sir. What should I call it?"

"Call it what it is."

"I'm sorry. I've never seen anything like this before."

"Consider yourself lucky. This used to be a mercury switch used in bomb making."

"Why would that be in a drug dealer's house?"

"I can think of several reasons, all bad." The detective walked toward the bedroom door. He stopped at the threshold and turned back to the uniform. "That's all you're doing here tonight. Get everything in an evidence bag back to the station ASAP. Make sure that whoever's pulled night shift in the evidence locker starts with that mercury switch. I want all the lab techs find out about it on Stallings' desk by noon tomorrow."

"If there is mercury, should I alert the hazardous materials team?" The officer stood.

"I'll take care of that." The detective turned into the doorway and called back over his shoulder, "Draw a map, so they look for the mercury in the right bedroom."

* * *

Stallings, Kerrigan, Martinez, and Mamba stood on the porch of the Lexington house. Tight smiles on the faces of the men were more eloquent than words. The operation netted three drug dealers. Two names were on the list Reed gave Mamba.

Nevertheless, the mood of the quartet was subdued. The tip of Sidney Brewster foiled what should have been a significant arrest.

"I think we're getting close. Real close," Stallings offered.

Three heads nodded in agreement.

Chapter 17

After being folded into the back seat of a black and white, Mary Carstairs recapped her performance. She was prepared to perform whatever emotional drama required to ensure her immediate safety and move her closer to her goal.

Mary sniffled in the back seat of the police car. After each sniffle, she noted the driver's reaction. His shoulders tensed with each one. Much like Martinez, the officer looked at Mary and saw what she crafted and heard only what she wanted him to hear.

"Are you all right?" the policeman called back to her.

"I, I don't know." She snuffled loudly. "I-I'm so s-s-scared."

"No need to be scared," the officer assured her. "We'll protect you. Sergeant Stallings said to give you special treatment because of your help setting up your supplier."

She smiled to herself. An enormous sigh preceded her next statement. "I h-hope I did the right thing."

"Hang in there. You've helped set up a terrible person. Don't worry. We'll catch the guy you identified tonight."

Another smile flickered at the corners of her lips. She'd hoped the cops would nail Sid Brewster for a long time. His organizational chart was simple: The more money an individual in any position made, the fewer of those individuals there were in the chart. She well knew that the only way to move up a notch in the organization was to replace someone above you.

She found that as a supplier, her current status was more lucrative than a dealer, her entry job. And the supplier's supplier was better yet. There was only one supplier's supplier. Sid Brewster was her current target.

At the station, the officer pulled as close as he could to what was euphemistically known as the delivery entrance. It was the door through which they escorted prisoners into central booking. However, after he helped Mary from the back seat, he led her around the corner of the building and into the front door to the station.

"Hey, Morgan," Sergeant Edwards called to Mary's escort. "That the last one from the bust?"

"Yeah, Eddie," Morgan responded. "Didn't expect to see you tonight."

"Tell me about it. Smitty left with the flu or something."

"Anyway, this is the house's owner. Stallings said to take good care of her, though. She fingered the next man up the ladder."

"Woo-eee," Edwards whistled. "Dangerous. You must be a brave lady."

Mary diverted her eyes, wishing the officer would hurry and book her. She turned her body away. The fewer people that knew about her collusion with the police, the better, even cops. She could assume that no one with untoward street connections heard of her betrayal. The others arrested at her house were in transit before she'd flipped on Brewster.

Morgan processed Mary personally. After fingerprints, pictures, and the obligatory offer of one phone call, he delivered her to a matron who supervised her change into the drab gray wardrobe worn by prisoners.

Twenty-four hours later, Mary Carstairs posted bail. She'd seen no one she recognized and had talked only to the guards—and then, only to answer questions. She walked from the division's holding cell with no intention of returning.

* * *

The fifteen-inch portable color television sat atop the dresser in the bedroom of Sid Brewster's temporary residence. The picture was small and grainy. The sound was tinny. Sid was unhappy about all that, and more. So dour was his mood that even long-time associates were steering clear of the man.

The *Five O'clock News* crackled into view on the TV monitor. Brewster paid close attention to the show's intro. He was interested in only one story. The anchor described it in the third teaser the broadcast team gave. He lay back on the mattress and stuffed pillows under his shoulders and head. He would wait.

The female anchor, a lean blonde with big hair, even when compared to other popular styles, introduced his target story coming out of the first commercial.

"This morning, Manzanita Police released news of a major drug bust. Our cameras were at the press conference."

The screen changed from a view of the TV studio set to a lectern before a powder blue curtain. A police officer, sporting perfectly coiffed hair and a dress uniform bedecked with medals entered through a slit in the curtain. After adjusting the microphone, the man flashed a dazzling smile at the camera. The camera's position minimized the effects of the five pounds the Chief had added to his waistline in his time in Manzanita. It was easy for any viewer to understand why Dwight Rogers was a media darling.

His expression morphed into an appropriate level of concern, and he began his statement. Although he had a copy on the lectern, he delivered the entire speech from memory.

"Fellow citizens of Manzanita, I am Police Chief Dwight Rogers. I am pleased to announce that through exceptional efforts by our officers, your police department apprehended several notorious drug dealers last night. Coordinated efforts between officers from our narcotics unit, our traffic unit, and our SWAT unit resulted in successful completion of two raids."

He paused and refocused his gaze on the camera before continuing.

"In addition, although not yet in custody, another key figure, the supplier to those dealers, has been identified and forced from his place of business. Rest assured that continued efforts by your police will result in more arrests and a decrease in the number of those corrupt individuals active in the poisoning of our city. Thank you."

"That was Police Chief Dwight Rogers with his statement to the press earlier today. We'll have more details of this situation, and highlights of the Chief's question-and-answer period, later in this broadcast. In other news—"

Brewster reached a hairy arm over and snapped off the set. Hair was Brewster's preeminent feature. He sported a shaggy mullet on his head and fur-like hair across the shoulders, down the arms back, chest, stomach, thighs, calves, and between the knuckles of his fingers and toes. During and after puberty, his nicknames included ape-man, Yeti, Sasquatch, and monkey-boy. The nicknames and fights resulting from those names hardened his outlook toward humanity and generated a speech pattern laced with profanity.

He grimaced. That was more than he hoped he would hear. He shrugged his shoulders. In his mind, it could have been worse. Rogers might have mentioned him. He'd thank his departmental snitch for his skills and remind all the cops on his payroll what happens if they violate the terms of their agreements.

* * *

Chief Rogers clicked off the TV set in his living room. As in his office, expensive designers selected décor to emphasize his taste. The woods were dark; the fabrics muted. The occasional pops of color supplied by pillows and paintings were subtle, yet effective in their portrayal of what he saw as his multidimensional persona.

While pleased with the coverage of his statement and the later footage of his Q/A session, he wished he'd been more animated. He feared he looked almost robotic in his gestures.

The ringing of his phone caused him to turn and look at the device.

"This is Rogers."

"I'm sure you know who this is," William Anderson told the partner he purchased. "Now that we've got the unnecessary introductions out of the way, you came across as a concerned public servant whose sole desire is to protect and serve today in your press conference."

"I made a statement outlining the progress of an important investigation and answered a few questions afterward. It was not a press conference."

"To-may-toe, tow-mah-toe. Since you brought up the subject, I was hoping, actually expecting, more progress in this important investigation. While I'm certain you've not forgotten our agreement, I find that details of such agreements are often best repeated. Shall I?"

"I can't help it if the big fish sometimes out-swim the fishermen."

"Quaint analogy. Allow me to continue it. I want that fish netted. Sooner rather than later."

"Information in that arena appears to be leaking to Garmel's people."

"Plug that leak."

"I'm working on it. However, I must use discretion. You should understand that neither of us can become the focus of any illicit event."

Anderson puffed out a breath through his lips before answering.

"Your eloquence is admirable. However, you are working for me, and I'm running short on patience. I don't want to hear excuses for sloppy housekeeping on your part. Accelerate the timeline."

"Or what?"

"Or what?" Anderson snorted as he cut off a laugh. "I'd hoped that my subtle reminder of our agreement would prove enough to avoid any messiness like this. But, since it was not, let me make this clear," Anderson said in a tone that changed from congenial to threatening in fewer than six words. "You have taken considerable amounts of my money to do things for me, things far outside the job description of Chief of Police."

"All I meant," Rogers started to answer.

"Shut up, Rogers! What I was saying, before being rudely interrupted, means this: You will do what I say when I say to do it." The words penetrated Rogers' psyche like arrows shot into a straw target.

"I'm doing all I can."

"I tire of this rhetoric. I don't think you're doing all of anything except milking me for more cash." The steel was back in the voice. "Move this along faster, or I will expose you."

The hum of a disconnected phone line ended the conversation.

Rogers stood with phone in hand. He said aloud, "Unless I figure a way to expose you first. If you think they'll take William Anderson's word over that of the Chief of Police, you're wrong!"

* * *

It didn't take long for Sid Brewster's mood to sour following his dinner. Considering his situation, the ebb and flow of emotions made sense on many levels. First, he barely escaped from his supply house. Second, he had to leave too much product in that house. Third, the place he occupied now was, in his view, a dump. The third issue was easily illustrated. He had a portable television in his bedroom.

In reality, the house was a small, detached single-family home. While it lacked the stereotypical white picket fence, it had an anonymous look to it from the outside. That was valuable. However, it looked like a set designer furnished it for a late 1950s sitcom and had not touched it since.

The most unfortunate aspect was the location itself. Anonymity came at a price. This house was on the south edge of town, less than two blocks off Highway 101. The location forced him to rent a hotel room in town for his cash business.

He despised commuting.

The evening of Mary's release, the phone rang. Rick Elkhart, Brewster's second in command, answered.

"Hello."

"Brewster. Now!"

"You want to talk?" Elkhart asked his boss while he held his hand over the phone's mouthpiece.

"Who is it?"

"He didn't say, sir."

"Find out!"

"Who's calling?"

"Tell Brewster to get his fat ass to the phone."

"He won't say," was the reworded response.

After a fit of foul language, Brewster picked up a phone extension from the table beside him. "Brewster here. This better be good!"

"Mary tipped the cops."

Brewster inhaled sharply. He recognized the voice of Eddie Edwards, his police contact. He shook his head. It was a shame. You just couldn't trust anyone any longer. And, she'd held such promise.

"She's out on bail," the voice continued after a brief pause. "My guess is she's lying low, waiting for this to blow over. I don't know if she knows you're not in jail. Either way, that doesn't matter. You need to find her and shut her up."

"Don't tell me what to do."

The line clicked dead. A torrent of profanity flowed into the unheeding phone receiver. Brewster hated being treated that way, but the price you paid for information often included less than desirable sources. He knew what he had to do. He took a deep breath and with utmost composure, Brewster instructed Elkhart to contract for a specific service from Oscar Briggs. He provided his associate with the number by memory.

Then, since he was in an evil mood anyway, he began preparation for the commute to his hotel room in town.

* * *

Petula Jacobs sat at her desk in Chief Rogers' reception area. Although unaware of her boss's dressing down by William Anderson, she knew something was bothering the man. He came in late and hadn't left the inner office. After months of carefully orchestrated moments of intimacy with the man, she read his moods as easily as she read the morning paper. Chief Rogers was ticked off.

She was skimming the memos and action reports that the Chief received in the morning interdepartmental mail. Most of it was routine, but the reports on the outcomes of two drug raids the night before caught her eye.

The phone rang.

"Chief Rogers' office."

"You can tell your boss I'm pleased with the way things started last night," Guillermo Arcenas said. "But, also let him know that I expect closure. Brewster's escape is, shall we say, unsettling."

"I'm not sure Rogers knew anything about those two events. I found out about them after the fact," Petula replied.

"That seems odd, don't you agree?"

"Sometimes, even the players aren't sure of what's going down until the last minute."

"I suppose that might be true."

Petula shook her head before she answered, "It's true. I'll let the Chief know."

"As I pay you to do," was Arcenas' closing statement.

Petula held the handset for several seconds while she considered her options. Before hanging up, she decided to work on something she could leverage when needed.

* * *

Oscar "Big 0" Briggs was an entrepreneur, although he did not understand the meaning of the word. Born into a lower-middle-class family, he grew up in and around tough neighborhoods. As a result, "you get what you work for or what you take" became his unspoken motto.

Although not a large person, he was intimidating in his mannerisms and had no trouble extorting schoolwork from his peers. He was a fourth grader in reading skill but could solve an algebra problem—given enough time and the proper incentive.

Soon after high school graduation, he was arrested and convicted of armed robbery of a convenience store. Prison hardened him in two ways: his body and his outlook. Physically, he lifted weights five times a week. His biceps were a sight to behold. Making himself happy defined his outlook. Whatever it took.

Briggs' idea of happiness almost always included women or drugs. The accumulation of money to disperse through those channels was his primary focus. But, with limited academic skills and even less desire to work set hours every day, he soon shifted to a life of a free-lance enforcer.

He rarely turned down a job that involved physical damage and pain for his target. The nickname Big 0 came from the preferred service he provided, hitman. The 0 was the numeral zero. It referred to the number of victims that survived his lethal attacks.

"Hello,"

"Is this Big 0?" Rick Elkhart asked.

"Yeah. Whatcha want?"

"You know Sidney Brewster?"

"I heard of him."

"And he has heard of you. In fact, you worked for him in the past through a mutual acquaintance. Now, Mr. Brewster would like to contract your services directly."

"This a job offer?"

"Yes."

"Doin' what?"

"Eliminating people causing problems for Mr. Brewster."

"If you want a hit, I get paid half up front."

"That is an acceptable condition. Do you have a pencil and paper?"

"Somewhere. Let me look." Briggs left the phone and rummaged through his limited cabinetry. After several minutes, he returned to the phone.

"Okay. What's the job?"

"It's two jobs. Will that be a problem?"

"Nope. I like what I do. Brewster can get the high-grade horse, right?"

"He can arrange that."

"I want my first payment in heroin. Not some low-quality stuff you've cut so much that it don't do nothin' when you hit with it. I want the good stuff."

"Understood. What is your normal fee?"

Briggs thought hard. He usually charged $300-400 for a job. He figured Brewster should pay more.

"How you know this be a normal job?" he asked.

"Well, uh, I guess I assumed that."

"Here's what I want. Six hundred dollars of horse—that's what you pay for it not what you sell it for. I get that before I do a thing. And six hundred dollars in cash, tens, twenties, and fifties, after they both dead."

"Done. Write down the names. We only have one address, so you'll have to find Mary on your own." He pulled the phone away from his ear when a full-volume wolf whistle greeted Mary's name.

"One's a woman. I like that."

Elkhart's blood froze at the coldness of Briggs' tone. He shivered but dredged up the courage to continue.

"Mr. Brewster's only request is that the woman know who's behind the hit." He stopped and listened while Brewster yelled something at him. "Mr. Brewster also requires that Mary suffers before you kill her."

"I can do that. Say the names and the address real slow so I can write 'em down."

* * *

It was mid-morning of the third day after the raid on Brewster's house. William Anderson sat alone in his private office. He had so many irons in the fire he'd lost track of what his wife knew and did not know about his business dealings. It was time to get the story straight in his mind before he told someone something they shouldn't hear.

His personal assistant buzzed him. He punched his intercom button.

"Yes, Eileen?"

"The secretary of the private detective you hired has called three times, sir."

"What did you tell her?"

"First time, that was three days ago, I told her you were out of town."

"Was I?" He flipped through his desk calendar.

"Well, yes, sir. At least technically. You were having a lunch meeting with a client at the lodge up in Ski Slope. That was eleven a.m. through one-thirty p.m."

"Fine." Anderson made a note of the time on that calendar page. "And the others?"

"Two days ago, you were in a meeting."

"And what time was that?"

"One-fifteen to two-forty-five p.m."

"Okay." He made another note on his calendar before he asked, "With whom was I meeting?"

"No one, sir."

"I understand. Perhaps a better question would have been, 'With whom might I have been meeting?'"

"Well, I'd suggest calling the HVAC company. They might have been meeting with you about upgrading our dehumidifiers."

"That's right. I remember now." He added a name to his second notation. "And the third call?"

"Just a few minutes ago, I had to tell her you were on a conference call. A long-distance conference call. I'm sorry, sir, but she's very persistent."

"No worries. I'll talk to some of our suppliers in the Midwest. I'm sure they'll verify that call if need be."

"Is everything acceptable now, sir?"

"Oh, yes. By the way, I'm working on something related to this case. So, when Mr. Mamba's secretary calls again, send it through, even if I am unavailable, technically."

"Yes, sir," Eileen said through a smile.

Chapter 18

Dancer thought his personal office at Mamba Investigations was an accurate reflection of him and his professional ideals. The private detective's old police badge and current license certificate hung to the right of the office door. A framed photo of Earth taken on one of the Apollo missions hung on the left side. Its purpose, as Hope explained, was "to balance reality."

On the credenza behind his desk was a display of Sherlock Holmes trademark tools. The focal points in the collection were a well-worn deerstalker's hat he found in a thrift store in Oregon and an oversized magnifying glass replete with tortoise shell handle. The magnifier was a gift from a grateful client.

He sat with both feet propped up on the felt pad that covered the top of his oak desk. As he sipped from a cup of fresh coffee, his mind wandered over various aspects of the partially successful buy-bust two nights earlier. When his thoughts turned to the mysterious tip-off Sidney Brewster received, it was enough to morph his positive feelings into full-blown concern.

He sighed, took another sip from his coffee cup, and determined not to let the one negative part of the otherwise successful operation ruin his good mood.

He heard the phone ring once before Hope answered.

"Good morning, Mamba Investigations."

"Hey, uh, I want Dancer." The drunken male voice mushed the words out.

"Hold a minute, please." Hope hit the intercom button. When Phil pick up, she said, "It's for you."

"Mamba here."

"Dancer, this is Reed. We gotta talk. Today!" Reed's speech was slurred. But, the tone indicated the man was scared. Scared more than Mamba had ever heard him.

"What's wrong?"

"Can't tell ya on the phone. We gotta meet. Today!"

"Where and when?"

"I don't know. Dancer, I don't know."

“Listen!” Mamba directed as his mind speculated on what Reed wanted. Since Reed was close to losing it, he offered one of two locations he figured Reed could find in any condition. “How about Tug’s?”

“Tug’s.” Reed’s monotonic response gave no sign he understood.

“Tug’s Pub,” Mamba expanded. “Down on Harbor Drive.”

“Is that close to The Jazz Machine?” Reed mumbled. “I’m at The Jazz Machine.”

“Stay where you are!”

“Sure. Uh, OK.” Mamba’s commanding tone cleared some fog from the musician’s brain. “You comin’ down? We gotta meet. T’day!”

“I’m leaving now.” Mamba hung up the phone and headed out of his office.

“I’ll be at The Jazz Machine,” he told Hope as he pulled his coat from the hook beside the exit door.

“Problem?”

“Apparently. At least it sounds like a problem. Whenever Reed calls me, it usually ends up a problem.”

“You know how I feel about Mr. Reed. Be careful.”

“Always.” He closed the door with surprising gentleness. There was no reason to infect Hope with his concern.

* * *

In an earlier time, The Jazz Machine was one of the premier jazz spots in all California. Many jazz legends played a set or two, or many more, in the original club. The ravages of time, and a fire, forced the owners to walk away. The current iteration of the name was at least five magnitudes of brightness below even the memory of the original.

Once in a long while, management announced some current name in the jazz community as “playing this Friday night.” More often than not, Friday arrived without the headliner musician.

The current remodel of the club was into its second year. In the first year, the Fire Marshall ordered the stage demolished. It was, torn down but not replaced. What now passed as the stage was nothing more than unfinished pine and fir two by sixes as floor joists partially covered with sheets of exterior plywood. An occasional nail pounded through the plywood into stringers below held the pseudo-stage in place.

Mismatched tables and chairs, a bar needing stain and a topcoat of epoxy, and a surprisingly well-maintained piano completed the interior.

Reed sat at a corner table in the nearly deserted club. His head throbbed. Sweet Lou the bartender refused to grant him credit, so the results of what liquor he bummed so far would have to tide him over until Dancer Mamba arrived.

As he tried to keep awake, his thoughts ran back in time. He remembered playing two sets behind Alice Coltrane. After John died, she traveled to his hangouts. Although he felt bad for her, her pain raised her playing to another level. In a flash of lucidity, Reed muttered, "I ain't never heard nothin' like that ever."

He moved his hands into position for holding his tenor sax. His fingers moved in well-practiced synchronization as the tunes of the past played with sweetness and finesse once again in his memory.

He ran his tongue around the inside of the empty glass sitting in front of him for the twenty-fifth time. He hoped beyond hope that somehow he missed a drop or two of the libation that once filled the shot glass.

He ran his gaze around the room. He knew they were searching for him. It was only a matter of time before they found him. Fear tied his intestines into a tight knot. Only the sedative effect of the alcohol allowed him to keep a loose rein on his rising panic. The effect was diminishing. He needed Dancer Mamba.

Mamba pushed open the door to the aging nightclub. Sweet Lou nodded his greeting. Two other patrons of the establishment afforded him unseeing eye contact. Only one person in the place expressed more than a passing interest in him.

Reed waved frantically. The PI returned a perfunctory wave and went to Reed's table.

"What's wrong?"

"Dancer. I got, I mean, we got trouble."

Mamba focused his full attention on the man's speech. Reed was drunk. Most of the words came out more mush than meaning.

"What kind of trouble?"

"Bi-i-ig trouble," Reed answered as he held his hands as far apart as he could. The effort caused him to wobble in his chair. He slapped both hands on the tabletop as he leaned forward and expanded his explanation.

"I need money."

"No deal," Mamba said and slid his chair back.

"Don't leave! I'll tell you what the trouble is for a drink," Reed whined.

"You tell me what's going on. After I hear what you've got to say, we'll discuss payment." Mamba slid his chair up to the table.

"Please, Dancer. I'm scared, man!" The man leaned farther forward, sending alcohol fumes into the PI's face with every breath. He grabbed Mamba by the shirtfront. "They know, man! They know!" He repeated the phrase with rising volume.

"Calm down!" Mamba barked with high intensity but low volume. He pried Reed's fingers away from his shirt and pushed the man's hands back down to the tabletop. He leaned against his chair back and surveyed the interior of the club as unobtrusively as he could.

Three people in the room appeared oblivious to their own existence. Two others were engrossed in conversation. The bartender kept time with "Night Train" as it played at moderate volume from the old-style jukebox against the wall opposite their table.

Mamba knew the music covered whatever they discussed, so he asked point blank, "Who knows, and what do they know?"

"They've got the papers."

"What papers?"

"The papers you wrote, man. They got the names."

"That's crazy talk, Reed. Nobody's seen those lists but the police."

"I'm tellin' you they're on the street," Reed insisted. "I seen 'em."

"Come with me." Mamba grabbed Reed's arm and stood. "We're getting out of here."

"What about my drink?"

"Later," Mamba promised. "You were right. We have to get out of here."

"I know. They goin' to come here lookin' for me." Reed's sudden flash of lucidity caused the PI to reassess the story. He decided haste was their best defense.

The two men left at the fastest pace Reed could maintain.

The next morning, Reed awoke to find himself in a strange bed. That the bed was strange was not unusual. The bed was clean; that fact that stood out in his slowly clearing thoughts. He sat up with a start.

He panicked as he looked around the room. Motel management mounted the front half of a suit of armor to the wall opposite the foot of his bed. Other decorative pieces suggesting life in medieval times lent an air of distorted reality to the scene.

"Dancer!" His cry of panic echoed through the motel room. Mamba awoke with a start. He'd spent the night in a chair next to Reed's bed in the cheapest motel he knew that didn't rent rooms by the hour. He shook his head and gathered his thoughts.

"Dancer! Is this your place?" Reed screamed.

Mamba took a deep breath and asked, "How're you feeling?"

"Dancer! Am I glad to see you!" Reed's head snapped left and right. "Where am I?"

"A Good Knight's Sleep Motel."

"Oh, man, that's good to hear. Some of this stuff is scary! I was afraid I was somewhere else."

"Where?"

"Where they are," Reed answered.

"Who are you talking about?" Mamba delivered the question with a frustrated edge. He was stiff and tired and wanted information, not more blubbering gibberish.

"The guys with the list," Reed repeated his story of the previous night. "You got a drink?"

"No drinks. Who told you about this list?"

"Nobody told me. I seen the lists. They showing them around so people know to skip. But, I gotta worry! I gave those names to you!"

"I wrote one copy of those lists, and they're locked up."

"I saw copies. They was made by one of them copy machine things."

"You saw copies? Where?"

"Hey, man," Reed said as he literally rolled out of the bed. He used the bedspread to pull himself into a kneeling position. Pushing off the mattress, his body unfolded until he stood facing the private investigator. The man wore boxer shorts. The effects of a long life of dissipation were clear. "I seen them at a party I was at."

He turned to the nightstand and picked up his pack of cigarettes. With shaking hands, he tried to light one. Mamba had seen enough drying out drunks to know the symptoms. The shaking is more than a drunk who needed a drink. The man was terrified.

"What's the matter?" Mamba demanded. "For real!"

"I'm scared, man. They're gonna get me."

"Why would they be after you?"

"The list, man. They must know who gave you the list."

"How could they know? I didn't tell them."

"Then how'd they get the list?"

"That I don't know," Mamba admitted. Only Mamba, Kerrigan, and Stallings had copies. While Martinez saw the pages, he never had copies of his own.

"That's why I'm scared, man," Reed whispered.

Mamba turned and looked at his CI.

"Get dressed we'll get some breakfast." He handed the frightened man his shirt and pants. "Hope washed these for you."

"Thanks, man." He pushed the shirt up against his face. "It's nice to smell clean."

Mamba didn't have the heart to tell the man it wasn't just his clothes that got washed. He didn't know if he'd ever forget the visual of the semi-conscious sax player swaying while he scrubbed the man's body with a soapy washcloth. He shivered.

"It's all good," Mamba mumbled as he waved aside the thank you. "I'll check out this list business. You lie low for a while. And, you've got to stay off the sauce."

"I can't do that," Reed whined. "I need the booze."

"When you're drunk, you might say something bad. Sober, you have a chance to keep away from whoever has the list."

"I know. But it's gonna be hard, man. I haven't been sober three days straight since '79."

"I know it'll be hard. But you have to stay sober for the rest of the week if you want me to poke around for you."

"Where will I stay, man? They know where I live."

"I talked to a friend over at the Rochester Hotel. He'll let you stay down in the basement if you stay sober and help with the cleaning."

"Thanks." He paused. Then he croaked out, "I'll try."

"I know you will. Finish dressing and we'll head to breakfast." Mamba swiped the cigarette pack from Reed's hand. "And don't smoke in this room!"

* * *

Three hours after breakfast with Reed, Mamba sat in his office. He'd lost count of the times he tried to dismiss the musician's fears as the ramblings of a hallucinating drunk.

On one hand, he had only Reed's word there was a copy of the list of names on the street, and Reed was hardly an unimpeachable source.

On the other hand, Reed was scared enough to consider staying sober for a week. That was a most convincing argument for the validity of his claim.

Mamba shook his head, hoping to clear his thoughts. He needed something to concentrate on and take his mind off the problem Reed brought up. He punched the intercom button on his phone.

"Yes, Phil."

"Did you check with Anderson about any new drug thefts?"

"No," Hope responded. "I've talked to the secretary over there three times with no return call. Frankly, although I can't imagine why, I think they're stalling."

"What?" Mamba recoiled at the impact of Hope's final word. Somewhere in his subconscious, the word had triggered the memory of an incident that took place on the night of the bust. "What did you say?"

"I, uh. I think I said that I thought Anderson was stalling," Hope stammered.

"That's what I thought!" Mamba slammed his hand down on the desk. "Get me Kerrigan! Reed might be right!"

* * *

Mary Carstairs' mind wandered as she thumbed through the phone book. She was looking for a cheap hotel where she could lie low until Brewster was out of the picture for good. Because of her self-imposed isolation in the division's holding cell, and her choice to spend thirty-six hours on the street after her release, she'd learned only that morning that someone tipped her boss. And he evaded arrest.

Since Brewster was on the run, she would be in a good position to take his place in Garmel's pecking order if he stumbled. She smiled as she finished marking hotel ads in a phone book and tore the marked page from the directory.

At the change booth in a video game and pinball arcade, she pulled an empty soda cup from the trash, then converted a five-dollar bill into quarters and dropped them into the cup. She carried the cup to the pair of pay phones just outside the arcade. Six calls later, she hung up the phone with a satisfied smile.

She started for her house to pick up an overnight bag. After walking about half a block, she stopped. If the cops weren't there, someone whom she didn't want to know of her whereabouts might be. She went back to the pay phone and called in a favor from one of her dealers. The woman would drop off a travel bag of necessities and clothing at her ultimate destination, the Royal Guard Hotel. That would complete the cheap, safe fix of her current homeless condition.

Anyone could lose himself or herself for a time in a place like the Royal Guard. The man she talked to on the phone guaranteed to be discreet. They'd been in business a long time, and she had to trust someone.

After paying a week's rent in advance plus an extra twenty-five dollars for the desk clerk's loss of memory, Mary retrieved the bag from the desk clerk. She asked the front desk to hold an envelope for the woman who'd return the next day for her compensation.

Carrying that bag, the sum total of her luggage, Mary climbed the stairs to room 214. She unlocked the door and paused in the doorway while she surveyed the interior. The kitchen area was straight ahead. To the left was the bathroom, something she knew because of the odor of fermenting urine. The bathroom door hung askew allowing a view into a crusty sink and water-damaged vanity.

Four tarnished posts of a brass canopy bed poked their ugly heads over the top of a partial wall that defined the bedroom. On the near side of the wall, her living room, she decided, a dilapidated couch and chair faced an ancient television.

Once inside the dingy flat, Mary set about making herself comfortable. She flushed the toilet and dumped some cologne in the bowl to mask remnants of the smell.

The dresser was stained and chipped. A phone book jammed beneath one corner replaced a missing leg.

Removing the top left drawer, she dumped the resident roaches onto the floor. She methodically stamped the life out of each of the insects that scurried around her feet. Most of the clothing in her bag went into what she decided was the clean drawer. She hung the remaining items, two blouses, on bent, rusting hangers in the dank-smelling closet.

It took only four steps to move from her bedroom into the kitchen. She opened the refrigerator door. While clean was a generous description, the interior was serviceable. The old-school freezer compartment inside the only door held a partially filled plastic ice cube tray. She flipped on one stove burner. It worked.

There was no telephone. She had to hunt for the on/off button on the television. Once she found it, she pushed it three times before abandoning her quest for an image on the screen. She decided that was not a problem. She'd catch up on her reading.

At the end of her housewarming, about ten minutes total, she stood with arms folded in the center of the room. Although it made little sense, she felt safe here.

No one entering the room would believe that the casual-chic Mary Carstairs, formally of 3717 Henry Court, lived in such a dive. She was pleased with her choice and knew she could tolerate the conditions for as long as it took the legal system to deal with Sidney Brewster.

Then, the memory of the report that Brewster evaded arrest in the raid she'd helped facilitate surfaced. She had target on her back. She flopped down on the bed and planned her next move.

She would work her street contacts and supply the police with anonymous tips about Sid's whereabouts. If all went well, the permanent removal of her former employer might not take long.

* * *

Peacock Feathers restaurant was not a restaurant Phil Mamba frequented. It was at the high end of his price range and longer than the distance he'd normally travel for a meal. He adjusted his tie. The action was unusual. He rarely wore a tie.

As he waited for the snooty hostess to seat him, he smoothed the front of his sports coat and buttoned the single button. A hostess in a short, form-fitting shirt dress seated him after a longer wait than the size of the crowd dictated.

Now he sat in a dimly lit rear booth keeping an eye out for Pat Kerrigan. A menu, a shallow bowl of breadsticks, and a glass of water were his only companions. He asked Pat to meet him for lunch after Hope's remark about stalling his investigation triggered a memory from the night of the bust.

What he had to say to his friend wasn't pleasant. It was also not for just any ears. This restaurant had a clientele that would frown upon hearing that a conversation of any such topic had taken place within its richly appointed interior.

A waiter materialized at his elbow.

"Are you ready to order, sir?"

"No. I'm waiting for a friend."

"Very well, sir." The waiter disappeared into the dim labyrinth of tables and chairs that surrounded the detective.

"This way, sir." A female voice attracted Mamba's attention.

A hostess was leading Kerrigan toward the booth and using a runway strut to do it. Mamba smiled at the uncomfortable look on his friend's face. Pat was doing his best to avoid looking at the strategically exposed anatomy of the scantily clad hostess. He was not succeeding.

"Remarkable scenery," was Phil's dry greeting. Kerrigan's face tinted red at the comment; the color change in his Irish complexion was obvious, even in the semi-darkness.

The hostess's radar picked up Mamba's innuendo. She placed her left hand on her hip, cocked her head toward Kerrigan, and winked blatantly at the thoroughly embarrassed policeman. Unable to maintain a straight face, she dissolved into giggles as she sauntered away.

"Thanks a lot."

"Sorry, Pat. But, I just couldn't resist."

"I would have done the same thing to you, given the chance," Kerrigan admitted with a wry grin. "I can only hope I'm the one with the next opportunity."

"Then I'll be extra alert around you."

An uncomfortable silence ensued before Kerrigan asked, "What's this all about?"

"Hope reminded me of an idea, an idea that's been bothering me."

"Sounds serious."

"More than serious. It could be catastrophic."

"You'd better—"

The waiter materialized.

"Are the gentlemen ready to order?"

"Two club sandwiches," Mamba answered as he handed both menus to the waiter. "I'll have coffee. What about you, Pat?"

"Do you have buttermilk?" Kerrigan made a face as he asked.

"I believe so, sir. But, I'll have to check."

"Buttermilk, if you have it. Otherwise, just water." Mamba's questioning look elicited a final phrase, "Doctor's orders."

"Very good." Both men followed the waiter's retreat with practiced eyes.

"I'm afraid that the Manzanita Police Department might have a leak."

Kerrigan fumbled the breadstick as that comment struck home.

"Jeez Louise, Phil, couldn't you wait until I'd eaten at least a lousy breadstick before dropping that bomb on me? He sighed and responded more professionally. "That definitely qualifies as a catastrophe, if it's true. What brings you to this accusation?"

"It's not quite an accusation yet. My case is purely circumstantial."

Kerrigan swallowed his first bite of breadstick before he said, "Let's hear it." He placed the breadstick on his napkin before he took out a small, black notebook and began to write as his friend narrated. Mamba reviewed the night of the bust reminding his friend of the tip to Brewster. Before he announced his belief in Reed's story of the copies of the names on the street, the waiter returned.

"Two club sandwiches. One coffee and one buttermilk." The waiter reiterated the order as he placed the food on their table.

"Let's eat," Mamba suggested. "I'll fill you in on my suspicions during the second half of the sandwich."

"You got a deal. I was hoping to enjoy at least part of this meeting."

"I think I'm offended."

"I would hope so."

Both men smiled and ate in relative silence for about ten minutes, each organizing his thoughts and consumed both sandwiches before the conversation resumed.

"I can't say I'm surprised by this news."

"I sort of figured that when you only dropped your breadstick when I first mentioned the leak."

"You noticed. I'm flattered."

"I don't miss much."

Kerrigan nodded and smiled. "You were about to give me your reasons for suspecting a leak."

"Fair enough." The PI pushed the empty plate to the center of the table. He pulled his coffee cup toward him and ran his finger around the rim while he explained.

"The contact who gave me the list of names came to me yesterday. He says there's a copy of that list out on the street."

Kerrigan raised his eyebrows.

"He says he's seen them. Actually, he said he saw copies."

"And you believe him." Kerrigan's response was a statement, not a question.

"Not at first. I figured demon rum had gotten the best of him again. But now." He paused, pursed his lips, and continued. "Now, I think he might be right."

"Why?"

"Fear. Pat, the man is scared. Terrified even."

"If he's a typical CI, he could be afraid of many things, people, or situations. It could even be the boogeyman."

"True. But, when you put what he told me together with the tip to Brewster, it adds up to more than the irrational fear of a drunk."

"Let's say you're right," Kerrigan proposed. "Who is or where is the leak?"

"Not so fast. You said you were suspicious, too. Tit for tat. Spill."

"Fair enough," Kerrigan mimicked Mamba's early prefacing comment perfectly. Mamba reacted to the mimicry with a half-smile. Kerrigan continued, "My suspicion is more feeling than fact. Just enough information seems to get out to sabotage one, maybe two major operations and a couple small ones a month. But there's no pattern or clear overarching motive. We can't find a common thread across the lost operations, but they're mostly drug related."

"Pat, you know I'd be the last person to point a finger at a cop. And, even though I want nobody to take a bum rap, I've got to say that Stallings looks good for this."

"Stallings a leak? Come on, Phil. Stallings is a real pro. He's got commendations and recommendations up one arm and down the other. I've seen his file. What's your reasoning?"

"Remember when the uniform mentioned Stallings took longer than he needed to get the warrant because he had to take a phone call?"

Kerrigan groaned. "That's weak."

"Maybe. More to the point, who else, besides you, me, and Stallings, had access to the list?"

"If the list is out." Kerrigan's tone of voice contradicted his words. He leaned back in the booth. "I can't do much with this."

"Let's ask him to see the list we gave him."

"Why? On what pretense? That I've lost my copy and you won't give me another one?"

"Don't be facetious."

"I'm serious," Kerrigan countered. "What do I tell the man? 'Hey, Stallings, we think you're leaking information to the street. Mind if we check you out?'"

"I know it'll be tough. Come on, Pat, you know you have to do it."

"You're right." Kerrigan sighed. "I just don't want to admit it."

Quiet enveloped the friends as they searched their brains for options.

"Maybe Martinez will help us out. I don't think Stallings is his favorite boss," Mamba offered.

"Martinez is a good cop. Maybe—" Kerrigan let the unfinished sentence hang. "I've got a thought. Pay the bill and let's get out of here."

"Where you headed?" was all Mamba had time to call out before Kerrigan was out of conversational voice range. He jumped up, frantically trying to attract their server's attention and get the check as he hurried to catch his friend.

"Division HQ," Kerrigan said as Mamba closed the gap between them. The Lieutenant looked at his watch. He turned and said, "Minor change in plans. Leave here in half an hour. Meet me in Stallings' office."

Mamba nodded. He checked the time as he returned to the booth. The waiter was still nowhere in sight. He motioned to a busboy for more coffee. He could kill thirty minutes here as well as anywhere. For the price he was paying for the meal, he might as well stay as long as possible. Besides, the coffee wasn't half bad.

* * *

Twenty-five minutes after Kerrigan left Peacock Feathers, a hostess informed Mamba he had a phone call. In one succinct sentence, Kerrigan told him they'd have to wait at least six days before they could meet with Stallings. Human Resources approved him to take today and the next as personal days and four vacation days after that. Kerrigan didn't know the reason.

Chapter 19

Enciso Martinez strolled down the unfamiliar street. He had no undercover assignment to fulfill. His task today was social. He was looking for Flatly Broke's place.

In contrast with other less desirable areas in town, the buildings in this community showed few signs of neglect. The paint was faded, but not peeling. Steps were smooth with no uneven surfaces because of unpatched cracks.

People who lived here might be poor in pocket, but they were not poor in pride. They made the best out of what they could control and didn't spend their days grumbling about how bad they had it.

Martinez was on this street today because he bonded with the ex-fighter. He would do what he could to cement their fledgling friendship. He admired how the man handled himself through a tense situation.

The big Latino stopped. He pulled a crumpled paper from his pocket. Checking the address written on the paper, he matched it with the stoop and started up the steps.

The door of the building burst open. Martinez flinched.

A disheveled young black woman stormed out. Fire blazed from her eyes. Martinez stepped back to avoid the woman.

Ignoring all impediments, including Martinez, she barreled down the steps. At the bottom, she turned and screamed up at a second-floor window.

"Don't nobody treat me that way! I'm not gonna take any of your slimy jive! I am too good for you! You a creep!"

Flatly's head appeared at a window on the second floor. He called down to the angry woman.

"All I'm doing is tryin' to help! You don't want no disease, and I don't want no disease neither! I can't help if you don't understand. I've got to protect myself. AIDS ain't nothin' to fool 'round wit!"

The woman aimed a crude gesture in Flatly's direction. She spotted Martinez, struck a pose, and adjusted her halter-top. The detective flashed his shield. The woman muttered something and hurried away, high heels clicking on the sidewalk. Martinez shouted up at the man in the second-floor window, "Hola, amigo. Can I come up?"

"Cue Ball! Sure thing, man. Come on up."

The undercover man went inside. He reached the second-floor landing and peered down a grungy hallway. One door stood partly opened. The smell of people crammed in living quarters too small for their numbers assaulted his nostrils. It reminded him of a thousand places he visited in his police career. It was also painfully close to the sights and smells of his childhood.

Flatly waved from the window alcove he used to call down to his date and the detective.

"Flatly," Martinez called. "It's good to see you."

"Follow me, man." The boxer led the way across the hall to his apartment door.

"You alone? I need to see you in private," Martinez told the ex-fighter as they entered Flatly's dingy apartment.

"Yeah. You saw her leave. What's happening, Cue Ball?"

"Well, first I need you to call me something besides Cue Ball."

Flatly's face radiated confusion.

"I only use that name when I'm working a case."

"Ooooh. I get it. That's like your other Bruce Wayne name."

"Bruce Wayne?"

"Man, you gotta know Batman. Bruce Wayne's workin' name is Batman."

"Yeah. Just like that," Martinez said, impressed with the connections to everyday things the man made with regularity. "I want to tell you what a great job you did on the bust."

"Thanks, man," Flatly glowed. "It wasn't no worse than some fights I was in. I ever tell you what a time I had with Crusher Carson back in '78?"

"No, I don't think so. Is it a long story?"

"Ac'chly, man, it's a real short story," was Flatly's sheepish admission. "He knocked me out in two."

"I thought this would be a story about something good," Martinez said through a laugh.

"I only got four, maybe five, good fight stories," Flatly confessed. "Four of the fights I won, and one got stolen from me. I only had ten fights before I had to get out the ring."

"What happened?"

"Got my bell rung too many times. Doctor said I was headed for some permanent eye problems, if I got knocked around another time or two."

"Sorry, amigo. I didn't know." As the massive, muscular detective looked down on the diminutive former prizefighter, he realized which of the two of them was the bravest. He waded in when maybe he shouldn't, but it was always because he had more firepower or more size. This man stood up with only his fists and took whatever he had to to make a pitiful living.

"It's okay, man," Flatly told him. "I don't let it get me down no more. How come you came to see me?"

Martinez shook his head to clear his thoughts.

"I was talking to Phil Mamba."

"The Dancer. He's o-kay. He tipped me off on the lady with AIDS. He saved my life."

"Actually," Martinez cleared his throat. "I'm here because Mr. Mamba asked me to come."

"Dancer's sent a message to me?"

"The lady's name."

"Oh, yeah. He never told me who it was. I 'member me asking after I got fake-arrested."

"There's a small problem."

"Can't be too much of a problem," Flatly assessed. "Dancer's one of the least problematic men I know."

"The problem has to do with the lady."

"What about her?"

"Well, uh. There, um. Well, there might not be any one lady."

"You mean there's more than one?"

"There might not be any."

"Whatcha mean?" Flatly demanded in the same tone he'd used in Weston's place when he thought he was being taken advantage of.

"Mr. Mamba sort of made up a little story for you."

"What you sayin'?"

"Mamba's not sure if anyone you know has AIDS."

"But he said they was."

"He said what he said because he needed your help."

"He lied to me?"

“Only kind of,” Martinez was in a quandary. He sighed. Even though it might put Mamba in hot water, he had to finish what he’d started.

“Mamba only knows that there’s a strong rumor that a woman named Sherleen, or something like that, was in for treatment for AIDS.”

“Sherleen! No wonder I ain’t seen her ‘round for a while.” Flatly finished with a whistle, all thoughts of treachery on Mamba’s part now behind him. “It’s good to know. She was my main squeeze for a time.”

“Is there anything I can do?” Martinez asked.

“Do you know where she’s at?”

“I can find out. Where’s your phone?”

“Don’t have no phone in my room, man, that’s bread I can’t spare. They got one downstairs, in the super’s place.” He scrounged around for a pencil and a scrap of paper. With labored effort, he wrote something down. He handed the paper to the Latino.

“Jus’ tell ‘em it’s for Flatly when you call after you find her. They’ll get me the message.”

“I’ll do it,” Martinez promised. He looked at the paper. In a childlike script, he scrawled a telephone number and name. It looked like a third grader wrote it.

“Sorry ‘bout my writin’,” Flatly apologized. “I didn’t get too far in school.”

“No problem.” Martinez made light of the obvious lack of literacy. “Is this a seven or a four?” he asked before he added a fabricated explanation of his own. “I don’t have my glasses.”

Flatly took the paper and stared hard.

“Must be a four,” he decided. He closed his eyes in thought. His head bobbed up and down as he recited a telephone number to himself. “It’s a four,” he confirmed.

“Good enough.”

“I didn’t know you wore glasses.”

Martinez froze.

“Uh, only to, uh, to read.”

Flatly nodded his acceptance of the reason.

Martinez started to leave. Then he turned and asked, “You had breakfast, amigo? I’m starved.”

“Well, it’s kinda late fo’ breakfast.” Flatly hedged.

“I’m buying.”

"Then, no!" The ex-fighter exclaimed, his face beaming. "I ain't eaten nuthin' since yesterday noon."

"Let's get going," the undercover man encouraged. "You like eggs?"

"I could live on eggs."

"Then I have got the place for you." Martinez sat on the only piece of furniture he was certain would handle his bulk and waited while Flatly dressed. As he waited, he described in delicious detail the size of the omelets at The Egg Shell Cafe.

By the time they left the building, he'd made himself hungry again even though he'd finished off two helpings of machaca, frijoles, and tortillas earlier that morning.

* * *

Three evenings after she moved into the Royal Guard Hotel, Mary Carstairs once again unlocked room 214. She waited until she closed and bolted the door before feeling around for the light switch. She snapped it to the ON position. Darkness kept its grip on the room.

"Figures!" Mary grumbled. She groped her way toward the kitchen.

She never made it to the linoleum flooring.

Strong hands grabbed her from behind. One hand clamped over her mouth. The fingers of another hand dug into her waist. She knew what was next. The attacker dragged her to her right. After an initial squirm, she let her body relax as much as she could. She understood that fighting a rapist almost always brought more pain and abuse than compliance did.

He headed for the bed. This happened to her once before. She decided to relax and pretend to enjoy what was coming but vowed to find a circumcision flint to exact her revenge.

"Keep quiet!" Her assailant spat out the command as he uncovered her mouth. His right hand moved to her arm. The sound of something tearing aroused her curiosity. Curiosity morphed into an infantile form of panic as a large piece of adhesive tape slapped over her lips.

She beat her hands against her assailant's chest. He continued as she hung limply in his grip. Her imprecations went unheard; the tape covering her mouth reduced them to meaningless noise.

She tried to scratch his eyes.

With a derisive snort, he grabbed both her wrists in one hand and squeezed. When she only winced at the pain, the attacker twisted her wrists to the right, spraining them both.

She willed her arms to relax, but that only fueled the sadist's desire. He gave a final twist, this time to the left. The pain intensified.

Mary felt her body folding into the fetal position.

Another snort. He released his grip. But, when she tried to move her hands, pain knifed up her arms. Her panic reached puberty. She wondered how Brewster found her. She knew why he hired this sadist to torture her.

Rough hands ripped the clothing from her body.

The same hands threw her naked form to the bed. Before she could react, the male's fully clothed body landed upon her.

She felt her muscles tense, but she didn't move, her attacker was too big. She tried to force her body to relax. She was unsuccessful.

The rapist wrapped one end of long pieces of adhesive tape around each ankle and wrist.

Shockwaves of pain burned through the nerves up her arms.

Tears erupted from her eyes. And, for the first time in a long time, the tears were genuine.

She began to sob as, one by one, he taped each wrist and ankle to its own bedpost.

Her panic matured from adolescence to a fully developed emotion. She twisted from side to side as she attempted to pull at least one of the tape-ropes loose from its bedpost.

A flash of her Catholic school training illuminated the prayer of the Rosary in her mind. "Holy Mary, mother of God, pray for us sinners, now and at the hour of our death." She prayed aloud, although her words seemed to stick to the duct tape over her mouth.

"Sidney Brewster hopes you don't enjoy this at all," the voice taunted. She heard a zipper opening. "But, I'm sure I will."

Mary prayed more fervently, trying to will the words through the tape. "O my Jesus, forgive us our sins, save us from the fires of hell, and lead all souls to heaven, especially those in most need of thy mercy!"

Her attacker rolled onto the mattress beside her.

She tried to scream.

Four sounds punctuated Mary's final earthly thoughts.

First was the squeaking of bedsprings as the attacker climbed off her and the bed. She squirmed trying to find the rapist, but the darkness prevailed.

Next was the speaking of a name, "They call me Big 0."

Third was the attacker's voice again.

"You're gonna bloat up real quick in dis weather. Kinda a shame, you bein' a woman and all."

Fourth was the muted sound of a single gunshot poorly silenced by one of Mary's pillows.

The too-short roller coaster life of Mary Carstairs was over.

* * *

Typical of Manzanita, California, the day was warm. Residents' wardrobes showcased shorts or flip-flops at least 250 days of the year. Although, they weren't particularly fond of the term, residents agreed that most of Manzanita's heat was a dry heat.

This day, the heat and humidity combined to make the day uncomfortable. The atypical weather had many residents out of sorts, even Flatly Broke.

The two days before had been good days for the former boxer. He learned the name of the woman with AIDS. And, he had the best breakfast he'd eaten in at least a year. This day was far from a good one.

He was never in a hurry to get home to his empty apartment. Sometimes, when he had a particular friend with him or waiting for him, his movement up the stairway was snappy. Today, there was no snap. There was no lady by his side or waiting. Sweat and the lack of female companionship had the ex-boxer depressed.

Because of the atmospheric oddity and his depressed state, Flatly climbed the stairs to his apartment slower than usual.

He was returning from a visit to Sherleen Hobbs, one of his favorite lady friends. Only she was not friendly anymore—to anyone. Sherleen was dying. The AIDS virus eroded her body's ability to fight certain infections. Diseases a healthy immune system would defeat were destroying her. It was a hopeless situation. And she knew it.

Flatly knew none of the details of how AIDS worked. All he knew was that a once fine-looking lady was now a thin, wasted shell of a woman. They told him she had only weeks to live. He could believe that. He'd seen people die before.

A store clerk shot his father attempting a robbery. Flatly'd been in the getaway car. He was five-years-old.

He'd seen a pedestrian hit by a car. She was dead before he got to her. He remembered the lack of blood on the street surprised him.

He knew dying was a part of living. It was the end part, and everyone had to go through it.

He reached the top of the inside stairwell and looked down the hallway in both directions. He almost always did that. The ritual started when he'd seen a perfectly good nightstand outside a door in his hallway. The sign taped to it read "Free." He knew that word and moved the night stand into his apartment post haste. It occupied a spot next to his bed.

In all the times he stopped at the top of the stairs and looked around, the nightstand was his only find. He continued the practice hoping to score another treasure. "Hey, man. You never know*,"* was his mantra.

Disappointed again by the lack of success in his quest for valuable items, he shuffled down the hallway. If a depressed state showed as a color, Flatly's aura would have been that hue.

He fumbled with his key at his apartment door. He usually had trouble with the ancient lock.

* * *

Big 0 Briggs wiped the sweat from his forehead. He'd climbed up two levels of the outside fire escape and now crouched on the narrow balcony outside Flatly Broke's flat. He wiped his brow again.

This was no social call. His deal with Sid Brewster had two parts. Part one was Mary Carstairs.

He licked his lips at the memory of her body as she thrashed on the bed while he fulfilled the first part of the double deaths contract. He smothered a grunt with the back of his hand while he rearranged his position on the metal platform. Periodically during the repositioning, he stared through the window at the door to the apartment. He didn't like the glare on the window.

The hitman pushed his fingers against the frame around the lower pane; then he pushed up. The window was unlocked and slid upwards with minimal force. Now he could see and hear without any barriers.

An unobstructed view was crucial to his plan to carry out the second death sentence on his list. The man living in this apartment was wired during the bust at Mary's place. Brewster decided to make an example of him. Briggs adjusted his body again.

Being exposed by something as underhanded as a police wire was offensive in the extreme to Brewster. He didn't believe in "no honor among thieves." That's why the elimination of Flatly Broke was part of Big 0's contract.

When he was content with his position and the line of sight to the front door, Briggs relaxed. He removed the gun he used to off Mary from his belt, checked the load, and disengaged the gun's safety.

A deep exhalation of breath and a second shake of his head cleared the mental residue from his mind and the residual sweat from his eyes.

The Big 0 turned full focus to his task.

* * *

"Hey, Mr. Flatly!" Marvin Dexter called out to his friend. The three-year-old boy lived across the hall from Flatly's apartment. The boxer's return always excited him.

Flatly pushed his door open and turned to see who was calling him. His depression lifted a little at the sight of the boy now waving his greeting with both hands. Marvin was one of his favorite people.

Flatly waved back and forced a smile. The boxer enjoyed hanging with Marvin. They both liked the same things: foods like pizza; TV shows like *Different Strokes, The Cosby Show,* and *The A-Team*, all on NBC, the only channel with a clear signal on Flatly's antenna; and taking a bath.

"Hi ya, Marvin. You lookin' good," he said with more enthusiasm than he felt.

He stepped into his doorway.

"Hey, Mr. Flatly. Look," Marvin called again. "Come see what my mom got me."

The boxer started the turn to his left to face the youngster. That partial turn saved his life.

The .44-caliber bullet from Briggs' revolver tore through his right shoulder obliterating the joint as it plowed its path of destruction then lodged in the wall across the hallway. Marvin's screams echoed in the hallway long after the echo of the gunshot died away.

According to the ER doctor, if Flatly hadn't turned to see what Marvin wanted to show him, the bullet would have killed him.

* * *

Martinez pulled up in front of the Royal Guard Hotel. The place was an eyesore and, most likely, in violation of dozens of health code statutes.

He was working out of homicide for a change of pace as he covered for a friend. Lieutenant Kerrigan okayed the arrangement.

His motorcycle needed enhancements. The extra shift would help cover the costs. Besides, Stallings was out of his office. New leads on narcotics cases were few, far between, and fought over by others in the unit. He made the unilateral decision to abandon his undercover identity for the time being.

As he climbed out of the black and white he requisitioned, he pulled a notebook from his shirt pocket. Both the notebook and the pocket were uncommon for the man who normally worked undercover in tank tops or muscle shirts and jeans. The collar on his shirt and the belt in the loops of his slacks also looked painfully out of place.

Increasing the discomfort was the combined high temperature and high humidity. Sweat soaked through the front of his shirt before he left the car.

He reread his notes on the call.

- manager contacted the police in response to a complaint about an odor from room 214.
- manager checked it out but would only confirm the smell.
- manager refused to open the door to the room, "because it stinks so bad."

Martinez tried filling the blank in the manager's censored comment he copied down as the dispatcher narrated. There were so many options.

"Let's get this done," he said to the uniformed officer they assigned him. His friend's partner picked up a lead on a cold case and hadn't been available to work this shift. That was fine with Martinez. He was working outside his usual haunts. It didn't matter with whom he worked.

The manager led Martinez, followed by the uniform, to room 214. Even with the door closed, the hallway reeked with the odor of decay.

"I can do this myself," Martinez said to the manager as he held out a massive hand for the key to the room.

"Drop it back at the desk on your way out," was the relieved directive tossed over a shoulder as the man hurried toward the stairwell.

"Glove up!" Martinez ordered. He pulled the XXL latex gloves he always carried from his pocket and onto each hand.

"On it, Sir."

Martinez gave a nod and turned the key in the lock. He reached for the doorknob.

"Unholster your weapon. I'll go in first and go to the left." He indicated the direction in which the door opened. "You wait 'til I clear the doorway. Then you come in and immediately sweep right. Got it?"

"Yes, sir! What about that smell?"

Martinez, who'd turned back to the door immediately after he finished his instructions, rolled his eyes and ignored the question.

As soon as the door pushed away from the jamb, the Latino regretted taking the lead. A monsoon of the stench of putrefaction engulfed him. He paused a beat, choked out a cough, and announced himself.

"Manzanita police!"

He stepped through the doorway and made his visual sweep behind the door and inside the bathroom.

"Clear!" he called.

The horrific odor permeated the studio apartment. Martinez's first glance did not reveal the source of the smell.

The uniformed officer entered. Martinez heard his gasping and choking before he coughed out a barely audible, "Clear."

The detective moved toward the kitchenette and waved his partner to check behind the half-wall. The uniform took a brief glance over the wall. He didn't quite finish his turn toward Martinez before he lost his just finished lunch on the dirty carpet in a series of gagging sounds.

The undercover man stepped around the pool of vomit to investigate. A quick survey of the bed was almost enough to trigger his own gag response.

Martinez saw the bloated, tortured remains of a naked female held in place between peeling bedposts with long pieces of adhesive tape. A brownish-red stain covered the pillow on which her head rested. A second pillow sporting a hole surrounded by black residue rested against the footboard.

The uniformed officer retreated to the hallway where he concentrated on taking deep breaths to settle his stomach. He heaved again. Martinez shook his head.

He picked up the purse that lay on the floor by the kitchen. The contents of the purse were untouched suggesting the attacker was a sex psycho.

He removed the leatherette wallet from the purse and stuffed the bag under his arm. He flipped through the contents as quickly as he could with gloves on, his goal to identify the body on the bed.

The purse dropped to the floor. Lipstick and a small package of tissues spilled onto the carpet. Unaware of the purse's escape, the giant stood, eyes fixated on the picture on the California driver's license. A smiling Mary Carstairs stared at him.

Tears welled up as he turned on his heel and left the room. He tried to convince himself the tears were from the odor, but he didn't succeed. He knew that Brewster found out Mary tipped the police and made sure that would never happen again.

"I'll call for the meat wagon." Martinez's voice was a monotone as he passed the pasty-faced officer in the hall. "You keep everyone away from this room."

Down at the car, he bent over and deposited his partly digested lunch, along with the tears in his eyes, into the gutter beside the front passenger tire of the squad car.

He called the homicide in. It was time to wait for the coroner.

Chapter 20

Two of Manzanita Police Department's finest pulled their black and white into the gated parking that accessed prisoner's entrance to the station. One rousted the prisoner out of the back seat. Each officer took a handcuffed arm, led and dragged the prisoner past the prisoner entrance. One officer opened the foot traffic gate to the front of the headquarters' building while the other shoved the handcuffed man through.

After manhandling him up the stairs, they shoved him through the double front doors. The doors swung shut behind them.

"Thanks, fellas," the handcuffed man said as one officer uncuffed him just inside the windowless hallway that led to the lobby.

"Always a pleasure working with you undercover guys."

"Put in a good word for me with the sergeant, will ya? I know Auto Theft is understaffed. We'd like to be part of the raid."

"I'll do my best," the prisoner promised.

Handshakes and waves ended the prisoner drop. The prisoner wore clothes and shoes that reflected his current assignment—mechanic and car thief. He walked to the tall platform desk that served as the welcome center for visitors.

"I'm looking for Interrogation Room 4."

"Access is restricted to departmental personnel," the desk sergeant answered and lowered his line-of-sight back to the report he was typing.

"I'm Deputy Howard Harris on loan from the Sheriff's Department. I'm undercover on a car theft sting. I'm about five minutes late for a meeting with Lieutenant Cummings in Burglary and Auto Theft."

"Ironic. I'm late on my car payment."

"Listen, I don't want to bother you any more than necessary, but—"

"You passed that mile marker when you came in."

"Could you at least call down and check my story?"

The desk sergeant glared over the top of his reading glasses, but he made the requested call. After a brief exchange, he put his left hand over the handset.

"Which Sheriff's station?"

"Santa Clarita."

The sergeant repeated the answer into the phone, nodded, and hung up the phone.

"Past me. Take the first right and the first left after that."

"Thank you."

The desk sergeant signaled the end of the conversation with a dismissive wave.

When the undercover officer reached the assigned room, he knocked.

"Geez, this isn't a bathroom stall, Harris. Haul your butt in here." It was a long verbal response from Lieutenant Cummings.

"Always good to talk with you, Lieutenant."

"Funny, funny guy. What'd you got?"

"Something's going down. Marco's acting odd, even for him. Is tonight too soon for the raid?"

"Nope. I'll lead the troops."

"Okay. We got a Dodge Challenger in Impound that's tricked out enough to make an impression on Marco. Since I bring in little merchandise, this should cause him to make a move with me there."

"And?"

"Get one of the mechanics to do whatever they do to the Challenger so it looks like I hot-wired it. Have him drive it to an isolated street."

"Good. Time?"

"2000. It'll be dark enough then."

"What about at the chop shop?"

"I'm guessing 2100 at the latest. If you're in place by 1930, that's plenty of leeway."

"Can do. You want 'Challenger' as the go word?"

"Naw. I've got to use that when I get there. Let's go with 'Corvette.' They never have many of those. Color doesn't matter. If I see one, I use Corvette and that color. If I don't see one, I'll use just Corvette."

"We'll breach all but one door. Make a run for that door. I'll be outside that door and tap you with my baton in view of the crew. You sell the tap and the cuffing."

"Make it the door closest to the rear of the building on the left side as you look from the street."

Cummings nodded. When the undercover officer didn't move, he spoke.

"You know your way out."

"I'll manage. Is there a Martinez working out of this station?"

"There's a Martinez in narcotics. Why?"

"I saw this god-awful motorcycle parked in the lot. Looked like the one Martinez had."

"He worked with a sheriff?"

"We were in a drug identification seminar for two days. He was my roomie. We split the money we saved. But, two minutes with Martinez is enough to remember him."

"The seminar lasted two days?"

"Yeah."

"They give you a medal?"

Both men laughed at the joke.

"Let Martinez know his drug partner says hello."

"I'll quote you."

The undercover officer's face morphed into an angry sneer as he exited the police station through the front door. Now back in character as a car thief, he stopped at the bottom of the stairs, turned around, and tossed an obscene hand gesture toward the front doors.

A sinister smile blossomed as he stomped across the parking lot to the pay phone. He called a fellow car thief for a ride.

* * *

Two black and whites backed behind the shrubs that screened the street from the chop shop. They kept backing until the front of each car was beyond the illuminated circle from the single light in the parking lot. No one entering the lot could see either vehicle.

Lieutenant Cummings and three uniformed officers parked in the shrubs off the road less than fifty-yards from the driveway. The quartet of officers pushed through the shrubs. A pair of uniforms went to the door to the right of the garage door. After leaving their sledgehammer flat against the ground, they moved around the corner of the building and out of sight from the parking lot.

Cummings and the remaining uniformed officer signaled to the officers parked inside the shrub line. Four officers and two sledgehammers joined them

"You two are with me." The lieutenant pointed to one sledgehammer carrier and the officer beside him. "You three, next door down this wall."

When all members of the assault team were in place, Cummings broke radio silence.

"Leave this channel open. I'll turn you loose and we go on my mark. Out."

Cummings assigned one door to the two officers with him. He moved down the building to the last door on the left side as you looked from the street.

* * *

The string of profanity ended with the words "stupid cop!"

"That don't explain why you're late with this delivery," the leader of the car theft ring barked at the driver who just delivered a Dodge Challenger to the chop shop.

"Shut your fat face, Marco! We do all the work and you get the biggest cut of the take!"

Two car thieves in the shop nodded in agreement. The others shook their heads in disbelief. Marco was a tyrant, but they were flush because of him.

"You stole your last car," Marco growled and walked toward his belligerent employee.

"I don't see a Corvette here."

The out of context comment stopped Marco in his tracks.

* * *

"Corvette" echoed in Cummings' headset.

"Go!" he barked.

As the undercover officer finished his sentence, three sledgehammers slammed three doorknobs onto the floor inside the chop shop.

Before Marco could react, two side entrances to the shop and the door next to the garage door burst open. Police officers poured into the building.

The Challenger thief bolted for the only unopened door. Without breaking stride, he shoved it open.

The crack of the Cummings' baton making contact with the forehead of the runner was heard throughout the chop shop. The car thief's body stiffened. He fell back inside. Several observers winced.

* * *

"Good work tonight." Cummings' congratulatory comments were hard earned and infrequent. His work philosophy was simple: If you weren't doing something wrong, he left you alone.

"Thanks, Lieutenant." The Challenger thief sat holding an ice pack on his head. "If there is a next time, please hit me with your forearm, not the baton."

Cummings shrugged his shoulders.

"Report back to the Sherriff's in Santa Clarita in the morning."

"I've got vacation time coming. They said not to worry about a new assignment until I'm back from that."

A blank stare indicating information overload was the lieutenant's response as he stood up.

"Got it. It's been a pleasure."

"Back at you," Cummings said while leaving his office before the sheriff's officer. "Pull the door closed."

Chapter 21

Dawn birthed another typical SoCal day: sun, low humidity, and a slight breeze. The occupant of one room in a rundown hotel had no interest in the weather or much of anything else having to do with humanity. Floor-length drapes covered every window. One electric bulb in the only light fixture in the room glowed a dim forty watts.

Oscar Briggs was the sole occupant of the room. He was aware of nothing except his desire for a hit. Every aspect of the room's décor supported Briggs' belief that contact with other members of humanity was neither essential nor desired in life.

He rationed white powder, part of the payment for his most recent job, into a scorched teaspoon. He then used his teeth to pull surgical tubing tight around his right biceps. For a moment, he stared at the candle whose flame flickered in the air currents stirred by the slow revolutions of an ancient ceiling fan.

He thought back to the phone call from Sidney Brewster. Brewster had requested his services in return for some first-line heroin.

Brewster said he contracted him to eliminate the woman because she tipped the police. But, he knew the real reason she was eliminated. She cost Brewster a bundle of money. The rape and beating before he shot her were his ideas. The smile widened as he recalled the terror that he felt in her through the torture. His breathing quickened as he remembered the last minutes of Mary Carstairs' life.

He had the good judgment to end the assignment with a bullet to the woman's head. Dead. Just as Brewster ordered.

The second job he pulled for Brewster was less memorable. He blew apart an aging boxer as he entered his apartment. That little man dropped like a rock when the bullet tore through his body. It was a thing of beauty in his mind. To Briggs, the boxer's hit was routine. He'd probably never think of it again.

Killing was Oscar Briggs' job. He was good at it. Pride was his failing. Pride and heroin.

His hand shook with anticipation as he held the teaspoon above the flame. The powder melted. He plunged a dirty needle into the liquid and sucked the depression dry. He cleared the air from the homemade syringe and jabbed the angled tip beneath the skin of his forearm. He squeezed the bulb on the end forcing the fluid through the needle and into his vein.

In a reflex action after the scores of times he mainlined, he released the surgical tubing and watched the color return to his limb. That was the last coherent memory he had for several hours.

* * *

In the six days Stallings spent away from the Manzanita Police Department, there was no progress in Mamba's case of the pharmaceutical factory burglary. He talked with Anderson. It was an uncharacteristically one-sided conversation, with the PI doing most of the talking.

He called Kerrigan the day before to ask him if the scheduled meeting with Stallings was on since it was his first day back. He learned Stallings was at the station for a meeting and decided to take advantage of the opportunity. As Mamba entered the station, he spotted Kerrigan standing at the lobby desk with his back to the door engaged in an intense phone conversation.

The PI waited.

Kerrigan slammed the receiver back in the cradle. When he turned around his face was a kaleidoscope of emotions.

"What's that all about? You don't look so good."

"I don't feel so good, either. That was Martinez."

"Something wrong with him?"

"Not him directly. He's upset, though."

"What about?"

"Remember Mary?"

Mamba frowned and shrugged.

"The woman whose house we busted."

"Oh, yeah. I got the impression Martinez kind of liked her, or at least he could get to like her, given any encouragement."

"That's part of the problem."

"How so?"

"She's dead."

"What? How?"

"Raped, beaten, and shot in the Royal Guard Hotel."

"Sleazy place. Sounds like somebody wanted to make a point," Mamba said. "I thought she was in jail."

"She made bail the day after we arrested her."

"Why? I thought she was afraid of her supplier."

"Maybe he wanted her out," Kerrigan suggested.

"That doesn't figure. If he knew she fingered him, he wouldn't wait a couple of days to kill her; he would have been waiting when you released her."

"Probably," Kerrigan agreed without conviction. "But, he might not have known she was in jail."

"How could he not know?"

"He was very busy that night. Remember?"

"What if she didn't know we missed nailing Brewster, either?"

"How could she not—" Kerrigan stopped himself. "You might have something. Unless someone in the holding cell told her, she couldn't see any news coverage; especially if she was hiding out somewhere."

"Why hiding out?"

"Wouldn't you? I mean you get arrested after ratting out your drug-dealer boss. You make bail and don't know if he knows you're the rat. If that's me, I'm not taking any chances on his associates cleaning house, or him coming after me if he knows."

"Good point. And I doubt she did much checking on the status of her former boss, considering what she did, or at least what she thought she did to him."

Kerrigan nodded.

"So, the whole Mary thing is tragic, but why's Martinez so upset?"

"I don't know him that well. What I know is Martinez was working homicide, covering a shift for some overtime pay. Anyway, he found a bloated body tied to a bed, raped, and shot in the head. He ID'd her from her driver's license."

Mamba winced. The boss would use Mary's death as an example of what happens to snitches.

"What did Martinez want with you?"

Kerrigan motioned his friend to silence. A second motion directed him to follow down the hallway.

"I don't think anybody back there would intentionally listen in, but I didn't think anyone would give away classified police information, either." He waited until they turned a corner in the hallway. "Remember when I told you I would try to get Martinez's help with this Stallings thing?"

"And now he won't," Mamba guessed.

"On the contrary. He asked for the chance to find Mary's killer." Kerrigan started toward Stallings' office.

"You lost me, Pat," Mamba admitted as he matched strides with the Lieutenant.

"Martinez worked the call from the hotel where Mary was hiding out. Remember, I told you he's the one who found her."

"And that's a problem because?"

"Might not be, but, as soon as the coroner arrived and confirmed Mary's death, Martinez walked away from the car and his partner. He called in from home, so we wouldn't think he'd bailed. They were talking about it at the desk when I came in. That's why I called him before you got here."

"And, when you told Martinez that you were out to find the department leak, he put two and two together and figured what was a leak once might have been a leak twice, with the second leak setting up Mary," Mamba summarized the theoretical sequence he assumed Martinez presented.

"Bingo," Kerrigan said without inflection.

"What's your plan?"

Kerrigan stopped and looked at his friend.

"For you, go back to your office and wait. Martinez will be here in about fifteen minutes. He'll meet me in Stallings' office and—"

"Hold on," Mamba interrupted. "I don't want to sit until who-knows-when in my office. Let me stay here."

With a sigh, Kerrigan held open the door to his office. "I figured as much. Go on in. I'll get you some coffee. But, you stay in my office until I come get you." While Kerrigan understood Mamba's desire to be part of Stallings' questioning, he wasn't willing to stretch his relationship with the captain that far by keeping the PI fully vested.

Yet.

* * *

Franklin Stallings sat behind his desk. An untidy pile of papers overflowed the tray designed to help organize his correspondence. Yet, he maneuvered his way through the tasks before him with an air of efficiency when alone. The clutter was an illusion. He'd found it an illusion that gave him an advantage in many conversations.

Feigning to search for a misplaced document provided him precious seconds to formulate responses to unexpected questions. Besides, the stacks of folders, piles of reports, and boxes on the floor allowed him to maintain the persona of an unorganized soul. Few co-workers ever realized the level of his intelligence or the amount of detail he included in his planning.

Just back from six days away, Stallings was looking forward to this morning. He had nothing scheduled until 1100 hours. That solitary blip on his radar was a briefing on how to complete the new evaluation forms for outside consultants. They assured him it would last no more than thirty minutes.

It took two of his personal and four vacation days for him to decompress enough to reach a state he judged as relaxed. He knew that the time away helped his wife, although he doubted she decompressed to any extent. Cancer, a disease whose purposes appeared to be to rob her of her strength and eradicate her ovaries, was taking its toll on the former star athlete. He did not understand how she coped with the nausea, the ache in her bones, and the debilitating fatigue that accompanied each chemotherapy treatment.

The couple rented a room in an inn nestled among the pine trees in the foothills to the east of Manzanita. They had no contact with anyone not part of the staff at the inn.

They'd walked trails, sat by the summer trickle that passed as a stream, and spent evenings on their balcony, speechless at the star-filled summer sky. Lizbeth smiled more in the last two days than in the two weeks leading up to their time together.

He felt almost human as they arrived home in the early evening of the sixth day.

He looked around the office again. He'd take the backlog he created by getting away in trade for Lizbeth's improved mental and physical condition anytime. After a moment of thought, he moved one manila folder from the top of his desk to the top of a pile that rested on one of his file cabinets.

Lieutenant Kerrigan approached the tiny office of the narcotics sergeant. He didn't relish what he was about to do, but he knew it had to be done. He also knew that he could trust no one else to do it. He knocked on the door.

"Yeah," Stallings called. "Come on in."

Kerrigan straightened his shoulders and entered.

"Oh, good morning, Lieutenant. What can I do you for?"

"I was just checking on the progress of the hunt for Brewster," Kerrigan lied.

"Not much to report there, I'm afraid." He dumped the contents of a manila folder on the desktop and shuffled through the loose sheets of paper. With a look of triumph, he held aloft two pages of a report and continued.

"We got the go ahead from the DA to prosecute the perps we arrested during the raids."

"Good to hear. But, no leads to Brewster at all?"

"I'm getting ready to put a tail on Mary Carstairs. Says here that she made bail. I figure she's our best potential to lead us to her supplier."

"I agree with you," Kerrigan concluded. "If you need any additional manpower, I'll put in a word with the higher powers."

"Thanks. The more help the merrier."

* * *

After the phone conversation with Kerrigan, Martinez made good time from his home to the station. He spent the entire ride focused on Stallings as the leak. Wisely, he stopped and composed himself outside Stallings' office.

"Got a minute, Sergeant?" The undercover man poked his head in the door and his booming voice filled the cubicle.

Stallings looked up. The paperwork he approved that morning granted the Latino two days off.

"Not now," he growled. "I'm meeting with the Lieutenant."

"Sorry," Martinez said, although he wasn't and entered the office. "All I need is one list of names Mamba's snitch gave us. I've got a couple names to check out. They look promising, but I can't remember if they were on that list. If they are, this might be even bigger than we first thought."

Stallings glared at Martinez. Although he knew the man was an excellent cop, he had doubts about the Latino's ability to act like an adult.

He shifted his gaze to Kerrigan. From the sound of things, he and Martinez were on the same page. The Lieutenant shrugged.

"I'm finished, but, I'd like to see if those names are on the list."

"It's up to you," Stallings responded. He rifled through a sheaf of papers on his desk. A puzzled look crossed his face. He went to one of the file cabinets behind the desk hoping he'd forgotten he stuck the list in a drawer for safekeeping. Opening each drawer in succession from the top downward, he rummaged around in all four cabinet drawers. When he completed his search, he turned to his visitors.

"I can't seem to locate my copies of the lists." Despite his intention to just lay it out, there was a detectable strain in his voice.

Kerrigan's spirits sagged. He hoped Stallings was guiltless. Even though all he had was circumstantial evidence, at this point it did not look good for the sergeant.

"I'm sure they'll show up," Kerrigan offered without conviction. He frowned as his glance swept the room.

"I still need to see the lists," Martinez insisted. Kerrigan's view from the side of the big man revealed cyclical clenching and unclenching of his jaw muscles as he fought to control the emotion in his voice. Kerrigan shot a warning look in the giant's direction.

"I'll keep looking for them," Stallings promised. "They have to be here."

Instead of leaning on Stallings, the Lieutenant acted to contain Martinez.

"Use my copy, Detective. It's in my office." He grabbed a thick arm and felt trembling beneath his grasp. "Walk with me."

"Yes, sir!" Martinez hissed at just above a whisper. "Let's get your list."

Martinez pulled away as they turned and left the room.

"I'll let you know about the extra men," Kerrigan called back before closing the door behind him.

"Liar!" Martinez spat when Kerrigan caught him in the hallway. "Does he think we're children?"

"You know, it's entirely possible he can't find his copy of the lists. You saw his office."

"Sure. And I might be the next Chief of Police!"

"Stand down, Officer Martinez," the Lieutenant ordered. "If Stallings is guilty, we'll get him. Our way. The legal way. Using police methods. Not by lynching. Not by circumstantial evidence. Not by innuendo."

"Yes, sir." Only after a tremendous sigh of effort did he manage, "What do we do next?"

"That's more like it. Our next move is to plant something we want to get out. We need to see if we can leak something."

Martinez agreed after a moment of thought. "Sí. We need to be sure."

"Come to my office. We can talk about it with the door closed."

They walked the rest of the way in silence. Kerrigan opened the door. Martinez entered first. Mamba sat in the chair by the desk; he was staring at the door without seeing.

"What's wrong?" Kerrigan asked.

"Flatly."

"What?"

"They've almost killed Flatly," Mamba said.

"Who? When?" Martinez demanded at near top volume.

"Departmental courier brought it in." Mamba roused himself and pointed to a folder on the edge of the desk. He added without apology, "He handed it to me, so I looked it over."

"Start at the beginning," Kerrigan instructed.

"Police responded to a call for gunshots fired from Flatly's building. When the police arrived the EMTs were nearly ready to transport. Flatly'd been shot in the right shoulder. The report indicates the shooter was close. That's not based on witness statements. A window on the apartment's fire escape was open along the path the bullet could have followed. They pulled a slug from the hallway wall."

"We gotta plug this leak!" Every muscle in Martinez's body shook with anger. "The only reason for trying to kill that man was because he helped us. Same with Mary Carstairs!" Thoughts of revenge for the brave little prizefighter's injury and Mary's degrading, tortured death scrolled through his mind.

"Come with me to the hospital," Mamba suggested. He looked at Kerrigan. Both saw that Martinez needed time to cool off. Mary's death and the attempt on Flatly's life knocked him off his center. Doing something for Flatly might help move him back toward the balance point.

Kerrigan gave a brief nod.

"If we hurry, we might get to see him before they dope him up for the rest of the afternoon."

Martinez turned to Mamba, and flashed a short-lived facsimile of his million-dollar grin. Mamba and Kerrigan exchanged meaningful glances. The call to action appeared to settle Martinez.

"I agree. Flatly's a good man." With speed that belied his physical size, Martinez bolted to the door. He spun, started to speak, and cut himself off. Kerrigan stared at him. The big man swallowed twice.

"Well, come on, Gumshoe. Who knows when they do the afternoon doping?"

"Who's driving?"

"All I brought is my bike. Want a thrill?" Despite the circumstances, the Latino winked meaningfully.

"I'd rather live until tomorrow," Mamba grunted. "We'll take my car."

* * *

The visit to the hospital by Martinez and Mamba was short. Martinez checked on Flatly's status while Mamba parked his car. Surgery would last several more hours, by which time visiting hours would be over. Despite his best efforts, the big Latino pried no more information from the receptionist in the surgery wing.

The Latino waited just inside the entrance from the parking structure until Mamba entered.

"Validate your parking ticket."

"Why? I just got here."

"We have to wait until tomorrow." Martinez held up his hand to prevent any argument. "Believe me, I leaned hard on the receptionist. He's in surgery. No one's gonna see Flatly before mañana."

Mamba sighed, shrugged, and shook his head in disappointment. He inserted his parking ticket into the machine by the door. A loud mechanical *cha-clunk* announced the placement of an ink stamp on the ticket.

The drive back to the station was a quiet one. Mamba spent the time mentally berating himself for involving Flatly in the sting.

Martinez mind was somewhere else. Mary Carstairs was dead. Flatly could have been. He determined to get out of undercover work and maybe ask Stallings for a transfer back to Southern Division.

Chapter 22

Hope Mamba checked voice messages that accumulated since she left the day before. Two messages were from solicitors. The third was from their insurance agent. None had any bearing on the one paying case her husband was working, or anything that might generate a positive cash flow.

She didn't mind that most of her husband's sleuthing was part of the pro bono work he was doing for the Manzanita Police Department. Greasing those wheels paid off several times in the past. However, there was not a lot for her to do when Phil had only one paying client.

She was filing documents that mysteriously appeared on her desk, grateful to her husband for giving her something to fill time when the sound of the front door opening stopped her. She turned from the filing cabinet. A man dressed in a seedy sports jacket entered.

"Is this Mamba the one they call the Dancer?"

Hope hesitated. The question was not surprising. Besides, she learned to go with the flow with her husband's nickname. But, something about this visitor set off alarms in her head. She stared at him with an expressionless countenance.

Some people that came in wanting to contract Phil's services were far from the type of folks she would invite to even drive through their neighborhood. This man was one of those.

"My name is Lester," the man continued even though Hope had yet to respond to his question. "Lawrence J. Lester. I have some important information for," he checked a folded paper he carried with him. "Philip Richmond Mamba. Assuming he is the Dancer."

"You have the right detective agency," Hope acknowledged, after another period of silence. "I'll get Mr. Mamba for you."

She went to the door of Phil's office. With a not so gentle knock, she pushed the door open, stepped inside, and pulled the door closed.

"Phil, there's someone here to see you. He says it's important."

"What's his name?" Mamba asked as he looked up from the papers that cluttered his desk. He was used to having characters drop by. He was not used to a reaction like this from Hope.

"He says he's Lawrence J. Lester."

"You're joking!"

"No." Hope gave him a quizzical look. "I'm sure that's what he said."

"It's not the name I was questioning. I thought Larry Lester was in prison."

"This one looks like he could—" Hope stopped and corrected her observation, "like he should be incarcerated."

"That's Larry Lester all right. You might as well send him in. He's the persistent type and won't leave until we talk."

"I'll send him in immediately if it means he'll leave sooner." She winked and went back to her desk, leaving Phil's office door open.

"Mr. Mamba will see you now."

"Thank you, Missy." He winked. "Maybe we could do lunch?"

"I don't think Detective Mamba would like that."

"He doesn't have to know, does he?"

"I usually tell my husband about my luncheon engagements."

"It's your loss, sweetheart." Lester shrugged. He went into the detective's office.

Hope rolled her eyes and headed to the restroom.

"Dancer, it's good to see you," Lester greeted the detective as he entered the office. He extended his hand.

"No comment," Mamba replied without standing. He kept his hands on his desktop. Lester was the type to keep at arm's length. Because he overheard the exchange between this man and his wife, his mood progressed from dislike to disgust.

"Mind if I sit down?" He had something Mamba wanted and would do whatever it took to change the PI's attitude.

Mamba shrugged and motioned toward a chair next to his desk. The visitor paraded over and took a seat.

"Mind if I smoke?"

"Yes."

Disregarding the response, Lester removed a cigarette from the pack in his pocket and lit up. He inhaled deeply and blew a cloud of smoke toward the ceiling.

Mamba waited until Lester's eyes focused on the smoke. He stood, reached across the desk, yanked the cigarette from Lester's fingers, and rubbed it into shreds of tobacco and paper between his finger and thumb.

"I'll bill you for the cleanup."

"Hey, Dancer. Back off a little! Cut an old buddy some slack."

"You reached the end of your slack the last time I saw you, Lester. And, you are no buddy of mine." Mamba bit the end off each word. "Why are you here?"

"I'm here because I was worried about you." Lester pushed up from his seat. "I thought you might want to know that certain people are out to get you. But, if you're not interested."

"Sit down!" Mamba snapped. While Lester repositioned himself in the chair, the PI closed the door to his office and returned to his desk. "What do you have you think I want?"

"With that attitude, maybe nothing!"

"I want to know what you've got. What brought you here?" The detective spoke through clenched jaws. "I want it now or you'll leave here with a fat lip."

"Now, now, Dancer," Lester cajoled. "Aren't we testy today."

Fed up with foreplay, Mamba flipped over the egg timer he kept on his desk to limit the length of consultations. Larry Lester was as aggravating as ever. Still, Mamba would let him run free for a controlled period. He occasionally provided high quality information. This time, Mamba wanted quality and speed of delivery.

"You see this?" Mamba pointed at the egg timer.

Lester nodded.

"When the sand's all gone, so are you. Talk."

"I hope I can finish in that arbitrary time limitation."

"Just get on with it. You had three minutes. I always start the egg timer when I ask a potential client what they want. The potential client has three minutes to convince me to take the case. You've got maybe two-and-a-half minutes left to do that."

The ex-con reached into his pocket and removed some folded sheets of paper. "I am holding copies of several pages of incriminating names, addresses, and the like. Rumor has it they originated here, in this office."

"Let me look at those," Mamba said with feigned indifference. If what he held was what he thought it was, the department's leak was more like a river.

With a smile, Lester handed the papers over to the detective. Mamba unfolded the stack and glanced at the top page. The glance was enough.

"Where did you get these?" His voice was low and hard.

"One of my employers provided me with those lists. I am to warn any of my acquaintances whose names appear in the queue. The intent of the warning is to provide them with adequate time to plan their escape from town and avoid prosecution."

"Does this employer have a name?"

"Not important." Lester knew that by contacting Mamba it was only a matter of time until the police traced him to his employer. For now, it was enough to use one hand to grease the other. If Dancer paid for information and Brewster still paid him to warn the troops, he could quickly and surreptitiously skip town if it all went south.

"Well." Mamba inhaled and exhaled slowly. "I know people who would beg to differ with you on the importance of the name of your employer."

"I'm not snitching."

Mamba saw fear in Lester's eyes. He went on the attack.

"What makes you think the lists came from here? Who started your rumor?"

"Perhaps I was inaccurate in my choice of words," Lester coughed discreetly. "Rumor was a bit weak. There is a fifth page to these lists."

"What fifth page? There were only four pages of names." Mamba paused as he realized Lester confirmed Reed's statements about origin of the lists and that they were on the street. He berated himself mentally as he realized he'd confirmed Lester's statement on the site of origin of the lists before opting to direct the burden of proof back to Lester. "There is no way on God's green earth to tie me to the lists by using the lists."

"True enough," Lester conceded. "There is not a clue to the origin of the lists on the lists I presented to you. The fifth page, however, is a different story."

Mamba didn't move a muscle. Lester shrugged.

"The fifth page is a copy of the Department of Motor Vehicles records of yourself and a gentleman named Patrick Kerrigan."

"Another rumor."

"Not a rumor, I'm afraid. I have seen the fifth page."

"Why come and warn me?" Mamba leaned back in his chair in contrived nonchalance.

"To be truthful, I am torn between conflicting loyalties. My employer can be very persuasive."

"You didn't answer my question."

"You were always square with me. You kept some of your less scrupulous associates from roughing me up when they arrested me, even when there were no witnesses."

"Everybody's entitled to a fair shake."

"Even you, Dancer. Even you."

"Thanks." It was time to end this. "Can I keep these copies of the lists?"

"Sure, although without them I won't get paid."

"I'll give you ten dollars a page," Mamba offered.

Lester wrinkled his brow. He slowly shook his head from side to side.

"Plus a ten dollar bonus for the information about the supposed fifth page." Mamba reached for his wallet.

"I'll need twenty for that information."

Mamba swallowed his rejection. While he did not like this man, Lester was sticking his neck out a long way for him. He cleared his throat. "Okay."

"Deal and done," Lester declared as he extended his hand to the detective.

"Thank you, Lester." He ignored Lester's hand a second time and handed him three twenties.

"Forget I came here, all right?"

Mamba nodded.

"I'm off then. Enjoyed our visit." The informant opened and closed the door more quickly than Mamba would have thought possible.

Lester paused at Hope's desk. "Last chance, honey."

"Not last. No chance at all," she muttered without looking up.

"You'll never know what you're missing." Lawrence J. Lester shrugged and strolled out the front door.

* * *

Mamba aired out his office after Lester's visit and did some hard thinking.

Having the lists out on the street was bad. Having his personal information on the streets is worse. Having Kerrigan's information on the streets was a disaster. He'd have to do whatever it took to prevent more attacks on people involved in this case. He punched the intercom button on his phone.

"Yes, Phil."

"Get me Reed."

She recognized the tone of her husband's voice. He was worried. She'd give him time before she asked to be filled in.

"And buy a bus ticket to Sacramento for Mr. Logan ASAP."

"Right away." Asking about Lester's visit moved behind the back burner.

When his phone rang five minutes later, Mamba snapped it off the base.

"Reed?" Mamba asked.

"Yeah. Who's dis?"

"Dancer. Just listen."

"I'm listenin'. Hard."

"Go to the bus depot. Ask the man at the ticket counter for the ticket reserved for Mr. Logan."

"Who's Logan?"

"There is no Logan. We don't want anyone to know you took the bus. You'll use the name Logan when you pick up the ticket."

"Where'm I going?"

"Sacramento. Someone will page Mr. Logan at the bus depot there. Answer the page and do exactly what the man tells you. You should be safe if you do what I say."

"That far north? Safe from what? And, how they know I'm this Logan guy? What's going down, Dancer?"

"You were right. The list is on the street. I have a copy."

Reed inhaled one quick breath.

"They know where it came from." He needed Reed's obedience.

"They fingered me!" Reed hyperventilated.

"No!" Mamba shot back. "Breathe slowly."

He waited for the man to obey.

"All they know is that Lieutenant Kerrigan got a tip. If you stick around, they might figure out it was you. I want you out of the way for a while."

"You bought the ticket already?"

"Why?"

"I'm on my way to the bus soon as I hang up!"

"Good. It'll be there. Remember you're Logan. And, Reed?"

"Yeah."

"Stay off the booze."

"I'll try. I promise."

"Stay off! It could mean your life!"

"Maybe it already has," Reed mumbled as he hung up.

Mamba hung up his phone with a sigh. He had done all he could for Reed. The rest was up to his informant.

"That ticket for Mr. Logan is at the bus depot will call, right Hope?"

"As of about ten minutes ago," Hope confirmed.

"Good. That's good. I want you to leave now." He stopped, kissed her on the cheek, then headed for the office door.

"Where are you going?"

"Northeast Station."

"Do I want to know why?"

"We'll talk tonight."

He was out of the office before she could respond.

* * *

The restaurant was at least two stars below Sid Brewster's norm. He learned that meetings like the one he was engaged in were ill-suited for rooms with tables displaying crystal goblets and silver flatware.

This meeting was an uncommon face-to-face with someone Sidney Brewster referred to as the necessary evils he employed. He was dining with one of his hired assassins. He never used the term hitman. That reeked of underworld collusion and brutality. Brewster's necessary evils involved both collusion and brutality. But assassin was less offensive to his psyche.

"Tell me, Mr. Briggs," Brewster spoke from behind a stuffed porkchop, the closest he could order to the Cornish game hen he preferred. He sat in an oversized rear booth of the country-themed restaurant. Surrounding tables were vacant, their vacancy ensured by monetary considerations to the owner. "Tell me how it went with our last transaction."

"Just fine, Mr. Brewster," Oscar Briggs replied. He sat across the table on the far side of the booth from Brewster. His position was so far from Brewster that an observer might conclude that Briggs' presence was unnecessary. "Parts was most enjoyable."

"Glad to hear that." Brewster took a drink of wine, winced, and vowed to have Elkhart bring his vintage to places like this. "Could you use more work?"

"Always can use your kind of work, Mr. Brewster."

"Good. Good."

"So, you need me again?"

"Yes, Mr. Briggs, I do. In fact, I have two more assignments for you."

"Shouldn't be no problem."

"Good." Brewster nodded to an associate standing as a silent sentinel during the meal. The man picked up an envelope from the table beside his employer. He walked along the front of the table and handed it to Briggs.

Big 0 ripped it open. Inside was a folded photocopied page. Briggs pulled the page out. Five uncirculated thousand-dollar bills and a dime bag of heroin slid onto the table top.

It was all Briggs could do to keep from dropping the envelope. This was an unheard of amount of money for two eliminations.

"The names on the copy of DMV information you're holding are the two men I want eliminated." Brewster relished the power he wielded over brutes like Briggs. The man had nearly soiled himself over a trifling amount of money and an even smaller amount of his drug of choice.

"Mamba and Kerrigan," Briggs read aloud. "Sounds like two uncool dudes." He stopped. A warning bell sounded in the hitman's brain. "Hey, this ain't Dancer Mamba is it?"

"I'm not sure. I suppose there's a possibility he uses that nickname."

"Then I, well, I don't know about this, Mr. Brewster. I mean he used to be a cop. He could be some trouble. I ain't never killed a cop before."

"I know that this Mamba is not a policeman, although he might have been. He's a private detective," Brewster explained. "Kerrigan is a policeman."

"This be too deep for me. I ain't gettin' mixed up with no hit on a cop and a rent-a-cop." Briggs began re-wrapping the money and smack with the photocopy.

"Before you turn me down," Brewster ignored Briggs' words and placed his fork on his plate. He waited until Briggs looked him in the eyes before continuing with icy emphasis. "Allow me to finish my proposition."

Briggs stopped in mid-fold. He concentrated on keeping his eyes aligned with those of his benefactor.

"I am prepared to offer you an enticement."

"What you mean?" Briggs asked. He had no idea of what enticement meant, but Brewster made it sound desirable.

"If you eliminate my problems, and they arrest you, I guarantee you the use of my legal team. If convicted of either killing, I guarantee you easy time." Brewster now spoke casually. "The money you're holding, and that bag of heroin plus two more bags whenever you want them, are yours to keep."

Briggs listened with little interest through the talk of lawyers and serving time. Promises like that could be broken. The lure of the money and smack in his hand, plus more smack. That was another thing.

"Five bags total," he decided. "By tomorrow, or I don't do nuthin'."

"Mr. Briggs, you are in no position to negotiate anything. It appears you've already done nuthin' on one of your assignments for me."

"What you talkin' 'bout? I offed the woman and the boxer, just like you said to."

"Not quite accurate."

"Huh?"

"Eloquent, Mr. Briggs. The boxer is still alive."

Briggs' mind raced, although his addiction slowed the speed of the race considerably.

"No way! I shot him point blank and skipped down a fire escape."

"I'm not arguing whether you shot the man. I'm saying you did not kill the man. He's in the hospital right now."

"I'm sorry, Mr. Brewster. This ain't never happened before. Lemme fix it!"

"Right now, I'm more concerned with Misters Mamba and Kerrigan. You finish those, or you'll never even think about working again." Brewster leaned forward. "For anyone."

"Why you sayin' that?"

"Because, Mr. Briggs. You. Will. Be. dead!"

"How 'bout I get only three bags."

"As you wish." Brewster was prepared to go two or three times what the hitman asked for. He loved the power fear held over those he scared. "I will deliver two additional bags to your place tomorrow by noon. When can I expect completion of these two contracts?"

"It's hard to tell, these guys bein' cops and all," Briggs mused. "Prob'ly take two, three weeks."

"Two weeks, Mr. Briggs." Brewster's voice hardened. "Longer than that smells like a stall to me. I will let you guess how I feel about people who make me wait."

"Two weeks." Briggs knew when it was time to fold and walk away.

"An excellent attitude, Mr. Briggs. And remember your priorities are the cop and the PI, not the boxer." Brewster turned back to his porkchop. "You may go."

It was times like this he missed the days when he dealt with problems himself. He figured two small bombs would solve this problem and remind his dealers who ran the show. He sighed. After all the hurried moves he made, he had no idea where any of his bomb-making supplies were stashed.

* * *

The window in Petula Jacobs' bedroom was open. A cool night breeze wafted through the portal. Two figures lay on the queen-sized bed that paralleled the wall with the window.

"You're unusually quiet this evening," she murmured. "A penny for your thoughts."

"You might not need that much," Dwight Rogers replied. "Most thoughts recently have been malformed, misinterpreted, or manipulated."

"I'm happy to provide a listening ear."

"I appreciate the offer. But, I don't think my administrative assistant needs to get dragged down by the stuff I'm dealing with." He rolled toward her, reached out, and pulled her close. "I know my mistress doesn't!"

She falsified a giggle.

He pulled her closer.

She didn't resist, but she made a decision. If her relationship with Rogers didn't move in the direction she wanted, and soon, this night would be the last time she played this game with the man.

Chapter 23

Franklin Stallings' head jerked upright. He'd finally gone to sleep but heard a noise in the master bathroom. He groaned and swung his legs off the bed and onto the floor. His wife was dry heaving. It was a residual effect of her chemotherapy. She always had nausea. Tonight was worse than most.

"How can I help?"

"Pray! Oh, I don't know. Why is it so bad this time?" Lizbeth was curled around the toilet bowl. She didn't look up when talking. It seemed like every chemo session selected some side effect and made it worse than it had been after other sessions. Tonight, it was vomiting. "I'm not sure how much more of this I can take."

Tears welled up in Stallings' eyes. He couldn't speak. He knew nothing coherent would come out if he tried. Stepping around Lizbeth's legs, he sat and slid his arms around her with all the love he had to give.

Lizbeth leaned back into her husband.

"Thank you, Franklin. Being held feels so good." She began to sob. Stallings adjusted his legs to better support his weight and began to rock her back and forth, as he hoped to rock his children someday.

An hour later he awoke with a start. He was still seated, for want of a better term, on the bathroom floor. One arm encircled Lizbeth's shoulder. The major difference from an hour earlier was that he could not feel his feet. They fell asleep while cramped beneath him.

Although he knew he'd pay a price when she awoke and they both stood up, he'd risk hurting himself to allow the woman he loved to get the rest she so desperately needed. He sighed and leaned against the bathroom wall.

* * *

Stallings rubbed his eyes, again. What sleep he got the night before was fitful. His drive to the station took longer than normal thanks to road construction and a three-car pile-up. He rubbed his eyes with increasing frequency as the morning progressed.

He felt himself nodding off. When he drifted into a light sleep state, he recalled the night before.

The ringing of his desk phone jolted him back to the present.

"Stall— Ahem! Stallings here."

"211. 555. 5219. Five minutes." The line went dead.

Stallings blanched. He had five minutes to get to a payphone. While the caller never identified itself or described the consequences if he didn't follow the directions, Stallings knew his past trapped him in this situation.

He had only one blemish on his record. It was a citizen's complaint about his actions during the rescue of several children trapped in a school bus. The bus rolled onto its side and slid into a pond. He did everything he could, and they rescued all the children.

However, the citizen's complaint implied he leaked her statement to the media. If even a hint of that got out now, given the current climate within Manzanita Police Department, he'd be branded as the leak before he had a chance to explain.

Pushing himself up from his chair, he limped towards his office door. Once outside, he turned and followed the sidewalk to the gate in the reinforced chain-link fence that surrounded the lot. He gave the crash bar a smack, envisioning his tormentor as the receiver of the blow.

Three minutes later, he stood inside a phone booth punching in the required numbers.

"This is Stallings."

"Great to know you made it into work today. I understand you had a rough night." The voice, which he now hated, demonstrated its omniscience by cutting to the source of his pain and fatigue without preamble.

The caller somehow disguised the voice; used an area code restricted to government agencies; never gave advanced notice; had a ridiculously short timeline; and mandated a payphone. Those two restrictions made tracing or recording the calls impossible.

"That's an understatement," he managed.

The electronically altered version of the voice of someone high in the Manzanita Police Department administration snorted a laugh.

"I'm glad to see you haven't lost your sense of humor."

"What do you want this time?"

"Ooh. Testy this morning, aren't we?"

Stallings did not respond.

"Be that way. Here's the situation. You will continue stalling the list of names investigation." The voice paused.

"I'll take that as a yes. Anyway, keep stalling, Stallings." The voice snorted out another laugh.

"Or?"

"Or, associates of mine will see that the side effects of your wife's chemo continue to increase in intensity and duration."

"Leave Lizbeth out of this!"

"It's my turn to ask. Or?"

Stallings knew he'd accomplish nothing by antagonizing the caller. It was clear the speaker possessed both position and power to do whatever it took for his compliance. His shoulders slumped.

"Is that all?"

"I'm good. You?"

"I hope you rot in hell!"

"You need to take a chill pill, Sergeant. That was both rude and offensive. But, if you'd prefer a physical pill, I have sources for that."

Stallings scowled at the innuendo.

"No? Well, it's been nice talking with you."

The line went dead.

Stallings hung up the phone and limped back to his office, avoiding the locked parking lot gate by entering the station's front door.

* * *

Mamba went directly to the station from his office after he set up Reed's bus trip. Kerrigan was gone and had a mandatory briefing the next morning. The PI departed without leaving a message. He worked his informants throughout the morning. He returned to the station around 2:00 p.m. and surprised his former partner. Kerrigan and Mamba sat at Kerrigan's desk.

"I know you had a briefing yesterday, but this is more important than whatever that was." Mamba's intensity surprised Kerrigan.

"You think it's more important than the briefing about security plans for the Governor's drive through next month?"

"It is! We wondered if the list of names was on the street. One of my CIs confirmed that. I've got the copies if you want to see them."

"That is bad. But, it doesn't trump protecting the Governor. And, I don't need copies to believe you."

"I'm not finished." Mamba leaned across the desk. When he spoke, Kerrigan felt his uneasiness build with each sentence. "Someone's targeting you and me. I confirmed that today. The bull's eye is our personal DMV information, including our home addresses. It's on a fifth page. And, it's out there, too!"

Kerrigan sat unmoving, barely breathing. It took several seconds for the implications of information to saturate his brain.

"This is bad. It's time to confront Stallings. If he is the leak, he's got to give up his handler and cooperate with the Department. Our lives are at stake!"

"Nothing's changed by this. Everything we have against Stallings is circumstantial."

"We've got no choice." Kerrigan stood. "Let's get it over with."

The men marched together to Stallings' office without a word between them.

* * *

It was late in the afternoon. Stallings remained awake for all but two short power naps. He looked at his watch for the tenth time in the last twenty minutes. The only thing keeping him going was the memory of the recent conversation on the payphone.

Kerrigan knocked on the door to Stallings' office.

"Come in," Stallings called, grateful for the diversion.

"Got a minute, Sergeant?" Kerrigan asked as he and Mamba entered.

"Always time for a Lieutenant." Stallings smiled, but his mind raced. He leaned back and put his hands behind his head, simulating a calmness he didn't feel. "What's on your agenda?"

"There are copies of Mamba's list on the street."

"What?" Stallings flailed his arms to keep from falling off his chair. His attempt at a calm façade was a dim memory. "How do you know that?"

"I've got a copy of the pages here," the PI told him. He tossed the copies onto the Sergeant's desk. "An informant got them on the street. He sold them to me."

"Why? What's his angle?" Stallings asked as he thumbed through the copies. Dozens, no hundreds of thoughts burst into the Sergeant's brain only to be replaced by still other thoughts like in a fireworks display on the 4th of July. As with those fireworks, none of the thoughts lingered long.

"Where's your set?" Kerrigan interrupted. While the reasons for selling a list like this might be of some interest and slightly more value, he was here to find and plug a leak.

"Huh?" Stallings looked up, shocked that the Lieutenant considered him a suspect. His expression conveyed the bewilderment he felt. "What'd you say?"

"Show me your copies of the list."

"I told you I couldn't find them the other day." Stallings stiffened as he answered. "Martinez was here, too."

"I was hoping you had located them by now."

"What are you implying, Lieutenant?" Anger and a sense of betrayal swirled in an emotional whirlpool.

"Nothing." Kerrigan's answer sounded calmer than the lieutenant felt. "I just want to be sure."

"I did not leak those lists, Lieutenant." Fear joined the mix of anger and betrayal. The sentiments merged forming a volatile emotional magma.

"I'm not accusing you—"

"Then what are you doing?" Stallings leaped to his feet, the residual pain in his extremities overcome by adrenaline. The Sergeant's face contorted, his breath came in shallow pants, his fists clenched. He stood, defiant, his shaking body displaying the turmoil within. "And what gives you the right to accuse me?"

"I'm not accusing you—"

"Then I guess I don't know what accusation means!" Stallings spat each word out like individual globs of fiery verbal lava. "What's the big deal? We've got Brewster's name. He's the lid on this cesspool."

"This, all this, is vital information." Kerrigan jabbed his finger at Mamba's lists where they lay on the desk as he fought to maintain his composure. "Martinez must feel the same way or he wouldn't have checked out as many names as he has."

"We can check out a lead in more ways than the list," Stallings countered. "It may come as a shock to you, but we rarely have a list of known traffickers dropped in our lap during an investigation." The thought that he was close to insubordination and needed to tread lightly flashed and evaporated just as quickly, reduced to a fleeting memory by the heat of his anger. "Narcotics uncovered a few suspects in other cases without them."

"Don't be sarcastic, Sergeant."

"What should I be? Gracious? Compliant?"

Kerrigan's gaze never wavered, and he offered no verbal response. Stallings clenched and unclenched his fists, an action Mamba hoped would defuse the bomb he'd become before he spoke again. However, for the second time in the brief shouting match, Stallings' actions ran roughshod over his thoughts.

"Well, I am neither gracious nor compliant. I am angry and insulted!"

"I'd bust your nose if you weren't!" Kerrigan barked back. "But my butt's on the line here, too."

"What?"

"They know about Mamba and me."

"Who knows? And what do they know? "

"Let me tell him." Mamba knew that unless he quelled the rising tension between the Sergeant and Lieutenant, both would regret this moment for a long time. He moved between the antagonists. Only then did he begin his explanation.

"There's another page on the street—a fifth page."

"What fifth page?," Stallings managed after a lengthy pause. The list is four pages long. There is no fifth page."

"But there is," Mamba said. He stared into Stallings' eyes until the man lowered his gaze. With Stallings' emotional state defused, the PI described page five. "It's a DMV printout on Pat and me."

He dropped his copy on top of the four pages of names.

Stallings glanced at the photocopy and his mind overloaded with frightening speculations. This news was much worse than a list of drug buyers and sellers leaked to the street could be. He took a deep breath. Only then did he feel he had enough control to speak.

"That's more than serious." He pointed at the DMV information. "You're setting up police protection, right?"

"I think it's a little early for that."

"Well, I don't think it is. Brewster's crew has shown it's willing to kill those who get in their way. It only takes one bullet."

"I think we're good for the moment," Kerrigan reiterated. He added what Stallings took as an attempt reconciliation. "But, thanks for the idea and the support."

Stallings' wry grin was a welcome response.

"But, keep trying to find those lists!"

"Starting now." His fatigue eradicated by adrenalin, Stallings turned to the row of file cabinets. He yanked open a top drawer, pulled file folders, and flipped through the contents of each.

Mamba retrieved the photocopies he got from Lester. He and Kerrigan completed the walk back to Kerrigan's office in awkward silence.

"Well?" Mamba asked after he shut the Lieutenant's door behind them.

"I don't know, Phil. He puts up a good front."

"Unless it's the truth." Mamba ran the conversation over again in his mind. All he saw in the Sergeant was a man angered by what he knew were false accusations.

"Yeah. There's that option, too," Kerrigan admitted with minimal reluctance. Stallings was a good cop. The last thing he wanted was to find out the man was a traitor.

They sat down. Kerrigan picked up a pencil and began to doodle on a scratch pad. Mamba idly fingered a stack of manila folders. They opened in succession as he lifted one side of the pile and let the folders slide back to the table one at a time.

"BALLISTICS REPORTS" caught his eye.

He removed the folder with that report from the pile and opened it. He read through three ballistics reports. Nothing stood out. He started to replace the folder in the stack. Whatever prompted him to select the ballistics reports for the past week was a bad hunch.

It was then he realized that a fourth ballistics report ran over to the second page. He read what was on the top sheet, flipped that report onto the inside of the open folder cover. He stopped reading when he saw Mary Carstairs name heading a fifth report.

"Pat, have you seen this?"

"I don't know what you're holding."

"They've run ballistics on the Carstairs case."

"Routine procedure. You know that."

"I do. Flatly's ballistics report is here, too."

Kerrigan nodded.

As evenly as was possible to speak, considering the implication of those reports, Mamba continued, "There's a match on the bullets."

"Let me see that!" Kerrigan snatched the folder from his friend. He skimmed the two reports. The same gun fired the bullets that killed Mary Carstairs and wounded Flatly Broke. "This is hard evidence that ties the two shootings to each other. It's about time we got something solid in this case."

"That also means that one person wanted them both out of the way. He may think he's accomplished that. My money's on Brewster, like Stallings said."

"I see where you're going. With two targets already eliminated, we could be next. We'll keep a lid on the boxer's condition and location for a few days."

"What if the leak's already delivered the news of Flatly's condition?"

"That's out of my control."

"But a security team for Flatly isn't. He deserves that."

"You're right. My homicide boys can start with this report." He held up the folder. "They need a challenge. I'll order a security rotation for the hospital."

Kerrigan hit his intercom button. He set up Flatly's security detail first. His second request was for one of his homicide detectives to come in.

The hunt was on.

Chapter 24

Big 0 pulled up to the curb in front of a house. He left the car running while he compared the house number to the number on the DMV report he held in his hand. He smiled instinctively, pulled his revolver from the glove box, cracked it open, and checked the cylinder. Six silver primers stared up at him.

The hitman smiled, but whether that was a smile of satisfaction or just the remains of a dissipating heroin high was impossible to tell.

After exiting the car and leaving the driver's door ajar, he looked both ways before strolling across the street. He disappeared from street view behind a stand of lantana and stared into the house.

"Look at them all peaceful," he muttered. "That's gonna end quick. Forever."

* * *

The Mamba's sat in the cozy living room of their ranch-style house. The neighborhood was quiet. It was quiet every other night, too, except for the few times a year when someone had a late party. But, as a courtesy, party hosts informed their neighbors about the event in advance.

He relegated being targeted by a local drug lord into the recesses of his mind. Tonight was family time.

He hadn't told Hope about the fifth page. It was best to wait and see what the homicide boys unearthed. If they were no closer to identifying Mary Carstairs' killer by this time tomorrow than they were today, he'd push until he got a protection detail for his family, and he'd push for Kerrigan to do the same.

"I'll put him to bed, sweetie," Phil said as he picked up their newly changed and pajama-clad son.

She kissed Jimmy. "Good night, munchkin. I'll be up in a few minutes."

"I'll be awake when you get up here," he called over his shoulder.

Shards of glass cascaded to the floor.

She knew that sound and hated it! She prayed what she feared wasn't happening!

As the glass shattered, the sound of a gunshot echoed down the street. Five more bullets screamed through the living room and slammed into the wall behind the sofa. Hope dropped to her knees, then threw herself face down on the carpet.

Her worst nightmare, a replay of the bomb blast she and the unborn Jimmy somehow survived, exploded in her mind exposing still raw nerve endings of shock, panic, and pain. Tears filled her eyes.

"Phil! Jimmy!" She screamed from her prone position.

Mamba heard the shots. Thinking first of his son, he sprinted up the remaining stairs and placed Jimmy in his crib. Then he heard Hope's screams.

"It'll be okay, buddy," he said with hardly a tremble in his voice. Jimmy sensed terror in his mother's screams and the tension in his father. He began to wail.

Hope heard her son's yowling. She pulled herself across the carpet until she faced the stairs. Fragments from the front window, as sharp as the point on a flint arrowhead, sliced into her right hand and knee. Although she left a bloody trail as she crawled, she was unaware of her injuries.

"Phil! I need you!"

"I have to go to Mommy," Mamba whispered in his son's unhearing ears. Without looking back—later he admitted it was the hardest thing he'd ever done—he left his son and tore back downstairs. Diving to his stomach three stairs from the bottom, he belly-crawled toward his hysterical wife.

"Are you hurt?" He demanded when he reached Hope's side. He felt something warm and sticky on one hand. He ignored the associated pain. Sympathy had to wait. He needed an accurate assessment of Hope's condition. He needed it now!

"N-N-No," she stammered. "Jimmy! Where's Jimmy?" She started to rise.

Mamba pushed her roughly back down. He saw blood on the carpet and her jeans. He knew she was hurt and running on adrenaline.

"He's fine. Jimmy's fine. And safe. He's in his crib in his room. I need you to focus. I need you to focus. Now!"

Venomous is an inadequate adjective for the look Hope shot at her husband.

"Good. You're back. Stay put until I get to the phone. Once I get there, you crawl to the stairs and crawl up those stairs to Jimmy. Do not stand until you're completely in the upstairs hallway. I'm calling the police. Then, I'll check out the yard."

"No, Phil," Hope pleaded, her focus wavering. "Leave the yard to the police. Please!"

"I'll just check from the porch. I'll wait for them there."

"You stay inside!"

"After I check the porch, I'll come back inside. I promise. But I have to know the porch is clear."

Hope nodded, but he couldn't tell if it was a nod of agreement or just an involuntary reaction to her situation.

"Change of plan. Go on upstairs. I'll watch 'til you're out of sight. Then, I'll call the police."

She nodded again.

"You're bleeding," he told her.

Confused by his comment, she looked for a wound. Adrenaline still blocked her pain, so she felt nothing.

"Just crawl. We'll worry about the blood later." She nodded once more. Once more, Phil could not tell whether it was a nod of agreement or a reflex action.

"Go now. Stay low. Get Jimmy. Go into the bathroom. Put him in the tub while you try to stop your bleeding."

"But—"

"He'll be fine in the tub. After you're bandaged, hug him all you need to. Once you pick him up, do not put him down until the police are here."

She crawled to the stairs.

He thought he heard her whispering a prayer as he watched her crawl away and up the staircase leaving a blood trail as she went. He shot a prayer upward, embarrassed he hadn't done that sooner.

The first thing Mamba did after Hope was in the hallway was pull the phone off the end table next to the sofa. He punched in 911.

"This is 9-1-1. What is your emergency?"

"This is Phil Mamba." He gave his home address. "Someone fired several bullets into my living room. My wife is bleeding. We need immediate police assistance and paramedics."

Mamba heard a click. He knew the operator was broadcasting the call on the dispatcher's radio frequency.

"How many people are in the house?"

"Three. Me. Wife. Son."

"Is anyone else injured?"

"No." He ignored the sliver of glass in the side of his hand.

"Please stay on the line."

"I can't do that. I'm going to clear the front porch."

"Sir, you need to stay away from—"

"I'm a private detective and a former Manzanita Police Department officer. I will clear my front porch to protect my family."

"Mr. Mamba, you need to let the police do their job."

The skills of 911 operators impressed Mamba. They were calm and professional, even in the face of critical emergencies. The woman already had cops on the way. And she remembered his name.

"One more thing." He interrupted for what he knew would be the last time. "Lieutenant Patrick Kerrigan needs a protection detail dispatched to his home immediately."

He dropped the handset into the cradle and crawled to where he stored his gun while he was in the house. After punching in the lock's combination, he slid the case open and pulled the Colt .38 Special from his shoulder holster. With gun in hand, he resumed crawling. At the door, he reached up and turned the knob. He first pulled the door open and then pushed it away from him while he remained out of sight. He pressed his body tight against the wall to the left of the doorway.

No bullets entered the open doorway. He rolled into the center of the portal. Silence. He clambered to his feet and stepped onto the porch swinging his gun from side to side. First left, then right.

"Clear!" he said, partly from habit, but more from relief. He walked back into the house.

While he waited for the police, Mamba pulled the shard of glass from his hand and covered the puncture wound with a Band-Aid. He gloved up from his stash in the case with his gun. He grabbed a steak knife and dug one bullet from the wall. Disturbing evidence was a flagrant breach of procedure. If the technicians linked the bullet to the homicide, it was a major break in the case. He went to the kitchen and dropped the bullet in a baggie.

It took less than five minutes for the police and paramedics to arrive in force at the Mamba home. The PI surrendered his gun to the first officer in. He directed the paramedics upstairs to Hope and Jimmy. His third, and last, official action was to offer the bullet in the baggie to the senior officer at the scene.

"How fast can you get this to forensics?"

"Sir, we have procedures for that."

"I'm a private detective working a case with Lieutenant Kerrigan and Sergeant Stallings out of Northeast. This shooting is linked to that case. The sooner we know if it matches the bullet that killed a woman, the better."

The officer frowned. It sounded plausible. But, the man admitted to being a private eye. That meant his words were suspect.

Seconds ticked away.

"If any Lieutenant agrees with me, let alone the Homicide Lieutenant on an active case, and you didn't shoot this evidence to forensics as fast as you should have. Do you have any idea what happens to you?"

"I guess it can't hurt." The officer took the baggie from Mamba and called a uniform over.

"Tag this and personally deliver it to ballistics. Put a rush on it!"

"Yes, sir."

Mamba smiled. It was good to know that being overly concerned with protocol in certain situations was still a liability.

Over two hours later, he maneuvered around Jimmy's portable playpen, which they took with them to the motel room. They were officially under police protection. A squad car sat facing the driveway of the parking lot just outside the door to the room.

Jimmy slept next to a wide-awake Hope in the queen-sized bed. Phil crawled into bed next to his wife. It was then he felt her body trembling as he stroked her arm.

"I love you," was what he said after filtering through a list of at least a dozen first lines in his mind.

"I know." She began to sob. "I feel like I'm a jinx."

"I love you," he repeated as he wrapped his arms around her. Jimmy, nestled between them, pushed against his father with his feet. Mamba moved back just enough to stop his son's action.

Hope sighed. But, that proved only a temporary respite for the sobbing and shaking.

He held his family for an hour, relaxing and catnapping only after the exhausted Hope fell asleep.

* * *

The morning after the attack on his home, Mamba was awake at six. After extricating himself from Hope and Jimmy, he used the bathroom, splashed cold water on his face, and replaced the Band-Aid on his hand. He felt almost subhuman after those actions.

He was pleasantly surprised to find that the motel room's phone cord was long enough to take into the bathroom. He grabbed the phone and phonebook and closed the door. He turned on the shower to muffle his phone conversation.

His first call was to one of Hope's college friends, the only one he had a phone number for. In minutes, he'd cleared an impromptu trip to visit her because "mommy has cabin fever." After that he made reservations for Hope and Jimmy to fly to Florida. His third call was to Kerrigan.

"I want Hope and Jimmy out of harm's way. I'm sending them out of town."

"I think that's wise."

"Send Kate away, too."

"I've got round-the-clock surveillance on my home."

"Only takes one bullet, Pat. You know that."

"I'll talk to Kate."

After Kerrigan said goodbye, Mamba made his final call. He left a message.

"Mr. Anderson, this is Phil Mamba. I'm afraid that I have to put your case on a back burner. There is a situation that requires my full attention for a while. Oh, yeah. Don't worry. You won't be billed for any hours until we both agree to reopen your case."

* * *

"I've made reservations to Denver for you and Jimmy. You leave in five hours from Los Angeles," Mamba told his wife after they finished breakfast. "You change planes in Denver to a nonstop to Miami."

"I don't want to leave."

"It's not a matter of wanting. Someone's after me. I have a better chance if you're not here. I'll be so worried about you and Jimmy that I'm afraid I'll miss something critical, especially after last night."

"What about my stitches? I've got over twenty stitches in my hands and knees."

"There are doctors in Florida."

"But I don't like leaving you." She offered another iteration of her primary excuse.

"I don't like it either, but it is necessary to get you and Jimmy away. Don't forget to pick up the ticket at the travel agent on your way to L.A. You'll be traveling as Mrs. Washington. I've booked a car for her, that's you, at the airport in Miami. Debra knows you're coming. She thinks it's a getaway time for you and Jimmy. Make sure you have her address and phone number."

"Why a phony name?" She listened politely to his spiel. That was the only question she came up with.

"As soon as whoever tried to kill you finds out you're still alive, they'll be hunting you. When they can't find you here, I want to make it as hard as possible for them to trace you." Mamba offered a crooked grin and added, "This whole trip is mostly for my benefit. It means less work for me if you're not here."

She hugged his neck as she said, "I love you, too."

He held her tight.

"Be careful," she whispered through the lump in her throat.

"Always," was all he could choke out.

* * *

Martinez found no time to meet with Stallings about his decision to quit undercover work. With Brewster on the run, arrests on drug-related crimes were down. He was back working the street for narcotics—from the front seat of an unmarked car in a neighborhood no different from where he worked at Southern Division.

Movement at the door of the building ended his musing. A scraggly, young man exited and moved down the sidewalk, his eyes darting furtively in all directions.

Martinez signaled his partner for the assignment. A veteran narcotics cop, Collins leaned against a doorjamb. After flipping away his cigarette to confirm the identification, the officer strolled along the street on the opposite side from the unsuspecting drug runner.

When both were out of sight, the detective started his car and tailed the pair staying a block behind them. He paused at an alley as though checking for cross traffic. As the car idled, unmoving for only the briefest instant, the back door on the passenger side opened and closed before Collins uttered a hoarse, "Go!"

The Latino sped up enough to keep the target in sight.

When the delivery boy entered a building, Martinez pulled a U-turn and parked. The officers followed the suspect up the front steps after he entered the building.

They watched the fumbling fingers of the boy touch the raised metal numbers identifying apartment doors one and two. After massaging the third set of numbers, he half-scratched, half-knocked on the door.

Oscar Briggs pulled the headphones of his Walkman off his ears. He listened intently. The sound came again. He grabbed his gun and pulled the door to his apartment open a crack while he stood off to one side.

"What you want?" Big 0 asked through the narrow opening between the jamb and the door.

"I got. Your smack."

"Hey, man, you look wasted." He opened the door, turned, and placed his gun on the table beside his faded couch. Turning back to the door, he helped the young man into the room.

"My, uh, your stuff is in pocket," the boy gasped and collapsed on the couch.

With a practiced hand, Briggs rifled the young man's pockets. He discovered two bags of smack in the kid's coat, payment from Brewster for the night before. He found another bag in a front pocket of the delivery boy's jeans.

One back pocket of the jeans yielded a wallet. Inside he found an expired driver's license and a single one-dollar bill.

The only other item the youth had on him was a crumpled envelope. Briggs tossed that aside.

"I need a hit. Please."

Briggs looked down on the slumped figure. The boy was desperate and crashing. Briggs looked at the bags of heroin in his hand. The kid's need was nowhere near as strong as him having possession.

"Hold on, boy. I'll cook your stuff."

"Thanks," was the slurred monosyllabic reply.

Briggs collected his paraphernalia. Opening the packet from the boy's front pocket, he tapped out a minuscule amount of the drug into the dirty spoon. He cut it with enough baby powder to fill the depression to its usual level. He only cut the smack he moved by fifty percent. This was a special situation. All he wanted to do was get the kid up and out of his room as fast as he could.

He grabbed a piece of paper from the coffee table. Twisting it into a skinny rope, he went to the stove and turned on a burner. Igniting the paper with the flame, he carried his torch over to the candle. Once the candle's flame flickered in response to the slow moving air in the room, he crushed the torch out against the dirty, threadbare carpet.

He wrapped his surgical tubing around the boy's arm. After melting the heroin/talc mixture, he sucked it into his syringe and pumped the pasty liquid into the boy's scarred forearm. There was a reflex jerk before the boy went limp.

Briggs swore. The kid wasn't supposed to die. Now, he had to drag the body out back. He swore again, louder this time. That made three mistakes in less than a week. Then he realized that nobody knew about this mistake. He'd make sure it stayed that way.

With a groan, he lifted the surprisingly heavy body. He made a note about hitting the weights more often. When he reached the door of his apartment, he shifted all the kid's weight to his right arm. Using his left hand, he opened his door and stepped into the hallway.

"Far enough, hombre!"

The barrel of a service revolver dented Briggs' neck.

"Back into the room!"

Collins materialized in front of Briggs who flipped the body he held into the man and shot his elbow toward Martinez.

Martinez blocked the attack with his forearm.

Briggs slumped to the floor when the butt of Martinez's revolver cracked his skull.

Collins, who deflected the body with his hands, moved to Briggs' unconscious form and leveled his gun at the prone figure in the doorway.

"You won't need that." Martinez knelt beside the hitman and unceremoniously placed his handcuffs on the man's wrists. "Use this guy's phone and call for backup."

"Check!" Collins stepped over the two bodies that littered the hallway and dialed a number on Briggs' phone.

Martinez finished handcuffing his suspect and recited the Miranda verbiage to the unconscious man. He would go through the recital again after Briggs woke up, but he made sure that somewhere among the first words he spoke to suspects as he handcuffed them were the required legalese.

"I told backup I'd meet them at the front door." Collins left without another word.

Turning his attention to the delivery boy, the detective felt for a pulse. His skin was cold.

Martinez made the sign of the cross and straightened up. He shooed the sets of eyes that peered out from two partially opened doors back inside with a brusque, "Police business." By then, Collins and two uniformed officers headed down the hallway in his direction.

"Call the coroner," he directed.

One of the uniforms spoke into the radio clipped to the collar of her tunic.

Collins bummed gloves from the uniforms. As usual, Martinez pulled a pair of XXL latex gloves from his pocket. A search of Briggs' body and the apartment yielded three bags of heroin and paraphernalia for mainlining, a recently fired hand gun of significant caliber, a new Walkman and its box, four thousand, two hundred and twenty-six dollars in cash, and a scribbled note: "Boxer – hospital – finish job."

Martinez went to Briggs' phone and dialed.

"Northeast Division."

"This is Martinez. Get me Sergeant Stallings."

"Right away, Detective."

Martinez counted to seven while waiting for his boss to answer.

"Stallings."

"Sergeant, this is Martinez. I just found a note in Briggs' apartment. Check our security on Flatly Broke Code 3."

"You're certain? We released no information about his condition."

"The note says, 'Boxer – hospital – finish job.' That's reason enough."

"Agreed. Make sure that note gets bagged and tagged."

"Already on it."

Stallings ended the call. As Martinez hung up his handset, he realized what Stallings said about the boxer.

"We released no information about his condition. More evidence of the leak," he muttered.

"You say something?" Collins asked.

"Nothing important. Let's finish this."

They bagged a wrinkled envelope with the apartment's address penciled on it, but it was a partially burned piece of paper found on the floor that moved the Latino to action a second time.

"Give me the gun," he demanded after looking at the printing on the burned scrap of paper. He secured two envelopes from the uniformed officer cataloging evidence and dropped the weapon into one and the burned paper into the other. He sealed them both.

"Tag these and log them as in my possession," he directed.

When the cataloging officer hesitated, Martinez explained.

"I want this run through ballistics right away." He held up the bag with the gun in it. "Stallings will want to see what's on this paper long before it goes into the evidence cage." He held up the second bag.

"Can do. Put 'em here." She pointed to the front of her line of evidence bags.

"Thanks. Collins, when you're finished here, type up your notes and leave all the paperwork on my desk. I'll wrap up the report when I get back to the station. I'm heading to the lab."

Nods of acknowledgment from all present indicated they heard and understood. Collins' nod was more one of appreciation than understanding. Martinez just volunteered to do the bulk of the paperwork on the case.

"Put in your notes I took the gun and this scrap of burned paper to the lab, Officer. Include the time. I never wear a watch." He took a final look around.

"Bring Collins back with you in your black and white." Martinez directed the cataloging officer and her partner.

He was headed out the door before the ink dried in the log after recording the numbers on the evidence bags he was delivering to the station.

* * *

Oscar Briggs had a headache. He lay on a too small, too hard bed in a too small, too tightly locked jail cell and pondered his situation in his usual manner, mumbling to himself.

"I screwed up bad. I killed that kid who's just doin' his job. I know what it means to do a job. I deserve to be in this cell. Hardest part's gonna be goin' cold turkey from the smack. I won't miss talkin' much, but I will miss bein' juiced."

He ran his fingers over the bump on his head from Martinez's gun. The headache would be gone in a day or so. In the meantime, he'd sleep on his back.

He finished his reflective session with a surprisingly complex ponder he'd need to remember.

"Life don't promise nuthin'. You got to get what you want any way you can. I'll be shuttin' up. But, if I don't get them lawyers and that easy time like Brewster promised me, Mr. Brewster is gonna wish he never lied and cheated the Big 0! Cuz' I'll be gettin' what I want. Whatever it takes."

"Prisoner Briggs!"

Big 0 took his sweet time to look at the officer outside his bars.

"Get your stuff stowed away. Lights out in thirty minutes."

"Shut your fat face up, cop!" Briggs snarled. They were the only words he spoke until his arraignment. But, he got his stuff stowed away.

At the arraignment, he delivered what was for him a soliloquy, "Not guilty, Your Honor."

* * *

It was an hour after Briggs' arrest. After dropping one evidence bag at the lab, Martinez stopped by Kerrigan's office.

"I figure I'll hear about removing the evidence from the crime scene before cataloging is complete. Sergeant Stallings will lecture me on that breach of protocol, but I want someone I trust to hear about this evidence right away."

Kerrigan nodded.

"And see some evidence, too." Martinez dropped the second evidence bag on Kerrigan's desk.

Kerrigan's eyes opened wide. The action was way beyond breaching protocol. Investigators always checked in evidence immediately upon arrival at the station. He wondered what Martinez risked an official reprimand to show him. He picked up the evidence bag. He maneuvered the contents while focused on the evidence. He inhaled sharply.

"Start talking, Detective."

He listened to Martinez's brief explanation of Briggs' arrest and what he left at the lab inside the other evidence bag. When the Latino finished, Kerrigan picked up the phone and called Mamba.

"Get down to the station," Kerrigan's words were more order than option. "Our friend, Martinez, told me a most interesting story. And, he brought with him an even more interesting item for show and tell."

"On my way," Mamba answered. He knew that tone. Kerrigan was too concerned to talk on the phone. He patted his shoulder holster as he headed out.

Chapter 25

Mamba's mind raced as he pulled into the Northeast Division station's visitors' lot. He found a spot without having to make a complete pass through the normally packed facility, and ended his introspection on his walk to the station's door.

He signed for his visitor's pass, walked straight to his destination, and knocked on Kerrigan's office door.

"Glad you could come so quickly," was the Lieutenant's sarcastic greeting when he opened the door of his office.

"Detective." Mamba ignored his friend and nodded to Martinez.

Martinez nodded back. He was in no mood for extraneous conversation. The longer he avoided meeting with Stallings, the worse it could go for both of them.

"Horrific traffic," he said as he took his place in the only vacant chair. There was no response to his excuse.

Kerrigan seated himself behind his desk. He motioned to Martinez who gave a Cliff Notes version of Briggs' arrest and the evidence bag he delivered to the lab. At the conclusion of the recitation, the Lieutenant picked up an evidence bag. "As you can see, this bag contains the scorched remains of a DMV report. The bottom of the page is missing, but the top half is pretty much intact. Look at the name."

"I don't have to. I know who it is. That's the reason for the shooting at my house and why my wife is no longer in Manzanita."

Martinez leaned forward.

"I didn't know she'd left town."

"You weren't supposed to. Now, three people connected with the case know." Martinez and Kerrigan caught the innuendo in Mamba's statement. Both let it pass.

"You think the shooter is Briggs?" Mamba asked, changing the subject as he handed the evidence bag back to Kerrigan.

"Most likely. I heard you ordered the senior officer who answered the call on the shooting at your place to get the slug to the lab as fast as possible last night." Kerrigan punched the intercom on his phone.

"Peggy, get me ballistics."

"I'll have them call you Code 3."

While he waited, he told the others, "Might as well put a little pressure on the lab boys from my end, too. Especially now that Martinez has something down there."

The phone rang. Kerrigan answered. Mamba and Martinez sat in self-imposed silence until Kerrigan hung up the phone.

"What'd you find out?" Martinez asked.

"Detective Martinez, you apprehended the person who killed Mary Carstairs, shot Flatly Broke, and fired shots at Hope Mamba. Ballistics on the gun and bullets found in Briggs' apartment match bullets found at all those crime scenes. His prints are all over the gun. He looks good for all three shootings."

"That's some good news. But we still have our leak to plug."

"We do, among other things." Kerrigan shoved his chair back and stood up. "Let's apply some pressure. We'll work together and see what we squeeze out of the Sergeant. Follow my lead. After the conversation gets rolling, go with what you think best."

"I'm for that," Martinez agreed. "He might have set me up, too."

"I know it looks bad for Stallings, but let's not convict anyone yet," Mamba cautioned.

Martinez grunted something in Spanish.

"We will follow procedures," Kerrigan said. He waited.

Mamba nodded his assent. Martinez also nodded, but with less conviction. Two men moved towards the office door.

"We will follow procedures," Kerrigan repeated with emphasis. He hadn't moved. "No information leak will get off on a technicality on my watch. I want a verbal response of agreement."

"Understood," Mamba said.

"I will follow procedures," Martinez responded without turning from the door.

Kerrigan shook his head at the uninspired responses to his order, grabbed the evidence bag off his desk, and followed the others out of his office.

* * *

Sid Brewster was in another bad mood. He was still living in the inadequate house he moved into following the raid on his house on Henry Court. And, now, he learned that the muscle-headed Briggs screwed up again.

That information wasn't reported by one of his employees. No. The shady information broker that stood before him would sell his mother for the right price. He was the one who delivered the news.

"Briggs did what?" A black and tan dachshund slunk out of the room in response to its master's shouts.

"I'm sorry, Mr. Brewster," Larry Lester apologized. For what, he wasn't sure. But, he learned that apologizing at the wrong time was much less an issue than not apologizing when expected. That applied to reputable employers like Phil Mamba and disreputable men like Sid Brewster. So, he apologized for what Briggs did. "I heard it from a lady that lives in the same building."

"That stupid Briggs killed the delivery boy and got himself arrested?"

"The woman said that there was a dead body taken from the building and that Briggs was handcuffed when the police led him out." Lester knew he was walking a tightrope by feeding information to both Mamba and Brewster. But, his mantra was "strike while the iron is hot," so he continued working both sides. Money was money.

A string of obscenities was Brewster's response. The kid was an addict, so it was possible he died of an overdose celebrating his payment.

"Did Briggs tell them anything?" he asked when he regained enough composure to articulate his thoughts.

"I don't know," Lester answered. "I would hope a man of Briggs' reputation would maintain a sensible silence on sensitive subjects."

"That was a rhetorical question," Brewster muttered. "But, Briggs better keep a cork in it. Thanks for the information."

"My pleasure, Mr. Brewster." When there was no immediate response by the drug trafficker, Lester coughed discreetly.

"You got a cold?"

"No, sir. I was just wondering about . . ." He let the sentence hang.

"You were wondering if your information was worth anything. Right?"

"Well, yes, actually. And, I'd like to slip my information source a token gratuity."

"Here's fifty for you and ten for your girlfriend." Brewster pulled two bills from his wallet. He pulled a third bill out and held it beneath

Lester's nose. "And here's another U.S. Grant, if you find out how much Briggs told the cops."

He placed the second fifty-dollar bill on an ornately carved oriental table, one of the few items Briggs felt gave the place from which he temporarily did his business a modicum of decorum. "President Grant will occupy that table top until this time tomorrow."

"I'll do my best, Mr. Brewster."

"Yeah, right. I expect nothing less," Brewster said before dismissing Lester with an offhand wave.

* * *

Stallings smiled a crooked smile as he walked down the hallway. His thoughts were on several devious methods of torture for the inventor of the coffee/broth dispenser in the break room. He was holding a cup in one hand and fanning his mouth with the other when he saw the three men waiting outside his door. He slowed his pace.

"You gentlemen waiting for me?" he asked as he pulled his keys from his pocket.

"No one else," Martinez answered for the group. Kerrigan shot him a look. Mamba realized he underestimated the tension, something he hadn't thought possible. Until now.

"Come on in." The apprehensive Stallings stood to one side while the three men entered his office in silence.

Kerrigan chose the only chair not covered with stacks of paper. Martinez opted to stand. Mamba shadowed the Latino to provide what buffer he could.

Stallings closed the door behind him, placed the cup of broth on the only uncovered space on his desk, sat down, and faced the tribunal.

"We found this," Kerrigan produced the evidence bag with the partially burned DMV report inside and tossed it toward Stallings. "It was in the apartment of the suspect now in custody for the murder of Mary Carstairs, the wounding of Flatly Broke, and the attempt on Mamba and his family."

"I've got a uniform at the hospital for Mamba's CI. It's my understanding you've accepted a security unit, Lieutenant," Stallings said without a glance at the evidence bag.

"I have. And I appreciate that, Sergeant. Although, my security detail only covers my house."

"You sure that's enough?" Mamba asked. He was grateful for Stallings' quick action but uncomfortable at Kerrigan's trivialization of the danger to his person.

"I'm a cop," Kerrigan said.

Mamba wanted to remind his friend that bullets didn't play favorites but Stallings spoke first.

"This is a DMV report on Mamba." He pointed to the evidence bag.

"Correct," Kerrigan again turned his attention to the focus of the meeting. "The burned portion of the page was information on me."

"Where'd you say this came from?"

"No games, Sergeant," Martinez snapped.

Mamba placed his hand on the arm of the big man. He kept it there until he felt the muscles relax a miniscule amount.

"This is a copy of an official government document. Outside the DMV, only departmental employees have access to this information. We think the leak's still leaking."

"So?" The word echoed through the office.

"So, if you add all the leaks together, Sargento. If you follow the trail, it leads here to this office!" Mamba felt Martinez's arm muscles tighten again as he presented his unauthorized conclusion several decibels above conversational level.

The PI pressed his arm hard against the Latino hoping to defuse the man's anger.

"That's a lie!" Stallings shot from his chair. "You're on a witch hunt, and I'm the closest thing you've got to a patsy. There's no way I'm leaking anything to anybody! Not before, not now, not ever!" His decision made, he fired his last bullet. "I will not be convicted by innuendo."

Mamba's ears perked up. First was Stallings' use of witch hunt, which he found coincidental. But, it was the "not before, not now" part of the denial of when he had not leaked information that had made the biggest impression. He wondered who thought he did something like what's going on here and whether it was before this accusation or before he got to Manzanita.

"Settle down, Sergeant!" Kerrigan managed to keep the volume of his voice low. He turned in his chair and spoke to Martinez while directing his words to Stallings. Even then, he continued at sotto voce volume. "Sergeant, the accusation just made was one man's opinion. If that man speaks out of turn again, there will be repercussions."

The giant opened his mouth but snapped it shut without speaking, jaw muscles contracting and relaxing with arrhythmic imprecision.

"There's no witch hunt," Kerrigan continued. "We're trying to determine what direction to take to plug our leak."

"Bull!" Stallings spat. "Get out of my office! Now!"

"Sergeant!" Kerrigan snapped back.

"I've got work to do, Lieutenant," was Stallings' icy end to the conversation. "You're welcome back on official department business, or to apologize, or to instruct me to contact my union rep. Otherwise—" He pointed toward the door with his thumb, figuratively throwing them out of his office.

Mamba made the first move. He tapped Martinez on the shoulder. Kerrigan caught the movement out of the corner of his eye. He stood and removed the evidence bag from Stallings' desk. The three men left before the room froze solid.

In the hallway, they dispersed without further conversation. Mamba headed to the parking lot. Martinez stormed off to complete his paperwork. Kerrigan ended up back in his office.

A uniformed police officer followed Mamba. A squad car sat outside Kerrigan's house. Protective details would continue until they plugged the departmental leak.

* * *

Hope and Jimmy were in Florida. The Manzanita Police Department cordoned the family home off with crime scene tape after the attack on Hope. Mamba avoided feeling sequestered by avoiding his motel room as much as possible. The beige rectangle with one of everything—door, window, sink, shower, bed, occupant—was nothing more than a grim reminder of consequences of his chosen profession.

So, although it was after 6 p.m., he sat at Hope's desk in the reception area of Mamba Investigations. He assumed there was a black and white squad car across the street in front of his building. While he was ostensibly trying to catch up on paperwork, he got only as far as opening the mail before he found he couldn't concentrate.

The sound of his office door opening interrupted his reading of the *Manzanita Daily News*.

"Dancer, we meet again," Larry Lester's sleazy voice announced.

"Hello, Lester." Mamba chose civility. He was too tired for anything else. "How can I help you?"

"Interesting that you should use that phraseology. This time you can help me."

"What do you mean?" Mamba's radar snapped on. Lester admitting that he needed help was a time to exercise extreme caution.

"My current employer asked me for certain information. It is my opinion that you are my best option for successful acquisition of that piece of intelligence."

Mamba sat in silence, his thoughts roiling. When he didn't respond, Lester massaged the back of his neck with the fingers of one hand, cleared his throat, and swallowed hard.

"Anyway, I am here to ask you about a man named Briggs."

"Who?"

"Oscar Briggs," Lester expanded. "He's also under contract with my employer. At least he was until the Manzanita Police Department arrested him."

"Arrested for what? And why would I care?"

"You don't know him?"

Mamba stared, stone-faced.

Lester's composure crumbled. This conversation was not going as planned.

"He made an aborted attempt upon the life of one of your family members, so I thought—"

"Go on, Larry." Mamba's tone left no room for doubt that Lester would continue his narration. "And I expect the absolute truth!"

"I can't. I've already told far more than I should have."

"Why are you here?" Mamba moved behind the snitch, blocking his exit.

Lester's shoulders slumped.

"I need you to help me get out of a big jam, Dancer."

"How can I do that?" Mamba's curiosity piqued. Lester's voice and demeanor implied that he was speaking the truth, and truth rarely passed the lips of Larry Lester.

"I need information on Briggs."

"You already asked for that. To be honest, that sounds like a lame deal. You get the information you need, but nothing's in it for me."

Lester took a deep breath. "In return for your information, I will work, um, undercover, for you, inside my employer's organization."

The offer stunned the PI. Whoever the employer was would not let such a transgression pass without severe, possibly fatal, consequences.

"Why?"

"Believe it or not, Dancer, I am frightened." Lester paused, appeared to consider something, then continued. "Actually, I am scared to death. These people are playing with stakes far too high for my liking. They treat human life like it is something to crumple up and toss in the trash. I don't want to end up in a dumpster somewhere."

"I believe you're scared. But, why come to me? The police will listen to you." Mamba returned to the chair behind the desk.

"It was hard enough to decide to cross these people. It's too big a risk to go to work for the cops. I remember what the screws are like in Quentin."

"I might be willing to deal," Mamba mused while he ran various scenarios through his brain. "What information do you want?"

"What did Briggs tell the cops?"

"That's simple enough."

Lester perked up at the word simple. It was a change in demeanor that Mamba did not miss. "But, if you want to work for me, you start now."

"What do you mean?"

"I want your employer's name."

"Brewster, Sidney Brewster." The name flew from Lester's lips. Then there was a slight pause. He coughed discretely and rephrased his question, "Now what did Briggs say?"

"Nothing, Larry. Briggs said absolutely nothing. I got the impression he would die at least twice before he'd talk to a cop."

"Are you sure?"

"Is Sidney Brewster your employer?" Mamba's accusatory tone reminded the man that questioning information the PI provided was unacceptable.

Lester looked away and mumbled, "Yes."

"Did Brewster supply Briggs with heroin?"

"If Briggs had smack, Brewster probably supplied it. He's one of the major suppliers in the city."

"Do you know where he lives?"

"I've only been to a hotel suite. I don't know if he lives there or if it's just a front."

"Write it down," Mamba slid paper and pencil across the desk.

Lester complied. He put down the pencil and stood up.

"I've got to go. Fifty dollars is waiting for me for the information on Briggs."

"You'd better not be working both ends against the middle."

"No way I'd do that to you. In fact, I hope you collar Brewster." He brushed the front of his slacks with both hands. "But fifty bucks is fifty bucks. The way I figure, it's severance pay."

"Good luck."

"Can't have too much of that," Lester called back as he exited through Mamba's office door.

The PI watched the man as he passed the large front window of his office suite. Lester, who would sell his grandmother's last bite of food if the price was right, was concerned because the people he was dealing with thought too little of human life. That was a surprise.

He shoved the paper with the address into his pocket and locked the door to the office. He would phone Kerrigan with Brewster's address first thing in the morning. He wanted a chance to swing by and get the lay of the land before he gave up his intel.

He began composing his rationalization for delaying going to the police while crossing the street. He stopped at the car assigned to protect him.

"Don't report the guy that just left."

"I'll need a reason."

"I understand. He's a former client back in town."

"Whatever you say, Mr. Mamba. But, I have to log a male as in and out."

"Wouldn't have it any other way. Just wanted to save you some time. Paperwork's a killer, isn't it?"

"You have no idea."

* * *

As the sun began its trek across the sky above Manzanita, not even the hint of a cloud obstructed its path. Although the morning was lovely, it was too early for Patrick Kerrigan's taste.

But work was work.

He stacked the paper he was studying on a pile at the extreme left edge of his desk's surface. Three homicide investigations were in progress. Only Mary Carstairs' seemed headed toward closure.

There was a knock on the office door.

"It's unlocked."

Eddie Edwards opened the door to Kerrigan's office.

"Hey, Lieutenant. You're at it early this morning."

"No rest for the weary. What brings you here?"

"Four evidence lists. I made the copies, and I thought you might like to see 'em before the rest of the troops came in."

"Thanks, Eddie. It's people like you that keep the rest of us going in spite of ourselves."

"I knew you'd appreciate my humble efforts." The Sergeant grinned. He handed several pages to the Lieutenant.

"Bye, Eddie." The Lieutenant's tone implied dismissal.

Kerrigan sighed and sifted through the papers Edwards delivered. They were lists of evidence from the scenes of Mary Carstairs' murder, Flatly Broke's wounding, the attempt on Hope Mamba's life, and Briggs' apartment.

"More paper." Kerrigan tossed the pages on the top of the already substantial pile of papers that filled his in-box.

His phone rang.

"Kerrigan."

"Pat, it's Phil. Got a minute?"

"For you, more than a minute. When I die, I won't need a grave, you'll find me buried in paperwork."

"I got a tip on Brewster's address."

"What kind of tip?"

"The address."

"Hold on! Let me get a pencil." He rummaged around until he found a pen and said, "Shoot."

"Regency Park Hotel, 54th Street. Probably suite 730."

"Wait a minute," Kerrigan's voice sounded perplexed. "I just saw that hotel name and street address." He grabbed the pages just delivered by Edwards. On the list from Briggs' apartment was an envelope with the address.

"I've got the same address from Briggs' place, but the name is Sam Brenner. Where'd you get your information?"

"Brenner must be an alias. I drove by early this morning. The place is nice, but there's a vibe that feels wrong. But now, since the same address comes from two sources, it might be enough for a warrant."

"I'll push it," Kerrigan promised. "Thanks. Even if you are holding out on me."

* * *

The Regency Park Hotel was an aging beauty. In its heyday, the 1940s and '50s, it had been one of the two premier hotels in Manzanita. Forty years after it opened, time had not been kind.

A nervous Larry Lester punched 730 into the house phone in the lobby. He was uncomfortable in this environment. Besides, the lobby was crowded for 9:00 a.m. The phone rang several times.

"Seven-three-zero."

"Is Mr. Brewster there?"

"Who is this?"

"Larry Lester. I have information."

"Shut up! Get your sorry butt up here!"

Something was wrong. While Brewster's associates never treated him with anything approaching respect, they had, at least, been civil in the past. He rode the elevator up to the seventh floor, his trepidation rising with each increasing number in the display panel.

One of Brewster's army of associates materialized when the elevator door opened. With sullen efficiency, he frisked Lester who stood unmoved and unmoving. This was SOP.

"Stay with me." The associate escorted Lester down the corridor toward Brewster's suite.

The corridor was as busy as the lobby. Men carrying bags and boxes hurried past.

Entering the bedroom/office of the suite, the informant dodged to avoid a man hefting an oversize box.

"What's going on?" Lester asked.

"Mr. Brewster will tell you what you need to know. He's in the bedroom."

Lester entered the suite where Sidney Brewster was packing a leather attaché case that lay open on the bed. He stood for several seconds waiting for Brewster to acknowledge his presence.

"What information do you have?" Brewster asked without looking up. He continued to place papers and plastic bags into the attaché case.

"I know that Briggs didn't tell the police anything."

"You are positive of this?"

"Yes, sir." Lester had yet to see Brewster's face. It was unsettling.

"That's good to hear," Brewster muttered as he rubbed his chin. "I expected as much." He turned toward the informant and asked, "What did I promise you for the information?"

"Half a C-Note," Lester answered instinctively. There was no temptation to lie. Working for Mamba against this man was the absolute limit of his courage.

"Rick," Brewster called to the man who had escorted Lester.

"Sir?"

"Find Mr. Lester a fifty."

"All we've got left are hundreds, Mr. Brewster."

"Give him one," Brewster directed after the slightest pause. He turned to Lester. "You owe me one piece of information." His tone left no doubt of his expectation.

"Yes, sir."

"I'll call you when I get settled in my new place. The cops have this address."

Lester's heart plummeted as he realized Dancer called his police buddies. He started toward the door of the bedroom.

"That's one question I have for Mr. Briggs," Brewster asked to no one in particular. "I don't know how this suite number got into his apartment."

"You can contact me at my regular number," Lester managed when he could breathe after realizing that the address comment wasn't directed at him.

"Mr. Brewster, we'd better be leaving," Rick said. "It's been over an hour since our man notified us that they were pulling a warrant."

Profanity was Brewster's response. Larry Lester made a silent, unobtrusive exit down the elevator and through the hotel lobby.

* * *

Franklin Stallings fumed the entire drive home after the meeting with Kerrigan, Martinez, and Mamba. He started with the accusations from Kerrigan and Martinez. Next was his disgust of that private detective's involvement in the case. The end result of his fuming was a determination not to return to the division for several days. He knew if he let anger have its way, he'd be looking for a new job.

He was glad he pulled himself together enough by the time he pulled into his driveway to hide most of his angst from Lizbeth. The last thing she needed was more stress.

Today, he'd gone in early. When he saw the report on the unsuccessful raid on Sidney Brewster's hotel suite, he knew what was coming his way. He locked his office and told the Desk Sergeant he was going home sick on his way out.

He arrived home before 7:45 a.m., called in, and officially requested a week of sick leave. It didn't take much acting to pull off the charade since he was sick of the entire situation.

"Honey, are you okay?" Lizbeth Stallings asked when she entered the kitchen and found her husband sitting at the kitchen table with the Yellow Pages open an hour later. The phone, cord fully extended, sat beside it.

"Yeah. No! No, I am not okay."

Lizbeth waited. She knew her husband. She knew when he had something to say he would say it. Until then, she'd let him process his thoughts. She sat down across from him.

"They think I'm the information leak in the department."

"Oh! That can't be true!"

"It's true all right. Whoever's pushing me from the top manipulated circumstances so well that sometimes I wonder if the leak is me. I mean, I still don't know where my copies of the lists are."

She reached across the table and placed her hand on his. A sudden wave of nausea triggered a reflexive jerk of her hand back to cover her mouth. She looked at him through widened eyes.

"Oh, Liz, I'm so sorry." He started around the table.

"No. I'm fine. It's just a false alarm, thank God!"

She reached out and slid the phonebook around so she could read the print. "Tell me why you have the Yellow Pages open to Truck Rentals."

"You know I love you," he said as he sat down.

"Yesss."

"I watch what you go through every other week. I'm just heartbroken each time. When I think of what I'm going through, there's no comparison to what you're handling with courage and grace."

"I think what you're going through is much harder than what I'm going through. I know exactly what the problem is and what to blame for every lost hair, and every other symptom of my cancer."

"I can't argue with that reasoning. I'd give a month's pay to know who the leak is and why I'm being manipulated," Stallings admitted.

"Tell me more about the manipulation. I don't think we've talked about that more than five minutes since you first said something."

"You must be feeling better."

"What? Why do you say that?"

"You want to listen to your paranoid husband rant."

"If I bolt from the room, only I'll know if it's the chemo or your story." She grinned. He rolled his eyes.

"You'll need coffee." He went to the cupboard and pulled two cups from their designated spots. Then he went to the coffeemaker, filled each cup, and returned to the table.

"It's been over a month now. I get a phone call from an electronically altered voice. I'm sure I've heard the unaltered version before, but I can't tell who it is. It gives me a 211 phone number to call and a time limit in which to make the call from a payphone."

"Have you tried tracing the calls?" She asked as she stirred cream into her coffee.

"I ran a hypothetical scenario by our tech people. They say they can't trace a specific number from the 211 service."

Lizbeth took a sip of her coffee.

"What does the caller want?"

"Depends. Most of it is for me to slow the progress of an investigation."

She thought for a moment and took a sip from her coffee cup before asking, "How do you know it's a male?"

"What?"

"You said 'every time he calls.' How do you know it's not a woman?"

"I don't know. But, whether it's a male or a female, they made it clear that I'm supposed to slow the investigation of a list of names this PI named Mamba collected from one of his informants. There are two or three dozen names of drug dealers, suppliers. The voice doesn't want us to get far into the investigation of the names. Every time the caller compromises a raid, it slows the investigation and stops our progress. I think he's the one. I mean it's the one leaking information I'm blamed for leaking."

He took another swig of coffee. When he continued, his words came so quickly that they merged into one long sentence.

"I found a truck and rented it. I'm selling our car and walking to the truck rental place. When I get back, we'll load as much as we can today and tonight. I want us on the road before daylight tomorrow."

"You can't mean we're leaving Manzanita?"

"We have to. I'm sure they'll be suspending me soon. Or arresting me as the information leak. Once that happens, even if I'm cleared, my law enforcement career is over. We'll make a run for it. I've done some preliminary looking at Canada."

"Why rent a truck? We can't take everything in this house. Loading a moving van is something we can't hide."

"I know. We'll leave a lot of the big furniture pieces. But, if we take the bed frame apart and—"

"You're serious about this."

"Never more so."

"What about my chemo?"

"We'll be stopping back home in Ohio. We'll find a doctor there. If we end up in Canada, they have excellent health care."

"I get the idea. It's obvious that you've been planning this for some time."

"More thinking than planning. But, you've been so ill, I just couldn't bring myself to add to your situation."

"Until today."

"You asked."

"What if I hadn't asked?"

"You'd have awakened tomorrow morning in the back of a rental truck on your way out of town."

"Since we are doing this, pick up some storage boxes when you get the truck. I'll sort stuff in the kitchen."

"I love you," he said, kissed her, and headed off.

"I know. I love you, too," she whispered.

Queasiness limited her sorting to a few drawers by the time her husband returned with a smallish moving truck. He said nothing about her lack of follow-through, for which she was grateful. They set about packing and loading the truck.

It took less time to load their things than he expected. When they finished, the house was devoid of all personal items. Only furniture pieces too awkward or heavy for the both of them to load remained.

* * *

"I don't understand, Lieutenant. We hit that address less than two hours after you called for the warrant," Martinez complained. "But when we got there, the place was empty."

"The leak's not through yet," Kerrigan's voice and body sagged. "I don't see how this can keep happening."

"Where's Stallings?" the Latino demanded.

"He couldn't have done it," Kerrigan sighed. "I called it in before seven-thirty this morning. I doubt if he was in the station that early."

"I'll feel better if we check him out."

"I suppose it can't hurt." Kerrigan picked up the phone.

"The front desk says that Stallings came in around seven this morning," Kerrigan mused. "He left for home about seven fifteen. Said he was sick. The Desk Sergeant says he looked like paste."

Martinez muttered something in Spanish, turned and punched the doorjamb. The thunk echoed through the office.

"I apologize, Lieutenant. That was—"

There was a knock at the door.

"Since you're close, get that Martinez."

Janet Cowan leaned forward and glanced in both directions before she hurried past the detective holding the door open.

"I have your copies of yesterday's shift summary reports." She slid a set off the stack she balanced on one arm and handed it to Kerrigan.

"That's quite an armful," Martinez offered, hoping the comment offset whatever thoughts Cowan had when she saw him holding the door open.

"I have ten other deliveries to make, Detective."

"Then you'd better get back at it, Officer Cowan."

"Let me know what you find out about the sergeant," Martinez called over his shoulder as he followed Cowan out of the office. As soon as he cleared the doorway, he turned back to Kerrigan and used both hands to make a gesture universally recognized by the male fraternity as showing an appreciation of a female figure.

Kerrigan shook his head and closed his office door. He started typing reports he had due, but the report on the unsuccessful raid on Brewster's suite kept resurfacing in his mind. He cursed the inventor of the copy machine. He slammed his fist down in a combination of frustration and anger.

"Get me Edwards in Records," he barked into the phone. He drummed his fingers on the desktop as he waited for the Sergeant to answer.

"Records and Copies."

"Eddie?"

"This is Edwards."

"Good. This is Kerrigan. Who else did you give copies of those evidence reports to this morning?"

"Geeze, Lieutenant," Edwards stalled as he thought. "I have to check my delivery list to be sure."

"Do that, Eddie. But, do you know off-hand if Sergeant Stallings got a copy?"

"If he had any reason to get a copy of the evidence lists, then he got them before you this morning. His office is always first on the delivery list. Not that I play favorites. His office is closest to the copy room."

"Thanks," Kerrigan mumbled. He hoped Stallings hadn't received copies of the list. Now, he had to check and see if Edwards was mistaken about the delivery schedule.

He walked to Stallings' office and knocked. There was no answer. He used his master key and entered.

The lists were visible atop a stack of copies near the center of Stallings' cluttered desk.

A dejected Pat Kerrigan returned to his office. He was glad Stallings was ill. At least that postponed the confrontation for a day.

* * *

Stallings knew the department would trace the rental truck. To delay that eventuality, he drove to the first city north of Manzanita. There, they rented a private storage space in Lizbeth's maiden name and unloaded what they'd just loaded. By then, they were exhausted. Against Lizbeth's advice, he drove another hundred miles before turning the truck in.

Their physical exhaustion stretched the night in a Motel 6 into mid-morning. After a fast-food meal, the couple purchased a used car for cash. This time, they used Lizbeth's mother's maiden name as that of the new owner. The salesman asked few questions. They offered no information.

By early evening, they were on I-80 and headed to Nevada. Reno was the target for their next night's lodging.

* * *

Petula turned the water on in the rain shower in her master suite bath. She inhaled sharply when she stepped into the downpour from the shower head. The cold water shocked her body and her brain, clearing her mind and allowing her to restructure her thoughts.

The focus of tonight's thought restructuring was her relationship with Chief Rogers. As she reviewed that relationship, him avoiding eye contact even when no one else was around and leaving his office through his private door at the end of the workday instead of through her office, formally uncommon occurrences were now normal. In her new view of the relationship, they were warning signs that the liaison was eroding.

As the water raining down on her warmed, she admitted that however she and her boss were connected outside of work, it was no longer a relationship.

She smiled a mysterious smile as she reached for her bottle of shampoo.

Chapter 26

Mamba was frustrated. His investigation into the thefts at Anderson Pharmaceuticals stalled. The list of names he pulled from Reed helped, at first. But with the lists out on the street, thanks to the departmental leak, most dealers and suppliers were lying low or had skipped town.

The PI's frustration showed in several ways. He was cranky and saw far more bad in things than good around him. He felt like every light at the end of a tunnel ended up a locomotive headed in his direction.

This morning, his first order of business was to contact Franklin Stallings about what happened during his last meeting with Kerrigan, Martinez, and him. This was not the first attempt at such contact.

"Sergeant Stallings, please."

"I'm sorry. He is still out sick. Could someone else in his department help you?"

"No. It can wait. I'll try tomorrow."

Mamba hung up the phone. Today marked the fifth time he called the division trying to talk to the Sergeant. It was also the fifth day Stallings was out sick. He called Kerrigan to see if he could get Stallings' home number.

"Pat, this is Phil."

"What do you want?"

"Nice to hear your voice, too." When Kerrigan didn't respond, Mamba continued, "I need Franklin Stallings' home number?"

"You know that I can't give out that information."

"Not even considering the leak?"

"I told you before, we're doing this investigation strictly by the book."

"Okay. Can you call him at home for me? I'd like to talk to him. Away from the job."

"I can do that," Kerrigan conceded. "If he wants to talk to you." There was a calculated pause while he decided on a minimalist approach. "You know it doesn't look good for him."

"That's what Martinez told me. He also mentioned something about evidence lists. I'd like to know more about those."

"I'll get back to you."

Fifteen minutes later, Kerrigan called back.

"No answer at Stallings' place."

"I could go and see him," Mamba offered. "If I had the address."

"Come on, Phil. Give me a break."

"What if I guessed it?"

"What?"

"Like twenty questions," Mamba warmed to his own idea. "I could ask if he lives on a street with a plant name. All you have to say is 'yes' or 'no.' That way you'd never tell me the name of the street. You'd be in the clear, departmentally."

"Why do you do this to me?"

"Is it the name of a President?" Mamba asked, ignoring the question.

"Phil!"

"Yes or no."

"Oh, hold on," was the exasperated response. Kerrigan got up, rummaged around, and pulled a folder from his lockable desk drawer. He removed one sheet and checked the part of the departmental list of names and addresses that contained surnames beginning with the letter S.

"No."

"How about between A and D?"

"No."

"E and J?"

"Yes."

"F?"

"Yes. You're so lucky."

"I like to consider it superior reasoning." Phil's voice sounded like the smile on his face. He consulted his city map. "Farnsworth Street?"

"Yeah. But I can't believe your luck." Without the usual courtesies, Kerrigan ended the call. As he pushed back in his desk chair he muttered, "I hope you get in touch with him."

Five minutes later, Mamba's office answering machine was on auto-answer, his office door was locked, and his car was headed to Farnsworth Street. He wasn't about to tell his friend that Farnsworth hadn't been a blind guess.

He turned on Farnsworth and parked close to the corner. He had no plan. He preferred making up a plan as he went along, something he'd never admit.

He stopped at seven houses before he found someone that knew which was the Stallings' house. He returned to his car and pulled up to 3550. He stared at the neat, stucco with brick façade house for a long moment. It looked unoccupied. Folded newspapers littered the driveway. No gap appeared in the drapes covering the front windows.

He stopped on the porch. Lifting the top of the mailbox, he noted the envelopes and mailers filling it. He knocked on the door. The hollow rapping echoed inside the house.

He waited for a few moments and knocked again. Again, no one answered the summons. He went around the side of the house. He peered in the only window without drapery blocking the view.

He saw a single room in its entirety—the kitchen. He craned his neck. His visual path led through a doorway into what might have been the dining room. What he saw was enough to confirm his suspicion. Save for a buffet along one wall, the dining room was empty.

The last place Mamba checked was the detached garage. The lift-up door was padlocked. He looked around to see if any eyes might be on him, then went to the single window in the side of the building. Although it was too high off the ground to see to the garage floor, he could see a black Crown Victoria. Stallings bolted.

"Excuse me," the PI called over the fence to a middle-aged woman removing dead blooms from her roses in her backyard. "Do you know if the Stallings are expected home soon?"

"I think not," she called back. She closed her pruning shears and approached the fence. Lowering her voice, she spoke as though including him in a conspiracy.

"It's very strange," she stage-whispered. "They just up and left three days ago. No, it must be four days now. He came home with a truck. When I looked again, they were gone!"

"Did they say where they were going?"

"They most certainly did not!" Indignation dripped from the words. "And I thought I was their friend. Why are you asking all these questions?"

Mamba didn't want to say he was working with the police. This woman must know Stallings was a cop and would expect the police to know where their employees were.

"I'm with the Census Bureau." He reached for his notebook. "I have one question that you can help me with."

"I'll do anything I can to help."

"Thank you. Could you tell if the truck was a rental?"

"I would think so. She drove a compact car. He drove a big black car most of the time."

"Oh, yes. I have that in my records. Do you remember any markings on the truck?"

"No," she started, stopped, and added, "I'm not a busybody, you know."

"Oh, I don't think that. I was just asking because you've shown yourself to be an outstanding observer," was Dancer's verbally choreographed answer.

"I think there might have been yellow or orange paint," the woman rephrased her previous answer, beaming at being considered an outstanding observer.

"Well, thank you, Ma'am. Oh, may I have your name? I like to verify my information sources."

The woman promptly and proudly answered and then spelled her name. Mamba dutifully made one dot in his notebook for each letter she provided. When she finished, he snapped his notebook closed.

"Thanks, again. You've been a tremendous help."

He glanced back as he headed for his car. The woman had cornered her neighbor on the other side of her house. He wondered what tale she was spinning.

The drive to the division station was uneventful. Mamba spent most of the trip trying to place himself in Stallings' shoes. Even with his often-overactive imagination, he couldn't imagine a scenario where he'd run like that.

His steps slowed as he walked across the parking lot at the station. He had bad news for Lieutenant Kerrigan and was in no hurry to deliver it.

When he got to Kerrigan's office, he opened the door without knocking. As the Lieutenant gave him a "you've got a lot of nerve" stare, Mamba spilled his bucket of information.

"Stallings has flown the coop."

"What?"

"His house is empty, at least there's not much furniture inside. A neighbor saw them loading a rental truck. I've called truck companies and found the one I suspect Stallings used. It should be easy for the department to find out where that truck is now."

"You think they're still running?"

"Most likely." He couldn't believe that Stallings, whether or not he was the leak, was dumb enough to leave town in a rented truck and not expect to Manzanita Police Department to find him within a short time.

"I'll put out an APB on the truck after I verify the rental," Kerrigan decided as his mind raced. "And another on his car, too. And, it's time to involve Internal Affairs in this mess."

"You need to send a car to Stallings house. Make sure they have bolt cutters. His g-ride's in his garage."

"At least he not up for grand theft auto," Kerrigan mumbled as he pulled his phone off the base.

Mamba sat in silence as he watched and listened while Kerrigan made a series of calls. At the end of the phone session, all state law enforcement agencies knew of the BOLO on the rental truck and Stallings' personal vehicle.

The PI didn't feel relieved.

* * *

"It's been a while," Petula Jacobs said upon hearing the voice of her current caller. "I was afraid I'd offended you in some way."

"That, Officer Jacobs, is something you have reason to fear," was Guillermo Arcenas' response.

"What do you want?"

"That's better. What is bothering your boss?"

"I don't—" She cut herself off. After performing a mental berating, she resumed her answer. "What makes you think something's wrong?"

"You are quite good at that, you know."

"I'm afraid you have me at a disadvantage," she lied.

"If you say so." Arcenas paused long enough to let Petula know he was aware of her deceit. He continued, "Two items for your boss."

"Should I be writing these down?"

"Don't get too cheeky. Remember, you serve at my discretion."

Jacobs fumed in silence.

"Again, that's better. First, tell Chief Rogers that I am pleased with his handling of Sergeant Stallings. He has removed himself from involvement in any cases. I was wondering if you know where he is."

She straightened in her chair. She thought the man was on sick leave.

"Because I'm in a good mood, I'll take your silence as a no. Second, tell Chief Rogers that I am not happy that Stallings has removed himself from the case he is supposed to be working to my advantage."

"Those two contradict each other."

"I hope you're able to resolve that issue before you report our conversation to your boss."

* * *

The Internal Affairs Division, IAD, of the Manzanita Police Department was not much different from their counterpart in any police department. Some officers assigned to the division were seriously anal, compulsive, rule-following social misfits that felt everyone was out to get them. Others were former, or current loose cannons relegated to the IAD to limit their contact with the public. Most IAD members considered their job essential in maintaining public trust in the local law enforcement agency.

Regardless of the reason for their placement in IAD, once entrenched, many officers morphed to fit the stereotype: arrogant, disliked imposers of seemingly arbitrary rules and regulations. Most line officers saw them as spawns of evil, or snitches, often shunned by those outside their division.

At least that was the opinion of those under scrutiny by IAD.

Senior IAD Officer Luke Hargrove glared at the rookie who placed the Stallings case file on his desk. He did not need more work.

"That'll be all!" Hargrove dismissed the delivery officer.

IAD's temporary lead officer for four months, the Chief's office informed Hargrove that a new Sergeant was pending appointment, weekly. He wondered how long would be before the department brought the staff in Internal Affairs back to full strength.

He picked up the folder just delivered, held it aloft, and called to the plainclothes officer sitting across the room from him, "We've got another one."

Officer April Desantos sighed. She walked over and took the Stallings folder from Hargrove.

"What do you want me to do with it?"

"Put it in the pending file cabinet. We'll get to it when we can."

Desantos forced a smile and stuck the file in the third drawer after highlighting the last name of the cover. She knew what pending meant.

The pending file cabinet in this division was always overflowing. Stallings' file would rest there until someone got around to investigating whatever the offense was. That could be a considerable length of time. With only Desantos, Freeman, and Hargrove, the Internal Affairs Division hovered near half-staffing.

Current investigations involving IAD included two firefights, an alleged rape of a female suspect in a holding cell by her guard, and a charge of sexual harassment by one member of the department against another. Pending files were of similar diversity and significantly larger in number.

Whatever the new folder held, it would have to wait until they reduced the backlog, unless someone higher up assigned another officer to the unit. Hargrove knew the chances of getting a volunteer added to this crew was were slim. Few officers looked upon duty with Internal Affairs as a plum assignment.

Hargrove reopened the active file folder on his desk.

* * *

In what some might consider cosmic karma, Phil Mamba brought Hope home the day after he learned of Stallings' surreptitious exit from Manzanita. Their reunion at the airport was minimal, thanks to the crowds and Jimmy's loudly repeated declaration that he wanted to go home.

Chapter 27

Erin Reilly, orthopedic nurse, pulled her stethoscope from her locker. She listened to the banter going on around her with mixed interest as she sanitized and hung the device around her neck. Just returned from a week's vacation, was still on vacation time, and was running behind her normal morning schedule.

"I tell you, last night was steeem-eee," one of her colleagues reported. She and her husband were trying to get pregnant. After eight months without success, she announced earlier in the week she'd rented some videotapes to spice things up.

"I figure more estrogen, testosterone, and adrenaline might be just the ticket!"

Erin moved into the break room that housed a small refrigerator with as much mold as cold inside. Also present was a microwave oven, the interior of which had food splatter burned into the plastic. The final appliance was a coffeemaker. Its carafe displayed the most disgusting stain patterns she'd ever seen. She never understood how nurses could let their break room become a Petri dish.

As she cleared the doorway from the locker room to the lounge, Erin found the concept of dating, pro and con, who was and who wasn't, was still on the table. The assault began as soon as the nurses spotted her.

"Reilly, welcome back. What's your position on dating?" the charge nurse called. Snickers, twitters, and full-on laughter greeted the innuendo-filled question.

"I'm in favor," Erin answered, choosing to take the conversational high road.

"If you're for it, then why don't you do more of it?"

"I date. A lot."

"Yeah, right. And I never ate a whole box of chocolates in one day," a third nurse chimed in.

More laughter.

"When's the last time you went on a date?" The charge nurse asked. Before Erin could answer, she qualified her question. "A real date, not 'I talked to a guy in a bar.'"

"Recently!" she shot back.

"When?"

"That doesn't matter," she pushed past the actual question. "For your information, I just might have something going on tonight."

At that point, seven nurses turned away after rolling their eyes or with waves of dismissal. They moved out into the hallway. It was time for work. Nurse Reilly's fantasies could wait.

"Well, I could have a date tonight. If I wanted to," Erin muttered to herself in the now empty, save her, nurses' lounge. She adjusted her name badge, tugged on the hem of her scrubs top, poured a cup of who knew how old coffee, and headed out in the direction taken by the others. She had a debriefing at the central nurses' station on the floor to attend.

She was almost late already.

* * *

Enciso Martinez pulled his motorcycle into a quasi-parking space in the Memorial General Hospital visitor lot. His stream-of-consciousness recall began with appreciation for his bike. It continued as he walked down the stairs of the parking structure and into the main building.

Included were recollections of Briggs' collar and how hard it was for him to control his urge to injure the hitman for shooting Flatly. He finished by recounting reasons the boxer was more a man than Briggs would ever be.

"Allow me, señorita." The detective interrupted his thoughts to hold the automatic door open for an elderly woman. She smiled her gratitude. He removed his bandana as she passed through pushing her walker. She smiled.

"Oh, my. I'd have to be fifty years younger to be anybody's senorita."

"You don't look a day over—"

"Watch out, young man. You could get yourself into trouble with some women if you go around guessing ages."

"Sí. You sound like you're young at heart."

"Oh. I like that. You be careful now." She shuffled away through the lobby.

After a stop at the reception/information kiosk, Martinez headed to the bank of elevators. He needed to get to the fifth floor and had no desire to climb that many stairs.

When he pushed the UP button for the ninth time he decided that the elevators in Memorial General Hospital were as slow as in every other hospital. The cynic in him was certain that in order for one of the two elevators in every side-by-side pair to go up, the other must be full and on its way down. He smiled a wry smile as he pictured a single pulley between the tops of both elevator shafts. He was still smiling when the elevator doors opened.

A young woman in hospital scrubs barreled out of the open doors and rammed headlong into the giant.

She glanced at him.

He held her gaze.

She looked down.

"Hold on, Chica Bonita," Martinez whooped as his huge hands deflected the young woman's course.

"Excuse me," the nurse apologized. "I'm running late. But, that's no excuse for running into you."

"That's not a problem." Martinez's teeth flashed his most macho grin. "But, it would be a shame to waste a fortuitous meeting, uh—" He read her plastic nametag and asked, "Erin Reilly, do you have any plans for this evening?"

"I don't think so," she said, hiding her surprise with a hint of attitude. But then, the conversations from earlier in the morning flashed through her mind. "I mean, I can't. I work tonight."

"You work every night?"

"No. I'm off tomorrow. I suppose I might have some time."

"I could pick you up at your place around 6:00 tomorrow evening," Martinez offered. He was on autopilot as he ran through his usual pickup line sequence. With a touch of self-consciousness, he added a hasty afterthought. "If you would like me to."

"I rarely talk to strangers. You know, like my mother told me. And you have me at a disadvantage in that regard."

Martinez's facial expression radiated confusion.

"Let me help you," she said with enough sarcasm to make it unmistakable, but not enough to bite too deep. "You know my name. I don't know yours. Ergo, you are a stranger to me, but I am not a stranger to you."

"Well played, señorita. I am Enciso Martinez. Detective Enciso Martinez, and I am at your service."

"Yeah, right. Let's see a badge, Detective Martinez."

He reached for his shield. His fingers touched his pocket and found it empty.

"I don't have it on me," he mumbled.

"No proof, no date."

"Can you wait here while I go to my motorcycle? I've got some ID there." He followed up with a caveat of his own, "If you're not too busy."

"I can't wait here. I have a job." She stole a quick glance at her watch. "Which I will not have much longer if I don't get going."

"What floor you on?"

"Floor number five, orthopedics."

"Okay. I'll get my ID and bring it to the fifth floor."

"I'm on duty until 8:30 p.m. If you're not back by my lunch, that's four o'clock, don't bother climbing all those steps to floor five."

Before he could respond, she sauntered off.

He returned to his bike and did a quick visual scan for eyes looking in his direction. Satisfied he was unobserved, he retrieved the copy of his ID hidden inside the gas cap. It smelled terrible. He pulled a latex glove from his pocket and stuffed the ID inside it, hoping to trap the gasoline fumes.

It didn't take long for Erin to finish her business on the first floor. Heading for the elevator, a thought occurred. She would check out Martinez. If he was a cop, which she doubted, no harm done. If he wasn't a cop, the police needed to know there was a poser out there.

She returned to the main records library to use the phone. Because of that delay, she missed sharing an elevator ride up to the fifth floor with her potential date for the next evening.

Apparently, the other elevator was full when Martinez pushed the UP elevator button after retrieving his ID. It was less than a minute from the time he entered the elevator until he exited on the fifth floor. After his ingrained visual surveillance sweep, he followed the wall signs to room 550. The door stood open. Flatly Broke lay sleeping on the nearest of two beds.

Martinez looked down on the ex-boxer and was amazed how small the man was. He acted bigger than he was without being overbearing. He was one of the nicest men he'd ever known.

The Latino sat down in a visitor's chair to wait. A hospital veteran, as both patient and visitor, he knew visiting hours were the only time the hospital staff left you alone long enough to sleep uninterrupted. Between pills, blood pressure checks, doctors' rounds, and persistent nurses, nights were more challenging than afternoons to find the elusive, restorative sleep. He usually tried to use his police ID to visit during off hours. This was his only window today.

He picked up a book from the table next to the bed. The half-naked form of a voluptuous brunette graced the front of a torrid sex novel thinly disguised as a detective story. He flipped through the obviously unread pages wondering why a man of such limited literacy as Flatly would have any book. A second look at the cover as he closed the book answered the question for him.

Movement attracted his attention. Flatly's left arm flopped off the bed. As Martinez gently replaced it on the mattress, he noticed the plastic nametag that encircled the man's wrist. "Waldo Winston Wiggins" was the name typed on the paper lining of the plastic tag. The detective shook his head. No wonder the man didn't mind being called Flatly Broke.

"That you, Cue Ball?" a raspy voice called in a hoarse whisper.

"Sí, amigo."

"Could I have a little water?"

"No problem." He poured a cup full from the plastic pitcher sitting on the table and pushed the button that elevated the head of the bed. Flatly took the cup from him and swallowed most of the contents in two gulps.

"Thanks, man." He handed the cup back. "You're here almost every day. How come?"

"You're my friend, mi amigo. A man visits his amigos when they're hurting."

"Dancer's the only other person visits me." Flatly's voice held no emotion. He was stating a fact.

"Your other friends just haven't gotten around here yet."

"Nah." He shrugged and winced at the effort. "They don't care 'bout me like you guys."

Phil Mamba walked in.

"Good to see you, Gumshoe," Martinez greeted him. "We were just talking."

"I won't be long," Mamba said ignoring the old movie descriptor of those in his profession. It was a descriptor he tolerated more than appreciated. He removed a tape recorder from the paper bag under his arm. He placed the machine on the edge of the bed.

"Remember, just push this button." He touched the device. "It'll play for forty-five minutes. Then, have the nurse turn the cassette over. It's all on these two tapes." He removed another steamy novel and a second cassette from the bag. He placed them on the bed next to the recorder.

"There's another book on that table, Dancer," Flatly's face beamed as he nodded toward the novel that Martinez examined. Mamba nudged the giant who handed the book to the detective.

Flatly pushed the play button. Mamba's voice poured from the speaker.

"The wind whipped through the trees and ripped at the fabric of Jocelyn's skimpy dress."

"Let's go," Mamba whispered.

"But I just got here."

"Just come along. He's in his zone now."

"Okay. Bye, Flatly," Martinez called as he followed Mamba.

There was no response from the man on the bed. The sounds from the tape recorder carried him to a different place.

"He can't read," Mamba explained once they cleared the doorway. "I read the books he chooses into the tape recorder. He plays them back."

"Amigo." Martinez's vast right arm half-surrounded the man beside him. With more than a hint of sentiment, he added, "You are one gringo that's familia in my book."

"Thanks," he grunted as he worked free of Martinez's vice-like side hug. "You headed down?"

Before Martinez could answer, he caught sight of Erin Reilly at the nurses' station.

"Not right now. I've got another stop to make."

"Okay. See you around."

While Mamba made his way to the elevator, Martinez headed towards the nurses' station. The closer he got, the slower he walked.

Before he could think himself into aborting the mission, Nurse Reilly turned around. She spotted the Latino and fixed him with an ambiguous stare.

"Hola, Nurse Reilly."

"Hello, yourself," Erin answered. She decided to give the nosy-Nellie nurses on her floor something to remember.

"I have my," Martinez started to explain after he pulled the smelly latex glove from his pocket. Erin cut him off.

"I know you're a cop."

"What? Why? You didn't believe me downstairs."

"I called the main police number. The operator must have looked you up because she transferred me to the Northeastern Division. Seems you really are a cop, even though you look more like a cross between a biker and a heavy metal band member."

"Interesting visual. Who vouched for me?"

"Officer Cowan. At least I think that's her name."

"Cowan? How'd you get hold of her?"

"She answered the transferred call. Let me see if I can remember how it went." She folded her right hand into the universal representation of a telephone handset.

What he observed was a one-woman reenactment of Erin's conversation with Officer Cowan.

"Ring."

"Northeast Division, Officer Cowan speaking," Erin said in a brusque tone.

"My name is Erin Reilly. I'm a nurse at Memorial General. I'd like to know if a man named Enciso Martinez works there."

"Oh, my, yes," she breathed. "He is a very special detective."

"That's enough. If that's the way you play, your game's gonna be solitaire. I can't believe you checked on me before you gave me a chance." He pivoted on his heel and started away from the nurses' station.

"Officer, wait!"

Martinez didn't break stride.

"Please."

The Latino stopped, but he did not turn back.

"Can we go to the family waiting area and talk?"

The big man remained stationary.

"I'm so terribly sorry. Please, I'd like a chance to explain."

He shrugged.

"You'll need to see where I go to follow me."

He turned as slowly as he could. What he saw when he faced her made him rethink his intended action. She was visibly upset. He decided to cut her some slack.

"I'm on my break," Erin called back to the nurses' station as she walked away from Martinez and continued down the hallway. He followed at a distance, until he heard the catty comments from the other nurses.

"Actually, I have that effect on a great number of women," he announced in a suave, man-of-the-world voice after turning back to face to the nosey nurses. He enjoyed the embarrassed looks on the women's faces. Silence reigned at the nurses' station. Martinez flashed his biggest smile before he took two steps backwards while facing the women then turned and resumed following Nurse Riley.

Once inside the smallish room, Erin stopped. She stood motionless while deciding she would thank him for squelching her colleagues after she apologized, then straightened her shoulders and turned around.

"I am beyond embarrassed by the way I told you I checked on you. I have no excuse to offer.

"I'll give you a chance to explain. While I applaud your initiative in checking me out, I expected you to give me a chance to show you my badge before you did anything else. So, if this sounds like a whining, poor little me speech, I never met you." Martinez's voice was as free of inflection as he could manage.

"Deal." She took a deep breath and exhaled. "I don't date much."

"Really?"

"Okay. I deserved that. But, I'd appreciate it if you let me finish before you rake me over any more coals."

He nodded.

"I find it hard to find men who aren't just looking for, um . . ."

"Pleasure."

"That'll work. Because of that, I don't have much to talk about at the morning 'let me tell you about my date/husband' rundown."

He empathized with her. He made a habit to deflect that kind of attention, too. It was possible they had more in common than he wanted to admit. He fine-focused on her monolog.

"First of all, Officer Cowan's only comment about you was that you were employed as a police officer."

By the end of her recitation, the monolog was a dialog, and they settled on a place to meet the next evening for dinner. Both agreed it was just dinner, not a first date.

* * *

There was a path in the carpet in front of the telephone stand in Lester's apartment. He was a fidgety man by nature, but this situation pushed his fidget into uncharted territory. He knew what he should do, what he promised Mamba he would do. Now it was time to do it. But, the evil visage of Sidney Brewster haunted him.

Lester's phone rang. Lester waited. It rang again. He waited again. After the third ring, he answered. The voice on the other end directed him to a location and hung up. Lester placed the handset back in the cradle. After taking a deep breath, he picked the handset up and dialed a number.

"Mamba Investigations. I can't come to the phone right now. Please leave your name and number or message after the tone. BEEP."

Lester disliked answering machines.

"This is one of your employees. You should call me today. It might be too late tomorrow."

He stood by the phone trying to think of another way to contact Dancer.

The phone rang. Again, he waited until the third ring to answer.

"Hello?" the voice on the other end questioned when he did not speak. "Are you there, Lester?"

"Who's this?"

"This is Mamba."

"I have a meeting with my other employer tonight at nine-thirty," was the rapidly delivered admission.

"Fill me in."

"Not on the phone. Let's meet at the deli on the corner by your office."

"Okay. Be there at four-thirty. Don't be late."

"I am a habitually prompt person," was the offended reply. Lester ended the call.

"You took your own sweet time, Larry," Mamba muttered as he hung up the phone. "Unless, you just found out about this meeting."

Mamba had been looking for Brewster for too long. Today's contact with Lester was his first lead. He called the station and got Kerrigan's answering machine.

"Pat, this is Phil. I'll have information on a meeting with Brewster tonight after five."

"That's good news!" Kerrigan's partly out of breath voice broke into the recording. "Sorry, I was just outside in the hallway finishing a conversation. What's your source?"

"Lester."

"I have limited faith in that source."

"He's slippery, I'll give you that. But I trust him as a source. We should have Brewster this time."

"That would be an excellent turn of events. I expect a call when you have the details."

* * *

Mamba knew a lot about Dominic's Deli. Much of his knowledge came from personal experience. The joint was a favorite for those wanting above-average, handmade, oversized sandwiches.

Mamba looked at his watch as he neared the door. It was 4:27. Lester wasn't at any of the sidewalk tables. He stepped through the entrance to the deli and scanned the dine-in area.

Lester sat at one of the few inside tables. He sipped coffee as he watched the door. He waved discretely.

The meeting was brief. Mamba ordered two pastrami sandwiches, both of which left the deli in bags after minimal consumption. While they sat without eating, Lester related the location of his late-night meeting with Sidney Brewster along with the details of Brewster's operation he collected since their last meeting.

After Lester exited the side door of the deli, Mamba placed a call to Kerrigan from the payphone on the sidewalk outside Dominic's. The call finished, Mamba headed home. They'd have to get along without him on this one. He owed Hope that much, and more.

Kerrigan took Mamba's information and jotted down the outline of a plan to bust Brewster's meeting with Lester. He left his office and was glad to see his secretary still at her station.

"Peggy, I know it's after your quitting time, but I need you to run this down to the copy center before you leave. I want Narcotics and Vice to have copies of this. And hurry, please."

"Yes, sir."

After Peggy departed for the copy center with the outline, the Lieutenant placed a call he hated himself for making. He waited for Kate to answer the phone.

"Hello, Kerrigan residence."

"Hi, Kate. It's me."

"Hi, sweetie."

"I hate to tell you this."

Kate sat in stony silence.

"Ooo-kayyy. Um, I don't know when I'll be home tonight. I'm involved in a big bust of the guy who's behind at least two deaths and two attempted murders, including Hope Mamba's."

Despite her best intention, Kate Kerrigan gasped.

"I understand. I don't like it when you go or when you're gone, but I do understand." She abandoned all her plans for amplifying her husband's guilt-trip.

"I love you."

"You'd better, buster. And you'd just as better come back home all in one piece." Tears welled up in her eyes.

"That's a 10-4," Kerrigan responded huskily before he hung up.

Kate stared into space for a minute before she replaced the phone in its cradle. She stared at the device for a long time.

* * *

Lester pulled his borrowed car into the driveway. The house was not what he expected. The exterior design radiated anonymity instead of curb appeal.

When he reached the front porch, he turned and looked around. Every house he saw looked the same as its neighbors. It was no wonder Brewster liked the place. Without an address, it could take a full day to find a specific house.

Lester knocked as instructed. After a quick peek at him through the security hatch, someone allowed him safe entry. He raised his hands for the frisk. The man who performed the task was efficient and quick.

The inside of the house bustled with activity. It reminded Lester of the most recent meeting with Brewster, but amped up.

"This is too short notice!" Brewster was complaining loudly to the man known to Lester only as Rick. "How does he think we can clear out this fast? We're not a moving company."

"Boss?" One of Brewster's minions called as he displayed a dozen pressure sealed baggies.

"Toss those in the fireplace."

"I'm sorry, Mr. Brewster. He said it was the first chance he had to call without fear of being overheard," was Rick's attempt to console his boss.

"For what he earns, there is no excuse for such a compact timeline!"

"Yes, sir."

"What do you want?" Brewster snapped when he spotted Lester.

"You called and set up this meeting, Mr. Brewster."

The front door burst open.

"Manzanita Police! Freeze!" Simultaneous with the announcement, several officers surged into the room, weapons in hand. The time was 9:24 p.m.

By ten o'clock the raid netted six suspects, including Sidney Brewster and Larry Lester. They also documented the relative dearth of evidence in the house.

Officers remarked on the marijuana odor that permeated the room. It didn't take much investigating to track the source of the odor to the fireplace. According to the final notation in Kerrigan's notebook, they doused flaming marijuana with water and bagged the ashes.

* * *

On the morning after the raid on Brewster's house, neither Hope nor Phil Mamba was in a good mood. Much to Phil's displeasure, Kerrigan called Mamba after arriving home the night before. The call awakened Jimmy. That resulted in an entire night of fitful napping and only two hours of sleep for Hope. She told Phil she'd reserve her final judgment on her mood until that night.

"Bye, Hope. I love you," Phil called softly as he left their bedroom. He took great care not to wake Jimmy, who was asleep next to Hope after spending most of the night burrowing between him and her.

"I hate your friends," was the barely audible dour response from Hope before she eased over on her side.

Phil smiled. "Sometimes I'm not so fond of them myself."

The meeting place Kerrigan selected was a restaurant far off the beaten path. It nestled in foothills due east of Manzanita on the road to the closest ski resort. It was a popular weekend breakfast retreat known for fluffy omelets and crispy bacon. Location, ambiance, quantity, and quality of food drew lines of customers from as far as Santa Barbara and Lompoc on weekends and holidays.

Weekdays were a different story. This morning, Mamba and Kerrigan comprised exactly half the clientele.

"I don't know how, Phil," Kerrigan complained to his friend as they ate. "Someone tipped Brewster. I'd swear it."

"It couldn't have been Stallings."

"Probably not."

"Cut the guy some slack, Pat. He has been nowhere near the station in a week."

"Just got these this morning." The Lieutenant shoved two sheets of paper across the desk to his friend.

"What are these?"

"A page from Stallings' personnel file."

"You gave me two pages."

"I know. I am the only person to request copies of his file since they hired him. Like all personnel files, they're kept under lock and key."

Mamba glanced at the documents. "These look like identical copies."

"Take a close look at the highlighted line of text on the second page. According to Personnel, that page is a copy of the other page. If you compare the highlighted line to the same line in the other copy, the type style doesn't quite match. The page without the highlighting has been in and out of Personnel for various reasons."

Mamba scrutinized the sentence on each of the two pages. "I don't see any difference in the type style."

“Neither could I. But the lab techs are positive someone altered this. According to them, there are two sets of depressions from typewriter keys on the back of the original page. That’s the one without the highlights.”

Mamba turned the offending page over. He pulled his fingertip over the back of the page. Then, he tilted the paper hoping to see something when the light hit the page from a steep angle. It looked like there might be more or deeper depressions from the letters in the highlighted line.

He read the first page again and then re-read the second page. Then, he spotted it. The whole sentence was worded differently. The tone in the highlighted page wasn’t accusatory.

“There’s more significant difference than type style in the documents.” When Kerrigan did not respond, the PI asked, “Internal Affairs thinks Stallings did this?”

“Who else? IAD called his last Lieutenant. The text in the part of the file that’s referred to in this sentence was altered, too. If you go to the page referenced in the highlighted sentence, you find that the current wording eliminates the only smudge on his record.”

“What was it? And, why do they think he changed it?”

“What was what?” Kerrigan asked. It was then that Mamba realized his friend had been on autopilot, repeating information he heard like a tape recorder.

“I was asking what something was changed in the file.”

“Oh, sorry. It was a citizen’s complaint.”

Mamba waited.

“Part of a witness’s statement was leaked and got reported in the local paper. Internal Affairs says it supports a pattern of behavior.”

“Sounds like the IAD mantra on this one is, ‘it’s only one step from a cheat to a leak,’” Mamba murmured.

“I missed that.”

“Just thinking out loud. Can I take these with me?”

“You know that answer, Phil.”

“I’m serious. I want to work on this. I’ve got a friend in the hospital because of a departmental leak, and the docs say that friend might lose his arm. Pat, I got him into this.”

“I still have to play by the book on this one,” Kerrigan insisted. “I heard that IAD says they’re on top of the case.”

"I can't guarantee I'll stay off this one," Mamba warned as he slid out of the booth. His friend was hiding something. "This meal's on you."

Outside the diner, he pulled the small notebook from his pocket. After glancing over his shoulder to make sure Kerrigan wasn't watching, he used a stubby pencil to write the name and address of the one reference he memorized from the page in Stallings' file. He had a long-distance phone call to make.

* * *

The arraignment for those rounded up in the bust at Sidney Brewster's last residence was on Monday. Because of the nature of crimes and the reputation of the defendants, the DA secured the courtroom. Uniformed officers restricted access to all but those directly involved.

Brewster's legal team went on the attack. The Assistant District Attorney was ill prepared for the onslaught of motions and writs presented at the arraignment hearing.

Brewster's brag about the abilities of his legal team was not an overstatement. After the presentation of arguments by both sides, despite the evidence collected at the scene and Brewster's sordid history, the court assigned him a bail amount he had no problem covering.

Also assigned by the presiding judge was a preliminary date for his trial. He was back on the street just over ninety hours after his arrest with no intention of appearing in any court on any date.

In keeping with Brewster's reputation for protecting those who were peripheral to his business, they released Lester without requiring bail or setting a trial date. Lester exited the jail as no longer a person of interest.

* * *

With Brewster's trial date set, the Manzanita Police Department pulled security details on Mamba and Kerrigan. It was more peaceful for Hope and Phil Mamba than for quite some time. Nevertheless, Phil was restless.

That worried his wife.

"What's wrong?" Hope asked as they lay beside each other. He remained silent. She paused before asking, "Aren't you glad I'm back?"

"More than you know," he answered with a kiss. "I've got a problem I can't seem to resolve."

"Do I know the case?"

"It's part of your, I mean our, case," he explained. "It's Sergeant Stallings."

"I thought you said he was a good cop."

"He is. At least, I think he is. There are irregularities in his personnel file, and nearly all leaks from the department involved information he had access to."

"Nearly all?"

"Actually, all but the last leak. But that's not what's bothering me."

"That means you have some doubts about his personnel file?"

"Internal Affairs seems to think there are enough irregularities to lead to prosecution."

"Shouldn't they know?"

"I suppose. But, it's too pat. It feels like a frame."

"Or else he is guilty," she responded in the role of devil's advocate.

"I suppose that's possible."

"What do you want to do?" She asked, although she already knew his answer.

"Who said I wanted to do anything?"

"You did when you said it was possible that Stallings was guilty."

"Your clairvoyance is maturing," he said before kissing her again.

"It's more Sherlock Holmes than Nostradamus this time," she admitted. "You are frighteningly predictable in situations like this."

"Ouch!" He grimaced and pulled away from her. "I want to follow up on his references. I want to get to know Franklin Stallings. The only name I could get from the pages of the file I saw in Kerrigan's office was a guy back in Illinois. I called him. Rather, I tried to call him. He's dead."

"How much did they cost?" She asked.

"How much did what cost?"

"The round-trip tickets to Chicago that you bought. The major airport in Illinois is there, right?"

"I love you." He pulled her back to him and kissed her. "We can talk more later."

"I still want to know how much you paid for the tickets," Hope deadpanned as she turned on her side away from him.

* * *

Kerrigan made the trip downtown to the offices of the Internal Affairs Division. He called ahead because he didn't want to wait. He had other meetings later in the morning.

"What've you guys got on the Stallings file?" Kerrigan asked Senior Officer Hargrove.

"Stallings?" Hargrove looked confused. "I don't recall that name."

"We sent the file down here at least two weeks ago."

"I still don't recall that name." He called across the room, "Desantos! Do you have anything on a Stallings?"

"Not that I know of, but I'll check." She rummaged through the active case files. "Nothing here."

"Check the pending cases."

"Sure thing." More rummaging preceded her next response, "Here it is." She held up the requested document.

"What does it mean to be in the pending file?"

"It means, Lieutenant, that I have neither the resources nor the manpower to handle all the cases sent to us. Therefore, the investigation is pending."

"Maybe if you were more— Oh, never mind." Kerrigan started, stopped, then turned and stalked away. He knew it was no use getting into an argument with a self-righteous and condescending IAD officer.

He spent most of his drive back to the Northeastern Division mentally, and occasionally verbally, regaling the IAD's methods and attitude.

Kerrigan stopped in the middle of the hallway where his office was when something dawned on him. He knew for a fact that IAD had nothing on Stallings yet; they'd just admitted it. It appeared that someone else sent the evidence of the discrepancy in the personnel file, knowing Kerrigan would assume it was from IAD.

"You're headed the wrong way, Pat," was the warning from Burglary Auto Theft Division's Lieutenant Cummings as he passed the stationary Kerrigan in the hallway.

Kerrigan's confused look was his only reply.

"Captain's Council." Cummings reminded.

"Oh, no," Kerrigan moaned. "Is it Wednesday already?"

"This time every week."

"Let's get this over ASAP."

"ASAP? Dreamer. Budget is the first agenda item."

Kerrigan closed his eyes and shook his head in misery. There was nothing worse than the Captain's Council on the budget.

"I've got to pick up my notes." Kerrigan made a beeline to his office. He switched gears and mentally reviewed the planned defense of his section's budget request. Stallings dropped off his radar screen.

* * *

In the days following his arraignment, Sid Brewster refused to set up an entire operation in a new location. Instead, he was reviewing what was selling and what was lagging. That would allow him to do two things. First, he would stock only what was selling in his current residence. Second, he would pressure his employees to push the low-sales products, particularly if they had high-profit margins.

As he rummaged through some paperwork, he came across the list of dealers and suppliers he received from his police contact. Rumor had it the Sergeant heading up Narcotics was AWOL. When he mentally combined those developments, it brought him to a decision.

"Get me our police contact on the phone."

"Of course, sir," Rick Elkhart responded. Minutes later, he carried a phone to his boss.

"Edwards is on the line."

"Humph," Brewster mumbled as he accepted the phone. But, he gave a thumb's up to Elkhart for his help.

"I owe you a sincere thank you," Brewster said.

"Oh?"

"Glad you appreciate my gratitude," was the sarcastic rejoinder.

Silence.

Brewster shook his head.

"I want you to know that I appreciate the list of names you got for me. And, thank you for getting Sergeant Stallings out of the way. That showed significant initiative. I like initiative."

"I'm glad to be of service. I'm sorry you had to spend the weekend in a cell after your arrest. I got you the information on the raid as soon as I received it."

"I'm sure the late notice won't happen again."

"I appreciate your confidence in me. And, I'll do everything I can to see you have more advance notice in future warnings. I don't like a short timeline any more than you do."

"That's all. I'm sure you're at least as busy as I am."

Chapter 28

"Get me two disposable assets willing to do one long-term job."

"Any other qualifications, señor Arcenas?"

"Tattoos on at least one. Drug-related tattoos."

"Easy enough."

"Limited ambition and minimal drug use."

"Harder, but doable."

"Hood them and drive to my office. Let me know when you're about 20-minutes away."

The associate nodded.

Arcenas leaned back in his chair and fleshed out the plan in his mind.

* * *

RossAnn Gilroy pulled into the horseshoe-shaped driveway of her 3,500 square foot home in Manzanita's most exclusive neighborhood. She turned off the ignition but left the key in the Accessory position while Willie Nelson and Julio Eglesias crooned the final stanzas of "To All the Girls I've Loved Before."

"In your dreams, guys," she said to the stereo speakers as she pulled her key from the lock cylinder.

Three steps away from her car someone grabbed her from behind. Before she could shout, a hooded figure shoved an ether-soaked washcloth over her nose and mouth

* * *

It was late. Chief Rogers nursed a brandy as he listened to one of his favorite piano concertos on his stereo. It was a relaxing end to a day where it felt like all he accomplished was fire suppression of interdepartmental issues.

He swirled the dregs of the brandy in its crystal snifter. As he drained the glass, his phone rang. He looked at his watch.

It was almost eleven.

"This is Rogers," he said as he brought the handset to his ear.

"You are predictable. You should try new verbiage in your telephone answering protocol. Or, oh, this is a better idea. You might even want an office protocol and a different home protocol."

"What do you want?" Rogers recognized the voice of his administrative assistant. "It's been a while, Pet. Do you miss our nights together?"

"Like a dog misses fleas. But, I digress. Mr. A called again today."

"And I'm finding that out only now because?"

"Because I am your conduit with him. I like that, and I will use this position to maximize what limited influence I have on anything that's going on."

"What's he want now?"

"Nothing. He had a comment and a question. Which would you like first? I'd pick the comment."

"Okay. I'll take the comment for five hundred, Alex."

"Cute. I never figured you for a *Jeopardy* kind of person. Maybe *The Price Is Right*, but not a game that requires organized thinking."

"Just give me the information." Rogers tired of their banter much as he had tired of his libido-driven companionship with her.

"The comment— Wait. Let me read it. I wrote it down." Rogers heard the rustling sound of paper being unfolded and smoothed.

"Ah. Here it is. Quote: I applaud you for setting up the Narcotics Sergeant and removing him from the cases involving Garmel. And, here's the question: How much longer do I have to wait for the removal of Garmel's errand boy?"

"Anything else?"

"Nope," she answered.

"I guess it's good night then."

* * *

"I told you she wouldn't have tattoos."

RossAnn shook the fog out of her brain while trying to determine how the voice knew that about her.

"That's one for you. She looks sexier on TV and in the paper than she does sitting here."

"Yeah, she's got skinny thighs."

The hooded males holding her captive laughed between catcalls and comments about other body parts. RossAnn flinched again when she looked down and saw a bra and panties and not the Armani outfit she'd been wearing when the men abducted her as she got out of her car in her driveway.

As the public image for Nancy Reagan's "Just Say No," anti-drug campaign in Manzanita, she was used to catcalls and worse. This was different. This pair removed the public trappings from her persona.

RossAnn was certain that the timing of her abduction was not accidental. Monday, kickoff assemblies in all public schools marked the start of "Just Say No" week. They booked her at an assembly at each school over the course of the week.

"You're so tough, aren't you?" The question came out sounding like sandpaper on wood. She tried to swallow but couldn't. "I need water."

"You hear something?"

"Sounded like the voice of someone in no position to make judgments about us or demand anything from us. Not only that, she's tied to a chair," the gray-hooded man paused. He walked behind the chair and flipped the elastic band on her panties back. "Maidenform panties," he paused again, and pulled her bra away from her back. "And a Janet Reger bra."

She twisted as far as she could in the rope restraints that held her wrists against the plastic-covered chair arms.

"I thought you said she had money?"

"She does," Gray-hood answered.

"Then why's she wearing somebody else's underwear?"

More raucous laughter reinforced that RossAnn was not in control of her situation. She was a woman of influence. Touted as the first homegrown power figure in years by local media, she made her fame, and her considerable fortune, as an advocate for women's rights and a time and money supporter of anti-drug use campaigns.

She asked again for water, this time using please in her request. The men ignored her.

"I'm hungry," the man in a blue-striped hood announced.

"I could eat," Gray-hood agreed. "But, what I really want is a glass of water."

"No problem." Stripe-hood left the room.

"What do you want?" RossAnn rasped for what seemed to her like the one-thousandth time.

Gray-hood looked right through her, stood up, stretched and sat back down. The simple move reminded her she had no control, no power.

"Hey, look what I found."

Gray turned and watched Stripe's return.

"Here's your water." The kidnappers sloppily passed a glass between them. At least a third of the water in the glass sloshed onto Gray's hand and the floor. He shook his wet hand. Droplets landed on RossAnn's naked knees before the man drained the remaining water from the glass in a series of noisy swallows.

"That hits the spot." Gray smacked his lips. "What'd you find?"

"You know how this place used to be a barber shop?"

"Yeah?"

"Ta-da!" Stripe held an electric hair clipper aloft.

"Nice. Do they work?"

"I didn't check." Stripe walked behind RossAnn and plugged the device into a wall outlet. The sound of an electric hair clipper filled the room. "Sounds good. Too bad I got my hair cut last week."

Gray rubbed his hand through his medium-length hair.

"I'm good."

"She has a lot of hair. Maybe we should give her a haircut!"

"Don't you dare!"

"Did you hear that noise again?" Stripe asked.

"I did. Sounded like someone just dared us to cut her hair."

RossAnn felt an ice-cold ball of fear form in her abdomen and radiate through her body. She was shivering within seconds.

"Please, don't cut my hair." The words were quiet. Articulate.

"I just heard 'cut my hair.' Did you?"

"That's what I heard," Gray confirmed. "It must be a sign."

The men's laughter was loud and long.

RossAnn's shivering kicked into overdrive.

"This haircut's gonna be uneven if she doesn't stop shaking."

"No! Oh, please, don't cut my hair!"

"Ya know, I've had hundreds of haircuts. It always grows back." Stripe motioned for his partner to join him. "You hold the head. I'll cut the hair."

He clicked on the trimmer.

She turned her head when the humming began.

"Look. She wants to start on this side."

He swiped randomly at the hair closest to him.

"Can I help?"

"You're holding her head. And you're not going a great job with that. How are you going to help me cut?"

"I was thinking I could grab her hair. Like this." Gray used his left hand to grab a sizeable lock of RossAnn's hair. "Start where it's sticking out the bottom of my fist."

Stripe grabbed the end of the hair sticking out of Gray's fist and obliged his partner. He held the hair in front of her face while he admired his handiwork.

Defeat overwhelmed the socialite. Her head dropped as close to her chest as it could with a hank of hair being held by Gray. "Not bad. Grab another handful."

The men repeated their grab, cut, hold, and show routine a dozen times.

"I wonder if she'll like this style." Stripe left the room and returned with a hand mirror. He held it in front of her face.

She closed her eyes.

Gray smacked the back of her head.

She moaned, opened her eyes, looked in the mirror, and abandoned all hope.

The men continued grabbing what hair they could and jerking her head from side to side and back and forth. After twenty-minutes, Gray grabbed her by her ears while the faux barber ran the trimmer along her scalp.

They swept the floor and emptied the trashcan.

Gray made a bathroom run and came back with a small pan of cold water, a can of shaving cream, and a safety razor. He shaved RossAnn's head. She sat stone-faced through the ordeal.

After wiping the excess shaving cream off with a towel, Gray splashed after-shave lotion on his hands and rubbed it on her scalp. Every nick caused by the barbaric shearing sent a pain message to RossAnn's brain.

Chapter 29

The sun began its push to crest the mountaintops to the east of Manzanita. The sky was clear with a slight tint of red. It had the makings of a hot September day. Enciso Martinez was unaware of any of the beauty or grandeur of the early morning. At least he wasn't until the first ring of his telephone punched the sleep out of his brain.

He delayed picking up the handset. Weeks of undercover work left him uncertain of his persona at any given day and time.

Another ring shook the sleep residue from his mind. He relaxed when he remembered his vow to stop his undercover work.

It took still another ring to coax him to yank the handset off the base of the phone that housed the offending ringer.

"Yeah." He rubbed his eyes and tried to focus on the digital readout of his clock radio. As the seconds passed, the numbers lost their feathery outline and could be seen with painful clarity. It was 5:07 a.m.

He heard a voice but no distinct words.

"This better be good," he growled as he slapped the telephone handset against his ear. "Do you know what time it is? Whoever you are."

"Martinez, this is Phil Mamba. I know it's early, but my flight leaves at seven forty-five, so I've got to get moving."

"It's not early; it's too early. I'm not your travel agent or your chauffeur," the Latino grumbled. "If telling me your travel arrangements is the only reason for this call, I can think of many, many ways to repay you."

"I have a favor to ask before I leave."

"What kind of favor?"

"Well, I'm hitting the road to try and find Stallings. The Department doesn't seem to be in a big hurry, so I'm going to see what I can uncover."

"So far, I hear no reason for you to wake me up or for me to help you. Stallings is the leak." The voice was hard and even.

"I don't think that's the case," Mamba paused. When Martinez didn't respond, he added, "I need you to read to Flatly."

"What?"

"I promised Flatly I would read to him as long as he was in the hospital. I can't record while I'm out of town."

"Wait! That's it?"

"Umm, yeah."

"I'll do the reading. Just hang up and let me sleep, amigo," the Latino growled.

"Thanks. I owe you." Mamba ended the call as requested.

Contrary to what he said about sleep, the undercover man lay in his bed staring at the ceiling for quite a while considering Mamba's comments. The PI was going to look for Stallings. Stallings needed finding. That would plug the departmental leak.

However, his wish for Mamba's success was not completely sincere. If Stallings was the leak, he had hoped to be the one that found him. He tossed and turned physically while his mind tossed and turned scenarios.

When he finally rolled out of bed that morning, he knew that there were two extraordinary things that he had to do. First was to stop by the hospital and see what literary masterpiece the ex-boxer chose for his next book on tape. The second was to buy a tape recorder.

* * *

Six members of Manzanita Police Department's seven-member Leadership Team sat in an unusual venue. Chief Rogers called an emergency session. Each member received a phone call before 6:00 a.m.

Deputy Chief Chalmers stood.

"Thank you for coming on short notice. I know you all have full agendas today. Chief Rogers wants to keep this brief, so I'll prime the pump for him."

"Thank you, Deputy Chief." Rogers pulled the door shut behind him. "I will be brief. RossAnn Gilroy was apparently kidnapped late last night. Her car was found in a ditch south of the 101 and South Fountain Valley interchange. There are no leads. Uniformed officers are canvasing her neighborhood asking about abnormal activity."

"Has the family been contacted by the kidnappers?"

"Not yet. It's early for that, so we're tapping their phones hoping to trace the call when it's made." The Chief paused. "I know we all hope for the best. I've got a televised briefing on this in," he looked at his watch, "eleven minutes. That's all. Dismissed."

* * *

"Rest assured that Manzanita Police Department is not treating this as a random abduction," Chief Rogers delivered his penultimate sentence with a steely stare into the camera lens. "We will solve this crime and return RossAnn Gilroy to her family and the community she loves."

The teleprompter faded to black. That was fitting. Rogers' mood mirrored the teleprompter's color.

* * *

Mamba's flight from Los Angeles to Chicago was routine. The landing in Chicago was smooth; the taxi time to the gate took forever; the wait to disembark longer than he expected; and, there was a long line at the car rental booth. By the time Mamba pulled away in his rental car, he was already tired of traveling. He was glad Hope booked a hotel room close to the airport.

He woke up refreshed and ready to go. The wind off Lake Michigan was as bad as Mamba heard it was. As he eased the rental car into the traffic on Lake Shore Drive, he was forced to make sporadic corrections in his steering to keep the vehicle in his lane. Familiar with Southern California's Santa Ana winds, he wondered how long it took the natives to get used to the gusting winds he now experienced.

He drifted into the wrong lane, and hoped his hand signal to the driver of the car he almost hit was taken as an apology. Minutes later, a car on the lake side of his car swerved into his path, and he concluded you never got used to freakish wind gusts no matter where you lived.

In the end, he found his way to the interstate without mishap, but he missed his Indiana exit. He looped off the freeway and backtracked almost five miles to Gilman where he turned east on US-24.

The non-bustling city of Illiana was his first stop. It was where Franklin Stallings began his career in law enforcement as a member of the Illiana Police Department.

While he waited for the town stoplight to change, Mamba couldn't help but think of Mayberry. He sort of expected to see the sheriff and his inept deputy pull up in a patrol car any minute.

The light changed.

He drove half a block to a large brick building where the words City Hall were chiseled in the granite facade above the doorway.

In spite of his general impression of Illiana, he knew he needed a credible cover story to get a look at Stallings' personnel file. Even a borderline incompetent personnel director would have second thoughts about showing a complete stranger a police officer's file without verifying his credentials. He decided to see how far the minimal clout his PI license had in Manzanita, California, would take him in Illiana, Indiana.

"Hi, Hope. It's Phil," he said into the handset inside the one phone booth outside City Hall.

"I figured as much, since only you and I know this phone line exists. Is everything okay?"

"Can't a guy call his wife without having a problem?"

The line was silent for a moment.

"Hope?"

"After thinking about your question, I suppose a man might call his wife in the daytime on his private line if there wasn't a problem. Yet, for some reason, I suspect that's not the case this time."

He could see her smiling in his mind.

"If all goes well, I don't need you to do anything. But, if you get a call on this line in the next half-hour or so, please answer the phone with 'Private Investigator's Regulatory Bureau. This is Ms. Stapleton.'"

"Hold on. I'll write that down. Do I want to know why I'm doing this?"

"Probably not. When asked about hiring currently active law enforcement personnel as assistant private investigators, please tell the caller that your agency requires the private investigator doing the hiring to submit a written report on the officer's personnel files as far back as he can track them."

"Is this illegal?"

"Well, not technically. I'm pretty sure it won't land us in jail."

"That's nice to know," Hope said without the faintest hint of enthusiasm. "What kind of information do you need to file with my agency?"

"Huh?"

"You heard me. Ms. Stapleton is never going to take the word of a man who'd do something that's on thin ice, legally-speaking, as this is. What will you bring back as proof of completion of the requirement?"

"Nice save. I hadn't even thought of that." After a brief silence, he asked, "Can you type up a fake form?"

"Of course."

"Well, since you had this brilliant idea, if you get called, I'll say I left the form in my office and ask you to fax a copy to Illiana. It's the first town on the Indiana side of the Illinois-Indiana border."

"I'll need ten minutes to make a form that might fool someone." She added another loaded question. "Why did you get computers for the office?"

"Well, that's random. Why do you ask?"

"Just answer, please."

"I know I've told you this before, but it's to reduce paperwork in the office."

"You do realize that all the paperwork you think you're reducing is now stored in a stack of floppy disks, right?"

"Okaaay. Is there a point here?"

"I guess not." Knowing she'd lost that round of give and take, she continued, "Unless it's this: without the computer, I wouldn't be able to make a fake form that would fool anyone. Not in ten minutes, or even in an hour and ten minutes."

"You're welcome."

"If you look into the phone handset, can you see my tongue sticking out at you right now?"

"No."

"That's a real shame. You deserve it."

"If you say so, and thanks! I love you."

"So that's the real reason that you called?"

"Huh?"

"Wow! 'Huh' twice in one conversation. Get some coffee before you go in."

Mamba laughed as he hung up the phone and decided that coffee wasn't a bad idea. He surveyed the square where he'd parked and spotted a coffee shop half a block east of City Hall. He headed in that direction.

After a cup of coffee and a donut, he retraced his steps to City Hall.

Once inside the building, he encountered an atmosphere quite different than the quaint, stuck in the past impression he first formed of the city. Chrome on the modern furniture in the lobby glistened. The receptionist looked up from her PBX board and smiled the first part of her greeting.

"Hello," she called. "May I help you?"

"I was hoping to speak to someone in the police department."

"Oh, my! Is it an emergency?"

"It's a personnel matter."

The young woman visibly relaxed and pulled a laminated map of the building from the top drawer of her desk. "We're right here," she said as she pointed to a red "X" in the lobby. "The police personnel office is upstairs and down this hall." She traced the route with her finger. "Room 225. 'Personnel' is written on the door, too."

"Thanks," Mamba told her. "You're most efficient."

"Thank you, sir," she replied. "I like working here. Good luck up at personnel. But, I don't think they're hiring right now."

"I'm looking up a friend who worked here once."

"Oh. Has he been gone long?"

"No, not too long."

"I'm glad. Some of our older records are being converted to microfiche. You won't be able to see those."

"I hope his is still available. Thank you." He started toward the door marked Stairs. "I was wondering if you could direct me to a restroom. I drove here from Chicago."

The receptionist demonstrated her efficiency in giving directions, even without a map.

"Good luck," the woman called after him.

The civilian clerk in the personnel office was far more cautious than the receptionist.

"My name is Phil Mamba. I'm a private investigator from California. I'd like to see the personnel file of one of your former officers. His name is Franklin Stallings."

"I cannot allow just anyone to see a personnel file."

"This one's not an active file. Officer Stallings hasn't worked here for at least four years."

"I'm sure that's beside the point."

"I understand. I need to see Stallings' file because I'm hoping to hire him part time at my business, Mamba Investigations." Mamba pulled out his wallet, removed his private investigator's license, and gave it to the woman along with a business card.

The clerk scrutinized the identification but said nothing. She returned his license. He slid it back into his jacket pocket.

"I'd really appreciate this. The regulatory agency for private investigators is very clear on the process we have to use when vetting an associate. It's because we're licensed."

To add substance to his ruse, he added, "I've got the regulatory agency's number if you'd like to call and verify."

"I believe I would," she said.

"Okay. Let me get that number. I don't call it that often." He reached into his shirt pocket and pulled out his notebook. Feigning to read what was allegedly written there, he gave the clerk his private office number.

She jotted down the digits as he read and then dialed the number. Mamba relaxed, Hope was his trump card.

"Private Investigator's Regulatory Bureau. This is Ms. Stapleton. How may I help you?" Hope started right on script.

"Good morning. I'm calling from the Illiana Police Department. A—" The clerk picked up Mamba's business card and read the information. "Philip R. Mamba from Mamba Investigations says he has to see the personnel file of one of our former officers before he can hire him. Is this standard procedure?"

"It is. But, before we go any further, I'll need to verify that you have this. I'm sorry, what did you say the name was?"

"Mamba." She spelled the name. "First name Philip."

"Have you seen his private investigator's license?"

"I have."

"Please give me his license number."

"They need your investigator's license number," the receptionist said to Phil after she covered the mouthpiece of the phone with one hand.

He raised his eyebrows in surprise. That wasn't in the plan. But, he handed his license back to the woman. She read the license number into the phone.

"One more thing," Hope said. "We've been experiencing complaints about persons operating with forged private investigator's licenses. I need you to check his driver's license and compare his face to the photo. After you do that, I'll check this investigator's license number out."

As requested, the receptionist checked Phil's face against his driver's license photo and read the license number to Ms. Stapleton.

"I'm sorry about the photo," he apologized after promising himself to plan revenge for Hope's ad libs.

"Actually, for the DMV, this is pretty good. No way you're getting a look at mine!"

They both laughed.

"Ma'am." Hope's voice interrupted their levity.

"I'm here. It's Philip R. Mamba all right."

"And I verified his license number. When he's finished with the file, please sign and date his VOI-297 form."

"I need to sign and date a form for you when you're finished." The receptionist relayed the information.

"Arraugh! That's on the desk in my office! See if there's another way to do whatever that form does, will you please?"

"Certainly." Her next words were into the phone. "Mr. Mamba left that form in his office."

"Figures. You cannot believe how unreliable some of these PI's are," Hope said in a voice reeking with disgust. "I'll fax you the VOI-297. We need you to verify that the information he collects is authentic."

The receptionist shot a disapproving glance in Mamba's direction, diverted her gaze when he made brief eye contact, and said, "Will do. And thank you."

"No. I need to thank you. You can't believe what some of these Sherlock Holmes wannabees do to try and circumvent the regulations. I could tell you stories."

"I'll bet you can. Here's my fax number." She recited the necessary ten digits.

"Thank you," Hope said.

"It's been nice talking with you. Goodbye."

She handed his driver's license and investigator's license back to him. Then, without a word of explanation, she left the room. Minutes passed. He began to worry.

"I've got the personnel file you need here," the clerk said when she returned. As she handed him the paper sleeve containing the microfiche, she added, "The records being converted from their paper format are from the pre-1970 era, so I didn't have any trouble locating Franklin Stallings' file for you."

"Thank you."

"And, here's the form I'll need to sign when you're finished."

The receptionist handed Mamba the phony form Hope constructed. The page he held in his hand looked for all the world like a piece of genuine bureaucratic paperwork.

"The microfiche machine is over there." She pointed across the room to a small desk.

"Thanks."

Mamba went over and sat down at the lone public reading machine. He placed the plastic rectangle into the holder and began his examination.

Everything in the file was routine. Stallings' hiring was done on the basis of his scores on the examinations taken at the State Police Academy. The records of his hiring interviews were complete and positive.

He was commended twice and received a citation for heroism in the rescue of a busload of school children when their bus had failed to negotiate a curve and had ended up in a farmer's pond. Stallings used the farmer's tractor to pull the bus to safety.

He dutifully noted Stallings' history in the appropriate spaces on Hope's bogus VOI-297.

The only non-positive comment in the file was a notation of a complaint filed by a citizen after the bus accident. Stallings was accused of leaking the woman's testimony to the media. That was the same as in the original Kerrigan showed him. There was no record of what discipline, if any, Stallings received as a result of the complaint. He chose to omit any reference to that event in the form.

The only information Mamba could use in his search was the letter of resignation Stallings filed. It directed him to the city of Lincolnvale, Illinois. And, it provided two references to check out. The first reference listed on the application was the man that Mamba already knew to be dead. He copied the second address into his notebook.

"Find what you were looking for?" the receptionist asked as he stopped at her desk on the way out.

"Just about," was the ambiguous response. "Here's the microfiche and the form you need to sign."

She took the form and checked to see that he had filled in all the essential information.

"You forgot the microfiche number and the street address for this building."

"I'm sorry. I didn't know the address. I just missed the space for the number."

She gave a short grunt and filled in the missing information on the form. After checking it one last time, she signed and dated it in the indicated locations.

"Would you like an envelope for this?" she asked.

"That would be appreciated."

She tri-folded the form and slid it into an envelope with the Illiana Police Department's return address printed on it.

"Here you go." She handed him the envelope.

"Thank you. You've been most helpful," Mamba responded. He turned and walked toward the stairwell.

"Have a nice day," she called.

Mamba grimaced as yellow smiling circles invaded his thoughts. He hated that phrase. He gave a head nod and a wave of acknowledgement only because those were the polite things to do.

Mamba waved to the receptionist in the lobby and pushed open the heavy glass door when he glanced at his watch. He reversed his direction.

"Excuse me."

"Yes, sir," the receptionist answered turning back to him from her typewriter.

"I'm heading over to Lincolnvale. I was wondering if you could help me with two things."

"I will surely try, sir."

"First, what's the best highway to take to get to Lincolnvale?"

"Well, that depends. Are you in a hurry?"

"No. Not especially."

"Okay. I'd take . . ." The woman proceeded to draw a map with arrows, approximate miles between landmarks, and notes on places he might find interesting. Eleven minutes later, she finished with, "I used to live over by Lincolnvale."

"I see. My second need is the name of a good place to eat lunch. Can you help me one more time? It's later than I thought."

At that request, the receptionist lit up. She described four local cafes and provided detailed directions to each.

Mamba thanked the woman and left the building. He considered calling Hope as he passed the phone booth. Toward the end of her conversation with the fictitious Stapleton, he'd seen the clerk's face lock into a less than approving look. She looked in his direction and quickly looked away.

He decided that getting even with Hope would wait until he got home. That would give him time to think of an appropriate retaliatory action.

* * *

"I'm telling you, Chief, don't threaten me. I've got enough on you to bury you in prison until not even your mother remembers you." Brewster ended his tirade with a string of profanity.

"I'll ask again, why did you kidnap RossAnn Gilroy without telling me about the plan?" Chief Rogers fired his words at the phone handset as fast as a machine gun fired bullets at a target.

"For the last time, Rogers, I don't know a thing about any kidnapping. I don't kidnap. It's too risky. If I want a someone out of the way, I hire people to handle that!"

The line went dead.

Although Rogers' hands were shaking from the anger he felt, he managed to punch the autodial number for his other supplemental income supplier.

"I told you this number was for emergencies only."

"If you don't think kidnapping RossAnn Gilroy without informing me doesn't qualify as an emergency, I don't know what you think an emergency is!"

Silence.

"You still there?"

"I am. When did this kidnapping occur?"

"Like you don't know."

"Humor me."

"Sometime last night. Her parents reported her missing. Uniforms found her car early this morning."

"My sympathies to the family. While I have no children, I know how my parents would feel if I were to disappear mysteriously."

"You're telling me you know nothing about this?"

"Only what you just told me."

Silence. This time from Rogers.

"If that's all, I've got a drug company to run."

The line went dead.

Rogers knew one of the men was lying through his teeth.

* * *

In the short time Erin Reilly dated Enciso Martinez, they learned quite a bit about one another.

She did not like leftovers. That was the takeaway when he tried to serve cold pizza from their first date for lunch. Of course, it might have been that the leftovers were from a week earlier that brought about the rejection. Whatever the reason, Martinez decided to play it safe and avoid leftovers when with her.

Enciso liked Mexican food. Any Mexican food, as long as there was a lot of it, and it was served with salsa hot enough to blister gringo tongues.

She liked movies. He liked sports.

She liked sitcoms. He liked sitcoms, too.

At this moment, the couple, which is what they had become, was engrossed in an activity dropped into their lives by Phil Mamba.

"Passion igniting a flame that threatened to consume them both," Martinez finished reading a chapter aloud in the book Flatly selected. He snorted before pushing the PAUSE button on his new tape recorder. After taking a deep breath, he asked his companion, "Can you believe this? How can they publish this garbage?"

"People usually buy whatever's advertised," Erin answered as she punched the OFF button on the recorder overriding his pause button push. In her mind, this recording session was over. "I see these things at checkout stands in every store."

"I guess so," Martinez grudgingly admitted. "I still don't want to believe that people think this is literature. Would your parents have allowed you to read this?" He shook the book. "I know mine would have pulled me to confession every day for a year if they'd seen me near a book like this."

"I'm not sure that most of the kids I went to school with know what literature is," she said. "As far as my parents, I suspect we'll find a lot of similarities between yours and mine."

As though they'd worked for weeks on the choreography, the couple looked at one another and hastily diverted their gazes. After a beat, she continued her response to his comment about parental approval and the nature of Flatly's literary preferences.

"You've got to remember, to a lot of people, a book is only something they use to look up the telephone numbers or prop up a piece of furniture."

"I guess you're right."

"What now?"

Martinez talked through his checklist.

"I deliver the tape to the hospital tomorrow."

She nodded.

"I give the recording to Flatly. Sorry, I keep forgetting that you know him as Mr. Wiggins, and he listens to the tape while we read the next book he chooses."

"I've wanted to ask something for a while."

"Okay. I guess." Uncomfortable with where the conversation might be headed, he shifted his position in his chair. "What is it?"

"What's Mr. Wiggins to you?"

Martinez's body relaxed. Her question was not the one he'd worried about.

"He's a guy I got to know on a case—a nice guy. A guy who wanted to help. A guy that didn't deserve to be hurt." Each phrase increased in intensity. His relaxed state evaporated. The veins on his neck were distended by the time he finished.

"I'm sorry, Enciso. I didn't mean to upset you."

"It's not you, Erin. It's the combination of a lot of different things."

"What was her name?"

"Mary." He stopped and stared at the nurse. When she didn't flinch, he asked, "How do you know about what happened to Mary?"

"I don't."

He looked skeptical.

"Honest. I don't know anything about any Mary you were, or weren't involved with. You looked like you might have lost someone recently. I know that look. And, since Mr. Wiggins is still alive, I put two and two together."

"She was never my someone."

He related as much as he could of the saga of Mary Carstairs and Flatly Broke. Because he had to filter out any mention of his undercover work, it took about half an hour to complete the story. When the big man was finished, his shoulders slumped. His eyes were glazed with a thin film of tears.

Erin moved to him and put her arms around his neck.

He looked at her anxious and inviting face. With deliberate gentleness, he lifted her hands and removed them from his shoulders.

"Chica bonita, there is almost nothing I would rather do than anything you want. And I do mean anything."

"But," she added for him straightening her body in a subtle move away from him. "There is a but, right?"

"Yes. There is."

"But, now is not the time or the place, right?"

"You may not believe this, but I really, really like you," he mumbled while avoiding all eye contact.

"Is this where I hear another but?"

He shook his head.

"I like you, too. So far, I've not heard any but that matters."

"I don't know quite how to say this."

"Give it a shot!" she snapped as she shot to her feet. "I'd like to know what's wrong with me. Or what's so right with whatever other woman you're thinking about! " She stared at him, hands on hips, eyes ablaze.

"There is nothing wrong with you, Erin. And there is no other woman." His voice was calm, an achievement that surprised him. He pursed his lips before he managed to dredge up the courage to look at her face to face.

"In fact, there is so much right about you that I will not do anything that would make me feel as though I violated you."

The quiet dignity of his words and delivery rocked Erin. Without thinking, she responded.

"But I want you. That should mean something." She took a step towards him and reiterated, "I want you."

"Maybe that's part of it," he admitted while gently placing one huge hand against her leg to stop her forward progress.

She stuck out her lip in a genuine, full-blown pout.

"That's not all, though." He stood, dwarfing her frame. He held her gently by the shoulders and added in a hoarse whisper, "I think I am in love with you."

She felt goosebumps all over.

"Then what is the problem?"

"I can't do—" He stammered. "I couldn't—"

She fought back tears.

"Enciso Martinez, you're a prude," she accused softly.

"No, I'm—" He let his hands slide off her shoulders. A wry grin turned the corner of his mouth.

"Sí. I am a prude," he admitted. "I'm not sorry that I am." He inhaled deeply and exhaled. "You can leave if you want to."

"I've never been rejected so beautifully before," she said as quickly as she could, hoping the words would precede the warm crimson tint that she felt migrating up her neck and face and the tears she knew would trickle down her cheeks.

"I never tried to encourage a man so blatantly before. I've always had to fight men off."

"I believe that, Erin." Then he asked, "How successful have you been?" and immediately regretted his decision.

She answered before he could think of an apology.

"Not that it's any of your business, but I am undefeated." Swagger supplanted the softness in her voice.

"I'd like to keep it that way."

She tried to look appreciative but knew she ended up looking confused instead.

"I meant that I think we might have the opportunity together. Later. If you still want to," Enciso added.

"I wasn't kidding around," Erin clarified. "And, I haven't changed my mind, amigo. If you want to wait, and will let me hang around, I will wait for you."

"Remember that I said I thought I was in love with you?"

She nodded.

"Well, I've changed my mind," he announced.

Before she could interject a comment, he finished his thought.

"From I think I love you to just I love you." Tattooed arms engulfed her.

They kissed, kissed again and headed to the hospital.

* * *

After a longer drive than he anticipated, thanks to country roads and other two-lane highways, Mamba pulled into the first motel he came to in Lincolnvale, Illinois. It was like returning to his childhood. Back in the day, when his father, a career Army Sergeant, received new orders, the family packed up the station wagon and drove to the next duty station.

He shook his head. The trip here had been a true adventure in Americana. The receptionist in Illiana's City Hall made sure he experienced dozens of decaying barns. He passed through towns with only one street, State Route 136. SR136 ran from one end of town to the other, usually with a stop sign or light.

Even though his trip down memory lane was over, he sat in his car for a moment surveying the establishment. This motel rented individual cabins instead of rooms in a single building. The dim parking lot light could not hide the fact that the cabins' pale green walls needed paint. Only two cars graced the gravel lot, even though it was after 9 p.m.

He got out, pulled his suitcase from the trunk, and checked in. He had to kill a spider and two roaches before he climbed into bed.

In spite of the surroundings, he awoke refreshed in the morning. He shaved, showered, and repacked his suitcase. He asked the owner to recommend a good restaurant and was directed to a small cafe three-quarters of a mile away.

Breakfast was Midwestern in scope and size. Once he saw the portions on plates delivered to other patrons, he ordered the special. While he waited for his food, he bought a copy of one of the Chicago papers. He had an hour to kill before city offices were likely to open, so he read as he ate his bacon, eggs, pancakes, and sausage. He found himself enjoying the massive plate of breakfast items he received and the ambiance of the experience.

The Chicago paper turned out to be a day old and a quick read. He had almost thirty minutes left in the hour when he left the cafe. A police car was parked across the street.

He walked over.

"Good morning, Officer. I wonder if you could help me?"

"That's our motto, sir." The cop had the freshly scrubbed look of a rookie.

"I was wondering if you keep departmental records at the station?"

"I don't see what that has to do with anything that could concern you, sir." The rookie's voice assumed the tone a twenty-year veteran would use with the answer.

"My name is Philip Mamba." He produced his investigator's license. "I'm working a case."

"You'll have to speak to the Captain, sir," the officer responded after a cursory glance at the proffered identification.

Mamba's hopes wilted. It was obvious that the idea of helping a private detective did not sit well with the young man. Even though he was a new hire, he'd heard too many stories from force veterans to be comfortable around any PI.

"He should be at the station by now," were the policeman's last words before starting the patrol car's engine.

"Thank you, Officer," Mamba said as he backed away from the idling vehicle.

On the good news side of the ledger, it wasn't hard to find the police station. The building was one of the newer ones along the easternmost end of the main street. Mamba gave an appreciative nod when he pulled into the parking lot. The location provided easy access to downtown and what appeared to be the developing end of Lincolnvale, even farther east.

He had to wait for ten minutes after asking the female receptionist to see the officer in charge.

"Mr. Mamba. Captain Darling will see you now."

He stood.

The receptionist smiled and pointed to a short hallway.

He smiled back and entered the corridor. Darling's office was the only door on the left side of the hallway. Mamba knocked.

"Come in."

He opened the door and went in. After a reserved introduction, he decided frankness was the best way to broach the subject of his visit. By the time he got to Stallings' part in the scenario, a feeling of camaraderie replaced Captain Darling's reserve. It was cop to ex-cop.

"Stallings worked for me for two years," Darling recounted. "Distinguished himself enough to be promoted to detective. Worked some cases with the state police. Had a hand in a big bust down in Decatur. It was our loss when he joined the St. Louis PD."

The civilian receptionist interrupted the monolog when she delivered Stallings' personnel folder.

"You're welcome to look through this," Darling offered. "Of course, I can't let you take it with you or make copies, but you're welcome to make all the notes you want."

Mamba accepted the invitation and was escorted to an empty room. He thanked the receptionist and took his time reading and taking notes. His review confirmed Darling's recollections of Stallings' stint with the Lincolnvale Police Department. There were no local references listed.

Mamba had two choices. He could follow Stallings' career move to St. Louis. Or, he could go in the other direction—to Stallings' hometown in Ohio and talk to people who really knew the man.

Because one reference from the personnel file in Illiana was from Stallings' hometown, he decided on the second option.

Mamba returned Stallings' file to the Captain, thanked him, went back to his car, and located Tifton in the southwest quadrant of Ohio on his map. He circled his destination in pen, filled the gas tank, and used the restroom. After purchasing a can of pop, he headed for the Buckeye state.

As he approached Indianapolis, the words "Check Engine!" appeared in red under the temperature gauge. He pulled into the first gas station he came to and looked up the address of his rental company. After calling and getting the okay to drive to their lot, he asked directions from the gas station owner. He stopped at two other gas stations and asked for clarification of steps in the original directions. By the time he arrived at the rental lot, it was too late to change cars and get to Tifton in time to interview anyone.

He drove his replacement car to the closest motel and checked in. After calling Hope and Jimmy, he grabbed dinner at Steak 'n Shake. He updated his notes, watched television for an hour, and turned in for the night.

He arrived in Tifton around 4:00 p.m. and drove down the straight-as-an-arrow Main Street. He knew it was a tribute to the original township, range, and section surveys from the late 1780s. He turned around at the eastern city limit sign, smoothed out the note with the contact's address he copied from Stallings' file, and headed west.

The town had a total of fifteen cross streets off Main. It took him ten minutes to find the house.

He parked in front of a small Victorian home. The white porch wood matched what looked to be the functional shutters on the house. The paint was faded, but not chipped or flaking. The lawn was trimmed; the flowerbeds weed-free.

Mamba dropped the old-school doorknocker onto the back plate attached to the door. Lewis Conner answered. He greeted Mamba cordially. Cordiality transformed into a potential relationship when he learned the purpose of the visit was Franklin Stallings.

"Come on in, Mr. Mamba," Conner invited. "It's a little early, but I'll see if Louise can't set another place for supper."

"Oh, I couldn't. I mean, you weren't expecting me. I feel like an intruder."

"Nonsense." Lewis brushed Mamba's protestations aside with two syllables. "When's the last time you had a homecooked meal?"

Mamba stammered a response. "I don't know exactly."

"Then it's settled. The day Louise can't feed one more with the supper she's made up for just the two of us is the day after they bury her. It won't be a problem."

Louise heard her name and stepped through the kitchen door.

"This is Mr. Mamba. I'm sorry, I don't remember your given name."

"Phil, Mrs. Conner. It's a pleasure to meet you, and I'm sorry—"

"No apologies for being a guest in my home, young man."

"He's a friend of Franklin Stallings." Lewis closed the loop on the visitor's presence.

"That's nice," Louise said before returning to the kitchen.

Lewis and Phil toured the tidy home and back yard before Louise called them in.

Louise Conner did her husband proud. By the time she brought in dessert, Mamba was so full he felt like he had eaten Thanksgiving dinner. He was about to decline whatever she was serving for dessert when he caught a whiff of apples and cinnamon.

"That's not apple pie, is it?"

"Why, yes, it is." Louise smiled, then her face took on a serious look as she asked, "You do like apple don't you? It's still warm. I've got some leftover peach if you'd rather. But it's from yesterday."

"No." Visions of two kinds of homemade pie flashed through his brain before he realized his verbal answer was incomplete. "I mean apple is great."

"Sounds like you're not sure about the apple? If you'd rather have peach, I can bring that out."

"Give the boy a slice of each, Lou," Lewis Conner directed. "Then he can make up his own mind on which he wants for seconds."

"Brilliant, as usual, dear." Louise proceeded to serve the fresh apple pie to her husband. Before Mamba could stop her, she disappeared into the kitchen with his plate to add a slice of the promised peach pie.

Mamba had to agree to take a piece of apple pie away with him before Louise would allow the two men to retire to the living room while she cleaned up after supper. Once seated on the sofa, he began to probe the relationship between his host and Franklin Stallings.

"Well, I was Frank's teacher over at Tifton High. He was a fine student. Won some awards in math as I recall. Fine young man," Lewis responded to the opening question. "

"Did he have a lot of friends?"

"Just about everybody liked Franklin. He was Captain of the basketball team. Ran track, too. Fine athlete."

"This may sound strange." The PI was about to take the plunge into the seamy side, if there was one. He anticipated everything to be 'fine,' but he was unsure of where this line of questioning would end. "Would you say that Franklin was, well, honest."

Lewis Conner studied Mamba a long minute before he answered. "Seems to me you should be talking to Franklin."

"I'd like to talk to him. But, I don't know where he is."

"Why didn't you say so?" Conner boomed. "I thought this was some hush-hush case he was involved in. He's staying over at Lizbeth's folks. His parents are dead you know."

"No, I didn't know. And, I'm sorry, but who's Elizabeth?"

"Just Lizbeth," the teacher corrected. "That's his wife. You did know he was married?" Conner gave Mamba a suspicious look.

"I did, but I've never met his wife. We only know one another through the police department. Can you give me the address? I'll go over and talk to Sta, um, Franklin right now."

"The Hopkins live over on Calhoun. That's three streets west. Corner house at Calhoun and Second."

"Thanks," Mamba said. "I'll not trouble you anymore."

"It's been no trouble to us, young man. I hope it's not going to be for Franklin, either."

"I don't think it will be," Mamba said as he carefully lifted the foil-wrapped paper plate that held his apple pie.

"Give my best to Louise, and thank her for dinner," Mamba said as he left.

"Where's he going?" Louise asked as she entered the room after finishing KP. "He didn't forget his pie, did he?"

"No, Lou. He snatched it up like a hungry bird on a worm. Seemed in a big hurry to talk to Franklin Stallings. Maybe I'd better call the Hopkins house and let them know that this Mamba fellow's on his way over."

He looked up the number and dialed. The line was busy. Louise called to him to take out the garbage. He decided to try to get the Hopkins after the chore. Once outside, he discovered that one of the neighborhood raccoons attacked a trashcan. By the time he re-deposited the trash that covered a sizeable area along the side of the house, he'd forgotten about making the call.

Chapter 30

The Hopkins' house was similar to the Conner home. The porch was bright white, and shutters were a similar style. A picket fence enhanced the welcoming first impression.

Mamba crossed the Hopkins' wide front porch and heard loud voices inside. He knocked on the door. The voices faded as the porch light went on. The wooden portal opened. A black woman in her mid-fifties stood before him.

"Yes?"

"Mrs. Hopkins?"

She nodded.

"Is Franklin Stallings here?"

"Why?" The question hit him like a bullet. The questioner was not the woman who answered the door. A second woman stepped out from behind Mrs. Hopkins. She was thin and harried-looking to the point of concern.

"Why?" She snapped again.

Mamba studied the second woman, thinking as he observed the newcomer, then answered, "I'd like to talk to him. Lizabeth, right?"

"Lizbeth," she corrected reflexively. "Talk about what?"

A ringing telephone interrupted Mamba's response.

"Lizbeth, be a Dear and answer that, will you?"

"I should stay here, Mom, until—"

Another ring. Lizbeth frowned, glared at Mamba, but went to answer the phone.

"I have important information for Franklin Stallings, Mrs. Hopkins. I work with him and need to talk to him about one or two things that came up since he's been here."

"Why don't you come in," Mrs. Hopkins offered. She pushed open the storm door. "It gets so chilly around here after dark this time of year."

"Thank you, ma'am." He entered the house. "My name's Phil Mamba."

"I'm Doris Hopkins." She offered her hand. "Franklin's not here right now. We are expecting a call from him anytime—from the bus depot. His bus should be in soon."

"Is that man still at the door?" Lizbeth asked as she reentered the living room from the kitchen. The sight of Mamba standing in the small foyer stopped her in her tracks.

"You shouldn't let strange men into the house," was her icy advice.

"Who was on the phone, dear?" Doris asked. Her daughter lived in the big city too long. Tifton had no strangers, only friends yet to make.

"Sears." Lizbeth recognized her mother's hospitable stubbornness. She also remembered her manners and added, "It was one of those automated messages. Your catalog order is ready."

"That's nice. I thought it might be Franklin." Mrs. Hopkins gestured toward the private investigator. "This is Mr. Mamba." She ushered them both into the living room.

"I'm here to help, Mrs. Stallings." Mamba's voice implored Lizbeth to listen. "That's the truth. All I'm asking is a chance to explain."

"Since we're both guests in my parents' house, I'm obliged to listen. But that's all I promise you—to listen."

"Fair enough. I'm here to ask your husband some important questions."

The bell on the telephone announced another incoming call. Lizbeth retuned to the kitchen. Mamba took two steps in the same direction, hoping to learn something from the conversation. He watched her glance back at him as she picked up the handset.

"Franklin?"

There was the briefest of pauses while the caller answered.

"You've-got-to-leave-again. There's a man here from the police back in," Lizbeth shouted into the phone, her words running together in her haste to warn her husband.

Mamba dashed into the kitchen and grabbed the phone.

"Stallings! I need to talk!" The phone was dead.

"I wish you hadn't done that." He didn't look at Stallings' wife as he hung up the phone. "If I could get answers to a couple questions, I might be able to clear your husband from suspicion in the department's information leaks."

Lizbeth's eyes widened. "You what? You're trying to clear Franklin?"

"Yes. And you made it more difficult than it already was. I wouldn't have thought that possible until this moment."

"I didn't know," she whispered before she collapsed into a chair by the kitchen table. Tears filled her eyes and trickled down her cheeks. Within seconds, huge sobs wracked her body.

"It's, it's been so, so terrible. Franklin's so unhappy. He thought they were going to arrest him. He is, um, we're both worried sick."

"Running away wasn't your best decision," Mamba continued in a quiet voice. He offered the crying woman his handkerchief.

"Oh, my!" was all Doris Hopkins managed.

"I'm okay, Mom." When Doris frowned, Lizbeth continued. "Really. This man is here to help."

"Well, thank heavens for that! From what you've both told us, it's about time someone started being rational."

"Mr. Mamba and I need to talk, Mom. Please wait on the davenport. I promise to fill you in after we finish."

With an "I'm doing this but I sure don't like it" look, Doris Hopkins did her daughter's bidding. When she cleared the kitchen door, Mamba resumed his questioning.

"Why'd you leave town?"

"Franklin heard about the raid on that drug dealer's hotel suite," Lizbeth explained. She blew her nose on Mamba's handkerchief. A shocked look flashed over her face.

"Don't worry about the handkerchief. Hope, that's my wife, always packs extras for occasions like this." He managed a smile.

What might have been a smile flickered over Lizbeth's face. She took a deep breath and continued, "He figured that his brief appearance in the office the day of that last failed operation was sure to condemn him. Running would buy him time."

"He had to know MPD would find him."

"I suppose he did. But he was so desperate. He was out of options." She grabbed Mamba's arm. "Franklin is innocent!"

"I like to think there are always options besides running from a problem." When Lizbeth started to respond, he raised his hand in a stop motion. "I also think your husband's innocent. I'd like a chance to help him prove it. Do you know where he is?"

"He was at the bus station when he called."

"Yeah, your mother mentioned that. Unfortunately, he's probably gone now."

"I know, and I'm sorry." Lizbeth's composure rebounded. "He could be any of a dozen places here in town."

"Make a list. I'll check out as many as I can tonight."

Minutes later, he left, armed with the list and an unnecessary map to the bus station hand drawn by Doris Hopkins.

It took five minutes to get to the bus station on Main Street. He asked the ticket agent if he had seen Stallings leave the station.

"Franklin Stallings?" the man asked. "Is he back in town?"

"Yeah, and I've missed him again. I thought I could catch up with his bus. It's just not my day."

"You might try Dawson's Diner," the ticket agent suggested as he pointed across the street. "Lots of people go down there to wait for their ride home."

"Thanks." The diner wasn't on his list, but it couldn't hurt to check. He jaywalked to the small eating establishment.

"Good evening, sir," was the greeting of the waitress as he entered the diner. It was easy to visualize high school students in "letter sweaters" and poodle skirts in a booth while the vintage jukebox blasted out early rock-and-roll tunes.

"Would you like a booth?" The question brought Mamba back to reality.

"No. No, thank you, um." He found her nametag in the middle of a poodle design. "Actually, Elyse, I'm looking for someone, not something to eat."

"I know almost everybody in town. Who're you looking for?".

"Franklin Stallings," Mamba replied. "But he hasn't lived in town for years."

"Oh, I know Franklin. We went to school together. Funny, isn't it?" Elyse added wistfully, "Our Senior class voted him and me Most Likely to Succeed. He made it. I'm still a waitress." She paused. A look Mamba recognized as retrospection flickered across her features. "Did you know I've worked here since before I graduated high school?"

Mamba didn't answer. He let the woman talk. He knew the type. She would get to the point in her own time.

"But, you didn't come here for a sob story. I'm pretty sure I saw Franklin hurry past here about ten minutes ago."

"Could you tell me if any of these places are in that direction?" he asked as he handed her his list of potential hiding places. "I'm sure you've noticed that I'm from out of town."

She accepted the list with an enigmatic smile and gave it a quick read.

"Larry Penrose's house is about two blocks south," she offered as she pointed. "But he left town on business this morning right after he ate here. He won't be back for two or three days. Why do you ask?"

"I need to talk to Franklin. It's important. Thanks for your help." Mamba handed her a five-dollar bill.

"What's this for?"

"Pretend I ordered coffee," he said with a smile of his own.

* * *

The Penrose house was noticeably newer than either the Conner's or Hopkins' home. The section of town where it stood made its appearance as part of the big push by the government for GI housing after WWII. Although this house had fewer years, it also had fewer of the charming features added by artisans of past eras.

Only the echo of his knock answered Franklin Stallings as he stood on what most townspeople considered a mini-porch. Standing at this door took him back to high school.

A dog barked. Stallings shook his head and forced himself to concentrate on the situation at hand. He'd been tracked down. He knew it was inevitable but hoped it would take longer. He swore softly.

Another dog barked, this one closer than the first. Someone, or something, was headed in his direction.

He stepped off the porch, started down the front walk, and glanced in the direction of the bus station. A solitary figure moved out of the ring of light from the street lamp on the corner. He ducked behind shrubbery on his right.

The figure kept coming toward him. He relaxed a little when it continued past the Penrose house. His relaxation was short-lived. The figure, now clearly masculine, stopped. He held a piece of paper up so it caught what light it could from the streetlight. After checking the house number on the mailbox, he backtracked and started up the walk toward the Penrose house.

Stallings forced himself deeper into the shrubs. The thick growth shielded him from the interloper. He gave silent thanks for Larry Penrose's lax gardening habits.

The man crossed the small wooden porch and knocked on the door. Stallings began working his way through the shrubs, hoping they ran all the way around the side of the house.

Slowly, and as silently as he could, he pushed through bush after bush. He finally broke out of the hedge just past the front corner of the house. He froze after his first step and swore under his breath. Where the shrubbery ended, a gravel path began. The crunch of his shoes on the small stones sounded like thunder in the still night.

He broke into a run.

Ignoring all noises behind him, he sprinted down the driveway that ran beside the house. He knew if he could reach the garages lining both sides of the alley before it ended at a stand of birch trees, he had a good chance of escaping. When he was growing up, he complained to his mother about how small the yards in the neighborhood were. He regretted his complaint. Now he desired a much shorter distance to travel.

Without slowing, he made the turn into the alley. He increased his speed as his quarter-miler training from high school kicked in. Fifty yards away was a small stand of birch trees.

"Hold it right there, Stallings!"

He stumbled but kept moving. The hammer of a revolver clicked into the firing position. He slid to a stop in the loose gravel of the alley, breathing heavily as he turned toward the voice. The dimly lighted figure of a man with a gun faced him.

"Hands where I can see them, Sergeant."

"Mamba? Why'd the department send you?" He expected the FBI or worse, not the PI friend of Lieutenant Kerrigan. When an unpleasant realization formed in his mind, he spat out his conclusion, "I guess they figured they wouldn't waste a good man on a squealer!"

"If it helps any, no one sent me. I'm here because I'm trying to prove you're innocent."

Mamba clicked on a flashlight. Stallings squinted and turned his head while his eyes adjusted to the light.

"Sure, 'you're on my side,'" he said in a nasal, singsong voice. "And, you're doing this out of the goodness of your heart."

Mamba stared at the man. His next words had a hard edge.

"I am here out of the goodness of my heart. I even paid for my transportation. But, if that's the attitude you're giving me, maybe I'll just turn you over to Internal Affairs. I've heard they're bragging that they've got you for sure."

The two men glared at one another through the near-darkness. Stallings blinked first.

"You really believe I'm innocent," Stallings stated instead of asked.

"For several days now." Hoping Stallings accepted his status as an ally Mamba holstered his revolver. "I have to admit that I was ready to string you up when the leak cost Flatly the use of his arm."

"I heard about that. He's the guy who helped us on the first buy, isn't he?"

"Yeah. But, I'm here to talk about you. Why did you run?"

"I had to run!" The gritting of Stallings' teeth as he spoke sharpened his words. "You know they weren't listening to me. The raid on Brewster's that didn't pan out was the last straw. I called in sick, but I dragged myself in to pick up files to take home. What do I find out? I suspect IAD thinks I came in to get the information on the bust so I could immediately leak it."

Mamba stood in stoic silence. He'd wait as long as it took for Stallings to finish.

"I'm a good cop. I paid my dues in Podunk towns. I worked vice in St. Louis for three years. My arrest-to-conviction ratio was the best in the department there. Then I go out west, out to the real action." He paused.

Seconds passed without a sound.

"I'm not there two stinking years, and I'm accused of being a stoolie. Not only that, but somebody upstairs has been harassing me for what seems like forever." Stallings' voice, which increased in volume with each sentence, went silent. His shoulders slumped.

"Why would someone alter your personnel records?"

"They haven't been altered, at least not that I know of. Why? Who says they have?"

"That's what IAD came up with in their investigation."

"What do they say was altered?"

"Two paragraphs of recommendation from your Lieutenant in St. Louis are in a different type style than the rest of the letter. It looks like someone tried to match and didn't quite make it."

"That's it? They're basing this witch hunt on typewriters?"

"I know it sounds sketchy at first. But after you think about it, such a difference throws a shadow of doubt on the authenticity of the whole file. Which font is the real one?"

For a long moment, Stallings stood, lost in thought.

"Yeah, maybe you're right. But, it still sounds like a witch hunt to me. Why else would an anonymous someone in administration keep threatening me?"

"That's twice you've mentioned pressure from a superior. I didn't know about that," Mamba admitted before returning to his line of questioning. "Do you have any idea why the document in your file has paragraphs by different typewriters?"

"No. But, knowing Lieutenant Kraft, there could be many reasons. I can't say I felt bad about leaving St. Louis. The man is not connected to reality."

Mamba smiled. "One prong out of the socket?"

"You could say that," Stallings smiled a wan smile in return. "What's next?"

"Where'd you go?"

"You'll think it's stupid."

"More stupid than a typewriter causing all this?"

"Point taken. I was at a mass interview for a multinational private police force. I was desperate and hoped to get placed overseas."

"Let's proceed like that won't be necessary. Out of curiosity, how'd you do in the interview?"

"Killed it." Stallings relaxed. "They might offer me a position by the end of the month."

"Let's hope it doesn't come to that. What if we head back to your in-laws and work up a plan?"

"I'd like that. Lizbeth must be beside herself."

"She looks haggard."

The Sergeant stared into space for a moment or two before he asked, "You remember my delay in arriving at Brewster's house on the night of the first raid?"

"I do. That's what caused everybody to figure you for the leak."

"Right. Well, I was late because of Lizbeth. I couldn't tell anybody before, it would have looked like I was covering up, but you might as well know."

Mamba offered no response. It looked like Stallings needed time to decide how much to confide.

The question triggered a series of memories. Mamba realized that it took time for Stallings to organize his thoughts. What appeared to be suspicious behavior or trying to stall his way out of answering was nothing more than his normal routine.

The AWOL officer took a deep breath and plunged into his explanation.

"Lizbeth has ovarian cancer. She's been undergoing treatment because she wants to have a baby someday. We're postponing surgery as long as possible. If we get a miracle, forever. The day of the raid on Brewster's house was one of her days for chemotherapy. I called to check up on her. She was feeling lousy. So, I called the hospital to try and find out the results of the latest biopsy, hoping good news there would help her through the chemo. It took longer than I expected."

"That's tough."

"Tell me about it."

"What about the biopsy results?" Mamba asked out of equal amounts of interest and politeness.

"Nothing that night. Kind of no news the next day. Nothing's changed since she started the treatments."

"Isn't no change better than getting worse with cancer?"

"I think so. The only words Lizbeth wants to hear, though, are 'cancer-free.'"

Mamba did a mental calculation.

"Hasn't she missed a treatment? Most people I've heard were on chemotherapy went about once a week."

"She goes every other week, but, she's missed one treatment. That's worrying her. And me. Her hair's gone. She's losing weight. She's a beautiful woman when she's well."

"I'll bet she is."

"You young people, just go on home now," the voice of an elderly female admonished from the other side of the gravel path. "You've had plenty of time to have your fun in my alley. Now git on home before I call the police."

"Yes, ma'am," Franklin called back. "We didn't mean to upset you, Mrs. Simpson."

"Just git on home, now."

"Good night, ma'am." He looked at Mamba, shrugged and said, "She hasn't changed in—" He stopped and replayed his life in Tipton in his mind. "She hasn't changed in over twenty-five years."

"We all crave stability."

"Believe me, crave doesn't come close."

They walked back toward the bus station and Mamba's rental car.

Chapter 31

Manzanita was hot and dry four days after Phil Mamba flew to Chicago. A high-pressure air mass sitting over Nevada blasted a desiccating Santa Ana wind down on the city and surrounding area. Santa Ana winds wound even easy-going people's nerves tight.

Hope Mamba was not one of those people. The evaporation of her composure resulted from listening to William Anderson's complaints about her husband's service, not the Santa Ana winds.

She wanted to tell the man what he could do with his money. Phil was just as eager to find the thief as he was, probably more so.

"I understand, Mr. Anderson," was her edited response. "But Mr. Mamba is not available for a phone conversation."

"That's unacceptable," Anderson intoned. "I am paying for his services. My payment of money is a tacit agreement that I have the right of access to his results and other aspects of the case he is working on for me."

"Mr. Mamba has completed all agreed upon services and provided all reports as outlined in your contract."

"I can see that furthering this conversation will accomplish nothing more. I expect to hear from my employee before the end of business Friday of this week."

Hope hung up the phone with a trembling hand. She hated being angry. She hated Phil being gone, too. Between single parenting for the second time in a month and manning the fort in the office, she was at the end of her rope. She sighed and booted up the office computer.

* * *

"Did that sound convincing?" William Anderson asked his secretary after he finished his conversation with Hope.

"A bit testy."

"Thank you. I'll keep that in mind next time." He returned to his paperwork sporting a Cheshire grin.

* * *

After visiting the restroom for what seemed like the tenth time in the four hours she worked, Hope returned to her desk. She took another sip from the glass of water—knowing it would send her back to the restroom.

But she needed the fluid to suppress the nausea, which she blamed on dehydration from the low humidity.

She slid a data disk into her computer and typed a summary of the conversation with Anderson. Phil could read it when he got back and decide whether to include it in the man's file.

* * *

Stallings and his wife spent a day on a lake. The following morning, Mamba and a relaxed Stallings made the six-hour drive to St. Louis, Missouri. In a diametrically opposed weather pattern to Manzanita's, it was muggy with thundershowers in St. Louis. They were grateful for the air conditioning in their hotel room.

The next morning, Mamba and Stallings sat in the air-conditioned office of Lieutenant Oliver Kraft. The three men were discussing the discrepancy in Stallings' file.

The discussion began in a spirit of cool congeniality. As they tossed more words about and expressed more ideas, the mood soured until it was neither cool nor congenial.

"I tell you this is not the same. This letter of recommendation is different from the one I read in your file in Kerrigan's office," Mamba told Stallings as he thumbed through the St. Louis Police Department's copy of Stallings' personnel file.

"What about it, Lieutenant?" Stallings asked. "I'm sorry. I just want to know what's been going on."

St. Louis Police Department Lieutenant Kraft responded without expression. "That's what I typed. That's what I copied. That's what I sent to your new employers."

"Someone in Manzanita Police Department must be responsible," Mamba offered.

Even if the Lieutenant was a tool, there was no obvious reason for him to change the letter in Stallings' file. The original, here in Saint Louis, and the copy back in the Department personnel file, communicated the same tone.

Overlapping monologs replaced dialog as the discussion continued.

Mamba watched Stallings continue to stress and Kraft continue to minimize. He dropped out of conversation mode and into his mental problem-clarification mode. He murmured his ideas under his breath. Hearing his thoughts helped him process quicker.

"There are maybe three reasons for this minor forgery. First, the forged letter could have just been a practice run for the forger. If this forgery went undetected, it would build confidence for other attempts. But there's no evidence of that." He paused and mentally underlined a phrase.

"Second, maybe some altered wording was essential to make another part of the file, which was also forged, believable. But, there's no evidence of that, either." There was another pause while he added a mental exclamation point.

"Third, the forged letter could have been inserted into Stallings' file just to set him up, if, or when, it became necessary to have a patsy." He put mental stars around that idea. Reason number three was looking more and more like the real reason.

Mamba smiled and resumed his contribution to the discussion.

"Unfortunately, Franklin, that doesn't get you off the hook. Internal Affairs will contend that you had access to the file."

"What?" Kraft asked.

"What is it that doesn't get me off the hook?"

"I was thinking about changes to your file being made in Manzanita, not elsewhere."

"But, what about the threats? This has to have something to do with the threats I've been getting."

Kerrigan's face flashed through Mamba's mind. It came unbidden and kept reappearing despite his attempts to erase it. "Harassment from a superior" was Stallings' claim. Kerrigan was his friend. But, how well did he know the man who replaced him as homicide lieutenant?

"Do you have a record of those threats?"

"You know I don't. If I did, I'd have gone to IAD myself!"

"Time out." Kraft stopped the escalating exchange between the two Californians. "I want my office back. Take this elsewhere."

Two pairs of eyes locked. Two heads nodded agreement.

"We get it, Lieutenant."

Twenty seconds later, Lieutenant Oliver Kraft sat alone in his office.

Stallings and Mamba began their return trip in relative silence until they found a place for lunch. After their food arrived, they reviewed the meeting with Lieutenant Kraft.

"The part of your file that differs was Kraft's commentary on your reprimand while you were in Illiana," Mamba began. "The new wording doesn't mention a reprimand of any kind. Does that sound like something he would agree to?"

"My heavens, no! That's about the most opposite of an action by Kraft that I can imagine. Why?"

The PI took a bite of his hamburger. Stallings took the hint and did the same. There was no reason to ruin lunch. After they swallowed another two bites, Mamba resumed the conversation.

"I've been thinking."

"Good thoughts?"

"I think so. I'm leaning toward the idea that the change to your file happened somewhere between the St. Louis and Manzanita police departments."

"What's your rationale?"

"More gut feeling than rational thinking. The department leak is sending information to names on Reed's list. Some of those names must have out-of-state connections."

Stallings' face reflected increasing hope. "Yeah. The drugs have to come from somewhere. So, it could be— No, it's reasonable to assume that someone outside California wanted me to be culpable for the leak. My culpability shifts the focus of the investigation away from the real crooks."

"Crooks? Really, Stallings?"

"Just shut up, Gumshoe. I agree with you. Enjoy the moment."

Both men laughed. Conversation for the rest of the ride back to Ohio focused on their families.

* * *

After two weeks with her kidnappers, RossAnn Gilroy was running on empty.

Fluorescent lights buzzed their illumination twenty-four hours a day. The only time she wasn't tied to what she now referred to as her chair were trips to the bathroom. They had allowed her two showers. The presence of a shower stall confirmed her theory. She was not in an abandoned barbershop.

They fed her periodically. Without the light/dark cycle, she didn't know if it was once a day or more, or less. She knew she didn't feel hungry like she had at first. She knew she lost weight.

She wasn't sure of anything else.

What she said and what her horrid captors said was not conversation. She was invisible to her kidnappers, except when they wanted to torture her. Even then, they paid no attention to her words. They talked about her as though she wasn't there.

* * *

Mamba and Stallings spent the evening of the day they returned from St. Louis reviewing and planning. Breakfast the following morning was homemade biscuits and sausage gravy. The PI helped dry the dishes and headed to Chicago for his return flight. The Sergeant promised to follow with Lizbeth within a week.

Two hours and forty-five minutes into the drive, Mamba wished he'd driven down to Cincinnati and changed his flight at the airport there. Spending the extra money would have been worth not having to drive across parts of Ohio, a long corridor of Indiana, and the congested northeast corner of Illinois to get to O'Hare Field.

He followed farm vehicles and stopped at the only stoplight in so many little towns he quit counting. He arrived in Chicago at the start of the afternoon commute and was frazzled by the time he returned his rental car.

His most germane observation of the journey: He didn't remember the drive in the other direction being as exasperating as this one.

The non-stop Chicago to Los Angeles flight landed early, just in time to catch the tail end of the Los Angeles commute. He arrived home haggard.

After spending time with a very sleepy son, he and Hope talked. But, she fell asleep as he was explaining the next move he and Stallings agreed on. That wasn't like her. He got out of bed and checked on Jimmy. After a hasty inspection for locked doors, he turned out the lights and climbed back into bed.

The next morning, Phil fixed breakfast for the family. Jimmy was ecstatic over his Mickey Mouse pancakes. The stack of buttermilk flapjacks he offered did not excite Hope. Instead, she opted for a poached egg and some juice.

His commute to the Northeast Division station was ordinary. He was grateful for that. Driving on his home turf with drivers who understood his techniques and strategies because they were also their techniques and strategies was a welcome change. He walked into the station with great expectations.

"Hey, Eddie," Mamba greeted Sergeant Edwards as he entered the Records and Copies office, his decision on the best place to resume his search for the truth.

"How're you doing, Mister Mamba?" Eddie responded with minimal enthusiasm. He was engaged in copying a massive report that the Captain wanted thirty minutes after handing it off, and the clock was ticking. He trusted no subordinate with the task.

"Fine. Just fine." Phil's radar pinged. Edwards called him Mister. The man was under some serious stress and his request wouldn't help. "Could I get a look at a file?"

"You got authorization?"

Mamba played his only card.

"I'm involved in an active investigation. Narcotics is short-staffed with Sergeant Stallings missing."

After a beat, during which Edwards glanced at his wristwatch, he said, "That's good enough for me. Officer Cowan will get whatever you need."

He placed another page on the glass surface of the copy machine and closed the top.

Mamba went back to the counter outside the copy room. He told Cowan that Edwards approved his request and asked for Kerrigan's personnel file.

Mamba spent an hour with Kerrigan's file.

* * *

Hope Mamba sat at her desk in the office of Mamba Investigations. Phil, while back in town, hadn't come in. She was alone. With little to occupy her morning, she allowed herself to daydream.

She was envisioning her husband gallivanting about on a quest to right the world's wrongs when the door to the office opened.

"Telegram for Ms. Stapleton."

"I'm sorry, but—" Stapleton rang a bell in her brain. "Never mind, I'll sign for it."

The deliveryman raised the clasp on his clipboard, pulled out an envelope, and handed it to Hope.

"Sign here, please."

She complied.

The deliveryman turned to go.

"Wait!" Hope called. "Hold on just a minute, please." She pulled out the bottom drawer on her desk and removed her purse.

"Here." She handed the man two one-dollar bills. "And, thank you."

"My pleasure." He folded his tip money with one hand. "And, thank you."

After the door closed, Hope opened the envelope and read the telegram.

FR: State Licensing Agency
TO: Ms. Stapleton
RE: Phone conversation w/ Illiana P.D.
Heard of your success <STOP> Congratulations <STOP>
Need information on details of conversation <STOP>
Licensee complains of "evil look" given by IPD staff <STOP>
Expect contact by licensee soon re this incident <STOP>
Love <STOP> PRM <STOP>

"Well played, Phil," she said aloud to the empty office. She replaced the telegraph in its envelope and slid it into her purse.

* * *

Mamba arrived at Memorial General Hospital at the start of Flatly's afternoon visiting hours. He missed spending time with the man. He also needed a distraction from the Stallings' case.

"Dancer, where you been?" Flatly called from the chair by his bed. "Cue Ball—" He stopped. A look of panic flickered across his features. "I mean, Officer Martinez, said you was outta town. He says I can't call him Cue Ball." He leaned in Mamba's direction and whispered, "He says he's not doing undercover no more. He says it's too confusing."

"I think I know what Martinez means. Undercover is dangerous work. I've been on a business trip. I'm back now. Got another book for me to record?"

The boxer's eyes dropped, diverting his gaze from anywhere close to Mamba before he asked, "It okay for you not to read no more books for me?"

"Yeah, I guess so."

"Y'see, Officer M—that's what he lets me call him—and Nurse Erin read so much more excitin' than you." The words poured out of Flatly with no offense intended. "And with the two of them, it's jes' like a old radio show. Nurse Erin reads the girl parts and Officer M most of the rest. Nurse Erin, she reads fantastic, if you followin' me."

"Can I still visit you?" he asked. He felt like a pervert as he read some passages onto the tape. Now, he felt like a veteran ballplayer, benched and replaced by a rookie.

"'Course you can. I still don't get many, y'know—viz'ters."

"Hang in there," Mamba admonished. "I'm sure more will come by before you're released."

"I'll be hangin' with one hand all the way." He raised a single clenched fist.

In a classic Flatly-ish maneuver, an instant later he changed the subject. "The doctor says it's lookin' better 'bout keepin' my arm."

Mamba thought it was too bad Flatly wasn't that quick with misdirection in the ring. He was sure he'd have never lost a fight if he moved like he talked.

"That's good to hear!"

"I get to start some ther'py or sump'n day after tomorrow."

"You do exactly what they tell you to do. You hear me?"

"I hear!" was his immediate response. "I will. Exactly. I promise!"

Mamba nodded and shifted the conversation to sports.

* * *

The Stallings arrived in Manzanita as scheduled. Franklin called Mamba from Reno. Mamba drove Hope's car to a parking garage and parked it on the agreed-upon level before the Sergeant's after-dark arrival. When the Stallings reached the garage, they arranged for long-term parking, not uncommon for those taking a shuttle to Los Angeles International Airport.

Franklin retrieved the key from a magnetic key box under the driver's front fender. After moving their luggage to the trunk, he climbed into the backseat and hunkered down out of sight. Lizbeth drove to

Mamba's home. Only someone looking for something out of the ordinary would notice neither Mamba was the driver.

The garage door was open when they arrived. Lizbeth pulled in. Phil entered the garage and pulled the door closed. He grabbed two suitcases and headed inside.

"Hope, this is Lizbeth and Franklin Stallings." Mamba introduced the couple that followed him in from the garage.

Hope's shifted into hostess mode. "I'm so glad you agreed to stay with us. I cannot imagine what you've been going through."

"Be glad of that," Lizbeth said. "I wouldn't wish what we've been going through on anyone."

"You'll be in our guest bedroom upstairs. It has a three-quarter bath of its own, so that will help with privacy," Hope explained as she directed the couple to the staircase.

* * *

After a planning session with Stallings the next morning, Mamba headed for his office. Hope wasn't at her desk when he entered. He considered tapping the bellhop bell on her desk. She'd put it there with a sign that read

If I'm not here, ring this once.

If I hear two rings, you'll be there by yourself a loooong time!

That's when he heard the fan in the restroom.

He went straight to his office. Minutes later he heard his wife open and close a drawer in her desk. By that time, he'd seen the memo she wrote about Anderson's hijinks.

"Hope," he called. "I need you to take a memo."

"And, if I don't want to take a memo, then what?" As her voice trailed, her face appeared in the doorway to his office.

She looked pale to him. After making the observation, he waited to see if she mentioned anything about how she was feeling. When that didn't happen, he opted for being himself.

"Then, I'll type it, and it will take you twice as long to fix as it would have if you wrote it the first time."

"Don't worry. I brought my steno book. But, don't go too fast. I think I might have eaten something that didn't agree with my stomach."

He hated to see her feeling less than one hundred percent. He waited until she settled herself and looked over at him.

"To: William Anderson. From: me. Regarding: Status of your case."

"Can I edit this if your version doesn't represent the position of the entire Mamba Investigations staff? I really want to let this man know he's being a big jerk."

"Only if I get to read the final version before you send it."

"Go on."

"I have been away from my office working an angle on a case that appears linked to ours. Information gathered during the investigation of that case will have no impact on the hours billed to your case, regardless of the amount of crossover between said cases. Sincerely, etc."

"Sometimes you amaze me," she said.

"Only sometimes?"

"Ha. Ha. I mean you told him to back off and made it seem like it was your fault there was a problem. How do you do those kinds of things over and over again?"

"Clean living."

Hope rolled her eyes and stood to her feet.

"Since you aren't taking me seriously—"

"Oh, I did," he said as he interrupted her. "You didn't let me finish."

Hope gestured for him to continue.

"I was going to say, clean living and a world-class secretary."

"Not bad." She turned to leave, stopped, and turned back around. "What are you doing for lunch today? I need to eat something I can keep down."

He pretended to check his desk calendar before he answered.

"It appears I'm free."

"Well, I'm expensive. I'll be ready for you to take me out for a classy luncheon in about ten minutes."

They lunched at *Martin's on Main*, a restaurant they liked for a modestly priced upscale lunch. The place decreased the portions and the price of five of their most popular items from 11:00 a.m. to 1:30 p.m.

The food was good, as always. The conversation between the couple started splendidly. But, soon after ingesting her tomato bisque, his wife excused herself and returned to their table with the same pallor he observed in the office. She was minimally responsive through the rest of his meal.

Hope ended up taking over ninety percent of her entrée home in a box. Phil drove her directly home. He could figure out how to get her car back to their house later.

"I hope you're not coming down with a bug," he said as he walked her to the door. He called Grandma from Martin's and extended Jimmy's stay for an extra three hours to give Hope time to rest.

"What's wrong?" Lizbeth Stallings asked as Hope entered the living room with an unsteady gait.

No one in the Manzanita Police Department, or anywhere else in Manzanita, knew that Sergeant Stallings and his wife were staying with the Mambas. Mamba's neighbors thought they were friends of Hope's from her college days. Mamba felt it important to have Stallings nearby. The live-in arrangement was a chance they had to take. He prayed it didn't blow up in his face.

"I think I'm coming down with something," Hope mumbled.

Phil grabbed her as her legs turned to rubber. Together, he and Stallings got Hope upstairs. Once Hope was settled in the master bedroom, Lizbeth took charge.

"We're grateful for your help, but the last thing this woman needs now is a pair of men hovering around. Go to your pool room or wherever men go now and do whatever men do. Leave the two of us alone!"

She ignored Phil's protests, shooed them out the door, and pulled it closed.

After helping Hope out of her work clothes and into a pair of pajamas, Lizbeth supported her hostess as Hope scooted up and leaned against the headboard.

"Thank you for helping me, especially when I know you don't feel well yourself."

"No worries. My chemo's not 'til Monday. I feel great today, which is more than I can say for you." After a visual assessment of Hope, Lizbeth added, "You look marginally better than you did downstairs. How do you feel?"

"Marginally better," Hope replied through a weak smile.

Lizbeth laughed.

"I saw you brought food home. How much lunch did you get down?"

"A little tomato soup. But, that all ended up in the sewer lines, if you know what I mean?"

"Oh, I know from experience."

The women small talked for several minutes. When Hope related a personal habit, Lizbeth responded with a similar habit and blamed it on growing up in the Midwest.

"Mine is a result from living with Phil Mamba too long," Hope explained.

"I hear you. You should see some stuff my husband thinks is art." Lizbeth grimaced at the visual in her mind. Hope countered with a description of the first dress Phil bought her.

The women continued sharing anecdotes about their husbands' lack of artistic and fashion sense. Each parallel description of their husbands' choices set the women into another fit of giggles.

"I'd like you to do something for me, Lizbeth." Hope redirected the lively conversation and tales about husbands and their foibles.

Sensing Hope's change of mood and vulnerability, Lizbeth looked into her new friend's eyes with open concern. "I'll do whatever I can."

"Phil's told me a little about your condition. I can't believe you're having your treatment Monday here in town. Not with the police still searching for your husband."

"Please, don't worry about that. All my treatments are in a research hospital in Simi Valley. I haven't seen a local doctor about my cancer since they referred me to that facility."

"Oh, good. That's a relief." Hope cupped her hand to her mouth. "That was just insensitive. I am so sorry!"

"Never apologize for being normal around a cancer patient. I endure way too much abnormality from Franklin as it is. Now, what do you want me to do for you?"

"Really, it's two things."

"Okaaay."

"First, I want you to finish my lunch. Today, or at least before Monday. Actually, any time before your treatment after which you won't want to eat."

Lizbeth nodded.

"Second, I want you to pick up something for me from the hospital pharmacy when you're there."

* * *

"There are some serious discrepancies in Kerrigan's file," Mamba told Stallings after they settled in the downstairs den. "They can't all be coincidences. I don't like it."

"This's gotta be tough for you. You're good friends, aren't you?"

"We were partners when he first came on the force."

Stallings needed no other explanation. To police officers, the concept of partner was self-explanatory. Your partner was more than your friend. He was a spouse, a mother, a sibling, a protector, and a confidant. When your partner got hurt, you bled.

"What do you know about Kerrigan the man?"

"He was military. He talked about Vietnam a few times. I know his family a little. I was single when we were partners, so I felt like an intrusion into his home life. He's a Lieutenant because I quit the force—" Realizing that sounded awfully self-serving, he added, "He was on track for that, anyway. Not right then, but eventually." After several seconds of silence, Phil grimaced. "I don't know another thing about Pat that's not related to police work. That's pathetic isn't it?"

Stallings shook his head.

"I'm going to Washington, DC."

"What? Why?"

"The FBI keeps tabs on any confidential police file transported." Knowing that was an inadequate reason Mamba added, "And, I want to check with the Defense Department about Kerrigan's military career."

"You can't do that over the phone?"

"Not like I want to. I have to see what the pages look like. I bought my ticket over the phone earlier today. I leave about noon on Monday."

"Ahh. Got it," Stallings commended, knowing a visual comparison might be the only way to know if someone changed something in the file. "Want me to drive you to LA?"

"I can't let you do that."

"We need a car. Lizbeth's got a chemo treatment in Simi Valley Monday afternoon."

"Okay. You meet Hope and Lizbeth on Hwy 1. Call Hope when you get about twenty miles out. Hope will hand Lizbeth off to you and return home. Her car needs to be here in the afternoon like it always is. And you can't risk being recognized in town. We'll leave early, so no one will care who's with me. But you won't get back until it's daylight. We can't have even a hint of your presence getting to MPD. That's why the rendezvous is on Hwy 1."

* * *

Anthony Garmel was finishing breakfast in his Chicago home. He liked breakfast: sausage patties, eggs over hard, and crisp, buttered toast with homemade jam. Any preference of his was a mandate to his staff, so they served him that breakfast every day.

He patted the corners of his mouth with the linen napkin and checked his calendar. When he read the first item on the day's agenda, he frowned and barked an order. He didn't bother checking if anyone was in earshot. He knew there was.

A figure dressed in waiter's uniform placed a phone on the table next to Garmel's left hand, another preference that always accommodated by staff. He slid his Hermes Platinum plate away from him. The waiter swept in and out, clearing the table. He scanned a list of phone numbers and dialed one.

"Get me Brewster." With those words into the phone's handset, all semblance of sophistication evaporated from the scene. It was time for business.

"He's not up yet. Do you know what time it is?"

"Do you know who this is?"

"No, and I don't give a baboon's butt who this is. If you think I'm waking Brewster, well, that's not gonna happen!"

"Considering this is Anthony Garmel, I suggest you think about another part of an animal's anatomy for any comparisons."

"Mr. Garmel?" Rick Elkhart, Brewster's terrified second in command gulped out the question. "I didn't know, sir. I'll get Mr. Brewster immediately!"

The sound of a telephone handset contacting a solid surface hinted at a hasty retreat by Elkhart.

"You bet you will," Garmel growled knowing full well no one would hear his comment. He heard several seconds of loud profanity in the background. A scraping sound informed him of Brewster's arrival.

"Mr. Garmel, this is Brewster. I want to apologize for my associate."

"Not necessary. I want his name."

There was the tiniest sound of a gasp from Brewster. The sound of a throat being cleared replaced the gasp.

"His name is Elkhart. Rick Elkhart. But, sir, he was acting on my orders."

"Shut up and listen, Brewster!"

"Of course, sir."

"The situation between you and the police has gone on far too long. You need to make a statement. And, you need to do it now."

"I understand, Mr. Garmel. I have been working on it."

"What you have been doing is neither successful nor efficient. Up your game. I'm tired of having to dial new phone numbers when I want to reach you."

"I will do my best, sir."

"If you haven't been doing your best already, we have a bigger problem than I thought we had."

"Sir, I didn't mean, ," Brewster babbled like a child in trouble. After mentally berating himself he asked, "Would the elimination of a high-level police officer directly involved in the, um, in the disruption of our services be sufficient?"

"I would accept that. See that it happens by the end of this week. Is that clear enough for you, or do I need to use small words and draw pictures for you to understand?"

It took considerable self-control, but Sid Brewster reined in his true feelings.

"Consider it done."

Garmel hung up.

Brewster fumed.

After fuming for almost two hours, he made a decision.

"Get me Rogers!"

"Chief Rogers' office," the female voice announced.

"My boss needs to speak with Chief Rogers," Elkhart said.

"What is the nature of his business?"

"Tell him that my boss is calling on behalf of Anthony Garmel."

That was a name she hadn't heard in a quite some time. Something serious was brewing.

"Please hold." Petula Jacobs pushed the HOLD button and the FORWARD CALL button in quick succession. But she did not hang up her handset.

After one ring, Rogers picked up.

"Rogers here."

"This is Brewster."

"What in God's name are you doing calling me on my work line? Are you crazy?"

"Mr. Garmel directed you to derail the investigation into our local business operations," Brewster said, ignoring Rogers' irrelevant questions.

"It's not as easy as you make it sound. The Chief of Police cannot say, 'Let's just let this one slide.' There are checks and balances."

"Less checking and balancing is what I'm expecting. So is Garmel. And soon!"

Petula held her breath as she waited for Rogers to hang up. When he did, she replaced her handset and smiled a sinister smile. The videotapes of her escapades with Rogers were good insurance. And, she just added a high-value rider to her policy under the name of Anthony Garmel.

* * *

As far as Hope and Lizbeth knew, both husbands were still ruminating and pontificating in the den/study downstairs. After Hope's nausea passed, the pair moved from the master bedroom into the guest room the Stallings occupied. They explored one another's likes, dislikes, peeves, preferences, and nail salons.

During the conversation, Lizbeth removed the bandana she wore when she was certain she'd be around no strangers. The mood was one of deepening trust.

Hope dove in.

"You had an Afro hair style when we met. Now you've taken off your headpiece."

"Wow! You need to signal before you make a turn that sharp in our conversation."

Hope blushed.

Lizbeth reached over and squeezed her new friend's hand with reassurance that any topic was welcome between them.

"Don't beat yourself up. I need to talk about this more than I do. At least that's what the hospital oncology advocate says." She picked up her head covering and folded, then unfolded it as she continued.

"You can see I'm bald as a bowling ball. When my hair fell out, I tried going places with nothing on my head. You know, to make it seem that things were still normal."

"Oh, I get it. The day after a new hairstyle is trauma enough for me. I can't imagine what bald is like."

"I don't imagine anymore. I know what people think when they see a tall, bald, black woman. So, I got an Afro wig for outside. I wear one of these when I'm inside. I call them head-kerchiefs." She ran her hand over her hairless scalp. "Chemo definitely is not normal."

A memory from two days after one of her worst chemotherapy sessions exploded in Lizbeth's brain. She saw herself shivering under three blankets in her bedroom in the house they abandoned.

The flashback roused a shiver of the reality her icy-cold pain. She tried to talk.

"I'm praying so hard this."

"What's wrong?"

"I'm praying so hard this." The obstinate memory swept her conscious control away.

Hope moved closer and put her arm around Lizbeth. After a time, Lizbeth continued, "Maybe getting it out in the open would help." She sighed, looked past Hope, and began.

"I keep remembering my reactions after one of my worst chemotherapy sessions. I can't forget shivering under three blankets trying to get warm. Another time I slapped a hand over my mouth, threw the covers off and staggered into the bathroom. I know Franklin heard the sounds of vomiting over the next several minutes, but he never let on. I washed my hands and face, and then gargled to get the taste out of my mouth."

Hope sat sharing the quiet stillness allowing the confidences that Lizbeth shared to reverberate in her mind. She finally broke the silence.

"Well, I don't know how you do any of it. I've heard enough about how a person suffers after those horrible cancer treatments to mean that."

"That. That is the part of this I could do without!" Lizbeth mumbled, her mind still living the flashback, her ears not hearing Hope's comment.

"Do without what? When?" Hope asked.

"Intense cold, nausea, and vomiting after the chemo." She recounted the flashback including only the highlights, or more accurately, the lowlights.

Hope tried to put on a neutral face. She failed miserably.

"Oh, Hope. I apologize. It's not always that bad. I have good days, too. I have flashbacks after some treatments. In fact, I just had one. It's probably because I missed a treatment while we were in Ohio, and I've got another treatment on Monday. My reactions to the drugs are getting worse. They tell me it's something to do with my resistance declining. My doctor explained that the chemo kills good cells along with the cancerous ones."

The women sat in quiet contemplation.

"How many more treatments do you have left?"

"One more in this round. Then, they'll do some tests. They tell me radiation might be the next step."

Hope shivered involuntarily. Lizbeth put her right hand on top of Hope's left and squeezed.

"I thought radiation was bad, but I learned that radiation means they think the chemotherapy did its job. It's supposed to be a good thing." She turned to look Hope straight in the eye.

"Problem is, I don't want radiation."

"Why not? It can't be worse than what you just described."

Lizbeth stared at the floor. She knew she needed to tell someone besides Franklin how she felt and why. The Mambas were taking a risk on them by allowing them to stay in their home. She would take a risk with Hope. She raised her head and whispered, "I want to have children."

"I, um," Although she tried with all her might, Hope couldn't think of an appropriate response. So, she sat, waiting for Lizbeth to continue.

"It's okay not to have words for what you're feeling. I'm so glad you're willing to listen."

Hope relaxed. Lizbeth continued.

"Radiation of the ovaries, where my stupid cancer decided to live, will kill my eggs, or damage the chromosomes inside them. I won't bring a child into this world knowing it might be damaged because of a choice I made, a choice that might not even help my condition." By the end of her explanation, she was crying.

"I can't understand all of what you're going through, Lizbeth." She handed Lizbeth a tissue. "But, I'm here for you."

Lizbeth grimaced more than smiled her thanks.

Hope pursed her lips and swallowed hard before blurting out, "Well, it sounds awful; but, I need to get some sleep, and I've got to get to the bathroom quickly."

"I don't know how to thank you for doing this," Lizbeth choked out as she fought back tears.

Hope fought back tears, too, and lost. "I'm glad to do whatever I can. I'll be praying, too." She pulled away from Lizbeth and almost made it to the toilet.

* * *

"You got a second, nurse?" Mamba and Erin Reilly left Flatly's room together after a visit by the PI.

"Not much more than that, but, sure. What's up?"

"I was wondering about Flatly's hospital bill. I know the boxing association paid for some of his expenses. But, he's been in here over a month."

"It will be seven weeks this Wednesday," she corrected.

"Wow! Time flies. Anyway, he's got zero money."

"Don't worry, Mr. Mamba. It's all been taken care of."

"But, that's thousands of dollars. How?"

"It's tens of thousands. And it isn't a how, it's a who."

"You've lost me."

"One of our donors selects two patients each year. She pays all the expenses for whatever treatment is prescribed for as long as it's needed."

"Why'd she pick Flatly?"

"Funny answer," Erin said with a short laugh. "Her husband is a boxing fan. He saw Mr. Wiggins fight. Did you know his nickname was Kid Wonder?"

"No."

"Well, it was. According to the husband, early on it looked like he could be a contender. Then he got hooked up with a crooked trainer. After a couple of fixed fights, his optic nerve was irreparably damaged. He had to quit or go blind."

"That part I knew about, the blindness part."

“Anyway, the couple supports Mr. Wiggins for what might have been.”

“Still, this seems like a longer than necessary hospitalization.”

“Maybe. But Mr. Wiggins has no one to assist him at home. He also lives upstairs. Until his rehab gets him back to where he’s self-sufficient, he’ll be with us.”

“I’d like to thank the donors.”

“Write a note. I’ll see it gets delivered.”

“Thanks.” Mamba stopped and pushed the elevator button. As he stepped into the elevator he said, “You know you’re a special person, Nurse Reilly.”

The glimpse he got of the look on her face as the elevator door closed was priceless.

Chapter 32

Mamba's flight to Washington, DC, was long and uneventful. He checked into a hotel close to the airport that had shuttle service. He ate dinner and went back to his room. Tuesday's agenda was too important to tackle unrested.

After checking out of the hotel Tuesday morning, he took the hotel shuttle back to the airport. From Washington National, he boarded the Metro's Yellow Line. As directed by a fellow traveler, he got off at the Archives station around 10 a.m., wishing he had a warmer jacket.

The roller bag he pulled behind him caused a delay at the FBI's security screening. As he approached the arch-shaped metal detector, he felt a hand grab his free elbow. He was firmly and quietly pulled out of line. After removing his belt buckle, they sent him through the scanner. He showed his PI license, allowed an agent to search his bag, and showed his PI license again before they granted him access. He hoped that experience was the worst part of his visit. It wasn't.

The FBI was not helpful. They were beyond reluctant to allow access to any file without police authorization. The Bureau's roadblock wasn't a surprise. It was a chance he had to take. Certain that someone in Manzanita Police Department would hear about his visit, he made a mental note to prepare a rebuttal.

As he entered the main reception area, he took one last shot at getting information from the FBI. He waited in the short line until a receptionist was available.

"How may I be of assistance?"

"I need to get to the Pentagon. Can you tell me the quickest way to do that?"

"That's not in my job description." She checked the length of the line behind him, which was no one. "But, I can accommodate you."

After a moment of brow-furrowing, she asked, "Do you know where the Archives metro station is?"

"I do. I came here from the airport on the Yellow Line."

"Then you've got it easy. Go back on the Yellow Line to the Pentagon City station. It's as simple as that."

"Thanks for your help," Mamba said with a nod.

The receptionist did not reciprocate.

After hopping on the Yellow Line, he sat, lost in thought during the ride to the Pentagon. He hoped to leave the Pentagon with something tangible. He considered the fact he didn't change subway lines a good omen.

When he arrived at his destination, Mamba went into the restroom and changed into a clean shirt. Because Hope packed his bag for him, he could use the same tie with this shirt.

After leaving the restroom, he found a bank of lockers and stuffed his roller bag into one. He was as ready as he'd ever be.

The Defense Department declassified many Vietnam era documents in the early 1980s. After conquering the challenge of finding those documents, Mamba spent the early afternoon sifting through files. Since Kerrigan worked in security during his stint in the military, his name was in many of the files, but references were vague. He had to see Kerrigan's personnel file. It was just after four when he knew he had to make a move.

He had a small time window to do this, but that was a good thing. He'd try to pull off being an overworked, underpaid assistant to some brass who forgot his paperwork and left his badge on his suit jacket. But, he needed a model to mimic.

Armed with his flimsy, fabricated story, he went down to the personnel division of the Defense Department. He waited several minutes, out of sight of the security desk. Finally, satisfied with what he learned through his surveillance, he timed his arrival to coincide with another civilian, keeping close to the man as they approached the security desk.

Since the credentials of the first man were in order and Mamba's proximity implied they were together, security waved them both through. Mamba's model continued to an area that did not deal with inactive files. Mamba stuck close anyway. He watched how the man, a civilian working with a Colonel Nicholson, treated the clerk at the counter. The civilian left. Mamba began his solo search for the dead file room.

He was fortunate. The third door he tried opened into a cavernous chamber. A counter separated rows of files from the small area reserved for those waiting for service. He could see row after row of filing cabinets behind a chain-link wall.

The PI pulled his tie askew, unbuttoned the top button of his shirt, and entered. The con was on.

"Colonel Nicholson needs the file on Patrick Seán Kerrigan. The a in Seán has an accent mark," Mamba informed the soldier who manned the counter.

"Thank you, sir. The Colonel doesn't do much business with us. Must be a special occasion."

"Something about a complaint about a medal that was never received. I'm to bring the file to his office."

"If you have the pass, that's not a problem."

"The pass! I knew he forgot something. Never offer to do a favor for someone who's disorganized. I told Corporal Huntley that I would pick up the file for him since I was coming down here. He had that deadline on the Colonel's Senate Sub-Committee appearance. And then he forgets to give me the pass to take it out with me." Mamba threw his hands in the air and announced, "I'll look at it, anyway. Maybe I can find out if this medal thing warrants further action."

"Yes, sir," the soldier responded dispassionately. "Fill out this request form."

Mamba printed Kerrigan's name and military serial number in boxes on the form. He listed the unwitting Colonel Nicholson as the requesting party.

Mamba stood at the counter and leafed through the massive file he received. He knew that bureaucracies ran on paper, he still had nightmares about his paperwork as a police lieutenant, but he hadn't realized the massive amount of paper it took to run the federal government.

Page after page of Kerrigan's file was of little or no interest to him. He was about at the bottom of the stack when he found what he was after.

Before leaving Manzanita for DC, he read Kerrigan's entire file several times. A copy of this page of Kerrigan's military file was also in his Manzanita Police Department personnel file. If Pat altered something, this could be the smoking gun.

After checking to see if anyone appeared overtly interested in his actions, he pulled three pages from the file. He looked around once again. Satisfied he was alone, he checked the time on his watch. He figured that he had twenty minutes at the most before they shooed all civilians out of the archives.

He began to read. Carefully. The entire first page he read was identical to the same page in Kerrigan's file at the police station.

He turned that page face down and continued reading on page two. There was a notation in a comment box halfway down on that page. His stomach turned in disappointment. The notation on the original government document he was looking at was not the same as the notation on the page in Kerrigan's police file.

Documented in the folder was an infraction. Not a major infraction by any means, but an infraction nonetheless. Knowledge of the infraction might have kept Kerrigan from making Police Sergeant and would have kept him from the rank of Lieutenant. Without the information included in this file, Kerrigan made Lieutenant more quickly than many.

Mamba felt the color drain from his face.

"Are you all right, sir," the soldier asked. "You look pale."

"I'm just getting over the flu. I've been queasy off and on all day. This job is killing me."

"Routine for us all, sir."

Mamba grimaced.

"Did you at least find what you needed, sir?"

"Yes, I did. There's no medal in this file."

"Is that good or bad, sir?"

"It could be bad, Corporal. Very bad."

* * *

Sidney Brewster was upset. He sat at his most recent acquisition, a metal desk. On top of the necessity to skip on his bail, and the recent incarceration of his hitman, he now had a metal desk. He hated metal furniture.

"With Briggs in custody, I need a new man for a job. Maybe two jobs," Brewster told Rick Elkhart in what sounded suspiciously like a complaint.

"I've got the names of several hit men. They don't work as cheaply as Briggs, but they seem to be competent."

"I want no foul-ups on this," Brewster was emphatic. "One chance, one result, the result I want. If that goes well, we may contract for a second hit."

"I'll take care of it, sir."

"Good. I want to see the man tomorrow."

"Here? I don't know if I can get any of them to come here. And I know we don't want to transport them here. That could end badly. I haven't got much leverage, and I'm out on bail, too."

"For which both of us can thank my lawyers. I still think they screwed up with Briggs, though." Brewster spat and unleashed a torrent of profanity blaming the judge and his mother for his hitman's continuing incarceration.

Elkhart braced for the next explosion.

"Just bring me a name and a picture," Brewster said with a sigh at the end of his tirade.

Elkhart nodded and left Brewster. He took the stairs down two floors, transferred to the elevator for two more floors. He ended his trip to the underground parking garage by walking down the entrance ramp. He saw no one who appeared out of place or interested in what he was doing. Whether or not Sid liked the accommodations, this hotel appeared to be off Manzanita Police Department's radar.

* * *

After his disappointing day in Washington, DC, Mamba found that the airline overbooked his flight. He volunteered to be bumped in exchange for a two-hundred-dollar travel voucher, a free hotel room, dinner, and breakfast. After calling Hope, he spent another night in the same hotel and headed home on the first after breakfast flight to Los Angeles.

Seldom talkative to those seated next to him on an airplane, Mamba was Sphinx-like during this flight. He landed having exchanged no more than two-dozen words with anyone inside the plane.

Since he checked no bags, he was at the curb waiting when Stallings arrived. He briefed the Sergeant as they drove to his office.

"The FBI finally acted interested when I told them of the differences in the Defense Department file and the one in the Police Department. Special Agent Greene met with me in his office." Mamba sighed. "I'm inferring interest. Greene implied syndicate connections."

"That fits with the drugs," Stallings thought aloud. "That's hard to believe about Kerrigan, though."

"I don't believe it. But, I'm going to Pat with this. I want to hear his side. Sooner rather than later."

"You're thinking the feds will contact Chief Rogers."

"Based on my interaction, I suspect I opened a can of worms with my poking around. It's hard to imagine a scenario where The Bureau wouldn't pass on what I told them I found. And I've got a good imagination."

"And the Pentagon?"

"Not so good there, either."

"No details to share?"

"Nope."

For the rest of the drive, Mamba was as conversational as on the airplane. His mind was busy constructing and deconstructing situations. A few scenarios were good. Most were bad. Some were awful.

* * *

Larry Lester had news. The news wasn't good: Brewster found a hitman to replace Briggs. He knew Dancer would flip him back into jail if he didn't keep his end of their bargain.

Lester dialed Mamba's office.

"Dancer, this is—"

"Thank you for calling Mamba Investigations," Hope Mamba's well-modulated voice informed the caller.

Lester cursed Mamba's answering machine. As much as he hated doing it, it forced him to leave what he learned on the message tape or leave no message at all. His information needed immediate action.

He left the message.

"Dancer won't like hearing this after the fact. But, at least he'll know for certain that Larry Lester is a man true to his word," he muttered after hanging up.

* * *

Woodrow "Whack" Evans was a proud man, but he respected tradition. He bowed to his sensei, although he could have defeated the teacher in a matter of seconds. He was a professional hitman—one of the best in Southern California. The session ending now would be his last in the region. His current contract was a Manzanita Police Department policeman.

Elkhart hired him after Brewster saw a photo of Evans demolishing an oak desk with his hand. The brief verbal résumé of his work sealed the deal. Although only five feet eight inches tall, Evans' chiseled physique combined with black belts in three Asian martial arts made him a sinister human weapon. Almond-shaped eyes hinted at his oriental heritage.

For Evans, the hit on the policeman was the break he was waiting for. He agreed to a lesser fee than his usual compensation since Brewster was the upper echelon of the criminal community. Doing a job for Brewster was a big step up the ladder, despite Brewster's current situation.

At the moment, Woodrow lay flat on the ground, his eyes locked on the pedestrians leaving the Northeast Station's employee exit. He compared each male that walked out of the police station with the DMV printout in his hand.

Evans considered himself the best hitman around. If Brewster was an upper echelon employer, those using Evans considered him to be upper tier in both skill set and price. Because of his one hundred percent success rate, he was in demand.

Kerrigan was the name of the cop he waited for. So tight was his focus, he was unaware of anything but his victim's picture, tightly gripped in his hand, and the last name of his target. He enjoyed the shocked expression on his victim's face when he called them by name just before they died.

He squinted at the photo again in the waning twilight as a suit exited the station. He belly-crawled to the back of the closest car and crouched behind the rear bumper. He watched his prey unlock his car door, slide in, and insert the key in the ignition. As Kerrigan reached for his seatbelt, Evans sprang forward and used his body to ensure Kerrigan's door would remain open.

Before the policeman could turn his head, Evans delivered a strike to his victim's left temple with his left hand. Blood spurted on Evans' hand as the skin beside his target's eye ripped open. He shoved the policeman against the passenger window then compressed the man's lanky frame between the front seat and the dashboard. Kerrigan's head bounced off the bottom of the dashboard with a thud. He didn't move.

"Whack!"

After a look around, the hitman shook blood off his hand out the open door and wiped more on the front seat. He pulled a strand of electrical cord from his pocket and tied Kerrigan's wrists together. The knots tightened until blood oozed from the grooves cut into his target's skin. He put on his seat belt, started the Crown Victoria, and exited the employee lot when the gate opened automatically with the car's approach.

Evans was careful to obey all traffic laws on his drive to Koufax Field. He squeezed the steering wheel tightly in exhilaration as he thought of what was to come.

* * *

It took Mamba more effort than he thought it would to sound casual when he called Kerrigan the morning after returning from DC. He didn't want to confront his friend, but, confrontation or not, he had to know how much his former partner knew about the discrepancies in his personnel file.

Kerrigan agreed to meet with the PI and discuss the case. Mamba suggested meeting for ice cream after dinner. Kerrigan was a sucker for Rocky Road ice cream. They scheduled the meeting for 6:30 p.m.

Mamba looked at his watch for the thirtieth time in the last thirty minutes. It was 7:00 and Kerrigan had yet to arrive. He walked to the counter.

"Hey, David," he called to the high school kid with the name badge manning the register. "Can I use your phone?"

"I'm not supposed to let anyone use the phone, sir."

"I'm calling the police department."

"Oh, no reason for that, sir! I'll let you use the phone!" He pulled the device from the shelf under the cash register and slid it over the PI.

Mamba considered explaining what he meant, but decided against that. What was happening made a better story for David to tell his buddies. He dialed the station.

"Lieutenant Kerrigan, please."

"He's gone for the day," was the reply. "I can take a message."

"No, thanks. I'll call back later." He hung up and dialed Kerrigan's home number. David, who stepped away from the counter after giving Mamba the phone, started forward when the first call ended. He jumped back when the PI dialed a second time.

"Hello, Kate. This is Phil Mamba. Can I talk to Pat?"

"I thought he was with you."

"He must have got hung up at the office. I'll try there. Sorry to bother you."

Despite self-comforting conclusions he fabricated in his mind, he slammed the phone down and headed for the police station at what the police department considered excessive speed for the road conditions.

After parking in the visitor's lot, Mamba peered through the fence into the police personnel lot. Kerrigan's car was not in his assigned space.

He walked to the entrance to the lot, slid around the motorized bar that blocked the driveway, and hurried to Kerrigan's space. He switched on his flashlight and surveyed the parking space. Light reflecting off a shiny blotch caught his eye. He pushed his finger into the blotch.

He sniffed his finger.

That was all it took.

The sticky substance was blood.

The PI sprinted around the building and into the station through the front door.

The Desk Sergeant saw him coming and met him at the door.

"You might as well come back to the force, Dancer. You're here so much that people are expecting to find you here. In fact, I got a message for you to call your office about an hour ago. I called and only got—"

"Which phone can I use?" Mamba demanded, immediately regretting his tone. If the message was from Kerrigan, there was no need to panic the troops.

"Sorry, Smitty. It's been one of those days." He punched in his voicemail retrieval code.

"No worries."

"BEEP! Dancer, this is Lester. By the time you get this message, it will be too late for your Lieutenant. You need to tell the cops that Woodrow Evans did the hit. I suspect the body's out at the ballpark since Evans fancies himself a ballplayer. He even calls himself 'Whack,' because he's a hitman and crazy as well. Sorry, but I tried to find you. Remember that."

The message smashed into Mamba with the force of a .45 caliber slug.

"Smitty!"

"Yo!"

"Get at least one car out to the Koufax Field, quick! And an ambulance, too!"

"What's going on?" the Sergeant asked as he patched into the direct line to the dispatcher.

"Kerrigan's been kidnapped and he's injured!" Mamba yelled over his shoulder as he sprinted toward the door.

"Code 999! Officer down! Any units respond! I repeat Code 999! Koufax Field. Code 3! This is an emergency! Officer down!"

In response to the dispatcher's broadcast, three patrol cars and two ambulances with paramedics simultaneously began their Code 3 trips to Koufax Field. Lights flashed and sirens blared as they wove through traffic.

* * *

A few cars littered the Koufax Field parking lot when Evans pulled in. He preferred empty parking lots and darkness, but this was a rush job. He negotiated extra cash to complete the kill by the end of the day.

Evans nodded in what passed as casual acknowledgment for him when a VW Bug passed on its way out of the lot. The only cars left were down by the kid's playground. He could see parents rounding up the children in his headlights as he parked. His mood improved.

When the last vehicle, a station wagon, pulled out of the lot, Evans jerked Kerrigan out the passenger door. It was fortunate for the Lieutenant that the hitman pulled him out by the shoulders because his feet were the last to exit the car. Those crashed against the pavement.

Evans dragged Kerrigan's still unconscious body several hundred feet across the parking lot, past the dugout, to the pitcher's mound of the baseball diamond. Once there, he released his grip on the electric cord around Kerrigan's wrists. The policeman groaned.

Whack smiled at the sound. He hated shooting unconscious people. He pulled his gun and sat cross-legged in the dirt cutout surrounding the mound. It was almost dark enough. He would wait as long as possible.

As Kerrigan regained consciousness and tried to sit up, he discovered his hands tied in front of his body. His wrists and shoulders hurt. A lot. When he tried to stand dizziness and nausea convinced him to reconsider. He folded his body back into a heap. He looked around out of his right eye, his left eye swollen shut from Evans' blow.

What the one good eye looked at was a baseball field. That puzzled him. Even though the darkness altered the perspective, he was certain he was on the pitcher's mound of a baseball diamond. Directly in front of him was a scorekeeper's booth. A painful turn of his head brought a dugout into focus.

"So, you're finally coming around." Evans stood up and prodded Kerrigan's prostrate form with a shoe. "It's about time. I was almost ready to give up on you knowing who killed you."

"I don't understand," Kerrigan mumbled.

"You don't need to. All you need to know is that I am Woodrow Evans. You can call me Whack because you, Lieutenant Kerrigan, are about to die."

"Why?"

"Why?" Evans laughed. "For eight thousand dollars cash and two grand of high-grade horse. That's why."

The hitman grabbed the collar of Kerrigan's suit coat and yanked him to a kneeling position.

Evans placed the barrel of his gun to Kerrigan's forehead. "You can thank the DMV when you get wherever you go when you're dead."

"Whack!" Evans pulled the trigger.

In an unintentionally simultaneous move with the trigger pull, Kerrigan lunged toward the man in a desperate attempt to thwart the killer's plan.

The explosion felt as though it blew off half of his skull and cut short his mental declaration of love for his wife.

After the blast, Kerrigan heard nothing but the echo of the shot that lingered, ebbing and flowing with his heartbeats. He crumpled to the ground.

* * *

Mamba's car roared into the parking lot of Koufax Field. He slammed on the brakes. The car screeched to a stop. Long, black lines of burned rubber appeared, smoking evidence of the car's speed upon arrival.

"Pat's car!" Mamba leaped from his car and sprinted for the player's entry gate. "God, help me not to be too late!"

Sirens wailed. He felt their sound waves pounding against him as the emergency vehicles moved ever closer.

The sound of a gunshot stopped him.

He forced himself to run again.

He pulled his gun as he ran, an instinct from his police officer days, and sprinted past the bleachers. He slowed to a fast walk before entering the field just past the third base dugout.

He saw someone moving through the near darkness down the first base line.

"Stop! Police!" He shouted the lie. When the figure kept moving, he fired. The figure changed direction. Mamba saw a flash of red and white flame. A screaming noise left a legacy of pain across his left biceps.

He dropped to his belly and squeezed off three quick shots. The figure staggered but kept moving away from him.

Without warning, light from police flashlights sent thin beams in crisscross patterns over the infield grass to his right. As the beams played across the pitcher's mound, Mamba thought he saw something there.

His right field target now pursued by the police, Mamba started toward the mound. He hadn't gone more than a half-dozen steps when two uniformed officers caught him from behind. One grabbed the detective by his injured arm. He winced and gasped in pain. The other trained his gun on him and directed him to drop his weapon. Mamba let his revolver slip from his fingers.

"Check the body," Mamba said without emotion. He motioned with his head toward the still form on the mound. "I think you'll find its Lieutenant Kerrigan of Homicide."

"How do you know that?".

"I don't know for sure," Mamba answered in a hoarse whisper. "I hope to God I'm wrong."

The officer holding Mamba's arm released it. He left the PI guarded by his partner. He crossed the sloping side of the mound in two strides.

"I can't tell who it is. Half his head is gone." He knelt down, leaned over the body, and played his flashlight beam on the victim's face. His eyes opened wide, and he screamed, "Oh, my God! He's still breathing!"

"Officer down!" Mamba bellowed and bolted toward his friend. The uniformed officer covering him called for him to stop. Mamba did not stop. When he reached his partner, he dropped to his knees and cradled Kerrigan's shoulders in his arms.

The policeman who checked the body reached to pull Mamba back. But, it was clear Mamba meant the victim no harm.

Tears gushed from Mamba's eyes and coursed down his cheeks.

As though someone flicked a switch, Phil offered words of comfort and self-deprecation.

"Pat, don't die. You can't die on me! Oh, God, save my friend! Please God! He saved my life when we were partners! Please, oh, please save him now! Please!" He repeated the phrases over and over.

"We've got a body over here!" The call came from down the right field line.

"It's the shooter," Mamba mumbled without looking up.

"Approach with caution!" The officer with the gun called from the mound area. "That one's armed and dangerous!"

The two paramedics from the ambulance entered the field by the third base dugout. One stopped at the mound. The other ran out to the collection of patches of light in right field.

The first paramedic jerked open his kit and tried to shove Mamba aside.

"He's my friend!"

"He's my patient!" The tone of the EMT's voice left no room for misinterpretation. He was in charge of this situation. "The best thing you can do for your friend is to let me save his life."

Mamba gave a mechanical nod. He lowered Kerrigan's shoulders to the ground, wincing in pain as his left arm straightened. He stood. The paramedic filled the void he left.

Mamba backed away, prayers streaming from his lips. He stared with vacant, unseeing eyes as the paramedic ripped packages open and poured antibiotics over the massive wound to the skull of the body that lay before him. He started an IV.

A minute later, a huge bandage enveloped what was left of Patrick Kerrigan's head.

A gurney arrived. Two EMTs lifted Kerrigan onto the gurney's padded surface and wheeled the stretcher to the waiting ambulance.

Mamba stumbled after them. He tripped, and came close to falling, as his emotional and physical pain overcame his adrenalin rush. A uniformed police officer moved to his side and supported him the rest of his trip to the ambulances.

The EMTs loaded Kerrigan into the first ambulance. One paramedic from each emergency vehicle clambered aboard after the gurney was inside. The siren began its fluctuating wail. With emergency lights flashing, the ambulance pulled out of the driveway and began the trip to Memorial General Hospital.

Mamba riveted his vision on the exiting ambulance. “That’s my friend.”

“He’s in good hands,” the paramedic charged with caring to Mamba’s wounded arm assured. “One of those guys is my partner.”

“Pat was my partner.”

“I understand.”

Mamba winced as paramedics worked on his injured arm. His brain registered no pain. His prayers escorted the departing ambulance.

Chapter 33

"The wound is superficial," the ER doctor told Mamba. "It'll hurt for a few days and you'll have a scar but no permanent damage. Have your doctor take the stitches out in ten days."

"Thanks," Mamba winced a little as he climbed down off the emergency room bed. Then, he asked at least the fifth medical professional since arriving in ER the same question, "Do you know how Police Lieutenant Kerrigan is doing?"

"I don't even know if we've admitted any police officers," the doctor confessed. "I've been working on several people besides you. There was a three-car pile-up on Highway 1."

"Pat would be wherever you do your trauma surgery. Seriously bad trauma surgery. He was in bad shape."

"I'm sorry. Get back up on the bed and stay there. I'll see what I can find out."

"Huh? Oh, thank you."

The doctor pushed aside the drape that surrounded Mamba's bed. He returned quickly, too quickly it seemed to the PI.

"Lieutenant Kerrigan is still in surgery."

"And? It sounds like you know more than that."

"I'm afraid that the surgeons were not optimistic before they began."

"In all honesty, I wasn't optimistic either. I held him in my—" Mamba's voice broke. He swallowed hard and finished in a husky whisper, "I'm thankful that he made it as long as he did. Is Kate here?"

The doctor ignored his patient's question. He stepped to Mamba's side and eased him back on his bed. The man needed to lie down.

"The police told me he was here!" Hope Mamba's voice was easily penetrated the thin curtain divider. "I will search each of these beds one at a time if I have to! Someone shot my husband, and I will see him!"

Phil smiled at his wife's tenacity.

The ER doctor moved to intervene. Mamba put his good hand on the surgeon's arm, made a halt sign with the other, and winced.

After a questioning look by the doctor, Mamba called out as he pulled back the drape surrounding his emergency room bed with his undamaged arm.

“In here, Hope.”

“Phil! Are you all right? Oh, that was stupid. You’re not all right. You’ve been shot!”

She darted through the gap in the privacy curtain Mamba created. Before he could answer, she dropped her purse and a gym bag to the floor and enveloped him in her arms.

“I’m fine,” he said. “Except for bruising from being hugged so tight. Oh, and the bullet hole in my arm.”

“Don’t try to be funny!” She warned as she took a step back from her husband.

“I don’t have to try to be funny. I just naturally am. Ow!” His attempt to dodge her slap at his good arm was unsuccessful. “Where’s Jimmy?”

“He’s with Franklin and Lizbeth. I can stay as long as I need to.”

“Good to hear. I’m glad you came.”

“Philip Richmond Mamba! I remember a time when I was in the hospital and you were like a human leech. That’s how often you were there. How could you even think I wouldn’t be here?” Hope’s resolve and bravado evaporated. Her eyes misted over before tears poured out as she sobbed.

“I’m sorry. I didn’t mean to imply anything.” He reached out and took his wife’s hand. “I’m trying to keep my mind off Pat Kerrigan.”

“He’s in here, too?” Sobs evaporated as Hope shifted emotional gears. “Oh, please tell me he wasn’t shot. He was shot, wasn’t he?”

“Yeah. It’s bad. They don’t know if he’ll make it.”

“I’m so sorry, honey. I didn’t know.” She draped her arms around his neck.

He hugged her in return and hoped she hadn’t noticed the wince.

“Where’s Kate? She must be here.” Hope asked as she pulled away. “I can hug you all I want to later. Kate can’t hug anyone now unless I go to her.”

“I don’t know. I might have asked about Kate. All I’m sure of is that Pat’s still in surgery.”

“You can’t go to see Kate the way you’re, um, undressed,” she said after backing away to get the full view of the hospital gown that almost covered him.

"I don't know what they did with my clothes," he explained. "They were covered with Pat's blood. I took them off in the restroom over there." He jerked his head to his left.

"It doesn't matter where they are. When the hospital contacted me, they told me to bring you some loose-fitting clothes." She reached down, hefted the gym bag, and handed it to her husband.

"Excuse me." The ER doctor interrupted the tableau.

Both Mambas turned in his direction.

"Don't take this wrong, but we sorta need this space. You know, for bleeding, sick people. Please, take this conversation over to the surgical waiting room where you'll most likely find Kate, if she's waiting for someone in surgery."

"You get dressed," Hope directed. "And just how do we get to the surgical waiting room, doctor?"

Phil rolled his eyes. The physician used his hand to guide Hope's elbow as he moved her to the hallway.

"Follow the green line."

Hope took off without looking back. Phil gave the doctor a quick thank you wave and a "that's just the way she is" look.

The doctor pulled the curtain aside and signaled. As a nurse entered the enclosed area he said, "Please help Mr. Mamba get his clothes changed."

"Yes, Doctor. Is this your bag, Mr. Mamba?"

"It is."

"Good. Follow me." She picked up the bag and headed for the bathroom. "I'll wait outside the bathroom door. If you need help, let me know."

As Phil passed the doctor, the physician smiled and flashed a thumb's up. Phil nodded and followed his nurse to the bathroom.

Inside the bathroom, Phil unzipped the gym bag and removed sweatpants and a Lakers t-shirt. He pulled on the sweats before he discarded his gown. His first effort at pulling the t-shirt over his head with his injured arm ended in a flash of pain down the arm. He opened the bathroom door with shirt in hand.

"Ahh, I think I know what you're going to ask. Hand me your shirt, please."

Mamba complied.

"Now give me your injured arm."

Phil extended his left arm as directed. The nurse rolled up the t-shirt so the opening to the left sleeve was visible through the large opening at the bottom of the shirt. She manipulated the garment over his arm without the shirtsleeve touching his bandage.

"If I was a betting man, I'd bet you've done this before," Mamba said once the shirt hung awkwardly from his left shoulder.

"You'd win. Now, bend at the waist, then, bend your head forward and stick out your right arm—like you're diving into a swimming pool."

Mamba did his best high-diver imitation. It took only seconds for the nurse to pull the shirt in place.

"Can you get your own shoes?" she asked as she tugged the front of the t-shirt taught.

"If you help me get them on, I think I can tie the laces. Thank you!"

"All part of the service. If I heard right, you'll want to follow the green line to the surgical waiting room when you're dressed."

"Got it."

Minutes later, Phil Mamba, dressed in sweatpants, a t-shirt, and wingtip shoes and carrying an empty gym bag followed the green line as directed. He found Hope standing outside the waiting room door.

"You okay?"

"I couldn't go in there by myself."

"We'll do it together." He pulled the door open.

Kate Kerrigan sat alone. She looked like she'd fought an entire army and lost. She barely stirred when Hope sat beside her.

"Kate, it's Hope Mamba. I'm so sorry about Pat. Are you here alone?"

She tried to speak and began to cry.

Hope's eyes filled with tears. She placed one arm around Kate's shoulder. Kate leaned against her, sobs increasing in number and strength. "The last I heard, the doctors were optimistic."

Phil moved into Hope's line of sight and shook his head.

Hope glared back. Kate Kerrigan was dying of grief. She would continue to do whatever it took to help her cope.

"Why don't you get us each a cup of coffee, Phil," she ordered with a jerk of her head towards the door.

"Yeah. Good idea." He left the room. As he walked away, he knew that Hope was doing what Kate needed.

By the time he returned, Hope was holding a tear-soaked, sleeping Kate Kerrigan in her arms. She only let go of her friend after Kate's parents arrived and promised to call the Mambas as soon as they had definitive word on their son-in-law.

"My car's at Koufax Park." Phil took Hope's hand as they walked to the hospital parking lot.

"We can't leave it there."

"I'll have an officer pick me up tomorrow to get my car."

She nodded.

"And, why don't you let me drive home?"

She thought about arguing. Fatigue won out. She handed him her keys.

The Mambas didn't get to bed until 2:30 a.m. Phil called the hospital just after sunup and talked with Kate Kerrigan's father. When Jimmy stirred, he got his son up and dressed while Hope slept in. He was in no hurry to tell her Pat's prognosis.

* * *

The hotel room was small and made smaller by the bulk of Darrell "Dispatcher" Evans. The man was nearly seven feet tall and weighed close to 300 pounds. He was one hitman Sidney Brewster opted not to use. He was also Woodrow "Whack" Evans' foster brother.

Woodrow and Darrell formed an unlikely pair and an even more unlikely set of brothers. Because they needed the money, the Evans, Darrell's natural parents, took in the most derelict of foster kids. The majority transferred out of their care soon after they transferred in. But, Darrell and Woodrow developed a bond. Their dissimilar size and skin color masked their kindred souls.

At this moment, Darrell's blue eyes stared at a slightly built man in front of him. Billy Kennedy wore oversized, unisex clothes. Until the raid on Mary Carstairs' house, he was her second in command. Although arrested with Mary and released on bail with her, he said nothing to the police. Guilt by association was guilt in his world. He was persona non grata to drug dealers.

He missed a court date trying to avoid a fate like Mary's. He was on the lam, trusting no one, and reduced to the status of a delivery boy, a title he considered degrading in the extreme.

To earn money, he delivered information to those he thought had interest. He worked free-lance with people who were sketchy. Guaranteed nothing, he hoped to receive payment for the intelligence he provided.

Evans' right hand clenched and unclenched in a steady rhythm as he squeezed a large spring-loaded hand grip strengthener. He stared into Billy's eyes. Billy shuffled his feet as he imagined the hitman's fixated gaze burning deep into his soul.

"I thought you'd wanna know about Woodrow's death before it hit the papers." The words spilled out.

"You're sure about this information." Evans accused rather than asked.

"Yeah, uh, I mean, yes, sir, Mr. Evans, sir. Mr. Brewster hired your brother, and the police killed him." Droplets of fear-induced sweat formed on Billy's forehead.

"You have no other reason for informing me of my brother's death? Nothing like, let's say payment?"

"Oh, no, sir." Even though Billy gave a herculean effort to mask his feelings, his face fell. To cover what he knew was disappointment showing on his face, he added, "I know how you must feel."

"I don't think so. I don't see how you can know how I feel."

"Oh, but I do."

"Squeeze this," was the command. Evans tossed Billy his hand grip strengthener. The tone of Dispatcher's voice did not leave refusal as an option.

Billy gave his best effort with his right hand. There was a minuscule, momentary bending of the chrome spring wire. It sprang back to its open position.

"I can't do it."

"I told you to squeeze it! Use both hands."

Rivulets of perspiration flowed down Billy's face as he strained. Using both hands, he depressed the spring about one-fourth the distance between the wooden handles.

"Th-That's the best I can do," he panted, fear-sweat now running down his face.

"Give it back to me."

Billy extended his right hand with one handle of the grip strengthener grasped in trembling fingers. Evans' hand engulfed Billy's hand and the device. Once again, Evans clenched his fist. The wooden handles closed against each other. This time, bones cracked as the pressure from Evans' grip intensified crushing the information broker's fingers.

Billy's eyes filled with tears. Bullets of pain shot from his fingers to his brain. The muted cracking sound continued from the cavernous darkness of Evans' paw.

"See? That's how you do it," Evans gloated. He released his grip on the man's hand. The device fell to the floor. Pain overwhelmed Billy's senses. Tears ran down his cheeks.

"If you can't squeeze my gripper, how do you expect to know how I feel?"

The only response Billy could offer was a shivering shrug. He reprised his self-loathing for being dumb enough to think he could gain Evans' favor, and some cash, by bringing him the news of his brother's death. He concluded that Darrell's nickname, Dispatcher, was well deserved.

"I gotta go," Billy managed through clenched teeth. He knew the closest Urgent Care was his first stop. He estimated that he had at least three broken fingers.

"Thanks for the information, Billy, wasn't it?" Evans broke into unrestrained laughter.

* * *

The afternoon was hot and dry. Santa Ana conditions returned after a brief respite. Temperatures soared into triple digits while the relative humidity fell to below fifteen percent. The water misters Phil installed on their back patio for just such occasions were spritzing.

Hope and Lizbeth sat on the patio drinking Arnold Palmers. It was a relaxing location, particularly with the misters going. Today, the reason they were on the patio was the seclusion it offered.

"I can't thank you enough for last night," Hope said.

"It was the least we could do, considering," Lizbeth answered.

They sipped from their insulated mugs for at least a minute. Lizbeth broke the silence.

"I'm worried, Hope."

"I wouldn't believe you if you said you weren't."

"I don't think we're thinking about the same thing."

"Your, um—" Hope stopped, uncertain of her next words.

"My cancer. You can say the word."

Hope blushed.

"But cancer's not what I'm worried about."

"What could be worse than that? In my book, cancer's got to be as bad as it gets."

"What if they find out you and Phil have been harboring fugitives?"

"They won't," Hope stated with feigned authority.

"But they might." Lizbeth hurried on before Hope could respond, "I know the Department still has random security drive-bys of your house because of the shooting. They'll probably increase since Lieutenant Kerrigan's been shot. Every time I go to the doctor or for a treatment or take a drive just to be out of the house, I expect to find someone waiting to arrest me when I leave or get back."

The two women sat in silence for a long moment, glasses unsipped. Hope spoke without making eye contact.

"Things happen that we don't understand and can't explain. What we are doing is supporting each through a difficult time."

"I don't know how to thank you."

"You just did." She swallowed to keep from crying. After a second swallow, she managed, "Would you like a refill?"

* * *

Following the drive-by shooting of the Mamba residence, the department ordered random sweeps of their neighborhood. The protocol implemented in the aftermath of Kerrigan's shooting increased the frequency of those sweeps. In addition, MPD required officers announce their presence and check that all was well three random times per shift. Phil hadn't told Hope. He wanted to be the one who answered the door on this first day of the new protocol.

While their wives reposed on the patio, Franklin and Phil hunkered down in the den, putting Phil closer to the front door than his wife.

The two men began reviewing the case involving Sidney Brewster. The conversation was superficial. Both men knew there would be a change in the discussion's focus. Neither wanted to be the one to open the fresh wound.

It was time to acknowledge the elephant in the room.

"I tell you, Franklin, it looked like an execution. I can't believe that Kerrigan's our man. This shooting was for show. No more, no less. Somebody's out to prove something or make sure MPD knows they're not to be taken lightly."

"You're convinced Brewster's behind all this?"

"I can't see another viable suspect. The other names from Reed's lists appear to be role players. None of them have a big enough, well, big enough anything to have top dog written on them."

"I can't argue with that."

"Besides, we're losing possible leaks left and right."

"Yeah. If I'm not the leak, and Martinez isn't the leak, and Kerrigan's not the leak, we're back to square one, aren't we?"

"It looks that way."

"Maybe it's time to set a trap to catch our rat," Stallings began. "I have an idea that could blow up in all our faces."

"That's better than no idea, which is where we are at this moment. What've you got in mind?"

"How about this?" Stallings leaned forward, his eyes on fire with anticipation. Mamba couldn't remember a time he'd seen the man so excited. "What if we leak false information and see if it hits the street?"

"Go on."

"We could plant a plan for a phony drug raid."

"And carry it out like the real thing to see if information still leaks."

"Bingo! If we limit the sources that know about this raid, we limit our suspects if the information gets out."

"Good. Good. I like it," Mamba muttered. Without explanation, he left the den. When he arrived at the sliding door to the patio, he opened it and called to his wife.

"Hope, where do you keep the backup Rolodex for my contacts? I can't remember the last two digits of a phone number."

"It's behind the income tax folders in the file cabinet next to the stereo console in the den." She didn't even look in his direction.

"Thanks." After returning to the den, he searched through his Rolodex for a phone number.

He yanked a card from the device and punched numbers into the princess phone that Hope used as a décor accent in the den.

"Martinez?" He asked as soon as the phone picked up.

"Yeah. Who is this?" the sleepy voice demanded.

"Sorry to wake you. It's Mamba. Oh. You were on a stakeout last night, right?"

"Yeah. Documenting some Mexican coyotes delivering illegals just south of town. What do you want, amigo? And, it better be something big."

"I need you to come to my house. But park on the street behind us and sneak in through the patio. We've got a plan to catch the leak."

"Stallings is the leak." As the PI's words sank into Martinez's still lethargic brain he added, "And who are we, Gumshoe?"

"Stallings and me. He's not the leak."

"What do you mean, he's not the leak? The boys in Internal Affairs seem pretty—" Mamba heard a sharp intake of breath before Martinez resumed the conversation. "Did you just say he's with you? He's like, AWOL and wanted, you remember that, right?"

"I can explain. Are you coming over or not?"

Martinez pulled the phone away from his ear and stared at it as though trying to see what was going on at Mamba's home through the phone line.

"If you don't want to come, I understand."

He put the handset back up to his ear. "Say again."

"If you don't come, I hope at least you won't rat us out. At least not yet."

"All right. I'll come. But, give me half an hour to wake up, clean up, fill up, and sneak into your house. Why do I feel like another stakeout's in my immediate future?"

"We're feeling generous over here. Take forty minutes." Mamba hung up the phone on the last syllable.

* * *

Lester sat in his small, stuffy apartment. Every window was locked, and the door was dead bolted. He sat at the small table that multitasked as a dining table, a card table, a buffet table, and a desk. He stared at a paper sleeve from a travel agent. In it was an open-ended bus ticket.

He dialed a now too familiar number. After the fourth ring, Hope Mamba's voice delivered the answering machines greeting and instruction.

"Thank you for calling Mamba Investigations." Lester zoned out, until, "BEEP."

"Dancer, this is Larry Lester. Word on the street is that Brewster's not happy that the police were at the ballpark so soon after Evans shot Kerrigan. So, I'm leaving town. If he starts looking, he'll find me if I stay here. Don't try to find me."

* * *

"Excuse me, ladies," Martinez said as he forced his way through the last of the hedges between the street where he parked his motorcycle and the backyard of the Mambas' home.

Hope and Lizbeth leaped to their feet at the sight of the giant, tattooed Latino. Hope dashed to the patio door.

"Phil! We've got a problem! Hurry!"

"Wait!" Martinez called. "I assume you are Hope Mamba, and you must be Sergeant Stallings' wife. Am I right?"

"There are lots of ways to find that information, all of them questionable!" Lizbeth shot back at him. She held the heavy glass pitcher of Arnold Palmer solution menacingly in one hand.

Mamba threw the sliding patio door open. He and Stallings stepped onto the patio, weapons in hand.

"Oh, geez, Martinez. Can't you ever do anything the simple way?" Mamba said in an exaggerated, exasperated tone.

"I warned you about him," Stallings said loud enough for Martinez to hear.

"I know you both think that's comedy, but do not quit your day jobs. Ladies, I am Detective Enciso Martinez of the Manzanita Police Department." He bowed.

Hope placed her left hand on her hip and stared hard at her husband. "We deserved a heads-up."

"Sorry. Time got away from us. This way, Martinez."

The Latino smiled at the women and followed the men inside.

"That was surreal," Lizbeth understated as Martinez slid the door closed with a wink.

"I agre—" Hope cut herself off in mid-word. She swayed slightly and grabbed the back of the closest chair.

"Oh, Hope!" Lizbeth moved close enough to assist.

Hope nodded. She closed her eyes to stop the swirling view of the patio.

"Do you need help to get inside?"

"No, but I'll take more tea."

With that thought hanging, she filled Hope's glass from the pitcher she brandished only moments before.

The three men regrouped in the den.

"I used up most of my good nature being polite to your wives out on the patio. I don't have much left, so if I don't hear some very convincing arguments why you, Mamba, think you, Stallings is not the leak, and why you are stashing Stallings at your house, I'm calling IAD." Martinez leaned back after the speech he'd punctuated with a pointing index finger.

It took some time to push the Latino's position on Stallings' innocence from one of skepticism to convinced he was not the leak. Mamba narrated a travelogue of his trip through the Midwest. He showed the big man copies of the documents he collected.

Stallings added commentary from time to time. At the end of the presentation, Martinez admitted that it didn't look like Sergeant Stallings did anything wrong.

"I'll give you this round, Gumshoe."

"Good. There's just one more thing."

Martinez slumped back into his chair.

"With Kerrigan in intensive care and Stallings still in temporary hiding at my home, you are the only police contact for this ex officio committee."

"As that sole contact, what almost legal activities am I expected to perform?"

"Detective, we want you to instigate a phony drug bust," Stallings said. "Narcotics must propose it, or, if someone leaks it, no one will buy it."

"Hold on," Martinez said.

Stallings looked at Mamba who shrugged. Martinez pulled a small notebook from inside his boot. He thumbed through the pages until he found what he wanted.

"That I can do. What about this?" He showed his partners the address of a house.

"I know for a fact this place is empty. Some avant-garde photographer was using it as a place to shoot *Nudes In Dangerous Places*. I think that's what he called it. We thought it might involve drugs, so my partner and I swung by. No drugs. We just rousted him."

"And."

"He was alone with his camera. The investigation of the photographer was before I went undercover, but I swing by occasionally. The house is empty."

"We're good then." Stallings looked from Mamba to Martinez and back.

"Sí. I'll set the raid." Martinez paused, his brow furrowed. "There's never have been any drugs in the place. That's what you want, right, Sergeant?"

"The more things that are wrong with the tip the better."

Martinez rubbed a hand over his shaved head. "I've got to run this through the Captain. He's heading Narcotics at the moment, so he's the only officer of rank that can clear the personnel for a bust. I can sell a new CI to him."

"He knows about the compromised raids," Mamba stated the obvious. "You think he might be the leak?"

"I suspected everyone at some point," Martinez replied.

"Why are you avoiding a direct answer my question?"

"I'm not avoiding anything. I know all the information from the station funnels through the Captain. I can't believe you think he has the time to sort through God knows how many reports hunting for things to leak to drug dealers. At least, I hope that's the case."

"I never had the Captain on my leak list. He's homegrown talent. He was a Commander when I was hired," Mamba elaborated. "Before that, he moved up the ladder from a rookie on a beat. If he's the leak, the department would have needed a plumber long before now."

Heads nodded in agreement.

"We have to include the Captain, so we might as well include the Chief's office too," Stallings decided.

"What about Dispatch?" Mamba added. "Almost every call goes through them."

"Not enough time. Dispatch is the last to know, besides the beat cops," Stallings answered.

"Okay. I count four suspects. The Captain, the Chief, Sergeant Edwards, and Desk Sergeant Smith."

"Why Edwards, Martinez? I know why I think he's a suspect, but what's your angle?"

"He's makes the copies."

Mamba frowned. "He doesn't always make them."

"That doesn't mean he doesn't know what they copied."

"Maybe. Sergeant Smith isn't always the Desk Sergeant."

"I'm viewing the Desk Sergeant position as suspect. If Smitty's not there the morning of this ruse, he might have left word to call him." Martinez's voice trailed away.

"It's up to you." Although he was certain the Desk Sergeant position was a dead end, Stallings did not want to make that call.

"Who else knows about all the compromised operations?" Mamba asked. He'd run through his memory bank of positions of rank that had access to that information and come up empty.

"What about Deputy Chief Chalmers?" Martinez asked. "I'll bet he's on everyone's routing slip."

"Yeah. Let's add him." Mamba did a quick mental calculation. "You need six copies."

"Why six?"

"We need to leave the extra one with the copies for Edwards' team to deliver."

"I'm hand-delivering them," Martinez corrected. "To ensure they get where we want in a timely fashion."

"Okay. Just leave the sixth copy in the copy room." Blank looks from Stallings and Martinez convinced Mamba to add, "Make a quick stop in that little back room where only Edwards and his team go. Leave the sixth copy there. But don't make it obvious. Fold it or something and put it where it looks normal."

"How will we know if someone takes it?" Stallings mused.

"I don't think the leak is dumb enough to take something in plain sight. But Martinez can check the duty roster, if the information gets leaked," Mamba suggested.

"Hold on. I know Officer Janet, um, Cowan delivers copies for Edwards, at least sometimes," Martinez added. "That makes her a suspect, too.

"Hmmm." Stallings frowned. "Hadn't considered the delivery people, but that's a good lead. If Cowan's on duty, get the last copy to her."

"Instead of leaving one in the copy room?"

"Yeah. No, wait! Edwards shouldn't need a copy. Like you said, if it's him, he's getting copies to leak some other way. I've watched him run copies for Kerrigan and me," Mamba reported. "I don't see how he can sneak a copy out of that machine. If we don't give him a copy, and all the others come away clean, that's pretty damaging."

"Enough. Make five copies and remember where you put them, Martinez," Stallings decided. "We want the news of the raid to get leaked. I say we stop planning and implement the plan."

"But not until Tuesday. We want all the players on the field."

"Good point. The Captain often works Saturdays and takes the next day off."

"I'll give this my best sell," Martinez promised.

"To be honest, I was mad at you," Stallings said as he stood. "That's not true. I was angry. Now, I can't blame you. I was almost beginning to doubt myself."

"After this is over and you come back to the division, anybody that doesn't believe you're clean has to answer to me." The Latino thumped his chest with a massive thumb.

Although, he did not share his unbounded optimism, Stallings shook the big man's hand.

"A little bad news," Mamba said after Martinez departed. "It doesn't impact Martinez or his role in what we've got going."

Stallings gestured to continue.

"I just played back my answering machine. Larry Lester left a message. He left town."

"Why do you think that's bad news? From what you've told me, it's just as well he's not around anymore."

"It's not the fact he left that's the bad news. It's why he left."

"So, why did he leave?"

"He's afraid Brewster will figure out who tipped the cops."

"I thought Brewster was in jail."

"Somehow his lawyers got him out on bail. I didn't tell you."

"Next time, don't spare my feelings."

"Message received. Anyway, the Department has no idea where he is. Lester knew he contracted the hit on Kerrigan. Now, Hope and Jimmy have to leave town again. Lizbeth has to go with them."

"We need to tell them now," Stallings said.

"I was thinking more you have to tell them."

"Together or alone it's all the same to me. But we can't send them far. Lizbeth's got a treatment tomorrow."

"How about Lompoc for a day or two?"

"I can do that." Stallings opened the door to the den.

* * *

Larry Lester stood in a phone booth. Although he was almost 500 miles from Sidney Brewster with a full day's head start on anyone looking for him, he was worried the man would find out what he was about to do. He stared at the handset for a long time until he worked up enough courage to dial.

"9-1-1. What's your emergency?"

"I have a tip."

"Sir, this line is for emergencies only."

"You tell Dancer Mamba that Sidney Brewster is at 1792 East 42nd Street. Room 1220. He will confirm this as an emergency."

"I need your name—"

The 911 operator stopped in mid-sentence. The line was dead. She shook her head and punched in the Division Captain's number. She'd let him sort this one out.

* * *

Alone in his downtown office the day after they'd hatched the phony drug-raid plan, Mamba ran scenarios through his mind. While he had complete confidence in the plan set in motion, it was best to prepare for glitches, especially the way this case was going.

The phone rang. He picked up the receiver.

No connection.

The phone rang again. The image of his wife swept into his thoughts. The phone rang again sweeping Hope's face out of focus. It was enough to jog his memory.

He punched the appropriate button on his phone and answered, "This is Phil Mamba."

"Mr. Mamba, this is Captain Abbott."

"Yes, sir. What can I do for you?"

"We got a 911 call for you from an anonymous source that says you can confirm information. I need to know if it's legit."

"I'll try. Do I need to come down there or can you play it for me over the phone?"

"Thought you'd never ask." There was a click and a scratchy recorded message began.

"I have a tip."

"Sir, this line is for emergencies only."

"You tell Dancer Mamba that Sidney Brewster is at 1792 East 42nd Street. Room 1220. He will confirm this is an emergency."

"I'd get a team over to that address ASAP, Captain! The man's one of my CI's. He's rarely wrong."

"Appreciate your help."

Although the line went dead, the PI's mind was alive with ideas.

Less than an hour later, bail-skipping, drug-dealing, killer-hiring Sidney Brewster was in police custody.

Chapter 34

"There must be something I can do besides sit at my desk and wait for information," Mamba said to his reflection in the mirror above the sink in the restroom in his office. He winced as he bent his left elbow to look at his watch. He agreed to use a sling for a week after being shot. It was day five.

Every time he moved his arm, he was glad the ER doctor convinced him he needed support for his injured appendage. He rubbed his shoulder joint above his stitches while he continued his monolog.

"It'll be awhile before there'll be a report from Martinez on any evidence of an information leak about the pseudo-raid."

He shook his head trying to shake an idea loose.

"I'll visit Pat!"

He locked his office and drove to the hospital. His original plan was to visit every day. He blew that the second day.

Mamba thought of two good points about going to visit Kerrigan. First, he was visiting Pat in the hospital and not visiting his headstone in a cemetery. Second, Flatly Broke was in the same hospital.

He would make two visits with one trip. But, nothing could offset the fact he had to visit his former partner through a window in a wall of a room in ICU.

As was his hospital visitation routine, after parking his car, Phil spent several minutes praying for both Kerrigan and Flatly. Spiritually recharged, he hurried to the hospital's entrance.

Since intensive care was on the top floor, Mamba stopped in to see Flatly on his way up. The ex-boxer was sitting in the chair beside the bed. He looked much better than the last time Mamba visited.

"You're looking good."

"Man, I am on top today, Dancer. This ther'py stuff ain't too bad. They say I'm doing good at it." His gaze locked on Mamba's sling. "Hey, man! How'd you get hurt?"

"I didn't dodge fast enough. A bullet got me."

"What you doin' bein' shot at?"

"Lieutenant Kerrigan needed my help."

"It don't look like you was enough help," the boxer said as he studied Mamba's face. "The Lieutenant's hurt, too, isn't he?"

Nurse Reilly entered the room, pushing an empty wheelchair. Her smile radiated happiness and good will. "Hello, Mr. Wiggins. Time for your therapy."

Mamba looked around the room. Except for Flatly and himself, the room was empty. He was about to inform the nurse of her error when Flatly spoke.

"You almost late, nurse," he chided. "I was beginnin' to give up on you."

"Don't do that! You can't give up," she sobbed and clutched her heart in melodramatic actress fashion. "You have to get better!" She gasped, "For me!"

"Hey, I was jus' kiddin'."

"I know. Hop in." She pointed down to the wheelchair.

Flatly's grin blossomed as her humor registered. By the time he settled into the wheelchair, an enormous smile crinkled his face.

"Where are you going, Flatly? Nurse Reilly said she was looking for Mr. Wiggins."

"That's me, man," Flatly said as he stole a furtive glance around the room. "Only don't hardly nobody know. 'Cept Cue Ball, and Nurse Erin here, and now you. Don't you go tellin' nobody 'bout that."

"I'll never tell." He nodded his head in amazement, an action the fighter interpreted as agreement to his request.

"Let's get a move on," he called to his wheelchair driver. Erin winked at Mamba and pushed her patient from the room.

Mamba went down the hallway and opened the door leading to the stairwell. He was in no hurry.

Opening the stairwell door at the ICU floor, he spotted Kate Kerrigan exiting the room where her husband lay. She looked more like an eighty-year-old woman than a woman in her early thirties. He asked God to help him say the right thing.

He stood for a moment, framed by the doorway. She glanced in his direction then stared at him with a look he couldn't classify. He straightened his shoulders and took his first step toward her.

"Pat's still alive!" Kate Kerrigan shouted as she propelled herself at Mamba. He braced himself. She engulfed him in a sobbing embrace.

Although Kate's arm pushed hard against his injured bicep, he ignored the pain.

At that moment he realized no words were necessary.

* * *

Despite Martinez's usual bravado, the Latino had to convince himself he was ready to sell the fake drug bust to his Captain. After riding side streets long enough to get the motorcycle's engine hot, he roared up to the front of the station. He jumped off his bike and sprinted up the front steps. By the time he reached the Captain's office, he was breathing heavily.

"I need to see the Captain!" His voice boomed in the small reception area.

"He's on a conference call, Officer Martinez. Why don't you get some water and relax until he's free?"

"Okay," Martinez panted. "I'll be down in the squad room. This is important! Call me as soon as he's available!"

Ten minutes after he bombarded the Captain's receptionist, she called the squad room. Two minutes after that call, Martinez was standing in front of Captain Abbott.

"I tell you, sir, a major deal is going down tomorrow. I want to be there!" It was a passionate conclusion to his overview of the fabricated information about the fake bust.

"This is hard to believe, Martinez. You say you learned all this last night? There must have been months of planning on the drug dealers' side for a deal of this magnitude. I say something's fishy." Abbott's tone of voice and the look on his face amplified the doubt expressed.

"This source hasn't missed yet!" The narcotics officer insisted, pushing as hard as he dared. If Abbott bought in, the plan would sell itself.

"All right, but I want this monitored closely. No mistakes! With Stallings who-knows-where and Kerrigan almost dead, the last thing I need is another blown bust!"

"Yes, sir! Leave it to me," Martinez boomed and beat a hasty retreat.

"I don't have a choice now," the Captain muttered to the detective's back.

Martinez found an unoccupied desk in the squad room, grabbed a piece of typing paper, and laboriously typed in several essential tactical points of the planned bust. He surveyed his handiwork, corrected two major misspellings, and added a notation to the end of the page.

Satisfied with the document, he watched while Officer Cowan made six copies for him and returned his original. She showed no interest in the content of the copies, and she wasn't scheduled to deliver copies that morning. He would deliver the local copies.

When Cowan was called away from the copy machine, Martinez ducked into the small office used by Edwards. He folded one copy and slid it in the middle of a stack of pre-folded copies. He made sure his copy stuck out enough to draw attention.

He headed from the copy room to the Captain's office and dropped off one copy. He continued to the station's reception desk, stopped, placed his stack of copies on the raised desktop, and spoke in hushed tones.

"I'm expecting a call," Martinez lied to Sergeant Smith. "It's from a CI of mine. Could be important considering the raid that's in the works."

"Copy that. Where do you want me to transfer the call?"

"If the guy calls, ring Stallings' extension. Cut off after three rings. When I hear that, I'll come back here to take the call. If I'm not Johnny-on-the-spot, it means I'm already on site."

"I made myself a note."

"Thanks," Martinez said. He scooped the pile of copies leaving the bottom copy on Smith's desk as though inadvertently left behind. He was in no hurry as he walked away.

The desk phone rang. Smitty picked up the call.

Martinez slowed giving the Sergeant time to alert him of the errant copy. The self-appointed delivery boy turned the corner of the hallway and disappeared from sight. Smitty didn't alert him to the copy he planted. Martinez didn't know if that was intentional.

Back in the squad room, Martinez slid copies into two routing envelopes. He addressed one to Chief Rogers and the other to Deputy Chief Chalmers. He placed both of them in the URGENT outbox in the mailroom and glanced at the clock. It was seven minutes until the next pickup. It was at least twenty hours until the fruit of his labor ripened, if it ripened.

He called Mamba's office.

He got the answering machine and left a message.

* * *

Eddie Edwards punched in a well-known phone number. After the sounds of a call being forwarded, someone answered the phone.

"Yeah?"

"Give me whoever thinks he's the new Brewster."

He heard a clank, several undecipherable voices, and the scraping sound of the handset's retrieval.

"This is Elkhart. Who's this?"

"Shut up and listen."

The phone line went dead.

Edwards swore, looked around, and redialed the phone.

"Don't hang up, Elk-something, right? I've got important news for whoever thinks they're in charge. And, I'm not used to being hung up on!"

"I'll try to remember that," Rick Elkhart said without a hint of sincerity before rephrasing his request. "My name's Elkhart. Who are you?"

"I'm on two payrolls."

"I don't have time for games! Give me what you've got, whoever you are, or get off this line!"

"Do the initials MPD mean anything to you?"

"You're the insider at the police station. What have you got for me?"

"I'm holding in my hand a plan to confiscate what appears to be a large quantity of your product. Cops will be at a house on 12th Street tomorrow morning."

"Hold on." Edwards heard a series of answers to the same question.

"Don't know where you got your intel, but we've got nothing going anywhere close to any address on 12th Street."

"That's odd, because there's a full-blown raid set for tomorrow. I'm telling you, I'm holding a copy of the strategic plan in my hand."

"I wondered how long it might be until another group muscled into our territory. They waited for Brewster's arrest to make their move."

"You're telling me this isn't one of Brewster's deals?"

"Are you arrogant and hard of hearing? I just said that. Get the details over to the Sleep 'N Snore Motel. And do it now. We can always learn from what the cops do in situations similar to ours."

"I don't appreciate your sarcasm."

"I'll add that to your growing list of complaints. I don't like being treated like a child," Elkhart barked. "If you plan on staying, how'd you put it earlier? Oh, yeah, 'on two payrolls,' then you'll get that plan to the motel on the double."

Elkhart slammed the handset back into the phone base. He impressed those in the room by acting like the boss.

Elkhart put on his best poker face and turned back to what were, at least temporarily, his minions.

Back at the station, Edwards slid the copy of the strategic plan back into a stack of copies Cowan prepared for his inspection and stapled the set as requested.

* * *

It was a slow day in the office of the Chief of Police. Petula Jacobs appreciated downtime, however, too much of a good thing had its drawbacks. Downtime led to boredom, which often resulted in unfocused action.

As she thumbed through the pile of routine reports for the third or fourth time, she noticed something out of place. She stopped thumbing and pulled a stapled set of copies from the stack.

Oh, my!

She dialed Anderson Pharmaceuticals and asked the receptionist to speak with the owner.

"This is William Anderson. How may I help you?"

"I just got a copy of the strategic plan for a major raid on what was Sidney Brewster's operation."

"I see. What's the timeline?"

"Tomorrow morning."

"Thank the Chief for me, please," Anderson directed.

"I'll be sure and do that," Jacobs said into the dead phone.

As soon as Anderson hung up the phone, Guillermo Arcenas made a call.

"Get me Reed. I've got another job for him."

"When, señor Arcenas?"

"Tonight. It's crucial he hit the pharmaceutical warehouse before dawn."

* * *

Darrell Evans entered Miss Kitty's Gunsmoke Saloon with no intention of purchasing a drink. Security tossed him from the place once for refusing to leave at closing time.

In his mind, the indignity he suffered when four, then five men muscled him out the back door more than justified his plan to even the score. He was making up for the affront. He also planned to leave the saloon in police handcuffs.

He walked to the bar, grabbed the first empty bar stool, and, accompanied by a visceral grunt, twisted.

The stool relinquished its grip on the wooden floor with the squealing sound of metal twisting. A series of snaps signified the four bolts in the stool's base surrendered to Evans' brute strength. He tossed the stool over the bar.

The projectile crashed into the mirror behind the bartender. The sound of shattering glass announced that shards of the mirror were in route to the bar top and floor beyond.

Evans ignored the debris, intertwined his fingers and straightened his arms with his palms facing out. Now fully loosened up, he moved on to the hastily vacated next stool.

He launched seven stools toward various locations inside the saloon before the police arrived. At the sight of the blue uniforms, he dropped an eighth barstool at his feet.

His face glowed with ethereal serenity while one officer placed handcuffs around his wrists. Another officer stood at a significant distance from the handcuffing with his weapon trained on the blonde man-mountain.

Verbal abuse from the bartender and the owner of the establishment rolled off the hitman's back. They could say anything they wanted. He accomplished his purpose. He repeated that purpose mentally and sotto voce as an acolyte repeats a mantra all the way to the station.

He demolished the bar owned by one of his least favorite people as his last act of freedom. That sweetened his revenge.

* * *

It was 7 a.m. the day of Martinez's raid on the imaginary drug stash. Eleven officers circled the target house on 12th Street. They breached two doors and the bathroom window in simultaneous coordination.

Officers cleared the rooms. Diligence on their part uncovered none of what they supposed to be one of the largest drug caches in the city's history. A sullen group of narcotics agents assembled in the front room of the house.

"I found something!" Two officers with weapons in hand rushed to assist the caller.

Less than two minutes later three officers entered the living room escorting a pair of naked young people. The girl held her clothes in an awkward attempt to cover her nudity. The boy reeked of alcohol and arrogance as he paraded beside his captors. The consumption of the lion's share of the nearly empty bottle of cheap booze carried in an officer's gloved hand bolstered his arrogance.

"We found two reefers and this." The officer with the bottle held the green glass container aloft. "There is some evidence of other drugs, but they're not here now."

"Do these two have ID?"

"It says he's nineteen." An officer held up a driver's license.

"I'm eighteen. Last month," slurred the young woman.

"Contact Juvenile about her." The officer in charge waved off her protestations. "Book him on contributing to the delinquency of a minor and possession. Add attempted rape. Maybe that will sober him up at the station. If he keeps the attitude, add public nudity and drunkenness."

The officer nodded. He pushed the boy out of the house ensuring the public nudity charge. A blanket appeared. The officers wrapped it around the girl and loaded her into a black and white.

"Not much to show for all this effort, is it?"

"Agreed," was the officer in charge's reluctant response. "Martinez has some fast talking to do on this one."

"Where is he?"

"He called in sick. I talked to him, and it sounded legit."

Awkward silence and shuffling feet cued the officer in charge.

"Wrap it up!" He waved his hand in a circular pattern above his head and stalked from the house. He had a serious bone to pick with Detective Martinez.

* * *

Kerrigan did not know where he was. He did not know what day it was. He did not know why he felt pain and couldn't isolate the part of his body causing it. He remembered being forced to kneel. He remembered lurching forward at the man with the gun.

Searing pain.

He tried to sit up. His left arm pushed off the bed. His right arm did not respond. He flopped to one side.

He tried to sit up a second time. Now, hands of a mob of people forced him back to a supine position. He directed his arms to push the mob away. Again, his right arm did not respond.

He shook his head in anger and frustration, cried out in anguish, and tried to grab his temples to stifle the pain, but only his left hand reached his head

He passed out.

* * *

"Brewster's in prison awaiting trial," Petula spoke distinctly into the phone. Answering machines had their purpose, like now, when she had no desire to speak with Guillermo Arcenas.

Arcenas smiled as he hit the erase button on his answering machine.

"Inform Ms. Gilroy's escorts that it's tattoo time."

"Is that all, señor?"

"It's enough. They know what to do."

As the associate turned to leave, Arcenas added a thinly veiled warning.

"Remind them that this is the end of their task. Their contract includes depositing their package at the baseball stadium, picking up their final payment at the drop, and driving North out of town before breakfast tomorrow."

"Anything else?"

"Yes. Tell the pyro to head to Redding tonight. He'll get his retainer and assignment in the post office's General Delivery two days from now."

* * *

Inker arrived where RossAnn was being held thirty-three days after her abduction. By then, she'd reached the pit in her psychological degradation. She was now a no one whose name was RossAnn.

"Tonight's the night, right?"

"Yep. Call from the boss. It's time for our tattoo party."

Despite the emotional detachment, the taste of fear filled her mouth.

Twenty minutes after Stripe took Arcenas' call, a walking tattoo catalog arrived. Inker was the tattoo artist of choice for unsavory characters in and around Manzanita. Only five-feet, seven-inches tall, two-hundred-fifty-five pounds filled his frame and made him look significantly larger. Then, there were the tattoos.

Inker wore a tank top whose sides were open to what passed for his waist. One eye socket and eyelid were jet black. When he looked right at you, one eye and a black oval stared at you. It was impossible to feel at-ease around the man.

"Who's my canvas?" The words rumbled out of Inker's mouth. RossAnn flinched as she felt the sound waves crash into her. Goosebumps covered her nearly naked body.

"That's it," Gray said with a head toss in her direction.

"Not much to work with."

A horrified gasp escaped her lips.

"She never was," Stripe cut her reaction off. "She had skinny legs when we nabbed her." The two sentences were enough to bury what indignation remained in RossAnn's psyche.

She began to whimper.

"She ain't gonna cry the whole time, is she?"

"Doesn't matter. Where you're inking isn't close to her eyes."

Inker's instant change in posture and the flex of each bicep in sequence several times brought smiles to the faces of RossAnn's captors.

"You need a chair?" Gray asked.

"Maybe." Inker shrugged. "Where's the tat landing?"

"Show him," Gray ordered his partner.

Two weeks earlier, RossAnn might have noticed the brief hesitation before Stripe followed the direction and the moment of embarrassment when he pulled her legs apart.

"No." She delivered the objection as a flat, toneless croak.

"Interestin'. What's the emblem?"

Gray rolled both hands to palms up. A stylized rattlesnake skeleton with evil looking eye sockets adorned his forearms. It was the required ink for all members of one of the local street gangs. Grey rotated his left forearm so RossAnn could see it.

She was more than familiar with the design. A chill of fear washed over her. She began to shake.

"Not that image," she begged. "Please, not that image."

"She don't look like that type."

"She isn't. This is a message."

Inker shrugged.

It took both kidnappers to get RossAnn's legs far enough apart for Inker to get his needle to the inside of her thigh. After two tries, both thwarted by a mix of frantic movement, sobs, and screams by RossAnn, Inker demanded they sedate her.

"I'm not doin' a crappy tat because the broad won't be still."

Gray shrugged and released her left leg. He looked at Stripe who nodded, let go of her right leg and went to their stash of barbiturates.

"This will be a good thing," Gray said as he forced two pills down RossAnn's throat. Five minutes later, RossAnn was unconscious.

"Yeah," Stripe agreed. "They'll find drugs in the queen of clean's blood. That should take away any sympathy she would have got."

Two hours and thirty-six minutes later, RossAnn's first tattoo was fully inked.

Satisfied they'd broken their victim, the kidnappers cut her hair with the clipper then shaved the scalp clean for the last time. After injecting RossAnn with a mild stimulant, they placed her clothes and emaciated body, clad only in bra and panties on the floor in the back of a white Ford van.

Gray and Stripe called their boss and received explicit instructions about where to drop RossAnn, who to contact about the location, and the order of contact. They drove to Koufax field and parked as close as possible to the baseball diamond. Stripe loaded the semi-conscious victim into a wheelbarrow and pushed her to the first-base dugout. Her designer clothes formed a crumpled ball beside her.

Stripe sat her on the bench and leaned her body against the wall in the dugout's corner. He crossed her pointed-toe leather pumps on top of her clothes on the ground beneath the bench.

While Stripe set the scene, Gray used the payphone by the bleachers to call the Manzanita media leaving a tip that he saw the missing RossAnn Gilroy naked in a dugout at Koufax field. He waited fifteen minutes before calling in a similar tip to 9-1-1.

After assuring their houseguest was coming out of her barbiturate haze, the kidnappers drove north on Hwy 101.

It was nearly 2:30 a.m. when officers from two patrol cars arrived at Koufax field. Remote units from all three Manzanita television stations were taping reports for broadcast on their morning news shows.

Four officers worked their way through the media circus and discovered the disoriented, pale shell of the women named RossAnn Gilroy. After moving her to their ambulance, paramedics did a complete assessment while the police finished their preliminary questioning. They transported her to the hospital and admitted her to a private room in the hospital wing named after her father.

* * *

Television reports focused on the abuse RossAnn endured. *The Manzanita Daily News* added a special interest column on other famous kidnapped victims and their lives after their ordeals. Only the local National Inquirer wannabe took the low road.

The top cover headline, "Naked RossAnn Found in Dugout," featured a photo of her in the dugout. Poor lighting and lack of camera expertise made it impossible to determine if she was naked. The other cover headline, "Kidnapping or Love Gone Wrong?" included a stock photo of RossAnn standing with an attractive corporate executive at a gala from earlier in the year.

The Gilroy family lawyers filed defamation of character suits and demands to pull all copies from circulation within minutes after the tabloids hit the shelves. They recovered sixty-seven percent of the magazines, but the damage was done.

* * *

The day after the staged drug bust went bust, Martinez stood before Captain Abbott.

"How could you be that wrong?" the Captain demanded. "We tie up eleven officers and come up with one misdemeanor drug charge."

"I don't know, sir," Martinez replied in a level voice. "That source has never been wrong."

"To top it off," the Captain started, stopped, and started over with the volume of his tirade rising with each phrase. "To top it off, while we're embarrassing ourselves in a deserted house, someone's ripping off Anderson Pharmaceuticals. Again. That's where the major drug action was last night, Detective Martinez. Anderson Pharmaceutical's warehouse!"

"Will that be all, sir?"

Abbott's neck veins bulged as he bellowed, "What? Didn't you hear me?"

"I heard you, sir."

"And, 'will that be all?' is all you have to say?"

"Yes, sir."

"Martinez, I, I ought to suspend you!"

"Yes, sir," the Latino bit off each of the two syllables in his response.

"However, I can't afford to lose another man now." He grunted, refocused, and added, "I'm letting you stay, but IAD will hear about this. There've been too many instances recently where set-ups you've been involved with went sour. Maybe they're barking up the wrong tree with Stallings as the leak."

"Is that all, sir?" It was all Martinez could do to keep from blowing up at his Captain in retaliation for the accusations.

"Dismissed!"

* * *

A sullen Mamba and an indignant Martinez shared the desk in Mamba's office with cups of cold coffee. Captain Abbott's implied accusation of him as the departmental leak incensed the detective. The PI couldn't understand what else Martinez expected, and he was unhappy with the contents of the paper in his hand.

Mamba broke the tacitly agreed-upon silence. "These are copies of our plan. Copies my CIs picked up on the street this morning. Supposedly, they were available before dark two days ago."

"That means information leaked within hours of when I delivered copies of the plan," Martinez complained as he focused on the problem. Then he reverted to what was, for the time being, his prime concern, his Captain's allegation.

"I can't believe Abbott thinks it's me leaking information."

"Well." Mamba hesitated. "Part of the problem may be that these are copies of your typewritten page."

"I've had enough!" A meaty hand swiped the pages from the PI's grasp. "Let me see those."

Mamba flexed his fingers after the assault.

"No way! There's no way this could happen." The Latino scrutinized the copies. A look of confused revelation crossed Martinez's face. He looked at Mamba.

"What?" The PI asked after several seconds of Martinez's trance-like silence.

"Looking at these made me think of something! Do you have copies of any other leaked papers?"

"Sure." Mamba went to a file cabinet and pulled open the second drawer. "If I'd known that staring at photocopies stimulated your thinking, I'd have had you look at these weeks ago."

"Did you guys hear the latest?" Stallings interrupted Phil's search as he pushed open the back door to Mamba's office.

"Not since this morning," Mamba answered without looking up.

"What latest?" Martinez asked.

"The news broadcast last hour reported an interesting story. Someone robbed Anderson Pharmaceuticals last night, just hours before our phony raid. How did those burglars know the Manzanita Police Department would be tied up on 12th Street? That's across town from where they hit."

"I didn't know about Anderson's place," Mamba murmured.

Martinez's brow furrowed in thought. "Once the news of the raid was out, the real dealers knew it was a phony. That's an opportunity for an uninterrupted drug heist."

"He's right. Dealers would have known that information was bogus." Mamba slapped the copies he retrieved to the desktop. "Sounds like our brilliant idea cost Anderson more of his legal drugs. We should have thought of that."

Martinez collected the copies from the PI's desktop and studied each page. He wasn't sure of exactly what he was looking for. He hoped he recognized it when he found it.

Stallings sat next to the Latino and stared at the pages with him.

Mamba watched.

"This is strange," the big man announced at length.

"What's strange?"

"Look at these two pages." Martinez slid copies of two different pages across the desk. One was a copy of the phony drug raid report that Martinez filed. The other was a copy of one page of Reed's original list.

The private detective examined the two pages for what he deemed an appropriate length of time. "What am I supposed to be seeing?"

"Thank you," Stallings said. "All I see is one copy each of two different documents."

"Maybe I'm seeing things I want to be there and not seeing what's really there," Martinez admitted. "But, these copies don't look like they were made on the same copier."

"So? That doesn't surprise me. There must be several thousand copiers in this city."

"I don't mean each copy isn't from the same machine. Maybe someone made the first copy of the original on a different machine than the other copies."

Blank looks greeted his revelation.

"I know a guy that works on copiers. Once he bet me twenty dollars that he could tell if copies were made on different machines. Twenty dollars buys a lot of Mexican food. So, I took him up on it. I went to four different places and made one copy of a piece of junk mail at each place."

"Is this going anywhere?" Stallings asked. Mamba flashed him a thumb's up.

"I'm almost finished. As I was about to say, I marked each page as it came out of the machine before I showed them to the guy."

"The suspense is killing me. Let me guess what happened," Stallings begged. Mamba smiled.

"Okay, Sergeant, what happened?"

"The guy knew they were all from different copy machines because he set you up. He knew you'd use different machines for each copy. You made it easy for him."

"Actually, that's close. I'm impressed."

Stallings gave him a hard stare.

Martinez expanded his comment. "I'm impressed with the logic employed. I thought the same thing, too, at first."

"I've got to get going," Mamba said as he stood. "Visiting hours are short in the ICU."

"And, I've got to call Lizbeth."

Martinez deflated. "Fine. Just let me take these with me."

"It's okay with me." Stallings said.

"Thanks. Give me the rest of the day to do some checking. Meet me here in the morning at eight o'clock." He added, "Mamba, please don't call me before then."

Chapter 35

Darrell Evans did all in his power to speed up his arrival at the prison where Brewster awaited trial. He accepted handcuffs that were too small and unnecessary prods from billy clubs without retaliating. He pled guilty at his arraignment.

His restraint and compliance paid off. In less than three days, he stood inside the same correctional facility as his nemesis.

"Where's Brewster?" Evans asked the first inmate he saw.

"Whacha want him for, man? He's bad. Plus, he's already got some boys that protect him."

"That may be so," was Evans' unconcerned comment. As long as they were unarmed, there weren't enough men in the jail to keep him from his achieving his goal. "But, I've got business with Mr. Brewster. It's important that I see him today."

"Just before dinner, he pays off for favors," the inmate whispered. "It's a big deal. Lots of the cons is there. You could see him then."

"That will work nicely," Evans said with a smile. The more people that saw Brewster get his punishment the better.

At four-thirty that afternoon, Brewster and his entourage congregated against one wall of the exercise yard. Brewster stayed toward the back of the group. He let his soldiers deal with most of those who sought an audience. Only those he deemed worthy were met personally.

"I want to see Mr. Brewster," Evans rumbled when his turn came.

"What about?" a screener asked.

"I have some information about that hit on the cop he ordered."

"What kind of information?"

"Are you Sidney Brewster?" Evans' voice was hard. His tone was his first hint at what anti-social behavior might result from noncompliance.

"No. But—"

"Then, you don't need to know." He added a menacing glare for emphasis.

The man decided to let his boss decide what to do with the blonde-haired mountain of muscle glowering at him. He shuffled over to Brewster.

"The big dude over there says he has information about the cop that got popped."

"What's done is done."

"I think you might want to talk to him," the screener pleaded, not relishing delivering a negative answer from his boss to the behemoth. "He could be a good soldier."

"He is a big hunk of meat. Send him over."

"I assume you're Brewster."

"Yeah, who are you?"

"My name's Evans. Darrell Evans."

"So, what's this information on the dead cop?"

"I never said I had information on the policeman." Evans moved a step closer to Brewster. "I told your man I had information on the hit."

"So?"

"The hitman was my brother." Evans mumbled.

"What?" Brewster took a step closer and uttered an obscenity. "Speak up. I can't hear you."

Dispatcher smiled a grim smile. He'd lured his prey into his trap. He took a last step closer to his target.

"You got my brother killed!" he shouted for Brewster's entire entourage to hear. Ham-sized hands closed around the neck of Sidney Brewster.

Evans' fingers tightened their grip and cut short Brewster's string of profanity. Witnesses said that they heard bones cracking.

Brewster's body went limp. Evans continued to squeeze. His thumbs pulled outward on the veins of Brewster's neck. Blood flowed down the prison gray shirt of Sidney Brewster and spattered onto Evans. The hitman dropped the dead man in a puddle of his own blood.

His revenge complete, Darrell Evans reached down and wiped his bloody hands on Brewster's pants. He straightened up. A pathway opened as he entered the crowd and headed toward the dining hall. The path closed behind him as he passed through. Not once was Evans' personal space violated. A few inmates gathered around the lifeless form of their deceased leader.

The sound of the sirens announced a prison-wide alert. Evans stopped walking toward the dining hall when a squad of guards entered the exercise yard. He shook his head. He was hungry. It was a shame he would miss dinner.

News of the death of Sidney Brewster reached Manzanita Police Department headquarters at 5:50 p.m. A phone call to Mamba Investigations delivered the news minutes later. He called Hope in Lompoc and told her to pack her things. She, Jimmy, and Lizbeth were coming home.

* * *

Stallings waited while two women and a small child finished packing clothing in suitcases in preparation for checking out of their motel room. With Brewster no longer a threat, the chaos left in the wake of his demise would deter thoughts of retaliation on Mamba or his family.

Stallings accepted the responsibility of escorting the families back to Manzanita.

"You ladies about ready?" he asked for the fifth time.

Lizbeth stopped and stared hard into the face of her husband. It was three days after her last scheduled chemotherapy treatment. She spent the day before in bed. Today, she felt like she should be in bed. But not just any bed. She wanted to get back to a real bed before she slipped between sheets again.

"Are you blind?" She snapped. A flurry of observations, complaints, and criticism flashed through her thoughts.

She swayed a little, fought to regain her balance, and then ran to the bathroom.

Hope grabbed Jimmy and dodged to one side allowing her friend a direct path into the lavatory. She knew that look. It was her look all too often recently.

"I'll put this stuff in the trunk," he called back as he walked out the door.

* * *

The phone in the motel where "Brewster's Survivors" were living rang nearly non-stop for several hours. All Brewster's phone numbers were programmed to forward calls to the last number in the queue when forty-eight hours passed without a completed call.

Most calls were regular dealers requesting product. Some were former associates wondering what the chances were of rejoining the organization since Brewster was dead.

The call in progress was neither of those.

"Who's in charge now?" the voice demanded.

"We don't know who'll be appointed permanent head of this branch," Elkhart answered. He assumed the mantle of leadership without challenge. No one knew more of the ins and outs of the operation.

"Now that Mr. Brewster's dead, we have to wait for word from Chicago. As it stands now, and like I told you the last time you called, I am in charge."

"Whatever. I want to know as soon as the next boss up the chain names the replacement. I mean as soon as that happens. I want to renegotiate my deal."

"The main office won't go for that."

"I'm taking a lot of risks here," Edwards snapped. "And it's not getting easier for me."

"You're paid well to take those risks."

"Shut up! I don't care if you think you're in charge or not, you're just a lowly employee like me. No! You're lower than me. Don't expect me to deliver items ever again. Oh, yeah. I almost forgot. Never lecture me."

"You talk tough on the phone."

"Just let me know when the new boss arrives. Remember, you can be replaced." The sound of a handset crashing into its cradle ended the call.

"So can you," Rick murmured as he replaced his handset on its base.

* * *

It was the day after Hope and Jimmy returned from Lompoc. The Mamba family headed home from church.

After the usual recital by Jimmy of what he did in Sunday School, all the Mambas spent the rest of the trip home in small talk. By the time they got home, Phil had phased himself out of the conversation. Something the minister said in his message stuck in his mind.

The sermon's title was "Third Party Grace?" What stuck with him was the idea that God's grace is only what you need and when you need it. He said, "There's no such thing as third-party grace in situations. Only the active parties in a situation need the amount of grace they receive."

He thought of Kate Kerrigan. Her husband was balancing between life and death. Mamba understood what she was going through. A terrorist's bomb put Hope in the ICU. It disturbed him that he didn't feel the same way about Pat.

"I thought I'd grown callous," Phil said to Hope after Jimmy was down for his nap. "Pastor helped me see I don't need the same grace now that I had with your situation."

"I noticed you'd stopped taking notes when Pastor defined third-party grace."

Phil shrugged.

"But, you getting calloused never worries me. I know you. You have a heart for people."

"Well, don't let that get around."

Hope rolled her eyes and kissed him.

"I won't tell a soul."

"I'm going to the hospital. I want Kate to know that I'm praying for and supporting her and Pat."

* * *

Mamba usually jogged three mornings each week. He described his routine as, "twenty minutes or two miles, whichever occurs first." While working overlapping cases with the Manzanita Police Department, jogging ceased. He needed to revive the habit.

His guilt-inspired promise to himself while he scanned the morning paper was to start jogging soon, but not today. His scan of the paper yielded two tangentially related articles that inspired him to physical activity.

"Chamber of Commerce Weather" was predicted for Manzanita. In addition, a parade in honor of the first Spanish land grant owner started at 10:00 a.m.

The smallest deviation from the normal morning routine snarled Manzanita traffic. He'd take advantage of the weather and walk to Memorial General Hospital.

He changed into a casual shirt and pants, put on his jogging shoes, and headed out. After a brisk half-hour walk, he arrived at his destination. He stopped in the first men's room he passed to rinse his face and hands and arrived at the door to Flatly's room as his orthopedic surgeon was in the middle of an explanation.

"The therapy has improved your condition, Mr. Wiggins. However, the choice has to be yours."

"What choice is that, man?" Flatly asked, unsure of the meaning of all the doctor related over the past several minutes.

Mamba stepped into the room.

"If you're a visitor, come back in five or ten minutes," the surgeon advised in a tone that implied it was more a directive than an option.

"Hey. It's okay, Doc. This is the Dancer. He's my friend. He can stay."

The doctor nodded indifferently to Mamba and resumed his explanation.

"If you continue with therapy, you will increase the limited mobility in your right arm. Therapy sessions will be weekly for at least a year. At that time, I will assess the extent of your recovery. However, no matter how diligently you work, Mr. Wiggins, your shoulder mobility will never return to normal."

"That just sounds like doctor talk. What's my choice?"

"If I amputate," the surgeon continued as though Flatly had not interrupted him, "I can rebuild the shoulder area and prescribe a prosthesis that will provide more mobility in the long run."

"What you sayin', man? Say it in English!"

"I think he means that you have to decide whether or not you want to keep your arm." Mamba offered his translation.

"At the simplest level, your friend is correct."

"But, that ain't no choice!"

"There are ramifications to consider either way," the surgeon picked up where he left off.

"Would you explain it to me in the hallway," Mamba asked. "I think I can make it clear to him."

"I doubt that," was the aloof reply. "If I do not explain the options to him, I am absolving myself of responsibility of this man's decision. You are a witness, nurse." He motioned to Erin Reilly.

She nodded obediently. She knew which doctors not to cross. This was one. She prayed that God would help Mamba survive this ordeal then prepared to help explain Flatly's options.

Mamba and the surgeon retired to the corridor. Several minutes passed. Erin read a passage of a new book to Flatly. Mamba returned, alone.

"Help me out, okay?" He nodded to Erin.

"With or without your asking."

He smiled his thanks, took a deep breath, and plunged into his translation of the doctor's explanation.

"If they don't take your arm off at the shoulder, you won't be able to move it enough to do many things you're used to doing."

"Like what?"

Mamba looked to Erin.

"Like pushing a door open using only that arm. Like reaching above your head for anything with that arm. Like pulling your pants up with both arms." Her voice was gentle but firm.

The boxer stared straight ahead, brow wrinkled in thought, his lips tightly pursed.

"But the doctor can rebuild enough of your shoulder to make a place for an artificial arm to rest. After you learn to use the artificial arm, you'll be closer to normal for some movements. You have to choose." As she finished, she gave the PI a 'how'd I do?' look. Mamba gave an affirming nod.

"If the doc cuts my arm off and I get me a artyfishul one, I'll only be closer? Not all the way normal?"

"Only closer," Erin confirmed. "No doctor is good enough to make your shoulder normal again. It would take a miracle for that."

There was a moment of silence. Erin's thoughts ran to how well she explained. Mamba's thoughts focused on how much Flatly understood of what he heard. The boxer's thoughts centered on the final phrase of Erin's explanation.

"I walked by a church on a Sunday mornin' once. I looked inside 'cuz there was lots of good singing comin' out. Over the stage where the preacher and a bunch of singers was, was a big sign. I asked one of the men taking up a collection of money what that sign said. He tol' me, 'Expect a miracle,' just like he really did. I think I'll go back to that church. I got me a miracle to expect."

"I don't think God works on demand."

"I won't be demandin', Dancer, I'll just be expectin'. I figure I need to be in church anyhow, just to say thank you for still bein' alive and all."

"That means you're keeping your arm?" Mamba asked. "You know it's gonna take a lot of hard work."

"Yep."

"That's a wonderful choice!" Erin hugged the ex-fighter. "Expecting a miracle is the right thing to do."

"You think so?"

"I do," she answered with another hug. When she passed Mamba on her way out of the room, her eyes were bright with tears. He wiped the tears from his eyes and smiled.

* * *

Martinez headed to the division station on his usual mode of transportation. As he steered his motorcycle through traffic, he formulated his plan for obtaining the photocopies he needed. His decision: take three original documents to the station's copy room and have them copied.

He would stay in the copy room and ensure the papers he handed over never left the room or his sight. When they returned his originals, he would make superficial alterations to them. If someone had the modified papers copied elsewhere, the changes he made would show up on the new copies. Copies of those copies would show the changes, too.

A close miss of his bike by a car changing lanes returned his mental focus to driving. But, after two blocks of obeying traffic laws, he was back to planning. He decided to take pages of three different files and have them copied at offsite copy machines. He would give those copies, what he called original copies, to the Records Division. They would copy the original copies under his surveillance.

Finally, he would have the Records Division make copies of one of the copied pages of Mamba's original list and the copy of his phony drug bust plan the PI got on the street. He'd deliver the copies he made to the lab. A technician owed him a favor for scaring guests at his kid sister's party straight. His analysis of the copies would pay back the debt.

Martinez needed answers to two questions. First, which copies came from which copy machine. Second, if a particular copy was a copy of a true original or if it was a copy of an original copy.

The blaring of a car horn and the sound of a shouted expletive forced him to abandon further planning. He shook his fist in retaliation at the driver who yelled at him and sped off—this time with his full attention on the road.

He skidded into the parking lot and brought his bike to a stop in its usual spot, parked illegally in one of the triangular areas at the end of a row of parking spaces.

Martinez checked in and went straight to the files. He rifled through one drawer and removed an arrest report and a report on an unprofitable stakeout. The second drawer produced two recovered property lists and two physical evidence lists. As an afterthought, he pulled a page from an old logbook. He removed the papers he tucked in his jacket at his meeting with Mamba and Stallings.

The bait was ready. It was time to go fishing.

He gave a wave to Nina in dispatch as he headed for the parking lot. He climbed aboard his bike and roared off. After stops at a supermarket, the library, and the post office to make copies of the documents he carried, he returned to the station and headed straight to the copy room.

"Whatta ya need?" asked the young officer behind the desk in the records division.

"Copies," Martinez answered with a wry grin. He held aloft his hand full of paper.

"What's the authorization?"

"SDA."

"Say again."

"Sorry. Spontaneous Division Audit. Lucky me won the random drawing for an audit this round," he lied. He was proud of his imaginary new requirement. SDA sounded like all the other official alphabet tasks assigned by those above him in rank.

"I've never heard of a Spontaneous Division Audit."

"Oh, you will," Martinez promised. "It's a new program from the Chief's office. From what I understand, we are the test division for the plan." He screwed his face up in a comic grimace. "You never know what those guys upstairs are thinking."

"I think it's an innovative concept. We should commend the Chief. I never understood how they expected to turn up irregularities in departmental policy with announced inspections. That gives everyone a chance to clean house prior to the inspection. Let me see your badge."

Martinez nodded courteously, smiled inwardly because he remembered to bring his badge, and complied by opening the wallet-like folder. The officer entered Martinez's name and badge number into his logbook and waved him in.

Sergeant Edwards stood beside the oversized copy machine. As a veteran of twenty years on the police force, he'd seen many innovations. From the standpoint of relieving some strain of mundane tasks from the regular officer, the copy machine was the biggest time saver to come along.

Without a word, an uncommon thing for Eddie Edwards, the Sergeant took the papers from Martinez. He scanned the contents of the pages. After the rapid perusal, curiosity got the best of him. "What're these for?"

"Spontaneous Division Audit." Martinez deadpanned.

"Another innovative new procedure, I'll bet," Edwards moaned. "How high did this one start?"

"Chief's office."

"Then I better alert my people. When something starts above the Captain, it's here for a while. How many copies you want?"

"Two of each, Sarge."

With a nod, Edwards picked up his logbook and wrote the number showing on the copier's counting device when he started Martinez's job. He added the number of pages to be copied and the number of copies of each page requested in their allotted columns. He also recorded the date and time.

Martinez was more baffled now than before. He was certain the leak was Sergeant Edwards or someone else in the Records Division. In fact, his plan sprang from the expectation of finding a glitch in the copy-making procedure that would allow Edwards to make unauthorized copies to sneak them out of the station.

The copy log procedure was tight. The Latino couldn't see how anyone could beat the copy counter. His shoulders sagged.

"Here you go," Edwards said. "And, buck up. You know better than to take this personally." He clapped Martinez on a drooping shoulder while handing him his originals and a stack of copies.

He straightened his shoulders.

"Yeah, you're right. I should consider myself lucky to be a test case. They can't have all the boxes to check figured out yet."

"That's the spirit! Your originals are on top. The copies are in the order of the originals underneath. Good luck."

"Thanks," Martinez answered with feigned enthusiasm, certain that his grand idea was nothing more than a dead end.

Chapter 36

The neurosurgeon hated conversations with the families of his patients. He wanted to tell them it was all up to their loved one. He learned, during twenty-six years and hundreds of brain surgeries, that recovery depended on the grit and determination of the patient.

What he needed to say was far from what the family wanted to hear. Today, he had his state-of-the-brain speech prepared for family and friends of the police lieutenant shot in the head at the ballpark. He was in the middle of delivering that speech to the man's wife.

"Because of what I just explained, I see slight improvement in your husband's condition."

Kate Kerrigan's face brightened. The brightness faded when the doctor added, "However, until we can check his eyes and vocal capabilities, he'll never score better than 'severe coma' on the Glasgow Scale. I'm not implying he will talk or he will wake up soon, but there are signs lessening depth of the coma."

The tired, disheveled woman sighed. "I know that's not much, but the way I see it is, some improvement is better than no improvement and a lot better than worse. I've got something now besides hope. God gave me a sign."

"I've got more rounds to make." The surgeon looked as his watch. "I've instructed the nurses to allow you to be with your husband as much as you like. I am continuing the restriction of only two visitors in his room at one time, though."

Kate gave the mechanical nod she perfected while listening to doctors.

"I'm also telling you to not wear yourself so thin that you end up as a patient here." He'd seen far too many wives, husbands, and children end up as psychiatric patients by the end of their loved one's treatment.

Kate nodded again.

Mamba and the doctor exchanged nods as they passed outside the door to Kerrigan's room. The PI arrived during the conversation between Kate and the surgeon. He waited outside. In direct contrast to his feeling of needing to help Flatly, he felt helpless when he visited his friend.

"Make her rest."

Mamba turned.

"I'll try. I've been in her shoes."

The doctor nodded and continued his rounds. Phil straightened his shoulders and looked through the wall of glass. Kate stared down at her husband.

Something made her turn in his direction. He noticed the look of optimism in the eyes of his friend's wife. He didn't have to wait to find out why. Kate motioned for him to come in, but hurried out the door to meet him.

"Oh, Phil, Pat seems to be getting a little better!"

"I'm glad to hear that," Mamba said with measured enthusiasm. He needed more information before he agreed, however, he wasn't about to let her know his doubts.

He hugged the woman with his good arm.

"Come in to see him with me."

"Is that allowed?"

"The doctor said I could go in as often as I want. I can take one person with me."

He offered her his right arm. She pushed open the door.

* * *

Kerrigan was awake again. He heard the same noises in his right ear. An acoustical void enveloped his left. He tried to imagine a place he would be that would fit the sensations he was experiencing.

Pictures flashed into his memory. He couldn't name any of them. That frustrated him. He considered sitting up and getting someone's attention regardless of the pain.

He heard voices. Yes, there were two voices. As before, visual images flashed before him. He could see the owners of the voices. Try as he would, he could not come up with the names of the man and woman.

"What did they find during surgery?" The man's voice asked.

"The doctors said that he would have to relearn how to do some things," the woman answered. "The bullet tore away quite a bit of the left side of his brain."

Kerrigan's heart went out to whoever they were talking about. He wished his throat was empty. Then, he could ask about the injured person. The man spoke again. Pat focused his attention on the conversation.

"Will he be able to walk and talk?"

"They're not sure."

"What about hearing?"

"They say he's deaf in his left ear. The bullet damaged the ear canal on its way in."

A light turned on in Pat's head. He knew what deaf meant. It could be a reason for the lack of sound on his left side. He struggled against his tubes and blanket.

"Phil! Pat's moving!"

"Doctor!" Mamba ran to the door, threw it open, and bellowed, "We need a doctor in here!"

Kerrigan wondered why it was so surprising that Pat was moving. And why would a doctor care?

He had no time to consider the reaction by the man and woman. As he moved, the pain engulfed him. He lost consciousness.

* * *

It was the end of a long day. Mamba tried to reconstruct what filled the time but came up with only routine events besides his visit to Kerrigan. He climbed onto his side of the bed.

He turned toward his wife who was reading a romance novel. Phil watched her until she tired of his stare and turned her head in his direction. He patted the mattress next to him to coax her closer.

"I want to bounce a few ideas off your pretty brain."

Hope reached over her head and placed the book on the headboard. She shifted her position slightly in his direction, rolled onto her back, and cupped both hands behind her head. "I'm ready."

"Here we go." He rolled onto his back. "At first I thought Stallings was the information leak. Then, when other people started to accuse him, I tried to exonerate him. The evidence against him was sketchy. It looked like a setup."

"I see," Hope murmured.

"Then, and I really didn't want to believe this, but Pat Kerrigan looked like the leak. Someone altered his military personnel file."

He paused. A vision of a gauze-covered head snapped into focus in his mind.

She stifled a yawn.

"Anyway, since someone ordered a hit on Kerrigan, I can't believe he's the leak."

"Then?"

"For the briefest instant, Martinez topped my suspect list. I mean he has access to all the information."

"But," she interjected for him.

"I don't know, Hope. He's done so much to find the leak, and he and Nurse Reilly took Flatly under their wings. Maybe I just don't want it to be him."

"I'm with you," she managed through a yawn.

"Thanks. That brings us to whatever Martinez is checking out in the lab. He's got some off-the-wall theory about the copy machine. I wish he wasn't so tight-lipped about it."

He turned his head in Hope's direction to continue his rambling.

She was asleep.

"Thanks for listening, Princess," he whispered and pulled the blanket up to her chin.

Chapter 37

"What's the latest on Reed?" Guillermo Arcenas asked into the phone while leaning back in his chair in his office.

"Nothing different from before, sir. He spends most of his time drinking, chasing women, or doing drugs."

"Then things are going just as we planned."

"It appears that way, sir."

"Excellent. Call me only if there is a significant change in this situation."

* * *

It was late afternoon. Martinez arrived at the station after taking his turn on a surveillance team. Tired and disappointed, he was ready to punch someone.

To avoid an enormous blot in his personnel file, he wandered the station's hallways in a random pattern. He had time to kill.

Finch, his buddy in the lab told him it would be 5:30 p.m. before he finished comparing the copies. He checked his watch. Even though it was 5:08, he headed down.

Martinez pushed through the door to the lab, stopped, and watched the man pick up the copy of the evidence list from the arrest of Oscar Briggs.

Finch placed the paper on his most powerful dissecting microscope. He studied the page for several seconds before his eyebrows rose, and he nodded and wrote something on a paper on the lab table. He looked at the clock. It was 5:12. He finished before his self-imposed deadline.

"Hola, amigo. Mind if I come in?"

"I should make you wait until 5:30. Lucky for you, though, I just finished."

"What's the verdict?"

"I've numbered the pages you gave me." Finch indicated the neat rows of paper on the table before him. When Martinez nodded, he added with more than a hint of condescension, "You might want to write this down. It gets complicated."

"This whole deal's complicated. Why should this be any different?" The Latino sighed. "You got any paper?"

"First drawer on the right."

He grabbed a blank sheet of typing paper and pulled a pencil from the pen and pencil holder.

"Before we get too far, I need to ask: Do you know how a copy machine makes a copy?"

"Sure. You put a file on the glass. You push a button. There's a flash of light and some noise, and a copy comes out in the little tray."

"That's what you see happen. How did the copy get on to the paper in the tray?"

"I have no idea."

Finch sighed. "You need to listen carefully, take notes, and ask questions when you don't understand."

"Or, I'll never be able to explain to anyone else what you're going to explain to me."

"Very good."

Martinez smiled a crooked smile.

"All right, then. Inside most heavy-duty copiers is a cylinder about the size of a large oatmeal container. That cylinder is the copy drum. Photostatic images attach to the surface of the cylinder. Every time the drum rotates, it transfers an image to a piece of blank paper."

"Photostatic?"

"Yes. It means that an image containing ink adheres to the drum by static electricity. Like a photograph's negative."

"Do the images stay on the cylinder?"

"No. It retains the image long enough to transfer it once—a single copy. Each flash you see is a picture of the master being taken. It's transferred to the copy drum for one turn of the drum." Finch stopped. "It's one picture, one turn of the drum, one copy." He held up one finger for each point.

"So, I couldn't steal the drum and get all the copies made on it?"

"Nope. Each new photo replaces the previous one."

Martinez grimaced.

"I assume you know that all the copies you gave me came from the same machine."

The big man nodded, but asked, "How do you know that?"

"Every copy machine has its own signature. See these faint lines traversing the page at an angle?" He pointed to the paper beneath the powerful magnifying lens. A polite nod provided the expected answer.

"The same machine produced all the copies, the papers you had in your pile labeled copies." He paused before asking, "The one in records?"

"Yes."

"The original copies, as you call them, are from four different machines. Three of them are from different, very poor-quality machines. The other two pages," he paused and handed them to the Latino. "These two are both from the same machine, originally."

Finch impressed him. The evidence list and Mamba's list of names were the only ones from the same copier.

"What do you mean by originally?"

"Well, they were first copied on the same machine, the one in records. That machine has rolled paper. You can see the uneven lower edge of the paper in the subsequent copies because the original copy wasn't quite a perfect eight and one-half by eleven-inch page."

Martinez examined the proffered documents. While he saw them because he knew they were there, he suspected not many people would notice the traces of the uneven edge. He asked his next question even though he knew the answer.

"You're sure these two are from the same copier?"

"Besides the lower border of the paper," Finch responded in an offended tone of voice. "There are the signature lines I told you about. Those aren't the same as the lines on the copies made in Records." He slid one page under the magnifying lens.

"Yeah, I see those." Martinez's excitement level spiked. If he found a copier whose signature matched the one on those pages, that would plug the leak. "Finch, amigo, we are even. In fact, I may owe you."

"Are you going to tell me what this is all about?" Finch's precise scientific brain reached its limit of Martinez-isms. He wanted one straight answer.

"As soon as I know," Martinez promised. "As soon as I know."

Martinez was at a full sprint as he barreled through the door of the lab and into the hallway outside it.

* * *

Reed surveyed his surroundings. The party was going strong. The apartment wasn't large, but it was a palace compared to his usual flop house. There was plenty of room for drugs, booze, and women.

He was grateful for Mr. Anderson's generosity. His take from the first drug company robbery set him up for a time, but he was tapped out when they delivered him to the pharmaceutical lab the second time. He didn't know how they found him in a dive in Atascadero, but he hadn't even blinked at the chance to score a second bonanza.

He thought about nothing but what to steal on the trip from Atascadero to Manzanita. He was sober enough to remember that most of the drugs he stole during the first heist were for his own use.

The second time he left the lab with more profitable merchandise. That's how he scored this fine apartment and enticed the people occupying the living room to come.

At the moment, a dozen associates surrounded Reed. There was a party going on, and he was the host.

Seated to his immediate left was an immensely obese woman. Her makeup was thick and her dress was barely appropriate on a much thinner person. The fact was, most in her line of work were much thinner. Rotunda, as they knew her on the streets, catered to a class of clientele that preferred blubber to bones. Reed liked what he saw. She shifted her bulk to reach for another handful of finger sandwiches. His pulse raced.

"Let's blow this joint."

"Not just yet. There's still a lot of good food here." She took an enormous bite of the sandwich stack and leaned forward as best she could.

"Be a Sweetie and hand me a beer, will ya?" she mumbled with a small burp.

Reed complied. He grabbed a second can of the beverage for himself, popped the top off, and took a swig.

"Let's dance!" Shouted one partygoer.

"Sounds good to me," Reed called back. He wobbled toward his stereo, his gait defined by the beers he consumed.

His collection of record albums was small but first-rate. He was a jazz aficionado, but he had samplings of several international artists of various genres. Fate directed his fingers toward one of the foreign records. He pulled it out and turned the album until he could read the cover: 'Favorite Mambos of Portugal.'

Mamba! The name burst into his alcohol-dimmed perception.

"Where's the music?" bellowed from a dimly lit corner of the room.

"Get a grip. It's comin'!" Reed placed the record on the turntable.

Movement behind Reed caused him to turn around. Rotunda stood behind him, tugging ineffectually on one side of her dress where it rode up.

"If you've got the money, honey," she offered. "I've got the time." A toss of her massive hip set off a series of reactions. Few parts of her body did not jiggle, wiggle, or wobble after the effort.

Reed shook with anticipation as he led her waddling form from the living room to the bedroom. As he passed his liquor cabinet, he grabbed a bottle of Gallo's Vin Rosé.

* * *

Mamba and Stallings sat talking in Mamba's office. It was 7:45 a.m. They were early. They learned to be on time for an early morning meeting with Martinez. He became less reliable at meeting appointment times as the day wore on.

"Hola, amigos. Have I got some news from the lab."

"Good or bad?" Mamba asked.

"Good, so far. I've got some things to show you." He held up a hand full of documents.

"Spread 'em out," Stallings invited. "I'll move my coffee."

Martinez obliged. Soon the desk was littered with the copies and originals he gave Finch to work with. Taking a deep breath, he began, "Let me explain. First, I had those papers I took with me from here, and some others from my files, copied by Sergeant Edwards on the big machine he uses."

"Why?"

"So that I could have a copy from his machine and get copies made of those on other machines."

"I'm not sure I'm following," Mamba admitted. He looked at Stallings.

"In all honesty, Detective, neither am I," Stallings admitted.

"Bottom line, these copies are all traceable to the copier that produced them. Finch, he's in MPD's lab, explained every machine has a signature it leaves on each copy made."

He grabbed Mamba's Sherlock Holmes magnifying glass and showed the men the faint tracings on each copy from the machine in the police station. "This is the first lead with the potential of tracking the leak."

Mamba turned to Stallings who gave a 'who knew' shrug. The PI extracted his magnifying glass from Martinez's meaty fist.

"The real problem is how the first copy of our originals is being made," Martinez continued, unfazed by the loss of the magnifying glass. "The original papers must leave the station because the copies on the street aren't from the departmental copier."

"If all you've told us is accurate, I agree." Stallings motioned for the magnifying glass without looking up from the papers on the desk.

"What I said is accurate, but I don't know how the documents get out. In fact, I can't even speculate on how. I watched the copying process yesterday. I watched like a hawk looking for a meal. There's no way the originals can slip through Record's security routine."

"Could someone remove originals from files at a later time?" Mamba asked as he handed the magnifying glass to Stallings.

"Maybe. But, remember that the copies sometimes appear on the streets within hours of their arrival at the station. It would take several people working together throughout the station to pull that off."

"Well, what about different security procedures at different times in the Records Department?"

"If that's true, though, the people down there would have to know when the information they want to leak was coming." Martinez sighed. "All I know for sure is it has to be someone with access to police records." He sighed again and added, "We've known that all along."

"My money's on Sergeant Edwards," Stallings offered.

Mamba frowned, retrieved the magnifying glass a second time and examined copies while he responded. "Not necessarily. It could be anyone that works in that division."

"I think Edwards is our suspect primero. Anyone but the Sergeant would have to circumvent his own protocols. Edwards runs a tight ship."

"Point taken," Mamba admitted.

If there was a conspiracy within Edwards' division, they had more to worry about than information on police tactical plans getting out. When the negative thought evaporated from his mind, Mamba jump-started the dead conversation.

"Okay, so all we've got, which isn't that much, points to Edwards. However, gentlemen, various people, even those in this room, have been certain that both of you were the leak at one time or another during this investigation."

He returned Holmes' magnifying glass to its rightful location. This meeting was over.

* * *

On the afternoon of the inconclusive meeting between Stallings, Mamba, and Martinez, Lizbeth Stallings finished her fifth reading of Farmer Grover to Jimmy Mamba. She put the boy down for his second nap, which usually was just long enough for Hope to sleep a little before he woke up. Since Hope wasn't trying to sleep today, Lizbeth figured the boy would sleep until dinnertime.

She heard the front door open and close. That could mean only one thing. She went downstairs as fast as her sluggish chemo-body would allow.

"So, how'd it go?" Lizbeth ambushed Hope who collapsed in her favorite easy chair after her visit to the family doctor.

"You were right. The rabbit died," Hope answered with a smile that grew and grew. "How come you, who've never been pregnant, were all over me being pregnant, and I, who already has one child, didn't catch on?"

"I want to be pregnant." Lizbeth turned away crying and choking out words that knifed into Hope's heart. "You didn't even think of p-pregnancy because you just figured it would h-happen when it h-happened."

Hope stood, waited for nausea to pass, and went to her friend. She wrapped her arms around the sobbing woman.

"Life is so unfair. I've almost died twice, but I have a son and I'm pregnant again. I'm so sorry."

Lizbeth groaned. Hope continued her embrace. Almost a minute passed before Lizbeth took one deep breath and removed Hope's arms from around her.

"Thank you."

"How do I tell Phil?"

"I'd skip the rabbit part," Lizbeth said with a twinkle in her tear-reddened eyes.

Hope laughed out loud.

* * *

RossAnn Gilroy was discharged from the hospital eight days after her admission. Her mother escorted her wheelchair to the curb. Both women joined her father in his Mercedes Geländewagen. She climbed up into the back seat of the imposing black vehicle.

On the drive to her parents' home, fatigue stealthily invaded cell after cell of her body. By the time they pulled into the oversized garage, fatigue rooted and blossomed into melancholy.

Her mother helped her into the elevator to the second floor and into the bedroom suite she occupied growing up.

"Rest up, dear. We're having a small gathering this evening to celebrate your return. It's a getting out party."

"I don't…" RossAnn rolled on her side so she faced her armoire. She let her mother speculate on the rest of her objection.

* * *

The Monday after Martinez's report on the copy machine and its operation, Mamba sat in his office at Mamba Investigations. He was early. The coffee was stale. His mood was poor.

The phone rang. He glanced at his wrist, precisely eight o'clock. He picked up the call before the third ring.

"Mamba Investigations. This is Detective Mamba."

"Anderson here. Mr. Mamba, I require your services again. As you undoubtedly know, those hoodlums struck my factory again the other night and stole valuable products. The police were nowhere to be found. And, once again, they have no suspects." He paused the tirade and inhaled deeply.

"I understand."

"I filed a complaint with the Chief of Police. Protection and a guarantee of safety for all citizens are obligations of police departments. I am not receiving those services."

"I'm willing to go back to work for you, Mr. Anderson. I haven't closed out your account. But, before I agree to anything, let me pontificate for a moment."

If telephone wires transported vital signs along with sound, Mamba would have seen a spike Anderson's pulse rate and blood pressure readings.

"If you must." The phrase hit Mamba's ear like a blast of Arctic air.

The PI waited a beat to sustain the mood.

"Obligations are not the sole purview of the police. Contracts between individuals or businesses also have obligations associated with them by law."

"What's your point." Glaciers thaw faster than Anderson's tone of voice.

"There's the matter of the current balance due on your account."

"Hold, please." The phone line went silent. Thirty seconds later, Anderson clicked back onto the line. "Remuneration will arrive by messenger within the hour."

"Thank you. Returning to your prior topic of conversation, I want you to recall that I had no more success than the police with the first break-in."

"Quite the contrary actually. It is my understanding that you obtained a rather lengthy list of suspects and turned it over to the police. They dropped the ball there. It's another example of the ineptness of our local constabulary."

Mamba filed "Anderson. List. How?" in the to do part of his brain.

"The police do a fine job far more often than they get credit for. It wasn't their fault—"

"I'm sure the police are competent in their own way, for routine matters," Anderson intoned. "This is a special situation and I want a special person working for me. You have carte blanche in terms of your investigation. Your methods during your previous time of employment convinced me of your capabilities."

"Thank you, Mr. Anderson," the PI replied in a carefully modulated tone. Something wasn't sitting right. His mind raced.

"I'll reopen your case right away."

"Of course you will. I require a written progress report every three days, nothing more. Goodbye, Detective."

"Goodbye, sir."

Before he hung up the phone, he called Hope.

"Hi, Sweetie."

"Hello, Phil."

"Vacation's over. I need you in the office."

"Oh, really. Starting when?"

"Tomorrow, day after at the latest. I'm back on the Anderson Pharmaceuticals case, and you know how he loves his reports."

"Sounds like a plan."

"That it is. See you tonight. Give Jimmy a hug for me."

* * *

Days morph into nights. Nowhere is this less noticeable than in the mind of a comatose individual.

Research shows that many coma patients are aware of varying amounts of what occurs in their presence. Yet, no studies show how much awareness of time those patients possess.

This day, Kerrigan emerged from the unconscious state faster than in the past. He remained rigid. He had no desire to risk another bout with the pain, at least not until he did some thinking.

He took stock of what he knew by reviewing the events leading to this situation. At the recollection of a gun firing, a new train of thought emerged from the dark tunnel that was his memory.

He ran through a checklist of what he remembered about guns and shooting. He knew being shot hurt and if he'd been shot, that's why he had pain. Sounds in his right ear suggested someone hospitalized him.

He devised a plan to get a person in white clothes to help him. The most important part of his plan required helpers to arrive before the pain caused him to black out.

He moved his left arm, bending it completely at the elbow with only a hint of pain. After waiting until he felt no pain, he slid his left hand toward his right arm. He wanted to know what kept it from moving. When his blind groping encountered a plastic tube, he grasped it firmly with the fingers of his left hand.

He took a deep breath and yanked on the IV lead. His yank was more a tug than a pull, but it accomplished the desired result.

The noise of an alarm filled his right ear. He relaxed. His plan was working.

"Any doctor!" an intensive care nurse called over the paging system. "Report to room six-zero-two. This is an alarm response!" She repeated the message.

Two white-clad figures raced to Kerrigan's room. As they entered, they saw the figure on the bed holding an IV tube in his trembling left hand. The doctor grabbed the Lieutenant's left arm. He unfolded the man's fingers and removed the needle-tipped tube from his grasp.

"What's going on?" the nurse asked.

"Involuntary spasm," the doctor diagnosed. He removed the needle from Kerrigan's grip and held the man's hand as he continued, "Perhaps not. I'm getting an irregular pattern of contractions from his hand."

The nurse nodded.

"Wait. It's not irregular. It's a repeating pattern!" He turned to the nurse. "See if you feel that." After holding Kerrigan's hand for several seconds, she announced, "It is a pattern."

The doctor moved close to Kerrigan's good ear. Leaning close to the patient's head, he instructed, "Mr. Kerrigan. If you can hear me, squeeze my hand until I tell you to stop." He waited.

Kerrigan knew the word hand. He closed his left hand.

"Stop!" The doctor commanded after five seconds. "Just like I told him. It looks like, or rather it feels like Mr. Kerrigan is on his way back to us."

* * *

The evening of Kerrigan's hand squeeze, after the dinner dishes were in the dishwasher and Franklin and Lizbeth Stallings had, at Hope's request, gone to bed early. She and Phil double-teamed Jimmy to bed. Now, they sat beside one another watching television.

"We'll be right back after these words from our sponsor," announced a break in the show.

"You should know I'm pregnant," Hope whispered.

Phil's head jerked in her direction.

"You're pregnant?"

She nodded.

"That's great! How long? When did you know? Is it a boy or a girl?" Phil fired questions at her at much more than a conversational volume.

"Hold on," she said as she pressed her fingers to his lips stemming the flood of queries. "I'll still be pregnant in the morning."

Phil took her hand in his and turned off the television as they headed toward the stairs.

* * *

Throughout the next week, Mamba was busy checking and rechecking Anderson Pharmaceuticals plant searching for evidence. He felt close to a solution but was certain he missed something.

Time and time again, Reed's name came to mind as he recounted a particular piece of evidence or remembered a name from Reed's list. He decided it was time to check on the progress of his CI's rehabilitation.

"Is Reed there?" he asked when his call was answered. "This is Phil Mamba calling long-distance."

"Reed? Hold on, please."

"Phil, how's it going?" A strong male voice greeted the detective.

"I'm doing pretty well, Father Henry," he confided. "Can I talk to Reed?"

"Not gonna happen. He left us, oh, must be at least two months ago. I figured you knew."

"Two months? I did not know that." After mentally berating himself for not checking on the alcoholic long before this, he asked, "Where'd he go?"

"Parts unknown. I got the impression he was not pleased about the selection of beverages we offer here at the mission."

"That, unfortunately, does not surprise me. Reed likes his booze."

"Is he in trouble?"

"Probably. But, I can't be certain with Reed. How much do I owe you?"

"I've still got money you wired before your friend arrived. He wasn't here that long."

"Keep it. I know you'll put it to good use."

"God bless you, Phil."

"Thanks. I always appreciate blessings and prayers, Father. Put in a good word, okay?" He flipped through his Rolodex file until he found the name and number of one of Reed's known associates. He tossed the card on his desk and dialed the number.

"Tell me where Reed is," he demanded. "Now!"

"Who wants t' know?"

"Dancer Mamba. Ring any bells?"

"Yeah," the voice replied with diminished confidence. Dancer busted her when he was a cop. She knew he would find out where Reed was, eventually. She knew where Reed was, and if she didn't tell Dancer, she could imagine what the ex-cop might have in store for her. "I remember you."

"Where's Reed?"

"He got a place down in South City."

"His own place?"

"That's what I hear."

"South City's a big place."

"He's livin' on Garfield Street. I think maybe even the Presidential Hotel. Leastwise, that's what I hear."

"Okay. If you're lying, the next time you hear from me will be through the bars of a holding cell." Mamba waited a full ten seconds before he hung up.

He knew the area known to locals as South City. Originally one of the more fashionable parts of town, it was now a breeding ground for illegal activity of all types.

The Presidential Hotel. It figured. The place had run down so far that it was nothing more than a house of prostitution with hourly room rates. He did not want to go there.

"Phil," Hope called over the intercom. "There is a police officer here to see you."

"Send him in," Mamba instructed.

A woman in a tailored outfit strode through the doorway.

"Desantos," the officer flashed her badge. "Internal Affairs."

"What do the boys— I'm sorry. What do the officers in IAD want with me?"

"We know you were in Ohio with Sergeant Franklin Stallings about five weeks ago."

"I was in Ohio around then." The timeline in the question convinced him that IAD finally got around to investigating Stallings.

"Sergeant Stallings is on unauthorized leave from the department," Desantos intoned. "And we have reason to suspect him of leaking confidential information. He is a fugitive."

“As far as I know, unless IAD filed charges, Stallings hasn’t been charged with any crime,” Mamba amended Desantos’ explanation, then asked, “What do you want from me?”

“I want to know if you know his whereabouts now.”

“I have no idea where Stallings is right now,” Mamba confessed.

“If you say so.” The IAD Officer’s tone of voice implied the PI’s answer was suspect.

She held out her business card, and added, “If you do hear anything of his location, give the department a call. That card has both the Division number and my extension.”

“Officer Desantos,” he said as he accepted her card. “I promise that you will be the police officer I contact if I hear where Sergeant Stallings is.”

Chapter 38

Martinez hated hospitals. Although he knew it was better to be treated for an injury sooner rather than later, being admitted for any extended time, which he defined as longer than overnight, was intolerable.

Visiting the hospital was tolerable. At the moment, he waited a short distance from the elevator for Erin Reilly to wheel Flatly out for his release from the hospital. The ex-boxer selected him to be his ride home. That choice provided him with the opportunity to set up a welcome home reception in Flatly's building.

The sound of a bell announced the arrival of the often-sluggish elevator. The door opened. Nurse Reilly backed out, pulling the boxer in a wheelchair behind her. She spun the chair in a graceful arc while she said something to her charge.

"Hola, amigo," Martinez called across the hallway. "You look good."

"Hey, man. I'm better than good."

"Are you the person to whom Mr. Wiggins is being released?" Erin asked.

"Yes, ma'am," Martinez answered with appropriate decorum.

The trio moved down the hallway. Their final destination was the curb where an unfamiliar car was parked.

"What did you feed your motorcycle to grow it into this?"

"Funny, Erin. You don't want to know what it's costing me to use this car."

She shrugged, but stayed with the wheelchair until they secured Flatly's seatbelt in the passenger's seat of the car. She gave Martinez a wink and walked away pushing the empty wheelchair before her.

"You know she's got the hots for you, right?"

"You want to walk home, amigo?" Martinez threatened without conviction.

Flatly laughed.

As Martinez maneuvered his borrowed car carefully through traffic, Flatly offered dry commentary.

“You ain’t never got to worry ‘bout gettin’ no traffic ticket. I been in buses moved faster than this.”

“I borrowed the car.”

“Actu’ly, ain’t no never mind to me. This beats layin’ in that ol’ hospital bed. And no matter how long it takes to get there, I’m goin’ home.”

“Here we are,” Martinez announced as he parked at the curb. “Remember, you can’t call me Cue Ball anymore like you did sometimes in the hospital.”

“Oh, yeah. I keep forgettin’. You not mad, are ya?”

“Not mad at all. But I have to be careful. You remember how it is when you’re undercover.”

“I surely do. I got to make sure not to out my partner.”

“Thanks. You need help getting out?”

“Nah. I can make it.”

“At least let me get the door.” Martinez opened his own door and waved to his accomplice inside Flatly’s building.

In response to his wave, a dozen people materialized at the foot of the stoop. Little Marvin, the unwitting savior of Flatly’s life, held a sign that read “Welcome Home.”

The boxer’s eyes went wide with amazement as he rounded the front of the car. Folks waved and called out encouraging remarks. When he reached the small crowd, his amazement turned into shock.

Marvin’s mother stepped forward and offered a pie she baked. The landlord presented Flatly with a certificate good for three months of free rent. Other neighbors offered various services.

Waldo Wiggins stood open-mouthed. Usually people ignored him or tolerated his presence. These people acted like they were glad to see him. For the first time in his adult life, he had neighbors.

He wiped a tear from his eye, as did Martinez. In fact, there wasn’t a dry eye on the stoop.

* * *

After IAD left his office, Mamba was tempted to hotfoot it down the Presidential Hotel. In fact, that was more than a temptation—he made it all the way to his car before he returned to his office.

He spent hours sorting, sifting, and rearranging ideas and facts in his mind. He knew he should have gone to Flatly's homecoming, but with IAD turning over rocks, clearing Stallings' name ASAP was imperative.

No matter how often he changed the order of his ideas and facts, Edwards and an unknown someone higher than the Sergeant consistently ranked one and two.

* * *

Anthony Garmel was at his desk. Instead of working, he was blessing Fall's arrival in his hometown. It was a cold November day in Chicago. He was glad to be rid of heat and humidity.

"Mr. Garmel, there is a call waiting on line one," crackled through the intercom.

"I've got it, thanks." He picked up his handset. "This is Garmel."

"Mr. Garmel, this is Rick Elkhart. I worked for Sidney Brewster in Manzanita, California, until, well, until his unfortunate demise. I'm sure you know about that."

"Yeah, I heard about Sid. Brutal way to end your life. Tough luck, I'd call it. What makes you think you need to call me?"

"There's a problem out here," Elkhart continued with his planned presentation. "No one man is ready to take charge of Mr. Brewster's operation. I've taken over the lion's share of the leadership, but I don't know if you have someone in mind, or if you're thinking of splitting the territory. I don't want to see all our hard work go down the drain."

"I've gotten reports from out there," Garmel mused aloud. "You've got moxie, and your call confirms a problem exists. But, you still have to earn the promotion. What's the status of your relationship with the police?"

"As far as I can tell, we're still getting the information you're paying for. But the inside man says he wants to renegotiate his deal with the new boss."

"I don't do that," was the rock-hard response.

"I tried to explain that, sir. He said he would wait and see."

"So, what do you want from me?"

"It's not my place to give orders, sir."

"I'm asking for your advice, Mr. Elkhart. What do you think should be done?"

Rick had considered what advice he might offer in the past, but only as a hypothetical scenario. He never expected being asked. The best he had hoped for by placing this call was to get his name in Garmel's mind.

"If you came out here and met with the guys that are fighting, I think that would settle the question the quickest."

"If that's not possible?"

"Mr. Garmel, the organization's in trouble without a visit."

"I see. I can't lose an entire operation. Give your number to my secretary," Garmel instructed. "You can expect a call within the week. Set your meeting up after my call. Be ready to pick up two passengers at the airport days after that call. And, make sure the meeting's not long after my arrival date." He switched Elkhart back to Jana.

Garmel sat for several minutes with his brow furrowed in concentration. It was over five years since he bought the man in the Manzanita Police Department. He was pleased that he was still getting the service he desired. He was not pleased with the reported developments.

There would be no renegotiation on any issue with anyone from Brewster's operation. If necessary, Garmel would bring in proven talent from elsewhere to replace Brewster. However, before going to that extreme, he'd give Elkhart enough rope to hang himself.

He wished for Gene Marcotti. But Gene was three years dead, killed in a war with the competition in St. Louis. He swore again. Bringing in another man would slow things down. He'd wait and hope that Elkhart continued his rise to the occasion.

* * *

As was his habit, Chief Rogers sat listening to a piano concerto on his stereo. He should have been relaxing, swirling brandy in a crystal snifter. But, the concerto was not one of his favorites; he was far from relaxed; his crystal snifter was empty; and his plan wasn't moving as planned

It was a schizophrenic time for him. On the sane side, a drug organization that plagued Manzanita for years was down and out, at least as far as the media was concerned. Lieutenant Kerrigan, who was shot execution-style, was making a miraculous recovery, and TV ratings of his press conferences were at an all-time high.

On the insane side, two issues cast shadows on his leadership. Evidence and testimony during the takedown of the drug operation exposed an information leak to the public. The bad publicity would take serious politicking on his part to overcome. Not only that, rumors abounded about who might benefit by the downfall of the reigning drug lords in the city. Current rumors were vague on that point. Rogers was smart enough to see implications from what was accumulating.

In the once positive, now negative column was his relationship with Petula Jacobs. What had started with unbridled passion and far different intentions on his part than hers degraded. Badly. All recent interactions were business.

He picked up the phone and left a message on the machine his administrative assistant checked the first thing every morning.

* * *

It was 5:30 p.m., not a late end of a workday for many people. For Officer Petula Jacobs, it was thirty minutes past her scheduled departure time. While a rarity, getting off late was not unknown for Jacobs. What was a rarity was the fact she had no clue why the Chief left a voice message that morning directing her to remain after hours.

Rogers had been distant from Petula for a while. She didn't mind that. In fact, she was glad he realized she was over him. She concluded this meeting must be departmental business.

She checked her regular end of the day to-do list items—for the fourth time. The coffee maker was clean. The shredder was empty with all contents of that device bagged in a sealed plastic pouch for secure disposal. She restocked the mini-fridge with sodas and water. She stacked the platters for serving pastries and placed a note to the custodial crew that the platters needed washing and the pastries still in the box from the donut shop were for them.

She straightened individual stacks of items on her desk. Two sets of meeting agendas and a complete set of blank officer evaluation papers with the names and badge numbers of the officers already typed in were ready for completion. The Chief opened the door between the two rooms in his suite.

"Jacobs, I'm ready to see you."

Petula shifted to high alert status, her earlier thoughts undermined by Rogers' tone. She walked past the man and into his office.

After she and Chief Rogers were seated, an emotionally charged thirty seconds of silence passed before the man spoke.

"You will do what I tell you to do when I tell you to do it, or I will bury you."

Jacobs paled. She ran a quick review of her recently assigned tasks. She'd chosen not to report one phone call to him.

"Regardless of your perceptions, our relationship does not exist outside your mind and your bedroom."

She stared at him.

"Surely you realize by now you've been nothing more or less than a pleasant diversion from reality for me," the Chief continued.

She exhaled the breath she'd been holding.

"But, Dwight, all I did—"

"I don't care about your rationale! You're this close to being fired. Fired. Do you hear me?" he roared as he held his thumb and index finger less than an inch apart.

Petula's mind raced. She recalled two other instances when Dwight Rogers yelled at her. The first was when she neglected to return the socks he left after one of their romantic interludes until two days after that evening. The second was when she tried the newly made key to the private entrance to his office without asking permission.

"And, after I fire you, if you go to any news outlet, who will they believe if you try to use our affair to smear me?" Rogers continued his tirade but at a lower volume and closer proximity. "Just who do you think will take your word over that of the Chief of Police?"

Jacobs stared past Rogers, focusing her vision on the wall behind the man while she considered the best way to respond to her boss's tirade. Every night they spent together was on its own videotape, changed out each morning after he slunk away. Each was labeled with the date, the time he arrived, and the time he left. If he took her down in any way, he would go down in flames.

Rogers mistook Petula's silence for submission. "Get out! And when you come in tomorrow, I expect you in uniform slacks, no more tight skirts!" He dismissed her with an emphatic hand gesture.

Chapter 39

The drive from Manzanita to Los Angeles took longer than Rick Elkhart anticipated, a lot longer. A semi hauling two trailers of gravel jack-knifed trying to avoid a minivan that swerved to miss a mattress that flew out of the bed of a pickup truck. Four lanes of I-405 funneled into the far left lane. He was almost an hour behind schedule.

He was tired, hungry, thirsty, and needed to use the bathroom. But, instead of meeting any of those needs, he squinted into the sun as his car prowled along the passenger pick-up curb. After two trips around the loop, he flipped down the car's sun visor to afford his eyes some relief.

He wrote an evening arrival time for Garmel's flight on his calendar. The phone call directing him to be at the airport five hours earlier than he planned stunned him. He rushed out of his place without his sunglasses and his wallet.

No sunglasses forced him to squint. No wallet meant he had no money to pay for parking. He knew how quick airport security was to tow a car. He couldn't afford to add that to a bad situation. So, he drove to curbside pick-up instead of meeting his passengers inside the terminal.

"Watch where you're going, buddy!" The angry voice of a cab driver snapped his attention back to the road. He avoided clipping the bumper of the cab and returned his focus to the sidewalk. He spotted Garmel and cut off a station wagon in his rush to the curb.

"Right here, Mr. Garmel," Elkhart shouted after screeching to a halt. "I'm sorry I'm late."

"Although we arrived over two hours ago, we've not been on the curb long," the man in the stylish clothes replied with more than a hint of annoyance. An equally stylish female stood beside him, her posture making it clear that she was unconcerned with such details."

"This is Jana. She's my traveling secretary."

"Let me get the door, Jana." The woman entered. Garmel reached past Elkhart and closed the door, leaving him wondering if he used the wrong protocol for assisting passengers.

Garmel started around behind the car, grabbed Elkhart's arm, and escorted him as he walked.

"I appreciate your help with both the information you provided and this taxi service. For now, I'll assume your lack of punctuality is an uncommon occurrence. I'll be keeping a close eye on you while I'm here. If all goes well, there might be a place for you at a higher level in my organization. But, I have to be honest with you. You haven't gotten off to a good start."

"Thank you. I know." He opened the rear door on the driver's side. Anthony Garmel climbed in. He put his passengers' baggage in the trunk and drove out of the massive airport complex.

"If it's not too much trouble, Rick, we'd like to stop soon, and at a nice place. We haven't eaten real food since early this morning."

"Yes, sir!"

* * *

Elkhart sat in the room he reserved for the meeting scheduled to begin fifteen minutes earlier. The plan was to bring together Garmel and the members of the local organization who were not playing well with one another. Elkhart looked at his watch for the seventh time.

Anthony Garmel waited in the chair beside his associate. The cigar clamped in his teeth evidenced his impatience. The end of the illegal Cuban panatella looked like someone pulled it through a garden shredder.

"Elkhart, are you certain that the time of this meeting was accurately communicated?" Although Elkhart was unfamiliar with Garmel's idiosyncrasies, the vocal inflection communicated the boss's rising anger.

"Yes, sir. Couriers delivered personal invitations to each of the men you requested be here as soon as you gave me your itinerary."

"Then it appears we are being snubbed deliberately."

"Garmel?" a voice asked from the door to the room.

The boss lifted his head. He did not have to turn in either direction to see the speaker. Garmel never sat with his back to the door. He positioned himself with a direct line of sight of the entrance to every room he was in, or he did not remain in that room. He had doors to this room blocked to ensure only one operable entrance and egress.

Four men entered.

"You're late," Garmel growled. "Sit down!"

"I don't think so." A gun flashed from beneath a suit jacket. Three other guns appeared in quick succession. "We're giving the orders now."

Garmel dropped to the floor. The percussive sounds of automatic weapons fire shattered the silence.

Elkhart threw himself down in panic simultaneously with the realization the traitors shot him. Wood from the table splintered into tiny fragments. Tufts of stuffing from the padded chairs floated through the air as though searching for a safe landing space. Bullet holes pocked the white walls above the paneling.

After the less than twenty second exchange of gunfire, silence regained control of the room. The four late arrivals lay dead on the floor.

Garmel's face wore a satisfied smile. Once again, it paid off to expect a problem instead of reacting to it. Elkhart was shaking and holding his arm where a bloodstain widened around the hole in his sports jacket.

"Come on out, boys," Garmel called. Five men carrying machine pistols emerged from their hiding places behind the decorative cloth wall hangings installed in the room at Garmel's insistence.

The look of astonishment on Elkhart's face was the only testimony required to confirm the fact he had no foreknowledge of the presence of the armed men. Or that those men, or any other men, would be required to protect him and his boss from the four tardy associates.

"Always have an ace in the hole." Garmel brushed the dust from his clothing while offering advice to Elkhart.

Elkhart's face was ashen. He trembled like someone outside in a freezing rain. Garmel recognized the symptoms of shock and made a subtle gesture that went unnoticed by the injured man. One protector nodded and left the room. A second protector helped Elkhart to a seat.

"The moments just experienced will be forgotten in time," Garmel continued. "For now, let's concentrate on finding suitable attention for your arm. After your treatment, we'll discuss our business arrangement. Let's start with the name of the police informer that wants to renegotiate his contract?"

"I think their name is—" Elkhart passed out and slumped forward in his chair. The shock of being in the middle of a live firefight, the blood lost from his wound, and what sounded like a promotion overwhelmed his nervous system.

* * *

Although there were bad days in Pat Kerrigan's rehab, there were good days, too.

"Mr. Kerrigan." Dr. David Liebowitz always started a follow-up visit by addressing his patient by name. "Raise your left hand."

Kerrigan complied. He wished whatever was in his throat wasn't there. He had a lot to say.

"Now, try to raise your right hand."

Kerrigan's arm didn't move. He heard the instruction. He didn't know how to comply. Either he could not remember how to do what the doctor asked, or he wasn't able to get his body to cooperate.

"Just as in the other attempts." Dr. Liebowitz frowned. "This confirms significant damage to the motor areas and processing areas in the left hemisphere."

"I agree." His associate slapped an x-ray up on the viewer in the room. "The damage must extend down to here," he said as his finger traced a large area over the picture.

"Yes, and that means extensive rehabilitation."

"I think that getting Mr. Kerrigan to the place where rehabilitation is a positive," the nurse muttered. The patient moved his left hand. "I think Mr. Kerrigan wants something, Doctor."

"Do you want something?" Dr. Liebowitz turned away from the x-ray viewer. "Squeeze once for yes and twice for no." He grasped Kerrigan's left hand.

One firm squeeze greeted the doctor's grasp. Kerrigan released his grip and curled his fingers as though grasping a pencil. He made what he hoped were writing-like motions.

The nurse hurried out to get a pen and some paper. Placing the pen in Kerrigan's left hand she slid the paper beneath the tip of the writing instrument.

"Go ahead, Mr. Kerrigan."

With an effort so great that Kerrigan sweated, Pat scribed letters onto the paper. Being a natural right-hander put him at a distinct disadvantage, but he continued his task with grim determination.

Tension built as the patient labored at the task. It took three pieces of paper to hold his scrawled message. The pen slid from his grasp as he finished.

Dr. Liebowitz took the three pages from the nurse. He spread them out in order on top of the oscilloscope that monitored Kerrigan's heart rate. Together, the three medical professionals determined the message to read, "WANTTOTALK."

"Do you have something to say?" Liebowitz asked.

When there was no response, the nurse asked, "Do you want to talk?"

The doctor felt one firm squeeze.

"You have a feeding tube in your throat. I will have it removed," Dr. Liebowitz told him. "While we prepare the equipment, I will explain where you are in your recovery." He summarized Kerrigan's injury, the extent of the damage, and the implications of removing the feeding tube.

What Pat heard shocked him. According to this man, part of his brain was missing. He would have to learn how to use his right side again. He would be partially blind and partially deaf. He could never recall certain things. Memories stored in the missing tissue were gone forever.

That's what the doctor said. How much Kerrigan understood was another thing. The left side of the human brain is the storage receptacle for most specific terms. Dr. Liebowitz would not know how much his patient remembered or comprehended until his therapy was much further along.

The Lieutenant gagged as they removed the tube. Once again pain swept through his mind. He fought it off, determined to talk.

The nurse put a straw between his lips. He sucked a mouthful of cold water. Swallowing was another painful experience, but his throat felt better after the drink. He opened his mouth.

"How is woman? No! How is wife?" were the first words he rasped out.

Kate Kerrigan stood by his bedside, just out of his line of sight. She'd been there throughout the doctor's visit.

"He's asking about me!" She burst into tears and nearly strangled the injured man with her joyous embrace.

The pain attacked Pat's brain. For the first time since Evans shot him, when the pain overwhelmed him, he lost consciousness with a lopsided smile on his face.

* * *

The first thing Elkhart remembered when he awoke to find an unfamiliar female face looking down at him was how loud the gunshots were. He remembered a terrifying variety of sounds during the gunfight. He remembered the pain in his arm. He remembered nothing else.

He pulled his eyes away from the female's cobalt-colored eyes and looked down at his painful appendage. Someone bandaged it.

He groaned.

"Anthony," the woman called over her shoulder. "He's waking up."

"Good. Good." The slowly focusing image of the man's face and body followed the sound of the voice of Anthony Garmel as he approached Elkhart's bed. "How do you feel?"

"A little weak." Elkhart paused and croaked out a correction, "That's not true, I feel a lot weak. Where am I?"

"At your place," Garmel told him. "I took you home after our escapade. My doctor says you'll be fine. He used more stitches than I thought you needed, but that's why he's a doctor. I flew him in from Chicago on the flight after mine. You can't be too well prepared for events such as that unfortunate gunfight yesterday. He gave you blood. You lost quite a lot."

"Drink a little of this," the female instructed as she held a glass to his lips.

He drank thirstily.

"Do you remember Jana, my traveling secretary?"

Elkhart gave a single nod.

"Good. I've instructed her to take special care of my newest regional manager." He winked at Elkhart and left the room.

The term regional manager triggered a spasm in his arm, and icy water sloshed out of the drinking glass. Elkhart handed the glass to Jana and used the bed sheet to dab water from his pajamas.

"Anything you want?" Jana asked. She flashed a smile and added, "A towel, maybe?"

"Just sleep. And the sheet's fine for right now." He looked at the door and asked, "Is he serious?"

"Mr. Garmel?"

He nodded.

"About what?"

"Being regional manager. About my taking over for Mr. Brewster."

"I would think so. He's not one to make jokes about business."

The conversation ended as Rick's painkillers pulled him back into unconsciousness.

The next morning, Rick Elkhart sat in his bed running potential scenarios as a regional manager through his mind.

Jana entered the bedroom with a breakfast tray.

"I hope you like eggs. I couldn't find any breakfast meat, so I made toast and a cheese omelet."

"Eggs are fine. Thanks. I don't keep a lot of meat in the fridge. Um, I buy fresh when I want it."

She smiled.

He ate with relish. Healing and the special care he received from the alluring Jana stimulated his appetite. As he finished the last of his toast, Garmel entered.

"I'll be leaving now. As regional manager, you have the authority to choose your own staff. But, remember, Rick Elkhart, you are responsible for all activity in this region, so choose your staff wisely."

"Yes, sir."

"Jana will stay the week to see that you mend properly. I added my private number to your personal telephone book. It's under Importers of America."

"Thank you, sir. I'll do my best."

"You'd better." Garmel gave Jana a knowing look. He turned and muttered, "Or I'll find someone who will," as he walked away.

* * *

The North Gang leader peered out the front window of his well-protected home. He watched his lieutenant ease the .38 caliber handgun from between his belted pants and the small of his back. He held it in plain sight, but with the barrel pointing at the ground.

Although this was as much a public meeting as the gangs would ever have, suspicion ran high on both sides, even though the North Gang called the truce.

A South Gang member marched up the ten-foot wide crushed brick path that spanned the gap from the sidewalk to the front porch. The crunch reminded the North Gang leader why he demanded that surface covering. There was no way for anyone to reach the porch without alerting those inside.

The silence after the crunching footsteps called the meeting to order. The two high-ranking gang members stared in stoic silence waiting for what only the North Gang knew.

The house itself sat atop a mounded section of the lot. Well-manicured shrubs comprised the strategically placed landscaping. Not a branch, stem, or leaf obscured the view from any window.

The North Gang leader pulled a .22 caliber rifle from the rack under the window. Pragmatism rather than fear dictated the move. If South Gang tried to flip this meeting into a massacre, retaliation would be immediate.

Holding his gun on his open right palm, the North Gang lieutenant reached into his left front jeans pocket. He pulled out a folded paper and handed it to the South Gang lieutenant who nodded, turned, and retraced his steps to a silver, 4-door Lincoln Continental Mark VI.

The South Gang lieutenant passed the paper through the car window and received it in return minutes later.

The courier crunched his way back to the North Gang lieutenant and handed him the folder paper. The North lieutenant turned and headed up the steps. The South Gang lieutenant walked back to the driver's side of the Lincoln and climbed in the back seat. The South Gang contingent eased itself away from the curb.

Inside the house, the North Gang Leader unfolded the paper. A grim, satisfied smile tweaked his lips.

"This meeting settles everything. We're making a contract. Exclusive rights to gambling, prostitution, money laundering, protection, and human trafficking in each territory."

"What about drugs?"

"There's two heavyweights in that fight already. Those people are ruthless. Let them have the drugs. We'll survive. I don't enjoy missing out on drug money, but, I don't want to lose good people in a war."

"Maybe someday things will change."

"Get this word out." The North Gang leader ignored the comment. "We meet at the Claymore building. Ground floor. Cabinet shop. Day after tomorrow. Two p.m. Make sure that information gets to everyone."

His lieutenant nodded.

Outside the house, just below the windowsill, obscured by one of the landscape shrubs, a nondescript figure frowned. The undercover officer assigned to infiltrate the North Gang waited until the lieutenant crunched his way to the sidewalk before he pried the suction cup of the stethoscope off the window and headed to South Division headquarters. This was the tip he would take to the captain. They had a little over forty-eight hours to pull together a SWAT operation.

* * *

"Please hurry, Phil. Please!"

Mamba finished listening to Kate Kerrigan's message on his office machine. He played the message again. It didn't help clarify why Kate needed help. He left after the second playback.

Fifteen minutes later, he was riding the elevator to the ICU floor. He reached the nurses' station when he heard a voice call his name.

"Phil, he can talk!" Kate called to him at full volume from down the hallway. "It's the miracle they said would have to happen!"

"It sure is," he called back to her and breathed a prayer of thanks.

"Come in and talk with him. Please!"

Mamba hesitated. Kate wasn't outside a regular ICU room. She waved for him to come to her. He complied. She held open the door to her husband's room.

"Lead the way." He reached over her and placed his hand on the door. Kate smiled up at him and headed in.

"Pat," she called as they neared the bed. "There's someone here to talk to you."

The PI stepped around Kate and stopped short. Most of the bandages were off his friend's face and head. The amount of scaring and stitches overwhelmed him. He took a deep breath and leaned over Pat's bed.

"Hey, partner, it's Phil. Phil Mamba."

"I know you. We can talk. Please send wife away."

"I'll leave you two alone," Kate told Phil. "Come and get me when you're finished."

"How are you doing, Pat?" Mamba felt like a fool as soon as he asked the question.

"I know you," was the best answer Pat came up with to that question. His annoyance intensified by the hour. He could remember many things. But some things that he knew he should know eluded his recollection. Frustration was his most common emotion.

At this moment, he knew the man talking to him. But he could not think of what to call him.

"I know you," he repeated. "But all I tell you is I know you. I don't know name."

Mamba repeated his name. Kerrigan repeated the name but could only associate him with the concept work.

Mamba affirmed their work relationship.

Kerrigan struggled to find a word for how he was injured.

"Shot," Mamba offered. "The man who kidnapped you shot you."

Pat pointed to his head with his left hand and stumbled through another word search before he did his best to explain that part of his brain was missing. He closed his eyes and panted for a full minute. When he calmed down, he attempted to tell Phil why they were talking

"Tell wife I—" He stopped speaking again. Tears of frustration trickled down his shrunken cheeks.

"I'll tell Kate you love her, Pat," Phil choked out the words before the emotions churning in his chest got the upper hand. He began to sob.

Sobbing escalated to crying as he realized how much Kerrigan had overcome. The next minutes were a time of increasing frustration for Kerrigan and increasing understanding by Mamba. The PI told Kerrigan about the people praying for him and that they would continue praying.

When Phil was reasonably certain Pat knew that Kate was his wife's name, he looked hard at his friend. The man's naturally pale complexion looked drained of what life it held. He knew it was time to leave.

"I'll tell everyone how well you're doing," Mamba promised. "You get your rest now." He patted his friend's arm and left.

He tried to wipe the tears from his eyes—and failed. Rationalizing that Kate would be crying, and would not notice his tears, he told her of the love that his friend was unable to communicate.

Chapter 40

"We've got solid information on the meeting time and place between North Gang and South Gang." The captain who doubled as SWAT commander started his briefing of the twenty officers available on short notice. He'd brief the other ten before the end of the day.

"The Claymore building isn't easy to approach without being seen. So, our two snipers will position themselves where they can eliminate the greatest threats." The captain paused and nodded toward the specially trained long-range shooters.

"You've all been on at least one SWAT assignment. You know it's essential to follow the plan as long as possible."

Perfunctory nods from all present.

"Captain, I have a question."

"Can't it wait?" The scowl accompanied what was not a question.

"I'd like to know the mindset of our targets before we talk strategy."

"Fair enough. Reports from informants and undercover officers confirm that a meeting between these gangs has one goal, to establish agreed upon boundaries for each gang's activity."

No smiles, no questions, only concerned concentration greeted that statement.

"The intent is to reduce casualties on both sides. My SWAT Needs Assessment Team confirmed the agreement allows each gang to focus resources now used against one another on illegal activities in the new boundaries. Crimes against the citizens of Manzanita will increase."

The Captain swept the room with a visual broom, his face frozen into a grimmer expression than normal.

"You will deploy at 1230 hours day after tomorrow in small numbers. Transportation will be unmarked vehicles to be as inconspicuous as possible in that area of town."

"I know it will be a long wait, but we can't risk being seen as we arrive. Check the rosters on the wall on your way out. There's a time and place for a final logistics meeting of each group below the names."

* * *

"Get whoever's in charge now that Brewster's dead on the phone." Chief Rogers did not break stride when he dropped one piece of paper as he passed his Administrative Assistant's desk. The information on the paper was time-sensitive.

Petula did a quick read of the memo about a planned SWAT action the Captain of South Division sent to his counterparts and the Chief. She'd make two calls. Elkhart wasn't the only player that might want this information.

* * *

"Why should I care about what these gangs do?" Arcenas knew his answer. He wanted to hear how much the woman on the phone knew about his organization.

"If I were trying to control traffic in this town, I'd figure a way to turn this police action into a shootout. Everyone in that three-way fight loses. You don't lose a thing."

"Bravo. Tell your boss I appreciate his thinking of me."

* * *

Rick Elkhart dismissed the news of the SWAT action. Word on the street was those gangs were staying away from all drug-related action. That suited him fine. He had plenty of fires to stamp out as it was.

* * *

After two weeks in her parents' guest room, RossAnn Gilroy's mother escorted her to the sunroom. Mrs. Gilroy made sure her daughter was comfortable. That was no mean feat, since RossAnn's side of all conversations since her hospital stay was a series of single word responses at most.

"The newspaper is on the coffee table, sweetheart."

"Thanks."

Not long after her mother left the room, RossAnn tossed the quilt off her lap and retrieved *The Manzanita Daily News.* The headline read, "Mobile Crematorium?"

The story above the fold featured a photo of a burned-out stolen car registered to a Manzanita family and reported stolen three weeks earlier. Tourists found the car in an unpaved parking area used by serious hikers in Castle Crags State Park north of Redding, California.

RossAnn's eyes widened as she skimmed the account of the discovery of what police thought to be two bodies burned nearly to ash inside the car. Investigators estimated that the car burned between three and four weeks earlier. One .38 caliber bullet was recovered from inside the driver's side front door.

She slowed her reading speed at the last paragraph.

Her left hand traced the outline of a rattlesnake skeleton on the inside of her right thigh. The act was part of the to do list she followed during her recovery. Each time she felt the corruption of her body, her resolve strengthened.

She re-read the last paragraph in the article aloud.

"Sherriff investigators recovered remains of a blue stripped hood or mask just outside the charred outline of the car. Investigators are calling it 'a potentially significant piece of evidence.'"

She smiled, something she hadn't done in six weeks.

"Someone went a long distance to ensure your silence, Stripe," she murmured. "I will find that someone, and they will pay!"

* * *

As was not uncommon for Manzanita Police Department's SWAT teams, all members were in visually protected positions and waiting for the order to approach the building before the announced deployment time. The captain radioed his coded ready word to the Downtown Station at 1300.

Each SWAT member had a partner. Each pair worked in tandem as fail-safes for their assigned responsibility. Among three uncounted Manzanita Police Department employees on site were two photographers. One photographed the face of every gang member who entered the building from the front and right side as you faced the front parking lot. The other covered the back and left side of the Claymore building.

The minute hand on the SWAT leader's watch crawled around the face. By 1400 hours, sweat saturated uniforms of all SWAT officers. Their Kevlar vests were invaluable, but hot. A Kevlar vest, as Casey Stengel said about the St. Louis Cardinals' stadium during the 1966 All-Star game, "sure holds the heat well." Everyone was tired, thirsty, and cranky by the time the captain signaled the other uncounted MDP employee to begin.

"This is Manzanita Police Department! We know who's inside and why. We have you surrounded. We want this to end peacefully, but we are prepared to stop what you are planning with all force required." A departmental psychologist used a bullhorn to begin negotiations with the gang leaders.

In reply to the psychologist's announcement, gang members fired a dozen shots from various windows of the Claymore building. Manzanita Police Department's response was intentional overkill. Fifteen seconds of firing from thirty rifles silenced the gang shooters.

According to both sides, after ninety-minutes of negotiation, they reached a non-violent agreement. The gangs threw several weapons out of cabinet shop windows. SWAT team members assigned first contact moved toward the building.

The sound of a shot fired from inside the Claymore building shocked police officers and gang members. The bullet struck a uniformed officer in the right eye socket. He died instantly.

The Captain called dispatch for "all the paramedics and ambulances you can reach that aren't actively treating or transporting patients!"

SWAT members retreated and opened fire. Return fire by the gang members, while no match for the SWAT volley over time, proved deadly to five MDP SWAT team members.

Snipers eliminated shooter after shooter careless enough to enter their line of sight.

After twelve minutes of live action, shots from the Claymore Building ceased. The Captain gave the stand down order.

Emergency vehicles arrived. Paramedics completed triage of MPD personnel and attended to Level 1 and Level 2 casualties.

* * *

"It wasn't supposed to hit anybody."

The man on the ambulance gurney mumbled the sentence over and over. He had bullet wounds in his right leg and his left arm pit.

"Hold up!" the Captain called to the paramedics.

"This guy's in bad shape. If we don't get him to the hospital soon, we might as well take a detour to the morgue."

"Thanks for waiting." The Captain muttered as he passed the paramedics. He stood for several seconds, looking down at the man on the gurney. The injured man continued repeating the phrase, either unaware of or uncaring about the police officer's presence.

"Why did you open fire on us? You agreed to surrender before we moved out of our secure positions. You even tossed out, what, a half-dozen rifles. As soon as my men cleared cover, you fired on us."

"It wasn't supposed to hit anybody." The injured man turned toward the police officer. "One shot. That's the signal for us in the cabinet shop to make a run for it and for those on the outside of your perimeter to just walk away. We knew we didn't have a cha—"

A fit of coughing filled the injured man's throat with blood. The paramedics shoved the police officer aside and resumed working on their patient.

The Captain turned and walked back to where his men expected his orders. He slowed his pace as he neared the carnage. Four uniformed and one plain-clothes officer lay in a macabre row. Someone covered three with what looked to be bed sheets. He knew he'd catch it tomorrow when the crime scene team filed their report and included how two corpses were—

"I need two healthy bodies!" he shouted to the cluster of police personnel at the edge of the parking lot.

Three uniformed officers hurried toward him. He waved the third away.

"I don't care if you buy tarpaulins, but I want every one of our people covered within the next twenty minutes. Is that clear?"

"Yes, sir!" The men sprinted to a patrol car, jumped in, and burned rubber leaving the scene.

"What do we do, Captain?" The plain-clothes lieutenant's arm was in a sling. A bloodstain the size of a football revealed the location and extent of the man's bullet wound.

"You're now in command of all ambulatory officers. If they can aim and discharge a service weapon, they're on your crew."

The lieutenant nodded. He turned and circled his upraised index finger toward the other officers. Injured and uninjured personnel qualifying for the lieutenant's crew segregated themselves from the invalids.

The Captain gave final directions to his subordinate.

"I'm not ordering you to kill anyone. And, if I find out anyone on your crew killed someone without reasonable cause, I will terminate that officer, arrest that officer, and charge that officer with murder."

The Lieutenant turned toward the men waiting for orders.

"I know you all heard that. We're on a search and rescue mission, emphasis on rescue. I want living gang members who can give us information. That's the only goal." The lieutenant paused, swept his gaze from one end of the line of officers to the other, and finished with, "If you're put in a position where you must defend yourself from an armed gang member, do what you need to do to protect and serve the citizens of Manzanita."

A dozen heads nodded their agreement, although the heads of those wanting to avenge their fallen brothers nodded only after a brief conversation with others in the group.

"That's all. Cover your sixes!"

* * *

"Who fired the shot that killed the first cop?" Arcenas asked.

"I don't know his name, but we paid him five large to start a gunfight."

"Where's that money now?"

"Somewhere in his house. I heard his own crew shot him. They were not happy he screwed up the agreement."

"They can't be crazy enough to think the police would slap their hands and let them go." The sentence was more a statement than a speculation. "I would have covered the exit streets, waited for the deal to go down, then created diversions behind the cops while the negotiators escaped."

"That's why you are the big boss, señor Arcenas."

"Not so," he corrected. "I am the big boss because I am ruthless and cunning. Never forget that."

The man's eyes widened. He nodded his head discretely.

"Go get the money. Keep $100 for your time."

"¡Gracias!"

The response interrupted Arcenas' instructions. He shook his head and continued, "Bring the rest to me."

After the man was gone, Arcenas decided to donate $5000 to the Manzanita Police Department officer's relief fund in the name of William Anderson to support the community's opinion of him. It would take only one transaction by Arcenas' cartel to more than cover that amount.

* * *

Crime scene investigators reported nineteen deaths on site including five police officers. Two officers died in route to the hospital.

Fourteen gang members died where they fell. The search and rescue team shot one gang member who refused to drop his weapon. Three gang members died either in-route to the hospital or in surgery.

The final death toll of twenty-four made the gun fight the worst massacre in Manzanita Police Department history.

Chief Rogers' office issued a special report to the media on what became known as the "Catastrophe at the Claymore." He concentrated on "the brave men who died keeping Manzanita safe." After a brief televised statement, he referred all questions to the special report for answers.

Chapter 41

Mamba paced in front of his office desk, uncertain of his next move after informing Manzanita Police Department of Reed's address. The SWAT team's shootout had all cops walking with one hand on their service weapon. Trust of outsiders was at an all-time low.

He'd been pacing off and on, in the office and at home, since he learned that Reed was back in Manzanita. After miles of pacing, the feeling hadn't changed. It was time to drop the hammer on Reed. He hoped Martinez was in the squad room.

He dialed Northeast Division and requested Detective Martinez.

"Anyone you know lost in the Claymore SWAT action?"

"One, but he and I weren't close."

"Even so, that's a hard pill to swallow."

"Especially after Kerrigan, Flatly, and…" Mary Carstairs face flashed through his memory. He shook his head to clear the image.

Mamba waited a beat before he revealed the reason for his call, "I've got a solid lead on the Anderson Pharmaceuticals jobs."

"Hold on. Let me get a pencil. Okay, amigo, shoot."

"Reed, you've heard his name, is down at the Presidential Hotel in South City. I'm headed there now. If he's got any of the stolen stuff still around, and I'm betting he does, you can pay him a visit right after I do."

"We could save you a trip. You know, get there first like the police are supposed to."

"While I appreciate your generosity, I want to be certain he takes the fall for these. When you go up to his room, you'll have him dead to rights. I guarantee it."

"I like guarantees. I accept your terms."

"Wait in the hallway outside his room. I'll leave the room number at the front desk."

"You can't trust the desk clerks down there to deliver a message."

"I know. Look for a long, bright green envelope in the mail slots. I'll be in the apartment with that number one floor above."

"Subtle and sneaky, I like it. I'm looking forward to meeting señor Reed."

Martinez ended the call and rounded up two Narcotics officers to assist in Reed's arrest. He was feeling magnanimous after orchestrating Flatly's homecoming. He would share the collar.

As they passed the Records room, Martinez glanced inside. What he saw stopped him in his tracks. A man in striped coveralls knelt beside the copy machine.

"You guys go on ahead. I'll catch up on my bike."

"I'm afraid it's down for a while," Sergeant Edwards greeted Martinez as he entered the copy area. "Weekly service check."

"Someone comes once a week to service this thing? That must cost a fortune!"

"Not as much as a major repair would," the repairman said from his position beneath the copier. "One big bill is more than many small ones. Besides, the department picked up the service contract when they bought the machines. You guys do so much copying that these babies would shut down with unwanted regularity without routine maintenance."

"Could someone take copies made earlier while working on the machine?" Martinez asked.

"No way!" Edwards' response was immediate. "I'm in this room during every routine servicing of the machine. All service calls occur during my shifts."

"What about emergencies?"

"They call me in from home. A departmental directive detailing servicing procedures for copiers in all stations is clear. The Senior Records Officer in each Division or his designee must be present during all servicing of these machines."

"You're in this room during all service calls?"

"From when the technician arrives until he leaves, like I said."

"What does he do every week?" the Latino asked and moved toward the machine for a look at its guts.

"It's technical." Edwards intercepted the big man and steered him away from the open panel where the repairman was working. "Mostly it's cleaning and checking for wear and tear, that's difficult for a novice to see. Let me show you the service manual."

"What's that big silver thing?" Martinez asked as he craned his neck for a better look.

"This?" The repairman asked as he held up a silver cylinder. Martinez nodded at his up close look at what Finch called the shiny oatmeal container.

"The copy drum. Pictures taken of the original document attach to the surface of this. When the drum rotates against a blank piece of paper, that picture transfers to that paper. That's the process you call making a copy."

"Wow! That's gotta be hundreds of pictures. How does the machine know which one to make a copy of?"

"It's not like that. Here look." The repairman held out the drum and continued his explanation. "The drum retains each picture long enough to make a single copy. You know the flash each time?"

Martinez nodded again.

"Well, each flash is a single picture. One picture goes on the drum. The drum makes one complete turn, and—"

"It makes one copy, right?"

"Yes."

"Hey, thanks for the lesson. I gotta vamoose."

Martinez thought about what he'd seen all the way to his motorcycle. After mounting up, he decided he and Mamba would do more than pass each other in the hallway of the Presidential Hotel.

* * *

Mamba performed a perfectly executed California rolling stop for the stop sign at the corner of Garfield and 10th. A right turn onto Garfield brought him within one block of the Presidential Hotel.

The deteriorated neighborhood was worse than he remembered. Teenage toughs leaned against a partially stripped car. Spray-painted graffiti decorated every blank wall space on the block. Debris ranging from newspapers to soiled disposable diapers littered the sidewalks.

He parked across the street from the hotel where he felt less contaminated than if he parked in front of the building. Out of habit, he checked his watch. It was 12:27 p.m.

He took a deep breath, unfastened his seatbelt, and climbed out of his car. He jaywalked across the empty street.

"Good afternoon," he called when he reached the registration desk. No one answered.

He tried again, "Hello! Anybody back there?"

"Pipe down, ya noisy bum," a gruff voice answered. "I ain't deaf. If you're in so big a hurry, find another hotel." A wizened woman hobbled through a door near the back of the lobby.

"Who ya wanna see?" she demanded as she limped over to the desk and fixed him with a bloodshot stare. "You ain't gonna stay here. You're dressed too fancy to spend a night in a dive like this."

Mamba waited.

She placed a pair of glasses on her nose, stared hard at the PI. "I get you, mister fancy dresser, you want to pay by the hour. That it?"

"I'm here to see Reed."

"Why?"

"I owe him money." Mamba reached into his back pocket, pulled out his wallet, and extracted two twenties and one five-dollar bill. "He got me some merchandise."

"I don't doubt that none, folks come and go at all hours with him. What's this Reed worth to you?"

"Abe Lincoln stays with you for his room number."

"You must not want him too bad."

"There's another Lincoln for stashing this in the pigeon hole I choose." He produced the bright green envelope and pointed to the boxes behind her. She turned her head in an instinctive maneuver. With the woman's gaze diverted, he feigned slipping the twenties into the envelope and palmed the bills.

"Lemme see the money!"

"Here's Abe." He removed a bill from his wallet while returning the forty dollars with a second simple slight-of-hand maneuver.

She snatched at the money. He held it out of her reach.

"Room number."

"Three-fifteen."

He lowered the bill. She snapped it from his fingers.

"Now put this in the box for two-fifteen," he instructed and sealed the flap before handing her the green envelope.

"This thing's too big for my boxes," she complained. "Look how it sticks out."

"Be sure it stays in that box until tomorrow. You get Abe's twin brother after you do what I ask."

"It'll be there, fancy dresser," she grumbled.

"If I come back before this time tomorrow and that envelope's not in box 215, you will get a visit from the Vice Squad instead of Honest Abe."

"Yeah, yeah. Like I haven't heard that before." The woman turned and stuffed the envelope into box 215. She turned back, folded her five-dollar bill in half, then waved him away.

Mamba climbed the steps to the third-floor landing. He stepped over two crumpled fast-food bags as he turned down the smelly hallway and walked to Room 315. He rapped sharply on the door. When there was no answer, he knocked on the door.

"Go away," a slurred and sleepy voice cried from within.

As his answer, the PI pounded on the door.

Muffled obscenities were distinguishable as the voice approached the door. A deadbolt turned, and the door opened a slit.

The heel of the PI's right hand slammed into the door. The wooden portal snapped back and cracked the bones above and below the right eye of the man who opened it. Reed dropped like a rock.

Mamba stepped over the moaning body and shut the door behind him. He prodded Reed with his foot. The man was stark naked and clutching a pair of boxer shorts.

The boxer shorts fell from Reed's hand as he rolled onto his back. Mamba saw a trickle of blood oozing from beneath the man's hands.

"Get up!" Mamba directed. "You're not hurt that bad."

"Man, my eye is broke," Reed slurred. Both hands clenched his fractured face. He wanted no part of another go-around with the door or its opener. "Who are you?"

"Get up and take a good look."

Reed struggled to his feet. He lowered his left hand and squinted at Mamba. His eyes closed. He rubbed his left eye with the back of his hand and squinted at Mamba again.

"Dancer?"

"Bingo."

"You crazy, man?"

"Put your underwear on!"

The order startled Reed into action. He labored as he pulled on his boxers. Thanks to his alcohol-induced vertigo, his first attempt ended with both of his legs in the same leg of the boxers.

"Sit on the couch and finish."

Reed pulled on the boxers, then leaned forward. As his body tilted, he gave what he intended as a surreptitious glance toward the bedroom losing his balance in the process.

"Who's in the bedroom?"

"Jus' a frien'. She's okay. Her name's Rotunda."

"I want her gone. What I've got to say is between the two of us."

Reed staggered toward the bedroom. He did not make the sharp turn and missed the doorframe. His shoulder ricocheted off the wood.

Mamba followed him. When he looked through the portal, he saw a grotesquely overweight female trying to pull a pair of stretch pants over hips large enough for two good-sized women.

Mamba didn't watch more. He scanned the room. The dirty window looked like it hadn't opened in years. There was no escape route. Traffic in and out had to use the living room.

"I want clothes on you, too, Reed," he called as he returned to the main living area. "And be quick—both of you. I don't have all day."

The obese hooker waddled from the bedroom and made a less than glorious exit from the apartment, slipping in blood pooled by the door and staggering into the hallway.

Reed appeared. He was zipping his pants when he got to the chair opposite Mamba.

"Sit down!"

Reed dropped onto the chair. The PI watched him squirm for a full minute before he spoke.

"I'm disappointed in you. I hoped you were on your way back."

"I am, Dansher."

"I talked to Father Henry." Mamba watched Reed's false bravado evaporate at the name of the priest that ran the turnaround mission.

"I tried," Reed whined. "I really tried."

"Bull!" Mamba snorted. "Shut up and listen. I'm here to buy some stuff."

"What?" Reed caught himself before he fell off his chair. After recovering minimal composure, he laughed nervously and said, "I thought you said you was buyin'."

"I did. You think that's funny?"

"No. Oh, no! You're so straight you make a ruler look crooked. What you want to buy stuff from me for?"

"I need money. Word has it you've done well recently. I want to buy for resale."

"This must be a setup." Reed narrowed his one non-swollen eye to a slit and studied the private detective.

Mamba shrugged at the suggestion of a setup. He stared into the man's good eye. It was focused beyond him toward the kitchen.

"Are you going to sell to me or not?"

"Ain't got none here," was the mumbled reply. "You call me in a couple days and maybe we can work sumpin' out."

Mamba offered a second shrug and stood.

"I'll get what I came for, Reed. I give everyone one chance. You've had yours."

As the door closed behind him, he nodded to the three Narcotics officers in the hallway.

"The stuff's in the kitchen, most likely right behind the green patterned overstuffed chair. He won't give you any trouble."

"Wait here." It was more than a suggestion from Martinez.

A uniform pounded on the door.

"Police! Open up!" As soon as he heard sounds inside, he turned the doorknob and shoved the door open.

"Freeze!" Reed froze, not three steps away from an open door in the kitchen's base cabinet. In his hand was a dilapidated shoebox.

"Glove up! I'll cover this guy," Martinez ordered.

Both officers complied. The first to pull on his second glove took the box from Reed's shaking hands.

"This is what we're looking for," the other officer announced. He held up a small container of pills with Anderson Pharmaceuticals, Inc. emblazoned on the label.

"I'll make you a deal," Martinez offered his associates. "You guys do all the paperwork on this. Leave my name out of the report, and the collar is yours."

"Why so generous?"

"I've got other frijoles to re-fry."

Both uniformed officers rolled their eyes, but neither smiled.

"Leave, if you're going."

"It's my pleasure. Adios, amigos," the Latino called as he shut the apartment door.

"Everything go okay in there?" Mamba asked when Martinez turned away from Reed's door.

"No problem. But it was difficult, and I do mean difficult, to walk away from a slam-dunk collar."

Mamba nodded. He understood. The importance of recording a clean collar for a detective was hard to overstate.

"Why'd you want Reed arrested?"

"Protection."

Martinez frowned.

"With Brewster dead, I think he'll have a better chance of staying alive inside than on the street. Besides, I'm sure it solves the Anderson Drug heists, too."

"Maybe." Martinez paused and shifted conversational gears. "Thanks for waiting. I know you weren't planning on that."

"It's all good. What's your big news?"

"Right. Did you know they service the copy machine at the station weekly?"

"No."

"Well, they do. And, get this, Sergeant Edwards is present, by departmental directive, during all service and repair work."

"So? It sounds like a good way to prevent unauthorized copying to me."

"If Edwards is our man, he could send information out with a bogus repairman. He gets called in from home for emergency repairs. It'd be easy as pie to fake a breakdown whenever he makes copies of important information and pass copies on to the repairman to sneak out."

"I suppose that's possible. But how does he get the copies he passes? We've both watched. There's only one set that comes out of that machine."

"That's the stumper." Then the Martinez grin blossomed to full size. "But I have a plan to check it out."

"Why am I not surprised." The sentence could have been a comment or a question.

"You want to hear the plan or not?"

"Sure. Just listen to my news before I forget about it."

"Fair enough."

"Officer Desantos from IA paid me a visit."

"What did she want?"

"Stallings."

"It took long enough."

"Not quite long enough, though. I'm certain they know I know where he is."

"But they don't know where he is, right?"

Mamba nodded.

"Then, we still have the advantage. Does Stallings know about that visit?"

"Not yet."

"You gonna tell him?" Martinez asked.

"Would you?"

"I don't know."

"Neither do I."

Both men lapsed into silence, their thoughts roiling. Mamba spoke first.

"Tell you what. You ride with me, and I'll listen to your plan for how to track the copies on the way to my office."

"No can do. I had to ride my bike here. I found out about Edwards and the service policy on the way out the door of the station. I sent the others ahead."

"Okay. Don't let this go to your head, but, I want to hear this plan of yours. How 'bout this? There used to be a kind of rundown coffee shop over—"

"Over on 9th. Right?"

"That's the one."

It wasn't long before the two men sat as the only patrons in the small, rundown coffee shop. Stallings' situation shifted to a back burner while Martinez filled the PI in on his plan.

* * *

It was one of those eerie coincidences. A coincidence that would make most people think differently about the space/time continuum if they knew the frequency at which they occurred. Franklin and Lizbeth Stallings sat on the Mambas' patio at the same moment Martinez and Mamba talked in the hallway outside Reed's hotel room.

"Franklin, I think you should turn yourself in to the police."

"What?"

"You've been running or hiding long enough. You need to come forward. Phil can clear you, can't he?"

"It's been more like too long," he corrected. "Mamba has evidence that supports my innocence, but I'll only go back if they'll listen. The jackals in Internal Affairs must be hungry for a taste of my blood. IAD is out to get cops they think are bad. Once they've decided, they don't listen to reason."

Lizbeth looked away from her husband.

"I promise to go back as soon as we find the real leak."

"What if you don't find that leak?" she whispered and turned toward him.

"Don't worry. I'll get off. I am innocent." He reached out and intertwined his fingers into hers. "Trust me?"

"Always." She raised their hands and kissed his.

* * *

"It's far from the greatest plan ever conceived, but it's better than winging it," Mamba said to Martinez as they walked from the coffee shop.

"For having only minutos to plan, my plan is exceptionally exceptional," Martinez insisted.

"How could I not follow an exceptionally exceptional plan? Meet me outside Records Division." Mamba unlocked his driver's side door as he finished.

"It is you, amigo, who will meet me there," Martinez retorted. He lumbered the last five yards to his motorcycle.

* * *

A familiar motorcycle sat parked illegally in one of the triangular areas at the end of a row of parking spaces. Mamba shook his head as he exited his car.

The PI joined Martinez in the hallway outside the Records Division. They entered the office in tandem. Martinez checked in as required and tossed a look in Mamba's direction. He nodded.

"You got any coffee?" Mamba asked the uniform at the counter.

"Not here. The closest is down in homicide."

"You know, if I stayed here and kind of kept house, you could hustle to homicide and rustle us both up a cup," Mamba suggested.

"I can't leave my post, sir."

"I can't get into homicide without my pass. I'm undercover and never carry it with me." Mamba wrinkled his brow. "I'll stay here. When someone comes in, I'll explain that they have to wait for you to return. That's better coverage of your post than during one of your normal breaks."

The rookie officer nodded his agreement and headed out the door.

While Mamba engaged the officer at the counter, Martinez visited Sergeant Edwards.

"I tell you, Sarge, this spontaneous division audit gets more complicated every day," the Detective complained.

"How so?"

"Now they want the complete case record from my first arrest. Something about comparing my work as my career progressed."

"You're telling me you need the entire file copied?"

"Sí, Sergeant."

"Come with me," Edwards directed. "We'll round it up pronto. You know I'm all for quality control, especially with all the negative press police departments get, but sometimes I think our administrative level has too much time on its hands."

"That's the truth."

As the two men disappeared in the stacks of case files, Mamba entered the copy area, pulled a small set of tools from his pocket, and extracted a thin, stiff wire from the leatherette case. He sprung the lock that held the access panel of the copy machine closed and swung the panel open. What he saw explained the leak and made him wish he had a camera.

There were two metallic cylinders inside the bowels of the copier and one tray that held an uneven stack of photocopied pages. He imagined both copy drums capturing the same image and each making a copy of that page each time the light flashed. One flash generated two copies, and one copy was unknown to the person who requested it.

After a quick look to see if anyone entered the room unannounced, he removed a flat blade screwdriver from his kit. He pushed the blade about one-eighth of an inch into the surface of the drum he reasoned made legitimate copies for the department and gave a quick twist. He smiled at the hole in the smooth, silver face of the copy drum. The sabotage complete, he closed the access panel. He was standing by the receptionist desk when the rookie returned with two steaming Styrofoam cups of coffee.

Chapter 42

It was almost 5:00 p.m. on the day Mamba damaged one copy drum in Edwards' machine. Martinez waited outside Mamba Investigations when the PI parallel parked.

"Am I late?"

"No. But, I'm anxious." Martinez looked left, then right in rapid succession. "We better get inside, pronto. Some of your business neighbors don't look too comfortable about a huge, tattooed Mexican hanging around."

"I haven't seen one of those," Mamba deadpanned as he opened the door.

Martinez snorted a laugh.

After the outside door was closed and locked, the men entered Mamba's private office. He described the double-cylinder setup inside the copier in the Records Division.

It didn't go well.

"That's what I saw!" Mamba repeated for the third time. "I'm convinced each flash of the camera light ends up as two copies of the image."

"That's just not possible!"

"One machine. Two copy drums. Two places where copies end up. Give me another option!"

"I don't have one."

They sat, each stewing inside for a different reason.

"Sorry. It's just so—" Martinez started, thought better of that, and asked, "Whatta we do now?"

"I made sure that Edwards will call for a repair. I modified one drum." Mamba held up his toolkit while making a scooping motion with his other hand.

"You dug a hole in a cylinder?"

"Seemed like the logical thing to do."

Martinez gave another snort. "Not very subtle, are you?"

"Only when it's necessary. I mean only when it's absolutely necessary. Actually, the hole's not that big. I suspect no one will complain about the gap in the print on their copies until it lines up with some critical phrase and renders it illegible."

"So, we know that Edwards will call for service. I'll stop in when the repairman's working."

"We will stop in," Mamba corrected.

* * *

Kerrigan's progress during his recovery exceeded the expectations of the doctors. He reached several milestones for patients with severe head trauma faster than anyone, other than Kate, imagined possible. His vocabulary of nouns was incomplete, but the physical side of his rehabilitation was ahead of projection.

This morning, he asked the nurse for a mirror although he couldn't think of the concrete term. He learned to substitute imprecise descriptive terms for concrete words missing from the damaged left side of his brain.

The nurse was hesitant to comply with his request—especially after she was certain that he wanted a mirror. The angry scars from the surgery were flame red, and lines of stiches from pre-reconstructive surgeries laced his swollen face. Most of his left ear was missing, as of yet untouched by the plastic surgeons.

The hesitation by the nurse to follow his directive brought the police lieutenant in him to the surface. He made it clear that she would bring him a mirror. If she didn't, he would climb out of bed, walk to the bathroom door, and look in the mirror attached to its inside surface. Of course, what he thought he said and what the nurses heard him say seldom aligned.

However, this nurse brought him a mirror.

Kerrigan stared at his reflection in the silver surface. A grim smile curled the functional corner of his mouth.

"I not look as bad as I think, no, thought," was his assessment.

The nurse holding the mirror shook her head.

* * *

As much as Martinez hated paperwork, he hated the thought of losing his job more. He tried to spend six to eight hours one day per week holed up in the squad room. The sound of typewriter keys punctuated a running commentary on the typewritten text and the sporadic burst of deprecating remarks against paperwork.

A phone call from Sergeant Smith at the reception desk brought the detective a break from the drudgery.

"Detective Martinez, please."

"You got him."

"Hey, Martinez. You wanted to know when the copier repairman got here."

"I do."

"He did." Smith chuckled at his repartee. It wasn't often he got one in on an undercover guy.

"Nice one, Smitty. I'll mark it on my calendar since it's the only one you'll get for another year."

Smith laughed.

"Did you call Mamba?"

"When the truck pulled up. I had to talk to his secretary. I found out he's tailing the repairman. Why would he be doing that?"

"He's a gumshoe. Those guys are all about half a bubble off."

"Roger that. Anything else the front desk can do for you, Detective?"

"You added concierge service like I requested?"

"Don't quit your day job."

"Then, nope. I'm good." Martinez hung up the phone. Sergeant Smith went to the front door and waved Mamba inside.

Martinez reached the hallway housing the door to the Records Division. He watched the repairman enter the copy room. Walking toward that door, he saw Mamba approaching and adjusted his pace to arrive simultaneously with the PI.

Without a sound, they stepped through the door to the outer office in tandem and watched the opening scene of the drama they created.

The repairman opened the copy machine with Sergeant Edwards standing close beside him. As both men peered into the innards of the machine, Martinez made his move. With amazing speed and grace for a man his size, he leaped toward the offending piece of equipment.

"Freeze!" he bellowed. He trained his gun on the repairman. The volume of Martinez's cry, coupled with the word he shouted pulled two uniforms in from the hallway.

Pandemonium ensued. Shouts and recriminations flew between the men beside the copier and the officers that gathered in the reception area. More uniformed officers crowded into the Records Division lobby.

It took Captain Abbott to restore order. After listening to a shouted explanation by Martinez and a vocal barrage from Sergeant Edwards, he demanded silence.

"Martinez. Edwards. With me," Abbott barked. As an afterthought he added, "You, too, Mr. Mamba."

The Captain directed two officers to detain the repairman and keep everyone away from the copy machine. He tossed a "follow me" gesture and strode through the surly but subdued crowd in the reception area into the adjacent supply room and closed the door.

"Detective Martinez, I want an explanation for your outrageous behavior." He stopped and stared hard at the man. "And it better be good."

"These men barged in here!" Edwards shouted.

"That's enough, Sergeant! You'll get your turn." He waved off the start of a second protest. "I said, 'you'll get your turn.' Continue, Detective."

"This whole thing started with a list of names."

It took forty-five minutes to relate the story of the leak and the search for the source. Mamba added to the length of the discourse by embellishing the narrative when Martinez reached the part about Franklin Stallings' disappearance. He included the cross-country odyssey he undertook to locate him.

Abbott asked one question during the recitation. He wanted to know if there were copies of the documents that would clear Stallings. Mamba assured him there were. The Captain's single comment during the prolonged explanation was a command that silenced Edwards' only attempt to interrupt.

"So, Captain," Martinez began his conclusion. "Inside the big copy machine are two cylinders, implicating Sergeant Edwards as the departmental leak."

Abbott waved off another of Edwards' protests. "I'd say the next step in the process is for us to return to the scene of the crime."

"Yes, sir."

"Let's move."

Once back in the copy room, Martinez turned the initial explanation over to Mamba.

"When you look, you will find a second copy drum with a connection to the copier's camera. There's even a separate paper tray for storing the copies out of sight. Every document copied for the Department has the potential of being copied on the unauthorized machine at the same time. We suspect they have a way to copy only what they want to leak."

Abbott peered into the access cavity. The second copy drum was clearly visible. There was no doubt of the veracity of Martinez and Mamba's narrative. He straightened up and turned toward Edwards.

"Get your union rep, Sergeant. You need to save your explanation for your lawyer." Edwards and the repairman were taken into custody by an overabundance of willing officers.

* * *

While basking in the success of what he considered his takedown of the Brewster organization, William Anderson neglected one very critical loose end. He picked up his phone and dialed.

"Is Reed still a potential problem?"

"Nice to hear your voice, too, Mr. Anderson," Petula Jacobs shot back. She was reeling from aftershocks generated when Rogers went ballistic on her. She was in no mood for more testosterone-induced attitude.

"I do not appreciate your tone."

"Yeah, well, tell it to the Marines."

Anderson waited for a wave of anger to pass. He took a deep breath and started over.

"I need to know if Reed might be a future problem as we move from where we are and where I want us to end up."

"Reed is in jail. He's got only a public defender. My guess is he'll plead out of whatever his maximum charge is and end up serving some lesser amount of time. Assuming that's agreed upon by all parties involved."

"That's far from a best-case scenario. Let me investigate. Can you find out the date of his day in court?"

"I can. When you call me back, I'll have that information. But, I want something from you in return."

"We already have an agreement." Anderson's voice was low and hard.

"Lighten up. It looks like they found the departmental leak for the copied documents."

Silence.

The silence encouraged Petula.

"I want a plane ticket to somewhere without extradition. By the time all this dust settles, I want to be out of here."

"That can be arranged. Will you need documents?"

"I'm sure I will. I'll check on destinations and see what they require. I look forward to hearing from you again."

Guillermo Arcenas immediately dialed another number.

"Who do you know that wouldn't mind staying in prison for life?"

"Hmmm. That's a tough one." Dead air. "I know a crazy hitman. He's the one that ripped Brewster's neck open, so he's a guest of California for life, anyway."

"He's not in isolation?"

"Don't know. But, even if he is, he has to know someone we can use. All we'd need to do is put some grease on his skids."

"Get me details and a timeline. I'll call you if I need this to happen."

"Is that all, señor?"

"I forgive your slip into español. This time."

"I'm sorry, sir. Is that all?"

"For now."

Chapter 43

News of the arrest of Sergeant Edwards for leaking departmental information spread faster than a wildfire through the chaparral-covered foothills east of Manzanita. By the end of the workday, news anchors from television stations as far away as San Diego and San Francisco were on the phone or in Manzanita Police Department's downtown complex. Police Chief Dwight Rogers was the most coveted interview target.

Petula Jacobs considered herself the eye of any media maelstrom. As Rogers' administrative assistant, she'd deflected more than her share of television, radio, and newspaper reporters away from her boss. A Rogers fan no longer, she was less concerned how this might end for him as she was for her own fate.

Her phone rang. The light from Rogers' private line blinked an invitation.

"Yes, Chief."

"I need your help."

"That's not how it's been in the recent past."

"Get over yourself. And get into my office!"

"Have a nice day."

"Now!" Rogers' tone left no doubt of his expectation. She locked her desk drawers and put her phone on Private. She wanted no interruptions to what she was sure would be a most interesting meeting.

"Edwards placed me in what has the potential to become a disastrous situation," were Rogers' first words after Petula closed the door to his office.

"That's a fair statement."

He glared at her. After a moment, his face relaxed.

"What are we going to do?"

"I assume you have a plan for such a contingency."

"I do. It used to include you. Now, I suspect you're more a liability than a liaison."

"You're not far off with that suspicion."

"What are the chances of reconciliation?"

She stared at him with her best poker face. Rogers tried another tack.

"I suspect you've calculated a monetary value for shoring up the business portion of our relationship."

"If you're referring to Anderson as the portion of our relationship, it has crossed my mind."

"You knew Edwards was the leak."

"Au contraire. I only suspected him as the leak. I never knowingly communicated directly with anyone named Edwards."

"You received copies of every leaked document."

"As part of my position as your administrative assistant. Listen, Dwight, don't try to implicate me as Edwards' co-conspirator. You really don't want to know what I can do, and will do to you, if I'm implicated by anybody."

"Fine. You work on keeping both our names out of the Edwards investigation. I'll work on freeing up some funds, enough for the both of us."

"If you do that, I might find it in my heart to work on that reconciliation you asked about. Compiling a file of documents that we need to shred is how I'd start."

Chapter 44

There were two pathways for the walk from the prisoner entrance of the Northeast Division station to the interrogation rooms. One was as direct as possible. Prisoners of little importance and criminals with the potential to cause disruption during their transport or incarceration followed that path.

The alternative route to the interrogation rooms was long. It meandered through several hallways. Arresting officers used it for prisoners they wanted to show off, or for those they wished to ponder their fate.

Sergeant Eddie Edwards sat in Interrogation Room 4. He arrived there via the short route. There was loud, emotional arguing over that decision among the officers charged with his transport from the jail cell to the station. A vocal minority wanted "the longest walk possible to show off his sorry butt to everyone he betrayed."

Cooler heads prevailed, but it took the assurance that Edwards would enter and leave the Federal Courthouse through a ceremonial blue gauntlet for all criminal action against him.

Edwards was not alone in the interrogation room. Three members of the Departmental Leak Task Force, a group convened after identifying the leak, sat across the table.

Edwards' lawyer occupied the chair beside him. A tape recorder rested between the two parties.

The door opened and Noemi Herrera, an assistant district attorney, entered.

"Gentlemen."

Four heads nodded, Edwards being the solitary non-responder.

Herrera took the remaining chair. Opening her briefcase, she pulled out a file folder. She opened the folder, removed one sheet of paper, and began her presentation.

"Sergeant Edwards, I am prepared to offer you certain immunities to prosecution for information on your part in this affair."

Two members of the task force frowned at the words. The ADA knew the opinion of making deals with a traitor to the badge and took note of their grim expressions.

“Look this over.” She slid the paper across the table. “If you agree to the terms, we will sign this document after we record your statement, and I verify the information provided in that statement.”

“I’ll play ball with you,” Edwards announced his decision without looking at his lawyer, who was reading the offer. The disgraced officer knew Brewster’s death and the current chaotic state of that group allowed him to recount all he knew about the drug operation. Little would come of it. He also knew that drug traffickers never forgave someone who talked to the police. “I want a guarantee that the time I have to serve will be as part of a witness protection package.”

Herrera frowned. As the most experienced member of the District Attorney’s staff, she’d handled such requests before. Her office believed Edwards’ testimony was key to dismantling the city’s drug trafficking infrastructure. Although she was prepared to go as far as needed to obtain the testimony her office sought, she pretended to consider the request before responding.

“I’ll see what I can do.” Herrera chewed each word before uttering it. “We might be able to work something out, after we verify what you provide.”

“I’m not worried about verification,” Edwards bragged. He motioned toward the tape recorder. A Task Force member pushed the RECORD button. Eddie began his tale.

“I was first approached by a man that I found out later worked for Sidney Brewster. That was about two years ago. He offered me quite a sum of money—”

“Not good enough!” The ADA slapped at the tape recorder’s OFF button. “I get specifics: names, dates, places, amounts, or you get squat—nada! If you expect immunity and protection, you will deliver far more than the generalities you’ve just tried to pass off as testimony. Is that clear enough for you?”

Edwards looked at his lawyer. At the nod of affirmation from the attorney, Edwards nodded to Herrera and began his revised recitation.

“I was first approached by a Richard Elkhart about two years ago. I later learned that he worked for Sidney Brewster. He offered me twelve hundred dollars per month for what he called ‘informational favors.’ It soon became obvious that the offer was syndicate-connected.”

Twelve hundred dollars per month was nearly half a uniformed officer's salary. Task force members gritted their teeth.

"How did you determine that the Syndicate was involved?"

"It was a hunch," Edwards admitted.

"What was your hunch based on? You provide proof of syndicate involvement, and that launches a full-scale investigation at several levels," the Deputy Chief interjected.

"Okay. I figured the syndicate was behind the offer mostly because of the information they were interested in. It was all drug related."

Members of the task force sighed. Their shoulders sagged. Edwards was a desk jockey for so long he was unaware of the number of non-syndicate people willing to pay for information about drug raids. His hunch about Syndicate involvement was just that, a hunch.

When Edwards detected lagging interest in his information, he played his last card. "I have one more thing."

"We'll listen, but this better be more substantial than what you've given us so far," Herrera warned.

"There's somebody up the admin ladder that got the copies, too. Not only that, but someone who's altering their voice called me with instructions several times."

"An altered voice? That could be anyone." The ADA wondered how Edwards ever made Sergeant. Herrera's tone was more respectful than she wanted to use when she added, "Go ahead."

Fifteen minutes later they switched off the recorder. Four uniformed patrolmen escorted Edwards back to his isolated holding cell.

The Sergeant's lawyer stood and asked, "Whom should I contact about the new identity?"

"I'll contact you after we verify Sergeant Edwards' information." The ADA tapped the tape recorder.

Edwards' lawyer nodded. He thought better of making a comment about alacrity in the matter. Faced with the overwhelming evidence against his client, any break Edwards got would be a godsend. He left without another word.

At the advice of his lawyer, Edwards pleaded guilty to one charge of Conspiracy to Commit a Crime and twenty charges of Obstruction of Justice. There was no godsend. The DA's indictments allowed the judge to sentence him to an out of state prison under a fictitious name.

Edwards was sentenced to five years for the Conspiracy to Commit a Crime admission and twenty consecutive three-year terms for the Obstruction of Justice charges. Parole would not be considered for thirty years. He was fined $36,000.

* * *

Following Edwards' session, another hastily compiled group assembled in Interrogation Room 4. As per his Manzanita Police Department contract, the panel of Franklin Stallings' peers and his union appointed lawyer would determine his fate. As in the Edwards hearing, the administrator present was Deputy Chief Chalmers. That did not go unnoticed.

"Sergeant, your conduct was unprofessional and criminal. Under ordinary circumstances, we would have no choice but to recommend prosecution to the District Attorney's office." Chalmers delivered his statement as unemotionally as one would order a burger and fries at a drive-through.

Stallings fidgeted in his seat, unhappy with the way the meeting started. He hoped for something besides guilt by association.

"However, it has come to the attention of this panel that you played a significant role in plugging this department's information leak. In fact, I have in my possession a passionate plea from a former police officer on behalf of leniency."

Stallings opened his mouth to speak when the Deputy Chief nodded to the patrol officer standing as sentry just inside the door. She returned the nod, opened the door, and motioned to someone in the hallway.

Phil Mamba walked through that door.

In less than half an hour, the former MPD lieutenant described his search for Stallings. He also accepted a significant share of the responsibility for Stallings' failure to turn himself in. The conclusion to his presentation was an admission that he had "knowingly and willingly" harbored Stallings in his own home.

After informing Mamba that charges against him were under consideration, discussion was brief and heated. The panel's final recommendation was the reinstatement of Sergeant Stallings with only a letter of reprimand in his file.

Stallings' suspension for unauthorized absence was rescinded. The panel's felt his contribution to identifying the information leak was enough to forgive of the transgression of going AWOL. His work on the case during that time swayed the naysayers.

Mamba's fate was quickly adjudicated. He was exonerated in a vote of raised hands.

"We have one more agenda item." The statement by the Deputy Chief seemed to lower the temperature in Interrogation Room 4 by twenty degrees.

"I have received correspondence from the Chief of Police in—" Chalmers placed his reading glasses on his nose and peered at the document in the only open file folder before him. "Ah, here it is. Illiana, Indiana is the site of origin."

Stallings' clenched his teeth to ensure he said nothing.

After a snort of impatience, the Deputy Chief removed his glasses and closed the file.

"Here it is in a nutshell. Although a complaint against then Officer Stallings was filed years ago, the witness in Indiana who filed the complaint about her testimony being leaked to the press admitted she sent that information to the media herself. She wanted her fifteen minutes of fame. Fearing she'd become just another witness in the case, she sent a summary of her testimony to the press anonymously and blamed you, Sergeant. Is that about right?"

Stallings' demeanor morphed from caged animal to proud papa during Chalmers' recitation. He answered without hesitation, "Right on the money, sir."

"Illiana PD sent a revised page for insertion into your personnel file." Ellerbe pulled a single sheet of paper from the folder.

"Sergeant Franklin Stallings, what was the single blemish on your record is on longer on your record. There never was a complaint filed against you." He handed the page to Stallings.

"Thank you, sir. Is this mine to keep?"

"It is," the Chalmers answered. He added with a wink, "Don't worry, I made a copy."

* * *

Two days after Stallings' hearing, Martinez and Mamba met him in his office.

The men were reading a copy of Edwards' statement by rotating pages between them. Stallings stated the obvious.

"Eddie was in deep."

"And Brewster was a bigger fish than I thought," Martinez added.

Mamba continued reading.

"I'm just glad I don't have to worry whether a copy of this transcript is already out on the street," Stallings' offered.

Martinez nodded.

Mamba continued reading.

"Okay, Gumshoe, what's stuck in your gizzard now?" Martinez asked.

"There's got to be someone higher than the division level involved in this whole business. I know I've said this before, but I don't think I'm beating a dead horse. Look. According to Edwards, somebody downtown got copies of all leaked documents, and the copy machine service contracts are citywide."

"You're on thin ice," Stallings warned. "That implies collusion from the Chief's office. Those contracts came from there. Besides, I know what it's like to be convicted by implication and innuendo. I still get sideways looks."

"I don't like it any more than you do. But, Chief Rogers, or someone close to him, is implicated. His office should be subject to investigation, like you were. Although this might just be pettiness, where was the Chief at your hearing?"

"He is the Chief of Police," Martinez offered. "My guess? He felt it more important to be seen as impartial in a decision of that magnitude."

"Could be," Stallings mused. "Anyway, Phil, we can't help you with this. If you investigate the Chief, you've got to do it with no active police help."

"I know. The last thing I want is for either of you two to get in trouble, again. Especially if I'm hiking the wrong trail." Mamba opened the door of Stallings' office. "Thanks."

* * *

"Tell me again where Chief Rogers went after Detroit," Phil asked Hope to repeat information she read to him earlier. He tilted back in his recliner. His eyes were closed as he visualized his thoughts.

"Detroit for three years; a year in Indianapolis. Four years in St. Louis. Then here three years ago." She retraced the police official's route to his current assignment as she read from old newspaper reports her husband photocopied.

"Wait a minute!" Mamba sat up. "Where was the Chief just before he came here?"

"Like I said twice already, St. Louis."

"Stallings' file was altered coming out of St. Louis."

"You suspect Chief Rogers of involvement with the syndicate just because two men worked in the same city once?"

"I know it sounds like that when you—"

"Repeat what you say," Hope finished.

"Touché! It's possible that's my reasoning," Mamba hedged. "I don't know. I might be grasping at straws. There seems to be something going on beneath the surface of this whole thing."

"How early can you be ready in the morning?" she asked as she picked up the phone book and began to flip through it.

"What do you mean?"

"I'll book your flight to St. Louis," she answered without looking up. "You're already there mentally."

"I love you," he told her and kissed her cheek. "First flight you can get me on Sunday afternoon. I want to go to church as a family."

* * *

Mamba's flight from Los Angeles to St. Louis was uneventful. He arrived at his destination Sunday night and took a cab to a hotel within walking distance of the St. Louis Police Department's central office building. He checked in and called home.

The next morning, he went to the St. Louis Police records' tomb. It took a call to Sergeant Stallings who had Deputy Chief Chalmers grant Mamba access to the room. He was told, repeatedly, that all documents were eyes only.

"Can I take notes?"

"We have to read them before you're allowed to leave with them. We have surveillance cameras in this room."

"Understood."

He spent the morning looking for something that might give him an idea of how to get to the pathway he was certain existed.

At 4:30 p.m., Mamba ran his fingers through his hair attempting to push the fatigue from his brain. The stuffy interior of the windowless room and the long day he spent there took their toll on his mental alertness and his confidence.

He studied the single scribbled note he jotted down while in the room during the six-hour search. The only irregularity in Rogers' tenure, if you could even call it an irregularity, was that the St. Louis Police Department switched special courier services after Rogers became Assistant Commissioner. Not much to show for a long day.

He sighed and turned to the final page in Rogers' file. It listed the last day of his service. Also noted was the day and time that a Sergeant Charles Drummond released the Assistant Commissioner's file to the Security Express courier service for transport to his new assignment as Chief of Police in Manzanita, California. Handwritten on that page of the file was the pickup time, 1115 hours.

He closed the file with more force than needed and jotted down the time of the transport as his second, and final, notation. It was time to go. Tomorrow he would check the courier service.

He dropped off Rogers' file at the desk in the records lobby and showed the single page of his notebook that contained his two notes. The Records Sergeant shrugged at what he considered innocuous notations and handed the notebook back.

"Long day for only that," he understated.

"Don't I know it! Thanks for your help."

The PI stepped into the world of Christmas decorations and lights. He shivered at the biting chill in the air. He passed the Gateway Arch as he hurried to his hotel. While he admired the architecture, he could not understand why anyone would want to go to the top.

After a hot shower, he speculated on what he might discover at the shipping company. By the time he climbed into bed, he had only a shred of confidence that the additional time he booked in The Gateway City would pay off.

* * *

Mamba checked his suitcase into stored luggage at his hotel. He asked the desk clerk for directions to Security Express's central warehouse. He stood at the front counter of the delivery company trying to explain his unusual request.

"I am working with the Manzanita, California, police. I want to look at the driver's log for a run that included a stop at a police station here in

St. Louis on August 11, three years ago." Mamba tried his best to sound legitimate.

"Now, that's interesting. Do you know that we are the exclusive delivery company for the police here in St. Louis?"

"Wow. That is interesting."

"I'm afraid the best I can do is give all log records for the month of August," the girl behind the counter apologized. "We merge everything by month at the end of each fiscal year."

"I'll take it. My plane doesn't leave until this afternoon. Thank you." As he carried a stack of oversized binders to the only table in the visitors' area of the office, he remembered a favorite phrase of his father. "Better than a poke in the eye with a sharp stick," he mumbled with a smile.

A quick flip through each volume confirmed his worst fear.

What the counter girl neglected to include in her explanation was the Security Express definition of consolidate. The records he sifted through consolidated the entire Midwest region's pickups and deliveries—by month. But the daily logs for August were a chaotic stack of days and times stored in four files, ostensibly one for each week of the month.

After staring at the mass of times, destinations, and initials, for far longer than he planned, he reconsidered his father's saying, and decided that maybe a sharp stick in the eye wasn't nearly as bad as his Dad made it sound.

He turned another page in the second thickly bound volume and allowed his finger to drift slowly down the columns of this August 11 page. He had to force himself to read each line.

"9 x 12 envelope, 1 Manila – SLPD Main Precinct Station – 3:35 PM." The entry was initialed, W.K.

That was the only entry from the SLPD's Main Precinct for August 11. He flipped to the next page and sat bolt upright. In his haste, he fumbled his notebook as he pulled it from his shirt pocket, finally trapping it against his stomach.

He took a quick look around to reassure himself that no one had seen his slapstick action. Satisfied that he had no audience, he opened the small, black book and turned to the last page of entries.

"Records out at 1115 hours – Drummond," he murmured.

That notation closed out Rogers' SLPD file. According to official records, the Desk Sergeant checked the file out of the station in the late morning, but the courier service had no official record of its arrival in their hands until mid-afternoon. He'd found over four hours of time for that file unaccounted for by either sender or carrier.

He considered possible explanations for the discrepancy.

The courier, W.K., neglected to log the package by mistake. He dismissed that since couriers couldn't afford errors in data entry. Big money depended on accurate records when a client tried to recover losses resulting from an alleged mistimed pickup or delivery.

Another option was that Drummond, the Desk Sergeant, logged the time incorrectly. He knew the desk sergeants at MPD were notoriously accurate people. Accurate to a degree that dismayed those working with them.

He lugged the four bound files back to the counter.

"Can I get a copy of one page?"

"I'll be happy to copy it for you. Which page is it?"

Mamba showed the page he marked by stuffing his hand in the binder. She nodded, made the copy, and handed it to him. He thanked the woman and headed back to his hotel.

* * *

After retrieving his suitcase from the luggage storage area, Mamba went to the front desk and changed two one-dollar bills into quarters and entered the phone booth in the lobby. He pulled open the phone book attached to the booth by a snake-like steel cord. He found the Yellow Pages and flipped through to the "C" pages. His eyes followed the tip of his index finger down the page until it touched the heading, "Copy Machine Rental, Leasing, Service."

He dropped in a quarter and dialed Manzanita Police Department's Northeast Division number.

"The rate for this call is thirty cents per minute. Please deposit coins to cover the expected length of your call."

Mamba pushed his remaining seven quarters into the slot on the payphone.

It took over one minute to connect to Franklin Stallings. After explaining what he wanted, he calculated he had a little more than a minute-and-a-half left.

"Franklin, please do what I ask!"

"You know I shouldn't be even talking to you about this." After sifting through several stacks of folders on his desk, the Sergeant located the page with the information Mamba requested and picked up the phone.

"Franklin, you still there? That's the fifth time I've asked that question. Come on! I've only got maybe half a minute left on my quarters!"

"Patience is a virtue, a virtue you are severely lacking."

"Did you find the company name or not?"

"Gar-Mar, Incorporated."

Mamba scanned the listed service providers in the still-open phone book. He saw that name on the page.

"Bullseye! That's the missing link!"

"Not that I'm all that interested, but when are you going to tell me why the company that owns the copy machine distributorship is so important?"

"As soon as I get back there. If I were you, I'd write up a file cover for Chief Rogers. I'll be shocked if IAD doesn't devour what I've got."

"Please deposit an additional thirty cents for one additional minute of time," the mechanical operator's voice intoned.

Dancer hung up.

"What are—" Stallings stopped. He was talking to the dial tone.

* * *

Guillermo Arcenas spoke slowly and distinctly into his office phone. Not that he was fearful of being misunderstood. He wanted to be certain that the recipient of his call knew the significance of his words.

"It is my understanding that Rick Elkhart assumed control of Brewster's remaining assets. I want that verified and I want a plan for his elimination in my possession within the week."

"I think that's doable."

"You'd better do more than think about it."

Despite her mental berating of the man, Petula Jacob answered Arcenas with only a hint of annoyance.

"You'll have what you want."

"See. That wasn't so hard, was it? What's the status of our disposable asset?"

"All they're waiting for is a time to finish him with the widest net of suspicion."

"I like that strategy, but remind them they have a deadline."

"I'll get a hurry-up order to them today via the prisoner delivery driver."

"Whatever it takes. You have until the end of the week."

Chapter 45

Brad Finch sat at his lab station two hours after the lab shut down for the day. He agreed to work overtime on a project for Narcotics. He knew this was payment from Detective Martinez. He didn't care what strings Martinez pulled to clear his overtime work. Money was money.

He hunched over several petri dishes. Each contained a single small scrap of paper. Finch's goal was to determine if all the paper was from the same manufacturer by analyzing the composition of the fibers in the paper.

He released one drop of a solution from an unmarked bottle on each.

Mamba, Stallings, and Martinez peered over the lab tech's shoulders.

"¡Ay, caramba! Look," the Latino breathed.

Two pieces turned a dirty orange color as the technician's solution saturated the paper. The three remaining pieces varied slightly from black to dark blue-purple under the same conditions.

"That clinches it." Finch straightened his spine and stretched his neck.

"What exactly did you prove?" Mamba asked. Different colors and Finch's comment suggested the results were significant, but his theory hinged on certainties not implications.

"It's a misconception that we prove anything here. However, these two papers." Finch pointed to the orange scraps. "These two are of an entirely different stock than the others. I'll testify to that in court."

"Good to know. You're certain these two papers are the same as each other and different from the rest?"

"I've testified as an expert witness on results not as definite as these."

"That's good enough." Stallings turned to the PI. "I'll take you to Internal Affairs about Chief Rogers now."

Finch raised his eyebrows at the mention of the Chief of Police.

"What about me?" Martinez asked. "You're not shutting me out now."

"You're our ace in the hole. Stay close to a phone."

* * *

"I think you want to see this," Petula said to her boss as she pulled the door to his office shut behind her.

"What is it? I'm kind of busy here."

"The kiss-up press conference can wait. Something's up in the lab."

Chief Rogers looked up but did not speak.

"Narcotics authorized overtime for a lab tech."

"Are they over budget, or what?"

"It involves testing copy paper," she said, emphasizing the last three words.

"Copy paper? Why should that . . ." Rogers' voice faded away. Edwards was in jail for his part in leaking information. Linking the copy machine contract from his time in St. Louis to any of his testimony would as good as convict him. "You've got my attention."

"You know those files you were supposed to prepare for shredding in just such a situation?"

Rogers glowered at her.

"I'm not stupid," he said.

"The jury's still out on that. I'll take your response for a no. I'd get hopping on it."

She sauntered out. She had files of her own to shred.

* * *

The morning after receiving Finch's lab report, Mamba and Stallings found the IAD ensconced in an interrogation room in the division station. Stallings insisted that Mamba not talk unless it was to answer a question.

Things weren't going well.

"Officer Desantos, this is the last time I say this. You need to inform Senior Officer Hargrove about the documents and test results we have with us. And you need to do that immediately." Stallings spoke with restraint he did not feel. He and Mamba had been getting the run-around from the Internal Affairs officer for nearly ten minutes. It was time to fish, not cut bait.

"If you'll show me what you've got, I'll see about getting you in to see Senior Officer Hargrove."

"I'm not about to reveal the reason for his visit to anyone but the Head of Internal Affairs. I'm living proof of where misinformation can lead!"

"The Senior Officer is out of the office on assignment," Desantos reiterated.

"He may be out of his office," Stallings fumed. "But I know he's still here in the Division house. You're both here interviewing SWAT officers involved in that firefight two weeks ago."

"Sorry, Sergeant."

"You will be," Stallings promised. "Come on, Mamba. We're going downtown."

The two men stalked away from the interrogation room and the recalcitrant Desantos. Without comment, they climbed into Stallings' car.

"This is a radical move." Mamba broke his self-imposed silence several minutes later as the two men entered the parking structure of the government building housing the Central offices of the Manzanita Police Department.

"We've got hard evidence of a significant crime." Stallings' voice was steel-edged. "Since the yokel IA officers won't listen, I'll find someone who will listen and will do something with this." He patted the laboratory report that lay between them on the bench seat. The Sergeant parked his car. The two men entered the imposing edifice that housed the Central office.

"Do you know which way we go?" Stallings asked. "I've only been here twice."

"Unless they've moved, IAD's Central Command is on the third floor," Mamba told him. "Not that I was here often, back in the day."

Stallings flashed a brief smile as he caught the innuendo. "Yeah, they make house calls, don't they?"

The PI grimaced.

They rode the elevator up to the third floor, checked the directory posted on the wall, and walked down to suite 325, the home of the Central Command of Manzanita Police Department Internal Affairs Division. After a brief wait, Stallings and Mamba entered the office of the ranking IAD officer.

"This is a most grievous charge," the Commander of Internal Affairs said. His tone of voice was as serious as the words he spoke. He re-scanned the documents they gave him. "Who did the lab work?"

"That's not important, is it?" Mamba asked. "You'll run your own tests anyway, right?"

"You know we will, Mr. Mamba. You haven't been off the force that long."

"Just protecting a source."

"Like all detectives—apparently both real and private," was the dour response.

Mamba felt his fuse ignite at the deprecating remark of his current line of work. Stallings, who'd also caught the Commander's meaning, made a small gesture with his right hand. This was no time for a confrontation.

"Finch from our lab did the work. It was overtime billed to Narcotics."

The Commander raised his eyebrows. It was obvious the two men were certain their charge would stick to Chief Rogers. For their sake, and the sake of the department, he hoped the board of inquiry wouldn't rule their expenditure premature.

"What are you going to do? We've got a lot of work tied up in this." Stallings came as close to demanding action as he dared.

"If my lab report matches yours, we'll take action tomorrow."

"Fair enough," Stallings said, hoping his tone wasn't noticeably condescending.

"Good morning, Gentlemen." The Commander rose in a gesture of dismissal. "For the sake of the Manzanita Police Department, I hope you're wrong."

"We're not," Mamba muttered under his breath. His tone of voice conveyed no hint of satisfaction.

* * *

To the surprise of neither Stallings, nor Martinez, nor Mamba, the lab work requested by Internal Affairs confirmed the work by Finch. The entire IAD contingent, with the Commander leading, was dispatched to Chief Rogers' office.

"Good morning, Commander," Petula said as the IAD team entered her office area. She hit the open intercom feed button on her phone.

None of the IAD officers acknowledged her greeting. The Commander went directly to the door to Rogers' office. He tried the doorknob. It resisted his efforts to turn it.

"This is locked," he said without looking at Petula. "Open it."

"I have strict orders—"

"Open this door now or I will have you up on charges of obstructing an IAD investigation."

She pulled her key ring from her purse and stared hard at the Commander while she extended the keys toward Officer Desantos.

"Which one?"

Petula slid keys around the ring until she segregated the desired one.

Seconds later, the Commander led his team into Rogers' office.

"You'd better have a very good reason for this intrusion," Rogers growled without looking up from where he stood feeding document pages into the shredder.

"Back away from the shredder!" The IAD Commander demanded.

Rogers' response was to stuff another page into the shredder.

"Hargrove, help the Chief comply with my order!"

"Yes, sir." Senior IAD Officer Hargrove tried to maneuver his body between the Chief and the shredder. Rogers fended him off with one arm and stuffed another sheet into the machine.

When Rogers shredded two more pages despite Hargrove's interference, the Commander acted.

"Desantos, take Chief Rogers' left arm!" Officer Desantos moved behind Rogers, grabbed his forearm, and pulled. The man reacted by shoving his arm back as he turned into his assailant.

As Rogers made his move, the Commander clamped both hands on Rogers right forearm. He gave a hard twist and pulled the arm behind the Chief's back. Rogers grunted and twisted away from the Commander.

Desantos used the Commander's diversion to her advantage. With a twist of her own, she pulled the Chief's left arm behind him and slapped on an open handcuff. The Commander grabbed the other end of the cuffs and slapped it onto his prisoner's right wrist.

Chief Rogers stopped fighting.

"I want my union rep and my lawyer," were the last words he ever spoke while in his office.

* * *

Petula watched from her desk as IAD escorted Dwight Rogers from his office. She planned her strategy for this day long ago. It was time to implement that plan.

"Leave, Officer Jacobs," the IAD Commander said once Rogers was on his way to a holding cell. "I want this entire office locked down."

"Yes, sir," she said. "I assume you'll want a statement from me."

"Don't leave town. We'll get your statement in the morning."

She nodded and pulled her purse from the bottom drawer of her desk.

"I'll need my keys. I've got to drive home and get into my apartment."

"Desantos, remove all departmental keys from her ring and return it to her," the Commander ordered. He took a step toward Petula and added, "While she's busy, I'll check your purse."

Back in her apartment, Petula opened the fireproof box safe she stored in her closet. She reached beneath her Last Will and Testament and pulled out the duplicate set of departmental keys she'd garnered over time through various questionable methods.

"No trail to me from these keys. Not one of them was illegally copied," she muttered as she shoved the keys into her purse. She thought about changing out of her uniform but dismissed that thought. Her uniform was better than any disguise for what she planned.

Petula returned to the Central Office as the graveyard shift was arriving. Since her undocumented set of keys contained copies of keys never issued to her, she could enter the building through a door from the parking garage to which only the Chief and his cabinet had keys.

She walked through the hallways keeping close to the walls and turning into every doorway as though she was about to unlock the door. Petula reached the hallway outside the Chief's office suite confident no one recognized her.

A uniformed officer stood in the hallway outside the office suite. She frowned.

She backtracked down the hallway until she found a door to which she had a key. Once inside, she pulled a small electronic device from a zippered side pocket inside her purse. After switching on the device, she held it over the mouthpiece while she phoned the front desk.

"Who's assigned to guard Chief Rogers' office?"

"I'd have to check the duty roster, but not until I know who wants the information," Sergeant Smith replied.

"This is Desantos from IAD. Now check the duty roster. I'm the eyes of the Commander tonight. I need you to go down to Rogers' office and have whoever's pulled that duty station check the reception area hourly. We can't have anyone, even custodial staff, in there until we've run our sweep tomorrow."

"Can do. You want a callback?"

"Only if he finds something. Oh, and, thanks."

She waited around a corner until Smith delivered her message and the guard was inside the reception area. With a grim smile on her face, she used a key to unlock Rogers' private door located just past the official office door.

She was lucky that the door was hidden in the hallway's wood paneling. She'd never discovered how Rogers pulled that off. It was before her time.

By the time she left the Chief's suite, the shedder basket in the Chief's office, once filled with freshly cut strips of an assortment of reports, memos, and miscellaneous in-house communiqués, was nearly empty.

Entering her office through the interoffice door, she retrieved papers she wanted shredded and returned to the Chief's office. She restarted the shredder, shredded her papers, and slipped into the hallway two hours after she arrived to ensure the guard was in the reception area as instructed.

She muscled two large trash bags filled with the shredder bin's former load down the hallway to the refuse chute. She held the door to the chute open until she heard the muffled thump of each bag as it landed in the dumpster in the garage.

The bag would be delivered to the recycling center before IAD arrived in the morning. There was not much physical evidence left in the building. It was time for Petula Jacobs to disappear.

* * *

Former Police Chief Dwight Rogers spent his first night under arrest in one of the Central office building's holding cells. His lawyer argued that it was a violation his civil rights "to be incarcerated with individuals we might assume wish harm upon him." It wasn't hard for the lawyer to find a judge that agreed.

They transported Rogers to his home. He spent two nights under house arrest. A pair of officers remained inside his house. One of the two had eyes on the man at all times. This strategy guaranteed that no potential evidence was changed or destroyed. When in the bathroom, Rogers left the door open.

As humiliating as it was, he would learn that it was far above the bottom of his pit of humiliation.

Chapter 46

Petula lounged on the full-sized bed in her motel room in El Cajon, California. It was early in the afternoon after she overheated Chief Rogers' shredder during her final hours with Manzanita Police Department. She packed lightly. A carry-on bag was her sole piece of luggage.

She ordered one of the electronic gizmos, her term, after she listened in on one of Rogers' conversations with Stallings. In her mind, it paid for itself the night before by clearing the hallway. Now it was time to add return to her investment.

Although distance calls from motel's came with a hefty surcharge, she needed to talk to two men about the same topic. She checked the time on her watch, picked up the motel room phone, pushed a button for the outside line, and dialed the first number. Holding the device in place as she had in the police station, she prepared for what she expected to be a profitable few minutes.

"For once don't talk. Just listen to me."

The faint crackle of background static was all Petula heard.

"Well done. You and I have never spoken before, but I eavesdropped on your conversations with my boss. So, I apologize for the first phrase of my opening comment. As a reward for good behavior, I'll get right to my first point. They've arrested Rogers. I have no doubt he'll go state's evidence. He will include your name in his testimony for a deal with the Feds."

"Why are you telling me this?"

"I want you to protect me."

"Why me?"

"Because I know who you are, Mr. Anthony Garmel. And, I know that the police know about Gar-Mar, Incorporated."

Static crackled in her ear a second time.

"How can I protect you?" Garmel asked. "It sounds like you have me at a disadvantage in terms of useful knowledge of this situation."

"I'll need an army of Ulysses S. Grants to ensure adequate protection. You will supply that army."

"How big an army?"

"It's negotiable, but I'm thinking in the neighborhood of 600."

Garmel did a rapid mental analysis and arrived at thirty thousand dollars. He pursed his lips. If what she said was true, that amount of money was a bargain. If it wasn't true, he would find out who she was and where she went and eliminate her for much, much less.

"I don't have all day, Anthony. My neck's on the line here, too. Or should I call you Tony?"

Garmel cleared his throat. Petula sensed she hit a nerve with the nickname and decided to reel in the sarcasm.

"Give me a routing number, and I'll wire twenty-five thousand dollars to that account within two days." Garmel's response was delivered through tightly clenched teeth.

"That's not 600 soldiers. It's not even a year's pay, and the timeline for the deposit is too long." She did some calculating of her own. "It now appears that I'll need an army of at least seven hundred Grants to protect me. So, the deal is thirty-five thousand. You have one day to make the deposit, or you'll be reading your name, and this phone number, in the newspaper before Rogers testifies."

The woman was tougher and smarter than Garmel gave her credit for. He changed his strategy. "I have a counteroffer for you."

"I'm listening, but not for long."

"How would you like to work for me?"

Petula Jacobs' laughter was loud and genuine.

"Fine, thirty-five thousand it is. But, if I ever hear from you again." Garmel made sure his tone activated the darkest side of the woman's imagination.

"Don't worry," Petula said after she caught her breath. "You won't. If I were you, I'd be looking for the best price for airline tickets to a faraway place tonight because I'd want to be out of the country within thirty-six hours." She shifted to her best impersonation of a telephone operator and added, "Please hold for my banking information."

* * *

"For once, don't talk. Just listen to me."

"I do not know who this is."

"Oh, my. Sounds like you're not used to being at a disadvantage."

"Do not play games with me."

"No games. But, you'd better listen, Mr. Anderson, or whatever your real name is."

"You better have some crucial information for me. Otherwise, your smart mouth will cease polluting the air with words very, very soon."

"Keep pushing me, and the police will know a lot about you, very, very soon."

"Why do you think that will happen? It would take a stupid man." He paused. Petula was certain it was for dramatic effect. "Or a stupid woman to do something so reckless."

"Save it! Chief Rogers is going state's evidence tomorrow."

"Rogers is under arrest." There was no hint of a question in the words.

"You figured that out all by your lonesome. Maybe you're smarter than I thought. I want thirty-five thousand dollars from you."

"I've already invested in an airplane ticket for someone with this kind of knowledge."

"Then, you know how the system works."

"Listen, you arrogant—"

"No! You listen! I have transcripts of dozens of calls to this number and one other number that I'm betting is on your phone bill, too. I made the calls. I made the transcripts. I control what happens to those transcripts."

"What am I buying with my thirty-five thousand dollars?" Anderson cleared his throat. "If I pay you?"

"I think you'll pay. You might even consider what I'm selling a bargain."

"I've heard nothing yet that is worth even the time I've spent on this phone call."

"I'm calling your bluff, Anderson. I think my transcripts are worth a lot of money to a man whose company makes drugs when the local drug lords are in shambles right now."

"No sale without knowing what I'm buying."

"Sounds fair, although I'm not sure your definition of 'fair' is the same as mine. I want ten thousand dollars for this warning to you. For the record, I'd say I've already earned that much. And, twenty-five thousand more for silence about all the things I've done for you that you don't want law enforcement to know about."

She heard breathing, but no words.

"In case I'm losing you, that would be the transcripts. Twenty-five thousand dollars purchases all my memories of you and your dealings with Rogers."

"And your hard copies," Anderson added.

"Ah, I love a man who listens. For being a good listener, I will include all hard copies of the transcripts I have in my possession for that price."

"You're the contact with the police department."

"Not exactly, and I've just posted a No Fishing sign on this conversation. However, since you've given me what I assume is your best guess, let's just say I've been privy to many of your conversations and leave it at that."

"If I'm hearing you correctly, it appears I'll be traveling soon. If that is true, I cannot spare that amount of cash."

"I figured you'd try to negotiate. Last offer: thirty thousand dollars total in cash and a fake passport in the name of Ilsa Jurgenson." She spelled the name. "Take it or leave it."

The woman sounded quite capable of leading the authorities to him, even if he accepted her offer. A passport cost him less than a grand. She phrased her answer about the transcripts cleverly, implying she had copies not currently in her possession. It was only money, and he would find her if she reneged on her promises, perhaps even if she did not.

"Since you've been so considerate, I will take your offer. You may pick up the money and passport, without a photograph, of course, tomorrow at—"

"I'll call back in an hour and talk to your secretary. I'll give her the details for the drop. Adios, señor Arcenas. In case you didn't think I figured that out!"

Before Guillermo Arcenas could reply, the telephone line went dead.

* * *

After cutting off Arcenas, Petula walked nearly four blocks east of her motel. She had a final call to make on a phone that, if traced, would not lead directly to her. She stepped into a phone booth, opened her purse, and removed the electronic voice distortion device. She inserted her four quarters.

"For once don't talk. Just listen to me."

"You know I'm under house arrest. They've probably got this line tapped," Rogers said without emotion.

"I'm using a payphone; I have access to a car, you probably noticed I altered my voice; and, what part of 'don't talk' are you having trouble understanding?"

"What do you want?"

"The direct approach. I'm proud of you. I guess I can forgive your vocal indiscretions."

"Just get on with it. I can do without sarcasm right now."

"Too bad. I'm not in the mood to alter my prepared remarks. Here's what I want. First, my name's not in any of your testimony. Not a single word about me. If you slip up, I'll release dozens of videotapes to the police with copies to the media."

"I don't know what you're talking about."

"I know. April Fools!"

"And, don't try to be funny. I'm not in the mood for that, either," Rogers grumbled.

"Funny is the last thing I'm being. I'm prepared to expose you, actually expose all of you, in several very compromising positions if I even sniff a reference to me in any report. I have sources—inside sources."

Rogers sat silent for several seconds. When he spoke, his voice was devoid of emotion.

"You videotaped our nights in your bed."

"What's the matter, Dwight? You really didn't think I'd do all I've done with and for you and not have my very attractive derriere covered, did you?"

Rogers maintained his silence. Too late, he realized that the woman was as tough as nails. He seriously misjudged her capabilities.

"Oh, my! You never even considered a woman might be smarter than you, did you? Then, this serves you even more right than I thought. Goodbye, Dwight. Don't forget your instructions."

Rogers sat holding the phone in complete silence for well over a minute. He knew that his administrative assistant had him by the short hairs. He had mixed emotions. On the one hand, he hoped they traced the call and would soon arrest her. On the other hand, he knew if they found her, she'd bury him so deep that he'd need a ladder to get up to the bottom of his grave. There was also the very real chance that some of what was just spoken over the phone would end up in the media.

He could think of only one outlet for his angst. He swore loudly.

* * *

On the morning after Jacobs contacted Garmel, Anderson, and Rogers, something more than the usual rumors spread through Reed's cellblock. A guard found a dead body in Reed's cell.

"Are you certain this is the prisoner?" the Warden asked.

"Yes, sir. We've double-checked. All we can find for his name is Reed. There's no other name in any of his paperwork."

"I know," the Warden replied. "We checked his prints with every known source and found no arrest record in any of them."

"That can't be right," the Senior Prison Guard objected. "Just look at the guy's body. If that doesn't scream 'addict,' I don't know what does. He should have been in the system years ago."

"All I know is what we didn't find, another name for these fingerprints."

"I guess it really doesn't matter," the guard said. "Dead is dead whether you have one name or five names, like my German Lutheran grandmother."

"Very philosophical. I'll get the Coroner out here. Try to keep a lid on this."

Five days later, the City of Manzanita laid Reed to rest. Mamba Investigations supplied a headstone. It was small and flat. The inscription was simple.

Reed
He played a mean tenor sax
Died 1984

* * *

Former Police Chief Dwight Rogers sat in stone-faced silence in Interrogation Room 5, the largest interrogation room in Manzanita Police Department's Central office building. Two officers guarded the door, one in the hallway and the other inside the door. Manzanita District Attorney Ellis Winston, an FBI agent, and now Acting Police Chief Nolan Chalmers sat across the table from the man. DA Winston was explaining Rogers' options.

"Mister Rogers, we will grant you certain immunities from prosecution for your cooperation," the DA said emphasizing the disgraced chief's soon-to-be civilian status.

"What do you mean by cooperation?" Rogers asked without expression. He knew his career was finished. The folder that held the report from the Internal Affairs investigation lay open on the table before him. It was disgustingly complete and one hundred percent accurate. His major concern was protecting himself and his wife in St. Louis from the revenge forthcoming from at least one of his illicit employers if he talked.

"We want names and dates and transactions. We want to know everything you did, what you got for doing it, and who you did it for."

"If I agree to do this, what are your plans for my safety?" As a veteran of law enforcement, he knew the answer to his question. What he needed was the assurance of hearing that answer spoken directly to him.

"You'll receive witness protection," the second of the three men facing him answered. The FBI Special Agent was authorized to offer relocation and new identification for appropriate testimony. "The government needs your help. A new life for you and your wife in another place is on the table."

"Would I get to choose my new place to live?"

The Special Agent snorted. "If what you give us is worth enough, you'll get the usual choices we give anyone we enroll in our witness protection plan. In most cases, it's a choice between two cities of our selection."

"All right." The disgraced Chief decided long before the interview began. He knew his chances of surviving in prison were nil. Any conditions imposed by the government were preferable to being shanked in prison or who knows what atrocities done to his wife. "Where's my contract?"

"You know that's not the way this works, Rogers," Chalmers said. He was angry that Rogers lied. Now he was angrier because, despite overwhelming evidence of his guilt, the man was still his arrogant self.

Rogers turned toward his former second in command, but said nothing.

"We need to hear the information first. The whole deal holds only if you provide appropriate, verifiable information." The Special Agent intentionally drew Rogers' attention back to the issue.

"So, are you in or out? I'm tired of waiting!" The DA's tone of voice left no doubt about how close Rogers was to nixing his deal by delaying the inevitable.

"You'll get all I know. Start the tape recorder."

The headlines in the local papers over the next few days followed the resignation of Police Chief Rogers. Some reports implied a connection with the underworld. The name, Anthony Garmel, head of the Midwestern branch of a drug syndicate, was linked to the man from as early as his days as Assistant Police Commissioner in St. Louis. They also hinted information leaks were part of the scandal.

However, neither the name Petula Jacobs, nor the title administrative assistant escaped Rogers' lips during his extensive recitation.

It seemed ironically appropriate how much information on Rogers' downfall found its way to the media—on radio, on television, and in the local papers.

After all, the departmental leak was sealed.

* * *

"All of them, Mr. Garmel?" The man in the expensive suit found one part of his employer's instructions difficult to accept.

"I want none of the regional managers in the present operation to remain," Anthony Garmel replied. He stopped packing his briefcase. "I cannot afford another Chief Rogers."

"But, we don't have any evidence that Rogers talked," the expensive suit insisted.

"Never leave a loose end," counseled Garmel. "If Rogers didn't talk, all this house cleaning will do is cost me replaceable people. I'll be back in operation within three to six months. If he talked, I figure to be out of business in the United States for a couple of years."

The expensive suit nodded sagely. He, too, was replaceable. "You can count on me, sir."

Garmel ignored the expensive suit's promise and continued as though the man had not interrupted him. It was an action that did not escape notice by the expensive suit. "Speak only when spoken to" was the boss's mantra.

"If I don't silence them all and some talk when arrested, I could be a fugitive for life. Even worse, I could be incarcerated." Garmel glared hard at his well-dressed associate before he added a meaningful conclusion. "I relish neither perpetual flight nor imprisonment for any length of time."

"I understand. We will eliminate all potential problems within the week."

"One week. No more. I'll be in South America," Garmel finished as he snapped his briefcase closed. "The only contact I will have in the immediate future will be through my secretary."

* * *

Rick Elkhart never got a chance to prove his business acumen or his loyalty to the syndicate.

Chapter 47

"Do you remember several weeks ago when you asked if I wanted to share what was on my mind with you?"

Hope stared at her husband trying to figure his angle. When she couldn't, she opted to play it straight.

"Yes, I do. You said it wasn't the right time or something like that."

"Well, now is the time. There are two questions I can't answer about this whole case. I'm talking Anderson Pharmaceuticals, ex-Sergeant Edwards, ex-Chief Rogers, the attempted hits on Flatly, us, and Pat—all that as one big case."

She nodded.

"I remember thinking something wasn't right after I gave Kerrigan the list of names. Anderson used a phrase that implied the police had that list. I remember thinking, 'How does Anderson know about this list?' It was one of those 'I'll get to it later' things that I never got to because of all the other stuff that went on."

"Number one: Anderson knows about the list," Hope said. "Do you think he knew about the fifth page, too?"

"I don't know. That doesn't matter either way. If he knew about any of it, the question 'How?' is still unanswered."

He stared off into the distance.

"What's the second question?" Hope whispered.

"Oh. Sorry. Reed was a drunken bum and an addict. Question two: How'd he get enough money to rent the places he did, entertain like he did, and spend money like it was water but not spend it all on drugs and booze? That question just came to me this morning. I don't know how I missed it."

"Pat Kerrigan. Franklin Stallings. Flatly Broke. Me and Jimmy," Hope offered.

"I don't follow."

"Those friends, your family, and Lizbeth Stallings were in jeopardy, or in the hospital, for all or part of this case. Personally, I'm glad I'm married to a man who cares so much about his friends that he loses track of someone else's financial dealings."

Phil kissed his wife.

* * *

Mamba called Anderson Pharmaceuticals from his office the next morning. The call had nothing do with the question he posed during his conversation with Hope. He wanted the man to expect a final statement in a day or two.

"I'm sorry, Mr. Mamba, but Mr. Anderson had to leave on an emergency. He left a message on my office answering machine last night."

"I see. Did he leave a number where I can reach him?"

"I'm sorry, no. Did he give you his home number?"

"I don't believe so."

"Well, I know he was happy with your work and was eager to get the account closed. I'll give you his home number. If he complains about my giving it out—"

"Tell him I forced it out of you," Phil offered.

The secretary laughed.

* * *

Christmas shopping crowds were growing, and the Parkway Plaza Mall, eighteen miles east of San Diego, was crowded. She saw an empty table in the corner and moved toward it as fast as she could through the crowded food court. Pleased by successfully attaining her objective, she placed the Woolworth's bag she carried on the table.

"Could you watch this for me?" she asked an elderly couple at the table next to hers. "I'd like to get a coffee and croissant."

"Of course, dearie," the woman replied. A smile lit up her face at the opportunity to be useful. "You'd be surprised how many people just ignore old folks like us."

"Now, Diane, don't grouse about your pet peeves to this nice lady," the man at the table said.

"It's not grousing when it's the truth!"

She smiled at the banter, hoping when she was old, she'd be feisty like that woman.

"Thank you. Can I get you something?"

The couple looked at one another with nervous glances.

"You know, for helping me."

The couple relaxed.

"Well, we both like apple fritters," the man said.

"But, we usually split one," the elderly woman added before she slapped her husband on the arm for his audacious behavior.

"Okay then. I'm getting coffee, a croissant, and an apple fritter."

There were smiles all around at her summation. She bought two fritters so the spunky, elderly woman and her husband wouldn't have to share. After assuring the woman that she could afford the additional pastry, she sat chatting with the couple until they finished the fritters.

The elderly woman got up first. She went to the wall behind the table and retrieved an aluminum walker. Back at the table, she held the walker in position while her husband labored to pull himself up from his chair.

"Don't rush, Bernard. It's not like we're in a big hurry."

"I don't need advice on how to get up from a chair, Bernice."

She watched the couple navigate through the crowd until they turned in the main corridor of the mall.

"You've been to Woolworth's."

The voice startled her. She looked up. A well-dressed Latina stood holding a fashionable purse still sporting the price tag.

"I have," Petula replied.

"Mind if I join you?"

"Do you know my amigo, señor Arcenas?"

"Sí. Do you know his friend, Petula Jacobs?"

"That's me. Sit down."

With the formalities out of the way, Petula and Arcenas' representative made short work of the meeting. When the representative left, the purse remained behind. It was custom-made, complete with five bundles of fifty-dollar bills and one passport in the name of Ilsa Jurgenson beneath the nylon liner.

Petula shoved the purse into her Woolworth's bag and left the mall. She drove to an address in East San Diego she got from a forger for a price, after assurance that her photo would be attached to the bogus passport with accuracy and efficiency.

"If the jacket is real, no one will ever know the passport's a fake," was how that phone conversation ended.

Petula opened the door to suite 7B and stepped inside.

* * *

Over the next week, Mamba called Anderson's home number daily. He left messages the first five days. By day number six, the answering machine was full.

He went to Anderson's home. Five newspapers littered the driveway. The mailbox was stuffed and shedding junk mail. Potted plants on the front porch needed watering.

He walked around the side of the house. He opened the gate. A voice called to him from the driveway.

"¡Señor Arcenas, usted es un hombre difícil de encontrar!"

Mamba turned toward the speaker, wondering who Arcenas was and why he'd been asked something in Spanish about that man at William Anderson's home.

"I'm afraid you have the wrong house," he said as he made eye contact with a pair of Hispanic males. "This is the Anderson's home."

"Lo siento. I mean, I'm sorry," the voice that called to Mamba by mistake apologized.

"No problem. I don't think I've seen you around here before."

"You haven't. It's the first time we've been to, uh, here. We thought this was where a, how do you say, socio de negocios?"

"Business associate," the second man offered.

"Of course. We thought this is where a business associate lives."

"Well, I hope you didn't come too far. The Andersons' are away on an emergency. I'm private security," Mamba said as he flashed his license. "I check on the house twice a day."

At the term security, the visitors glanced at each other. Mamba made a mental note.

"We must be going now. Thanks for the information." The two men returned to a Chevrolet parked against the curb.

Mamba memorized the license plate and climbed into his car. He reported the exchange and the license plate number to Stallings from the first phone booth he came to.

* * *

Mamba thought about the odd meeting with two men who appeared to be Mexican Nationals at William Anderson's home the day before. The event generated a new question: What was Anderson up to that brought people looking for a man named Arcenas to a house in suburban Manzanita?

He stretched his arms to increase blood flow to his tired brain.

He sat up with a start. Hope breathed out a low groan of unconscious irritation at being pulled from her sleep by his sudden movement. He slipped out of bed so not to disturb her more than he had.

He grabbed his pocket notebook, tiptoed downstairs and into the den, sat at his desk, and began pulling thoughts he had about oddities during the investigations. Several minutes later, as he rubbed his eyes, flashes of light morphed from loops to arches to whorls.

Fingerprints! Actually, the lack of fingerprints, any fingerprints. Anderson Pharmaceuticals' crime scene was devoid of fingerprints, including those of current employees. Anderson said it was because the warehouse workers wore gloves.

Mamba smiled. He suspected Reed wore gloves when he took the drugs from Anderson's factory. If that was true, he knew why Reed was easy to turn. He was on Anderson's payroll.

Chapter 48

In the weeks following Chief Rogers' statement, police in cities from California to the Mississippi River reported finding dead bodies of known or suspected drug dealers. Rick Elkhart was among the confirmed identities. A spokesperson for Manzanita Police Department reported that the body count was evidence of a major drug kingpin's house cleaning. Despite the disdain for the former Chief among the rank and file, many acknowledged he manned up in the end.

Enciso Martinez looked like a new man, literally. His scalp no longer reflected sunlight when not covered by a bandana. Along with his hairstyle, the Detective changed his wardrobe to slacks and collared shirts when it wasn't an MPD uniform. He was still in negotiations with Erin Reilly about a mustache.

Manzanita Police Department hired a lieutenant to head narcotics and bring that department back to full-strength. After talking with Captain Abbott, Stallings began studying for the lieutenant's exam. He transferred to Homicide as Sergeant-in-Command of that division to fill Kerrigan's open slot.

One month after Rogers' departure, Nolan Chalmers, the newly appointed Chief of Police called a meeting of selected personnel. The Chief, Stallings, Martinez, and other officers from the Narcotics Division were the attendees.

They invited Phil Mamba in an observational capacity.

After Chalmers completed his opening comments, he called Mamba to the front of the room.

"Mr. Mamba— Dancer, I can't call you Mr. Mamba. Not even at an official event. We worked together. How about just Phil?"

"That works, Chief."

"Okay. Let me start again. Phil, it has been brought to my attention by both Sergeant Stallings and Detective Martinez that you logged some billable hours working with this police department investigating a drug operation, searching for a missing officer, and tracking down the source of a leak of sensitive information to criminal elements."

Mamba turned an evil-eye stare toward Stallings and Martinez. Both men focused on their new Chief. The PI saw them sneaking looks at him while they pretended to listen to Chalmers. He vowed to get even.

"It is my understanding that one hundred percent of those hours were pro bono. Is that the case, Phil?"

"I, uh."

"I'll take that as a 'yes.' Although I've been on my new job less than four weeks, I discovered several things about my predecessor. First, he really liked pastries."

Snickers all around.

"Second, he was very, very good at hiding funds in officious sounding accounts that had no link to actual police business. While I've found no records of how he spent that money, I assume it went for his pet projects."

Mamba shifted his feet nervously.

"I've heard from our Accounting Section that Officer Petula Jacobs, Rogers' administrative assistant, had such funds, too. Officer Jacobs went missing the day Chief Rogers made his statement to the District Attorney. She's not been heard from since. We located her car in a long-term parking lot in San Diego, but there is no record of any Petula Jacobs flying out of Lindberg Field, or purchasing a bus or train ticket, or crossing the border into Mexico."

"Excuse me, Chief," Mamba said during a pause in Chalmers' recitation. "I was wondering if I could sit down now."

"In a minute, Phil. I'm almost there. A check of Jacobs' bank account showed that she received a thirty-five-thousand-dollar transfer of funds on the day she disappeared. I am forced to assume, even though not implicated by Chief Rogers, that Officer Jacobs was a part of several illicit actions during her tenure as his administrative assistant."

The Chief picked up a ledger.

"Phil, your bookkeeper was kind enough to provide your accounts payable desk with this. It's your company's financial ledger." He opened the ledger to a bookmarked page and handed it to the PI. "Please, read the highlighted column headings and the totals for each of the highlighted columns on that page."

Mamba looked down. He saw Hope's summary page for his hours on the Anderson Pharmaceuticals case and an estimate of hours donated to Manzanita Police Department for his work on the Manzanita Police Department cases.

"I'd rather not read this out loud."

"I understand. I was hoping you would read it because I wanted the members of the group gathered here to realize how many hours you donated to help us with two very complicated cases." He retrieved the ledger.

"Chief Chalmers, I have an issue with the term donated," Stallings said.

"And what might that be?"

"Why can't we pay this man?"

"Franklin, it's okay. I really don't—"

"Now, that's a first-rate idea, Sergeant. Phil, do you remember those hidden accounts I mentioned?"

Mamba nodded.

"Good. What is your fee schedule?"

"Why would you—" The PI cut himself off when the Chief cast a stern look in his direction. "I don't enjoy doing this." Another look elicited an answer. "My fee is two hundred dollars per day plus expenses, but I—"

"Oh, my." The Chief mugged an expression of shock. "So." He opened the ledger and muttered as he ran his finger down the page.

"Divide by twenty-four. Multiply by two hundred. Add plane fare, and another plane fare, and car rental, and hotels."

Mamba's discomfort increased with each word.

"I'm afraid I don't have the money to cover all these costs. Not even Chief Rogers squirreled away that much."

Smiles and chuckles greeted the Chief's observation.

"Well, I've had my fun, Phil. I hope you didn't mind."

Mamba gave a chagrinned shake of his head.

"I'm hungry, Chief. Can't you just give him the money now?" Martinez called out.

The sound of the door to the room opening drew all eyes in that direction. Pat Kerrigan shuffled in behind a specially modified walker. The right handgrip looked more like the hand guard on a military officer's sword. Mamba watched his friend push the guard with the back of his hand while holding the left handgrip normally.

It was the first time he'd seen his friend with the walker. He recalled wondering if Kerrigan could ever walk again.

No one moved. Faces of those present registered shock or surprise at Kerrigan's arrival. Only the Chief knew of this agenda item. Mamba's former partner would play Chalmers' trump card.

"Welcome home, Lieutenant," the Chief said.

"Thank you, um, wait. I know man. Thank you, Policeman."

"Do you have something for me?" Chalmers asked through a lump in his throat.

"Yes," Kerrigan answered. Using his good arm, he reached down into the walker's storage compartment and pulled out an envelope. "For my, friend!"

More shuffling of his feet maneuvered the walker until he was facing Mamba. Kerrigan stretched his good arm out and offered the envelope to the PI.

"Take the envelope, Phil," the Chief directed. "It's as close as I can get to paying you half the amount you'd get from a client for your work with us. I wish it was more."

The applause was loud and lengthy.

For the first time in a long time, Dancer Mamba was speechless.

* * *

Stallings was now more discriminating of what he agreed to do that kept him away from home at dinnertime. The list of activities outside work was a short one. Tonight, he made sure he was home earlier than normal. He had a feeling.

"The doctors are ready to start my radiation."

Franklin's fingers intertwined with hers as they walked to the sofa. He helped her sit, and then he eased himself down onto the cushion beside her.

"The biopsy showed no cancerous cells."

"I know. I was there. Remember?" While his wife went through the chemotherapy with a stoic resolve, there had been times her chemo-brain, as she called it, did not retain pieces of information.

"I want to be a mother."

"I know."

"I don't want the radiation."

The words stunned Stallings. In all his mental machinations about this conversation, he hadn't anticipated a flat-out rejection of the radiation therapy. When he recovered enough to speak, he said, "The radiation treatment doesn't mean you can't be a mother."

She fixed him with an angry look.

"I know you know that. We've talked about adoption in the past."

Her angry stare vanished. She leaned toward him.

"And, you're okay with adopting a child? Really okay?"

"I'm okay with you being alive to be the mother of as many children as we want to adopt. There are hundreds, no, there are thousands of children who need parents. We can be those parents for one."

"Or more."

"For one or more of them. Lizbeth, I love you so much. I want you to be well." Franklin barely finished before he began sobbing, huge, aching, heartbreaking sobs.

* * *

Lizbeth Stallings' radiation treatments were three days each week for four weeks. A biopsy performed following the final week reaffirmed there was no sign of cancer. After several more weeks of prayer and legal consultations, the Stallings began adoption proceedings of twin boys from an inner-city orphanage. The adoption agency informed the Stallings that Lizbeth's medical history triggered a mandatory delay in the process and adoption through them was unlikely.

The delay did not sit well with Lizbeth. Her motherhood had been delayed enough already. Franklin Stallings saw his wife's competitive zeal reignite. He experienced that zeal when he watched his wife playing basketball in college. He experienced it in bruises received while playing one-on-one with her.

He knew the adoption agency was in for the fight of their corporate life.

Chapter 49

Enciso Martinez and Erin Reilly were married in a Catholic mass. After weeks of surreptitious planning, Hope and Phil joined Martinez's fellow officers in donating money to transport over seventy of his family members by bus from Calexico to Manzanita in time for the ceremony.

When the day ended, the guests agreed it was the best Irish-Mexican wedding in history. They were unanimous that Waldo Wiggins looked outstanding in a tux.

* * *

Joanna Louise Mamba was born without complications two days before her projected due date. At seven pounds and seven ounces in weight and twenty-one inches in length, she was an adorable bundle of joy.

Jimmy got to hold his sister, with plenty of Daddy's help, the day after she was born. Much later in life, Jimmy described that experience as the formation of a lifetime bond and the moment he decided he would protect his little sister from bullies and bad people.

* * *

After eight months of physical therapy, although he insisted it must have been eight years, doctors released Patrick Kerrigan from their care.

"I going work," he told Kate on the morning of his second day home. At his physical therapist's recommendation, he read about James Brady, President Reagan's Press Secretary. The man sustained damage similar to Kerrigan's during John Hinckley, Jr.'s assassination attempt on the President.

The courage and commitment to a full recovery and the effort Brady exerted to make that happen inspired Kerrigan to similar commitments and efforts. The hard work paid off.

"I will drive you to the police station. That is where you used to work," she said. "But, I will also go into the station with you."

Kerrigan started to protest, but thanks to the lag time between his healing brain's decision to do something and any action related to doing it, Kate was able to divert his protest.

"Don't even start with me, Patrick Kerrigan. I know your doctor told you what you could and could not do. Going by work is okay. Going to work is not okay! I will go in with you. When I decide you are too tired to stay any longer, you will go home with me. Do you understand?"

Kerrigan smiled his crooked smile.

Now and again, to reinforce the extent of his progress to himself as much as anything, Kerrigan would make a statement straight out of his early recovery time. Unintentional gaffes were decreasingly frequent but not gone. Many missing neural pathways were not yet reconstructed.

Kate pulled into one of the two handicapped parking spaces at the Northeast Division station. While Pat worked on getting the passenger door open, she reached into the glove compartment, removed the temporary handicapped parking tag. Wishing they had a handicapped license plate, she placed the temporary tag on the dashboard where it was visible through the windshield.

Most of the officers in the station made a trip to the lobby for a few words with the popular Lieutenant. The departmental position on the recovering Kerrigan was he could work in a consulting capacity only. He would continue to receive full pay; his disability was determined to be one hundred percent.

He greeted few officers by name. Other officers he recognized, but, as with his wife and Phil Mamba, he would have to relearn the names blown away by the bullet. Most officers and staff in the division reintroduced themselves.

* * *

Throughout the next year, Kerrigan continued to improve. Plastic surgeries completed the rebuilding of the left side of his face and head. He was happy with what Kate called his rugged countenance.

Biofeedback techniques assisted in learning motor control of his right side by the right side of his brain. Hours of intense mental concentration helped him to store concrete nouns he lost with the destruction of his left-brain tissue.

He would always limp, and he would be a southpaw for the rest of his life. The doctors and Kerrigan were pleased with the level of rehabilitation achieved. The habitually stoical Dr. Liebowitz admitted his amazement. "I expected to sign a death certificate on the man when they brought him into the ER. Now, I am signing off his back-to-work release."

Eighteen months after the shooting, Departmental Consultant Patrick Kerrigan established his regular hours at the station. He was on site Monday, Wednesday, and Friday from nine o'clock to noon. He was on call during the rest of those day shifts.

His desk was in the common area in the squad room, making it easier to maintain contact with the rank and file. To keep his muscles in tone, he found his way to the therapy pool at the hospital's rehab center for a part of each of his workdays.

Chapter 50

There was one loose end that Mamba couldn't ignore any more. The discrepancy between Kerrigan's official Army file and the copy of at least one page of that document that rested in his police application folder gnawed at him. He knew he'd never report his findings to the Department. But, he had to know.

A phone call to Kerrigan's now retired CO from Vietnam provided him with the name and phone number of the Company Clerk of Kerrigan's unit. On a morning in March the year after Kerrigan returned to restricted duty, Phil made the call.

"This is Philip Mamba. You don't know me. I'm a private investigator in Manzanita, California. I know that you may not be able to tell me what I want to know, or you may not want to tell me. Regardless of either of those conditions, I've got to ask the question."

"Mr. Mamba, I hope you're not always as confused as you sound now," Master Sergeant Eugene Owens (Retired) chided. Then, in his best Sergeant's voice he ordered, "Spit it out!"

"Yes, sir!"

Mamba relaxed and continued.

"I'm sorry, Sergeant. It's just that this issue is sensitive. Actually, I suspect it's very sensitive."

"It's Master Sergeant, Mr. Mamba, it'll be impossible for me to comment on your situation."

"But—"

"I do not have any information on that situation. Tell me the issue."

"Yes, sir," Mamba said with a grin. He outlined the situation as briefly as possible. He included his partnership with Kerrigan, Kerrigan's promotion to Lieutenant, and his viewing of Kerrigan's file in the Pentagon. He chose not to describe how he accessed the Army personnel file, and he omitted Kerrigan's attempted murder, which he deemed irrelevant to the situation. When he finished, there was silence on the end of the line.

"I guess I struck out," he concluded.

"No, sir," Owens responded. "I was reminiscing. I'm the one who changed the document you found in the police file."

"Oh."

"Facts be told, sir, Sergeant Kerrigan was a company favorite, the entire company, except for one 90-day wonder."

"I was never in the service. I'm not familiar with that term."

"Ah. A 90-day wonder is what those of us in 'Nam called 2nd Lieutenants. Most 2nd Lieutenants were straight from ROTC. Those that fit the description were the least likeable of all the butterbars. I could go on."

"That's plenty. Thanks."

"Anyway, that raw kid couldn't see how valuable Kerrigan's assistance was to him—to all of us. He was one big hard case. None of the men liked him."

"I see," Mamba commented, although he didn't.

"Well, after this one patrol, the butterbar comes back all riled up. Somebody did what you read about in the official file. I suspect it was our favorite Lieutenant himself, but no one's ever said anything to me officially."

The line went silent. Phil wondered if he'd flashed back to Vietnam and hoped what he asked wouldn't haunt him after today.

"Regardless of who was responsible, whether out of spite, or in a cover your ass maneuver, the Lieutenant placed the blame on Kerrigan." Owens picked up as though he hadn't paused. "We all knew it was a bogus report, but no one could do anything about it. Except me."

Several seconds passed.

"I sat on the report until the Lieutenant caught it. That was about three months later. He pulled a John Wayne maneuver and stood up when he should have been belly crawling. After his death, I re-issued the document in its revised state and gave it to Kerrigan. I told him I couldn't stop the paper from flowing, but he could divert the flow if he ever needed to. And I guess he never thought he needed to."

"I guess not."

"I sent an amended copy of the report to Division HQ. Wasn't that in the personnel record?"

"Huh? Oh, uh, no. It isn't there."

"I could follow up again if you think it's necessary. Even though I'm not on active duty anymore, I am in the Reserves."

"No. I think we'd best leave well enough alone, Master Sergeant. The last thing Pat needs is any worry outside of his recovery."

"Recovery, sir?"

"Um, yeah," Mamba stammered as he realized his mistake. "Your Sergeant was shot in the line of duty about two years ago. He almost died. He's lost some memory and most of the use of his right arm. He's still working his way back."

"Sorry to hear that, sir, the shooting part. But glad to hear about his recovery. Did our conversation help you?"

"Just re-affirms my opinion of the man. Thanks a lot."

"Give my best to Sergeant Kerrigan, sir. Tell him Ollie hopes he heals completely."

"We all hope that, Master Sergeant."

"You wouldn't have his address or phone number, would you, sir?" Owens asked.

"I would. You wouldn't have a pencil and paper, would you, Master Sergeant?"

Owens chuckled. "On top of it, sir. Fire when ready!"

After giving Kerrigan's contact information to Owens, Philip Richmond Mamba hung up the phone. He made a fist and crumpled the paper that held the last two phone numbers he dialed. He tossed the wad into the trashcan beside his desk as he headed home.

THE END

COMING SOON!

Mamba Mysteries

Chapter 1

The quaint village of Gachupin is nestled in the rugged hillsides near the intersection of the borders of the states of Sonora, Sinaloa, and Chihuahua, Mexico. Occupied long before Hernando Cortes arrived in the New World, Gachupin is an enduring example of the heritage of the indigenous populations in what remains a dangerous, undeveloped area of Mexico.

That is what a travel brochure might read if anyone had the desire to travel to such a desolate location. Gachupin is roughly one hundred and ten kilometers east of the Gulf of California and five hundred seventy kilometers south of Nogales. The best travel time from the US Border is eleven hours in a 4-wheeled drive vehicle with extra-high clearance and twenty gallons of gasoline strapped to the back. Less arduous routes might take as many as eighteen hours to traverse, assuming the driver has access to gasoline en route. Four-wheeled drive vehicles are recommended on those routes as well.

One native puts it, "You don't need four-wheel drive, unless you want to get to Gachupin."

The Arcenas family was part of the final wave of Spanish immigrants to Mexico before the first revolution for Mexican independence. These pure-blooded Spaniards, known as Gachupines, were an elitist caste.

The story behind the name Gachupin is rarely discussed. The village became one of the last strongholds of the Spaniards when a contingent of Spanish infantry massacred the indigenous villagers. The victorious Spaniards discarded the traditional name for the village and chose Gachupin to emphasize their caste.

The direct descendants of the Gachupines, also known as criollos, were more elitist than their ancestors and were the target of the Miguel Hidalgo y Costilla led revolution of 1810-11. The city of Gachupin is the only remaining city of refuge of the criollos from the 1800s. Their goal was to remain Spanish at all cost.

Guillermo Arcenas carries that banner. He traces his family tree to gachupin and criollos roots. In his mind, Gachupin is a city of refuge for descendants of his line born in Mexico.

Gachupin is close enough to the Cerro Prieto fault line that extends into the Gulf of California that earthquakes are a concern. For a brief time, it was an outpost for discontented Mexican soldiers. Such soldiers were knocked unconscious and transported in windowless wagons to Gachupin. The malcontents who spent time in this purgatory returned to duty with a much more positive outlook on military life and discipline. Either that, or they disappeared without a trace.

La Casa Grande is the largest building in the village. Technically part of the military complex, in reality, it was and still is a single-family residence. The house has six thousand square feet under the main roof and four acres of grounds around it.

El Rancho Arcenas, as the entire walled compound is known, includes a well that is deep enough to allow access to water even in the driest summers. Perched atop the highest point in the village, La Casa Grande is a most impressive sight.

La familia Arcenas is the owner of the rancho, allegedly purchased by la familia from the Mexican Military during the American Civil War. Servants and staff occupy the grounds year round. Family members visit at their whim.

On this day, dust generated by the oversized tires of two Range Rovers was seen on the road leading into el centro de la ciudad, the town square. The dust arrived with the vehicles—a choking cloud of grainy brown settling slowly as the Range Rovers slid to a stop. After drivers and staff of La Casa Grande opened the passenger doors, three men exited each vehicle and made their way to chairs on a shaded portion of the patio.

"Buenas tardes, señores. Yo soy, Guillermo Arcenas. I thank you for traveling all this way to meet with me today. I hope your journey was not too unpleasant."

Suspicious head nods greeted this unknown man and his elegantly delivered welcome.

"This meeting will be brief. I know you all would much rather be enjoying the party." With a dramatic sweep of his hand, Arcenas directed his guests, attention to the Olympic-sized swimming pool at the far end of the courtyard. They scanned the pool and the nubile females adorning floatables in the water.

At ninety-seven-degrees, it was unseasonably hot and had been for nearly a week. Even the thick adobe walls of La Casa Grande could keep the temperature no better than tolerable on this windless day.

"I have a question and a proposal for your consideration."

A triumphant smile flickered across Arcenas' face. He began, "First, the question: How many of you are satisfied with your current financial condition?"

Not a hand moved. Arcenas knew they were greedy men. Men who might have coined the answer, "Just a little bit more," to the question, "How much money do you need?" if John D. Rockefeller hadn't said it first in the early 1900s.

* * *

Two hours later, empty tequila and cerveza bottles littered the patio around the pool and the shaded hallways where misters attempted to defeat the sun's heat. Squeals of delight, surprise, and, at times fear echoed off the stucco walls. Two bikini tops and one bottom floated in the shallow end of the pool.

The major domo was worried. He was nearly out of limes and the men showed no sign of slowing down.

* * *

While the noise and other activities distracted the guests and their host, a score of men in unmarked khaki uniforms crept across the hot sand. Wide-brimmed khaki hats shaded the direct sunlight from reflecting off the Foster Grants each man wore.

The strike force leader stopped, rolled over to his back, held up five fingers and waved to his right. Five khaki uniforms belly-crawled fifty yards and turned toward the outside wall of El Rancho Arcenas. While five men moved to the right, twice that many headed to the leader's left. Once the twenty attackers were in position, the leader counted "one, two, three" with his fingers and closed his hand into a fist.

Gunshots echoed through the patio. Six men inside the wall dropped to the floor, sobered by the familiar sound. They knew they were targets. They'd created such scenarios elsewhere.

"Stop them!" Guillermo shouted to his chief of security. "Keep one alive! I want information!"

"Sí, señor!"

The security chief yanked a walky-talky from its holder on his belt. He barked out a series of commands.

Two attackers were late arrivals. They manhandled an M72 anti-tank rocket launcher in position against one man's shoulder. Used extensively in Vietnam, the M72 held a single rocket and was as accurate as the man holding it was stable.

The manufacturer labeled the launch tube as disposable. Its structural integrity decreased with each rocket launched. The number of rockets launched before compromising a tube's structural integrity varied. An unwritten understanding among users ensures that no one launches over two or three rockets before passing the weapon to another increasingly reluctant soldier.

The gunfire increased in intensity as Arcenas' men returned fire. The volume ebbed and flowed as slight changes in position brought the attackers closer or moved them farther from the walls of the estate.

The strike force leader gestured, "Well?" to the M72 team.

The man without the M72 flashed the "go" sign. One rocket was inside the launch tube. The man flashing the "go" sign held a second rocket in his free hand.

The strike force leader feigned pulling a trigger with his right hand.

The launcher spat its rocket at the three-foot thick adobe wall surrounding La Casa Grande. The recoil knocked the shooter to the ground.

"Kaboom!"

The sound of the rocket exploding combined with the shock waves it produced rattled the chandeliers beneath the patio cover.

The seventeen remaining amateur soldiers stormed the wall.

"¡Usa los lanzallamas!" Arcenas bit off each word. The control their host exhibited impressed the men on the floor. The flamethrowers were more impressive to them.

"G'thump!" A sound similar to that made if ten thousand gas barbeque burners were filled with propane before flaring up in unison announced the igniting of the outer wall's built-in flamethrower jets. Milliseconds later screams of agony replaced the sound of incoming bullets.

The assault ended in a whimper.

A moan came from the throat of the only surviving attacker. His facial features melted and formed an irregular landscape of charred flesh out of what had been forehead, nose, eyes, and cheeks. There was no screaming. Half the burn victim's larynx was singed.

Arcenas knelt beside the deformed body.

"I need one word. If it is the right word, I will put you out of your agony. You have little time left. The pain will only increase. Understand?"

Arcenas took the gurgle in response as yes. He hoped the man could articulate a name. While the suffering of other people rarely bothered him, this man's condition was exceptionally bad.

"Who paid you to attack my house?"

It took all the concentration the drug lord could muster, but he got the name of the adversary responsible for the attack on his home.

A single gunshot to the forehead area of the informant marked a total victory for Arcenas' men.

"Find the hole Tomas Garcia lives in. Erase the town and those supporting Garcia by living there." Arcenas scanned the faces of his men before he ended with a specific instruction. "Leave no memory of the names of my enemies or of the city in which they died! Is that clear?"

Arcenas' soldiers nodded.

After ordering the annihilation of his enemy and his headquarters, Guillermo changed into fresh clothing and returned to his invited guests. The spring in his step reflected his appreciation for the unscheduled demonstration of his commitment to his cause.

"I am sorry," he offered in apology. "Let me assure you that whoever committed this act of treason will pay in full for their disloyalty."

Heads nodded. The guests understood the code by which they lived. "Señores, once again I ask: How many of you are satisfied with your current financial condition?"

Shaking heads and knowing smiles of anticipation answered.

"I thought so. Now, the proposal. I invite you to become members of a new business group. The purpose of this group is to export chemical products to our rich neighbors to the north."

Nervous rustling noises greeted this information. If he heard those noises, Arcenas ignored them.

"There will be significant hurdles to overcome in the shipping and receiving of what the Americanos call drugs. However, I am confident that my group." Arcenas paused and feigned embarrassment. "Perdóname señores, I should have said our group. I am confident that our group will become the most powerful cartel in all of el norte de México."

Heads turned side to side as the six men began closer evaluations of one another. Cartel was a term they all knew and respected. Being included in creating a new cartel was what dreams were made of. After a time, what appeared to be the oldest man asked a single question.

"Señor Arcenas. You describe a bold and potentially lucrative undertaking, but the term advisory group is vague. How exactly do we fit in?"

"Is that a question you all wish answered?"

"Sí," echoed through the room six times.

"Very good! Let us continue our time together by getting to know one another. A meal awaits you in the dining room." Arcenas flashed a smile. "Enjoy a time of fellowship and feasting. After you have satisfied yourselves, we will discuss our arrangement."

* * *

Two days later, headlines across Mexico and the rest of the Western Hemisphere reported a horrific attack on a village in south central Mexico.

Unknown attackers destroyed the village of San Luis Alcazar early this morning. Two jet fighters strafed and leveled buildings before napalm bombing the village. The attack killed all 137 residents between 3:45 a.m. and 4:00 a.m. No humans escaped the carnage that included burning an estimated sixty bodies. Perhaps not coincidentally, sixty residents of the village were thought to be the family of suspected drug lord, Tomas Garcia. The fate of Garcia himself is unknown at press time.

Guillermo Arcenas read the headline story. An angry look usurped the flicker of a smile. The names of the dead were not listed. There was no evidence that Tomas Garcia or any of his family died.

He vowed to learn the names of those who died in the attack.

"Guzmán, you are my new worst enemy. If you are still alive, I will kill you myself."

She stopped at the beveled glass-paneled French doors. Guillermo looked upset. She was sure she could change that. She pulled the door open and stepped onto the portico where Arcenas ate breakfast nearly every morning.

"Buenas dias. Can I share a cup of coffee with you?"

Guillermo turned his chair around.

"Of course, my precious, Petula." He gestured for her to sit on his knee.

Garcia could wait.

End of Preview Chapter

Selected Cast of Characters – Alphabetical by First Name

Name	Description
"Captain" Abbott	Captain of Manzanita Police Department's Northeast Division
Anthony Garmel	Head of drug trafficking syndicate.
April Desantos	Officer in MPD's Internal Affairs Division officer
Brad Finch	Lab technician that owed Martinez a favor
Darrel Evans	Hitman and Walt Evans' brother: Dispatcher
Dwight Rogers	Manzanita Chief of Police
Eddie Edwards	Senior Records Officer in the Northeast Division
Enciso Martinez	Detective in Narcotics, Northeast Division AKA Cue Ball when undercover
Erin Reilly	Nurse for Flatly Broke
Flatly Broke / Waldo Wiggins	Former boxer. Mamba's informant and undercover buyer
Franklin Stallings	Sergeant of Narcotics in Northeast Division. Transfer from St. Louis
Gray	One of RossAnn Gilroy's kidnappers
Guillermo Arecnas	Blonde leader of a small Mexican drug cartel. Dual Mexico/US credentials. The same person as William Anderson
Hope Mamba	Phil's wife and secretary. Mother of Jimmy
Inker	Tattoo artist who tattoos RossAnn
Jeffery Ellerbe	Assistant Chief and later Chief of MPD
Kate Kerrigan	Lt. Kerrigan's wife
Lawrence (Larry) Lester	Mamba's CI - playing both sides of this story
Lizbeth Stallings	Wife of Franklin Stallings Sergeant of Narcotics – Northeast Division
Mary Carstairs	Mid-level drug dealer
Oscar Briggs	Hitman for Sid Brewster. Goes by Big 0
Pat (Patrick) Kerrigan	Former Mamba partner. MPD Lieutenant Crimes Against Person in Northeast Division

Petula Jacobs	Chief Rogers' admin assistant and mistress
Phil Mamba	Private Investigator, former MPD officer in Manzanita, CA
Reed	Saxophone-playing addict, snitch, informant. Provides list of names of drug dealers
Rick Elkhart	Brewster's #1 associate
RossAnn Gilroy	Manzanita socialite and anti-drug campaigner
Sid Brewster	A notch higher than Mary Carstairs in Garmel's drug syndicate
Stripe	One of RossAnn Gilroy's kidnappers
Weston	Name on Reed's list. Low-level drug dealer
William Anderson	Blond owner of a pharmaceutical company. Dual US/Mexico citizenship. Same person as Guillermo Arcenas
Woodrow Evans	Hitman hired by Brewster. Goes by Whack

Other books by C. R. Downing
Amazon Author page: https://tinyurl.com/y4k4dkfd

Science Fiction

Traveler's HOT L - *The Time Traveler's Resort*
Traveler's HOT L Volume Two - 2nd Ed. - *New Tales from the Time Traveler's Resort*
egamI esreveR - *A Timeless Tale from The Traveler's HOT L Vol 3*
Patterns on Pages - *Secrets of the Sequenced Symbols - Traveler's HOT L Vol 4*
Insecticide - *A Science Fiction Thriller*
The Observers - *A Science Fiction Odyssey*

Anthologies

A World Unimagined: *An Anthology of Science and Speculative Fiction*
Mindscapes Unimagined: *An Anthology of the Supernatural, Science Fiction, and Horror*

Humor

Sir Isaac's Car - *9 Tales of Daring and Disaster*

NON-FICTION

Tune Up Your Teaching and Turn On Student Learning
NICU - *An Insider's Guide*
Idea Farming - *A Science Guy's Read on Writing – Volume 1*

Lizbeth Stallings is a composite of the many relatives, friends, former students, and colleagues, both female and male, who have battled, or are battling cancer. It is my prayer that research will soon produce a true cure for this affliction.

Acknowledgements

The following individuals provided comments, critiques, and composition ideas as beta readers for this book. Their input was crucial in elevating the quality of this manuscript.

Preya Goyal, Mark Baker, Renee Bautista, Lizzy Harding,
Paul Coffman, Cody Jelsovsky, Donna Jones,
Kathleen Fransway, Chandra Morton,
Police Officers Nicole Campbell and Robert Filley,
Former Homicide Detective Keith Newman

C. R. Downing
Photograph by Victor S. Sotelo, Photojournalist, San Diego, CA

C. R. (Dr. Chuck) Downing is a retired nationally recognized science teacher and author living in San Diego, California, with his wife and a small, feisty dog named Hogan.

Author of 8 fiction books, 3 non-fiction titles, with stories in 2 anthologies, he enjoys spending time with granddaughters, gardening, and working on Bible lessons for his Sunday school class and his My Christian Context blog.

https://www.crdowning.com/

Made in the USA
San Bernardino, CA
04 June 2020

72709902R00293